When the Tide Rushes In

Book Two

GRAVE ENCOUNTERS

If the precarious young heiress had known the truth, perhaps she wouldn't have fallen in love with the mysterious bindle stiff. But she didn't know, and those who knew weren't willing to tell.

KAY CHANDLER

A multi-award-winning author

This is a work of fiction. Characters, places and incidents are the products of the author's imagination or are used factiously.

Scripture taken from the King James Version of the Holy Bible

Cover Design by Chase Chandler

For Bill

The tide came rushing in the day you came into my life.

PROLOGUE
Goat Hill, Alabama

Lizzie Lancaster announced her death with the following obituary and had it printed in the morning paper on October 15, 1932. She thought it fitting. Her mama was not at all amused.

HEIR TO THE GLADSTONE PLANTATION SUCCUMBS
Eliza Virginia Lancaster's spirit departed this earth at the setting of the sun October 14, 1932. She was a mere eighteen years of age with cherished dreams for a long and wonderful future. But alas, the romantic dreams led to her untimely demise. Lizzie, as she was affectionately called, was a Lancaster and Lancasters are forbidden to dream. If you choose to mourn, don't mourn her death. Mourn her life.

Robert Loch was fired from The Tribune for printing it. Lizzie's daddy owned the paper, and her mama said Robert should have known better. Eliza cried for days when she found out she caused Mr. Loch to lose his job. An older man, he lived alone—the newspaper was his love. She understood too well, the pain that comes from losing something or someone you love.

Chapter One

Seven Years Later

Eliza Lancaster parked her shiny new Packard behind the hearse. "Congratulations, Mama. You had to go and die to get your way, but you finally got us together."

Throngs had gathered in the Gladstone Cemetery, but the first face Eliza recognized was Oliver Weinberger's. She slumped in her seat and groaned when Oliver waved and sprinted toward her. With his long, skinny legs and big, brown doe eyes, he looked like a panic-stricken whitetail deer on the first day of hunting season.

She glanced at the hordes of people staring in her direction and wondered how many had come out of sheer curiosity to gawk at a marked woman. Or at least one presumed to be marked. Privy to the nasty gossip that had continued to circulate through the small town, her pulse raced. Eliza didn't need to hear the whispers to know what they said about her. *Surely, Oliver knows. He lives here. Jeepers, has he no pride?*

He hunched over with his head slightly leaning toward the open window and panted. "Ah, my sweet. I trust you received my telegram."

Eliza feigned a smile and nodded. She hadn't responded to the wire. Now, sensing a flicker of hope in his high-pitched voice, she wished that she had. He seemed to interpret her failure to reply as an affirmative answer to his request. Eliza had no desire to create the illusion they were a couple and give rise to his fantasies, but neither could she humiliate him by spurning him publicly before a mob of curious spectators. She'd accept his offer to escort her to the memorial service and deal with the consequences later. At the moment, it appeared she was holding up a funeral.

Oliver jerked open the door. "I was beginning to worry, Eliza. We mustn't tarry. The preacher's waiting." He lifted his felt hat and blotted his damp forehead with a handkerchief. "I'm sorry about your mother—she was a grand lady. We were quite close, you know."

Eliza nodded. "Yes. Mama reminded me often."

His face lit up. "She told you we were close?"

"No. She reminded me often that she was a grand lady."

His brow furrowed.

"I'm teasing, Oliver. Yes, she was quite fond of you." Eliza had known since grade school that Oliver was everything her mama had ever wanted for her. But she wanted much more—or according to one's viewpoint, perhaps she wanted much less. In either case, Eliza knew what she wanted and Oliver Weinberger was not his name.

"Eliza?" Oliver's treble voice lifted. "I don't mean to rush you, love, but we're late."

She reached up and placed her lacy-gloved hand into his outstretched palm. Without a word, she shifted her body and stepped out of the car. Her peep-toe heels dug into the soft dirt. She grimaced when sweat from Oliver's clammy palm penetrated her thin glove.

With his head tilted back, Oliver peered down his long, Roman nose and with his index finger, smoothed his pencil thin mustache. "Ready, my dear?"

Her gaze met his. When a childhood memory invaded her thoughts, she gasped and tried to shove it back where it belonged—in the past. The timing couldn't be worse. She clinched her lips tightly. *Don't think about it, Lizzie. Don't! You know what'll happen . . . Armadillo face . . . now you've done it. Armadillo face. I can't make it go away. Don't start laughing. Not now. Armadillo face.* The name she called Oliver in the sixth grade stuck through the years. *It's not funny.* She swallowed hard. *Think of something else. Mary had a little lamb, his—*

Oliver tugged at his pinstriped waistcoat and crooked his arm. With her composure regained, she looked into his woeful eyes, smiled slightly and slid her arm into his. As they strolled past, the crowd parted, creating a narrow human avenue. Nauseating smells filled the hot, humid Gulf Coast air with the stench of cheap perfume, body odor, and stale tobacco mixed with an overwhelming fragrance of far too many floral sprays. Eliza winced and held her breath.

Oohs and ahhs followed them as Oliver escorted her toward the dark canopy located in the center of the graveyard, where generations of Gladstones lay buried. On a mound behind the freshly dug grave, stood a life-sized statue of a man on a horse—Papa Gid—holding a cotton boll. Etched on the impressive marble slab were the words "Gideon P. Gladstone III, Alabama Cotton King, 1852-1918."

As they inched their way toward the tent, Oliver stooped and whispered, "Eliza, I do hope it isn't inappropriate for me to say at such a somber time—but you look lovely, my dear—even in mourning. Oh, how I've missed you."

Eliza tried to muster a smile. She whispered out of the corner of her mouth, "Step it up, Oliver. This is taking far too long." When a gust of wind blew a wavy strand of platinum blonde hair into her eyes, she reached up and gently tucked it beneath her gray slouch fedora. Dressed in a Madeleine Vionnet Original, Eliza selected the black silk shantung suit with metallic cloth trimmings exclusively for Aunt Merle's benefit. Although Eliza preferred her red Chanel halter-neck, which showed off her tiny waist and newly acquired tan, she knew her aunt wouldn't consider it proper attire for a funeral. Her aunt had already worked herself into a dither over what people were saying. According to Aunt Merle, rumor had it that the Gladstone heiress left home seven years ago after a young hoodlum took advantage of her. Exactly what it meant, no one seemed to know for sure, although there'd been much speculation as the nasty rumors circulated. But Eliza had no intention of satisfying the gossips with any sort of explanation.

Arm in arm with Oliver, she strolled with her head held high and nodded when men tipped their hats as she walked past. *Don't look so smug, people. I know what you're thinking. Frankly, I wish every word of the gossip were true.* She bit her tongue to keep from blurting the words aloud. Eliza sucked in a deep breath, conscious by the women's uplifted brows and the men's shameless smiles that a sudden puff of wind had caused the bias-cut skirt to cling to her shapely body. She rolled her eyes and considered giving them something truly shocking at which to stare. She thought of her father lying on his deathbed at the manor, and out of respect, quickly dismissed the idea. Eliza adored her daddy.

Oliver thrust his chin forward and pulled at his tie. "Ah, the breeze is a welcomed relief." He lifted his eyes toward the sky. "We could use a good rain to cool things off a bit."

Not in the mood to indulge in idle chatter about the weather, Eliza felt no urgency to respond. Four chairs sat under the canvas tent and only one empty. Oliver stepped back into the crowd when Eliza let go of his arm and took her seat—twenty minutes late.

Pastor Hawkins' jaw dropped and his eyes bulged when Eliza sat and crossed her legs, revealing shiny silk stockings. She bit the corner of her lip and adjusted her skirt.

Cousin Bonnie sat in the slatted wooden seat next to Eliza. Aunt Merle and Uncle Henry occupied the other two chairs. Aunt Merle pursed her lips and made a point to look at her watch.

Eliza reached for Bonnie's hand and gave it a little squeeze. She mouthed the words, "Good to see you, cuz. I've missed you."

"Lizzie. I'm so sorry—"

Eliza smiled slightly and acknowledged the expression of sympathy with a nod.

Pastor Hawkins stood behind a wooden podium with his arms tightly folded. He cleared his throat and lifted a Bible from the pedestal. With his brow furrowed, he peered over the top of his wire-rimmed spectacles and glared in Eliza's direction. "May we begin?"

Eliza fidgeted with her earbob, aware that his comment was not so much a question, but an acknowledgement of her inexcusable tardiness.

The elderly, rotund preacher pulled a large handkerchief from his back pocket and wiped sweat from his bald head. With a perfected pastoral quiver in his voice, he began. "Our hearts are deeply grieved as we gather here today to commemorate the life of Alamanda Victoria Gladstone Lancaster, a precious saint if ever there was one. A true Biblical scholar, I venture to say the dear lady wrote more of my sermons than I did and with amazing unction, I might add."

Eliza shifted in her chair and glanced about as heads bobbled up and down in apparent agreement. Her lip curled at the notion that her mother may have written the flowery eulogy.

The preacher continued to read from notes stuck between the pages of his Bible. "A pillar of the community, this dear, generous sister shared her wisdom with us all—bold and unwavering in the face of opposition, she stood firm in her beliefs."

Unwavering. What an accurate word. Eliza couldn't deny the one thing she and her mother had in common was their stubbornness.

Pastor Hawkins blew his nose and flipped a page. His voice trembled. When he dabbed his eyes and drew a deep breath, Eliza suspected the sympathetic gestures were in his notes.

His voice lifted. "Ah, yes, Mrs. Lancaster personified the virtuous woman described in the book of Proverbs. Surely, her worth was far above rubies . . . strength and honor were her clothing; and in her tongue was the law of kindness—"

Eliza crinkled her brow and tilted her head toward Bonnie. "I think I may be at the wrong funeral," she whispered while listening to the glowing attributes Pastor Hawkins credited to the dearly departed. "He can't be talking about Mama. Can he?"

Bonnie hid her mouth with a lace handkerchief. Aunt Merle stretched her neck and gave both young women a stern look.

The Reverend paused and nodded toward the widow Blanchard, who stood and proceeded to play a mournful sounding tune on her accordion, while a men's trio belted out the words to

"Will the Circle be Unbroken." Eliza swallowed hard. *Our family circle broke seven years ago.* Though she could never forgive her mama for ruining her life, she had no doubt her mother made her peace with God—just not with her. Her thoughts drifted to the Lord's Prayer. *Forgive us our trespasses as we forgive those who . . . No, Lord. I can't. It's too much to ask.*

Aunt Merle reached over and nudged Eliza, who understood it to be her cue. She stepped up and dutifully tossed a rose atop her mother's casket. As she gazed into the dark hole, Eliza determined that even on 2,000 acres, there wasn't enough room in the ground for Mama and all the secrets buried long before her death. Why did Kiah Grave leave without saying goodbye? Eliza made a silent vow to stay in Goat Hill until the grave secret could be unearthed.

Pastor Hawkins had barely begun on Part II of his Farewell to Alamanda, when an unexpected cloudburst had the people scrambling for cover. Thunder boomed as streaks of lightning flashed across the sky. The crowd scattered, seeking refuge as the rain peppered down. Everyone disappeared except the four surviving relatives and the preacher. Gusts of wind whipped underneath the canvas cover, causing it to billow, while sheets of rain rushed in, drenching the seated occupants.

The eloquent orator appeared oblivious to the hammering downpour and continued to read from his notes. "In addition, our dear departed sister leaves to mourn her devoted sister-in-law, Merle Lancaster, who shared Alamanda's love for the arts.

Together they—"

With the rain stinging her face, Eliza glanced over at Aunt Merle and supposed someone should tell Pastor Hawkins to cut it short. Poor grieving Merle appeared too distraught to notice they were getting soaked. She sobbed hysterically, while Henry wrapped his arm around her, trying to offer comfort. Yet it seemed the harder he tried, the louder she wailed. Aunt Merle's crisp, black taffeta dress—now limp—clung to her tightly corseted body.

Uninvited comical mental pictures popped into Eliza's head, prompting an irrepressible urge to laugh. She could almost hear her mother's voice, scolding. *Stop it, Eliza. You're acting like a Loudermilk.* Her mother always used the poor Loudermilk family as a measuring rod whenever she wanted to reprimand her daughter for uncouth behavior. Eliza pressed her lips together in an attempt to stop the inevitable giggles, which seemed to take root in the pit of her stomach at the most inopportune times. After the first little tee-hee escaped, there was no stopping the embarrassing snickering. Lizzie lowered her head when her body began to shake.

Bonnie's brows arched. "What's funny?" she whispered.

Eliza cupped her hand over her mouth and replied, "Absolutely nothing, but I can't stop laughing." Mortified, she slipped a monogrammed handkerchief from her clutch bag. She slid the dainty linen cloth under the veil and clasped it tightly over her mouth. What could possibly be funny? Her mama was dead. Aunt Merle was overwrought with grief, and the preacher was not yet finished with his elaborate farewell.

A gust of whirling wind blew rain in from Uncle Henry's side. If given the opportunity, surely he would opt to leave, although she knew him well enough to know he wouldn't feel it his place to suggest it. She decided as the nearest kin, it was her call. Eliza bolted from her seat.

"Let's go people!" She blurted, right in the middle of "dust to dust."

With neither protest nor delay, Pastor Hawkins lifted a sanctimonious brow and snipped, "Shall we pray." Eliza was convinced the brief prayer would go down in history as the shortest one he'd ever uttered. At the sound of "Amen," Bonnie grasped Lizzie by the hand.

"Thank you, Lizzie. I'm glad you shortened the rites. Lightning scares me."

Eliza chuckled. "Everything scares you, Bonnie. You look swell, kiddo. I hope you'll stop by the manor so we can visit."

"Oh, honey, I'd love to, but Joe's going out of town tomorrow. I need to get home. Lizzie, I wish ..." she paused. "Never mind."

Eliza lifted a shoulder. "What's bothering you, ducky? Go ahead and say it."

"Lizzie, you may fool some people with your fake smile, but you aren't fooling me. Where's the fun-loving girl I once knew? It's been seven years. It's time to forgive."

Eliza bristled. "No, Bonnie. Mama ruined my life. I have no

idea what she held over Kiah's head, but she ran him out of town. I know she did. I'll never forgive her!"

Bonnie's eyes glistened, as she opened her arms. "One thing about you has never changed. You're still stubborn . . . but I love you." She turned and waved as she ran.

Eliza's throat tightened. If only she could turn back time. She approached her vehicle—and stopped short—startled to see Oliver standing beside the automobile, water dripping from his black felt hat. "Oliver! I thought you left."

"I waited for you, my dear." He gestured toward a 1938 LaSalle parked at the bend in the road. "That's my coupe. May I drive you to the manor?"

"I have my car, thank you."

"But, dear, you shouldn't be alone at a time like this. Perhaps I should ride with you."

"No, Oliver." She winced at the coldness in her voice. Was she turning into her mother?

He nodded. "I understand. We all have to mourn in our own way, I suppose."

"Yes. I suppose," she murmured. She wasn't sure what he meant, but she had no desire to have him expound on the subject. *Jeepers, Oliver, what do I have to do for you to catch on?*

Oliver opened her door and she slid in. She tossed her hat on the seat, removed her gloves and attempted to reset the finger waves in her wet hair. Eliza didn't want to be mean to Oliver, but she wished he would share his affections with someone who could appreciate them. She groaned, as she watched him trudge toward his vehicle, hat in hand. Poor Oliver. It wasn't his fault. He was caught in the middle of a feud—a feud that even death couldn't squash.

She grumbled aloud, "You're dead, Mama, yet I'm still trying to beat you at your game. When I sent Oliver away, I gave myself a notch. But I can't win, can I? Thanks to you, I lost the only love I've ever known—or ever will know. But you won't win, either, because I wouldn't marry Oliver Weinberger if he were the last man alive."

In no particular hurry to leave, Eliza sat in the parked car, remembering things she spent seven years trying to forget. Raindrops trickled down the windshield, like giant tears. She dreaded going back to Gladstone to face Aunt Merle, after the shameless way she giggled at the funeral. But Eliza knew she'd go back. She had two very good reasons and neither of them had anything to do with Aunt Merle. Her father lay dying at the manor, and Eliza wanted to be by his side. Then, there were the secrets. She pounded the steering wheel and screamed, "Why, Mama? What did you do to make him leave?"

Eliza loved her mother, although she never expected anyone to believe it. Yet she didn't like her. She never believed her mother loved her, although she found it conceivable that Alamanda might've been proud of her—proud that her daughter wasn't homely so she could show her off. But Mama was also proud of her Rolls, her fox stole and the diamond necklace Papa Gid gave her on her fortieth birthday. Mama took pride in Gladstone and all the trimmings. Eliza was a trimming.

The sun peeked from behind the clouds, as the rain slackened to a drizzle. Millions of tiny white marble chips surrounded each burial plot and glistened like diamonds as the light reflected off the wet fragments. She rolled down the window and sniffed. The shower left a clean, fresh smell.

Eliza glanced around the cemetery and sighed. No doubt she'd be planted there one day. She may as well be lying in the grave now. She wasn't alive—not really. A person without a heart ceases to live. She stared at the countless stone angels hovering atop the huge marble headstones, marking the graves of infamous blood relatives. Eliza surmised there were more angels in the cemetery than there were in heaven.

She gazed across the field at her grandfather's imposing statue and shivered. "Ridiculous," she muttered. "If anyone marks my resting place with a sculpture of me riding to heaven on a stone stallion, I'll beg permission to return from the dead, long enough to swat the guilty party with my burial shroud." An amusing idea caused her jaw to drop. Before leaving Goat Hill, why not choose a tombstone and write her epitaph? She'd already written her obituary. The thought of the impetuous act years ago caused her to laugh, but the laughter faded into snorts, which soon evolved into soft sobs. She felt a warm wetness on her cheeks as tears trickled down her neck.

"What's wrong with me?" She laughed when there was nothing funny, and now she cried when there was no need. All the tears in the world wouldn't bring Kiah Grave back into her life. "Oh, Kiah—"Saying his name aloud made cold shivers trickle down her spine.

Eliza dried her face and pondered over a suitable epitaph. Her lips pressed together when she thought of the ideal lines: Eliza Lancaster, daughter of Will and Alamanda. Born: The day she met him. Died: The day he left. Cause of Death: SSM (Silver spoon in mouth.) "Perfect!"

Eliza didn't dispute the fact that according to the latest census, her birth took place on May 2, 1914. Yet, she didn't begin to live until eighteen years later—May 4, 1932. That was the day she and Bonnie went joy-riding in Lizzie's new Model A and met Kiah Grave on a narrow dirt road near the railroad tracks. Had it really been only seven years? It seemed like such a long, long time ago. But she remembered it well—

"Did he get it? Did he?"

"He did, Lizzie. The scarf flew in his face." Bonnie squealed. "Isn't he a dreamboat? You think he jumped off the morning run, or do you reckon he's waiting to hop the next train?"

"Why don't I turn the car around and ask him." Lizzie

snickered.

"Are you crazy? You can't turn around here. If you get out of the ruts, we're likely to slide in the ditch, and we'll be in big trouble—Uncle Will warned you not to cross the tracks."

"So he did." Lizzie crinkled her nose and grinned.

"Lizzie, I don't like the expression on your face. I hope you aren't planning something stupid."

"Stupid? Of course not." She clutched the steering wheel tightly and stomped the brake to the floorboard, causing the car to come to a jarring halt.

Bonnie buried her face in her hands, slumped down in the seat and moaned. "Eliza Lancaster, you know your mama will have a conniption fit if she finds out you flirted with a hobo—and you know she'll find out. You can't spit in this town without someone reporting it. "

"All the more reason to do it, dear cuz—let's give them something to talk about."

"Lizzie, no. Don't. It's not proper. We don't even know him. He's a . . . a tramp, for crying out loud. Let's go. Suppose someone sees us? What if your daddy takes your car away?"

"I'll cry." Lizzie chuckled. "Daddy can't stand to see me cry." The gears made a loud grinding noise when she jerked the shift into reverse. "Besides, we can't possibly leave," she said as the car shot backward. "He has my favorite scarf."

Bonnie screamed. "Watch out!"

Lizzie's shiny new Model A Ford, which her daddy had given her for her eighteenth birthday, spun around on the wet clay road and slammed into the ditch.

Bonnie clasped her hand over her heart. "I knew this would happen. Lizzie, we're going to be in—" Her eyes widened. "Oh no! He's running toward us. What are we gonna do?"

"Flirt, silly." Lizzie pinched her cheeks and fluffed her hair. "How do I look?" She glanced in the rearview mirror. "Oh, Bonnie, catch me, I think I'm falling in love."

"And what's new?" Bonnie rolled her eyes. "I declare, you're so dramatic."

"I mean it this time. Isn't he dreamy? Take a gander at those arms."

"I see them. They're red . . . just like his neck. Lizzie, you can forget him. I can imagine what Aunt Ali would say if you brought *him* to the family picnic."

Lizzie smiled and batted her lashes when the handsome fellow approached the vehicle.

He propped his bare foot on the running board and bent forward, his head slightly leaning into the window. The hairs on the back of Lizzie's neck bristled, when she felt his warm breath on her face. Slung over his shoulder was a red bundle and a pair of worn brogans tied to the end of a pole.

"Can I help, ladies?"

Lizzie tucked a strand of hair behind her ear and flashed a

quick grin. "Why, thank you. I certainly hope so."

He stepped back and eyed the embedded tires. "Don't worry, Miss. It's not as bad as it looks. I'll run up the road and see if I can find something to put under the wheels." After taking a few steps, he turned around and pulled a scarf from his pocket. His blue eyes twinkled. "I believe this thingamajig belongs to you. Maybe you should tie it next time."

"Thanks. You can throw your—" She eyed the pole and fumbled over her words.

"Bindle? Is that the word m'lady's choking on?" His fingers raked through a mass of inky black curls.

Lizzie's face burned. Yet, in an odd sort of way, she found it quite charming that he wasn't afraid to speak his mind. "I wasn't choking. I simply didn't know what to call it."

"Try clothes." His square jaw jutted forward. "I gather you don't know the difference between a vagabond and a banker. We men of distinction pack our morning coats in red flannel when we travel, to keep from lugging around a smelly old cowhide suitcase."

"No need for such haughtiness. I merely wanted to tell you to toss it on the rumble seat."

He stiffened. "I suppose you're accustomed to telling folks what to do, but I'm not in the habit of taking orders." He shoved his bindle against the fence post and stalked down the road, looking madder than a run-over dog.

Bonnie crinkled her brow. "Lizzie, I can't figure him. He's almost rude."

"Don't be silly. He's playing hard to get."

"But isn't that what we're supposed to be doing?"

Lizzie gave a short laugh and took a second look at her reflection in the rearview mirror. "Well, I think he chose first, but I invented this game."

Within the half hour, the handsome hobo returned, carrying two four-foot long boards on his shoulder. After making a track in the clay, he said, "If you ladies will kindly step out, I'll crank 'er up. I think I'll be able to get it out."

"You *think*?" Lizzie cocked her head to the side, attempting to look coy. "Do you know how to drive?" It seemed a logical question, since he obviously didn't own wheels.

His nostrils flared. "I wouldn't have volunteered if I didn't know how to operate an automobile Miss, but if you think you can get the car out of the ditch, I'll not trouble you further." He threw up his hand and with a smirk, muttered, "Toodle-do, ladies. Have a nice day."

Lizzie flung the door open and leaped out. "Please! Don't leave us stranded. I'm sorry."

He trudged back to the vehicle, slid in and sat on the soft, gray seat covers. The motor revved and the car rocked. Then with a jolt, the Model A made a quick lunge and settled into the well-traveled ruts. Sporting an arrogant grin, he stepped out and strutted like a proud banty rooster. His gaze traveled from the front bumper to the rumble seat as he strode around, admiring the car.

Lizzie whispered, "If only he'd look at me the way he's eyeballing this piece of metal."

He gasped. "What a beauty. A real sweet patootie."

"Why, thank you. I thought you'd never notice. Oh, silly me. You were referring to the car, weren't you?" Lizzie shrugged when he ignored her. "Where are you headed?"

"Miss, do you have a habit of making everyone's affairs your own?"

She feigned a pout. "Forgive me. I didn't mean to pry. I was offering you a ride."

His blushing face grimaced. He grabbed his bindle stick and mumbled an apology, albeit a weak one. "Thanks. A ride would be swell." With his head lowered, he added, "If it won't put you out." His next words caught her by surprise. "Would you happen to know the whereabouts of the Gladstone Plantation?"

Chapter Two

Lizzie glanced at Bonnie and mouthed the words, "Is this a dream? I get to take him home with me?"

Bonnie shook her head furiously, but Lizzie paid her no mind, not even when Bonnie whispered back, "Don't be fooled. It's the makings of a nightmare."

"Gladstone?" Lizzie managed to keep a straight face. "Sure, we know where it is. Everyone from these parts is familiar with the place. Hop in. We happen to be going that way."

When the handsome stranger stepped up on the running board with his bindle stick and plopped down on the rumble seat, goose bumps raced across Lizzie's arms, causing her to shiver. Cleoda, the maid, called such shivers "a rabbit running over a grave," which didn't make a dab of sense. Lizzie knew exactly what caused her to tingle all over, and he looked nothing at all like a furry little creature with long ears.

"How far is the plantation from here?" He asked.

"Not far, but you were headed in the wrong direction." Her pulse raced. "What brings you to Goat Hill?" Before he could answer, she thrust her hand over her mouth. "Oops! Sorry. I forgot. You don't like questions." She glanced in the mirror and saw his lips stretch into a funny little grin.

"I'm looking for work. I hear the old man Lanchester hires this time of year. I'm hoping I can get on as a field hand."

Lizzie said, "For starters, maybe you'd better learn to pronounce his name. The name is Lancaster—not Lanchester."

"The man who owns Gladstone? You sure?"

"Quite sure. His name is William H. Lancaster IV. Everyone in Goat Hill calls him 'Mr. Will.'" Lizzie smiled. "Good luck in getting a job."

"Thanks, I'll need it. From what I hear, I'd have a better chance of getting elected mayor."

"Oh? And why is that?"

"The word at the yard is that the ol' man's wife wears the pants and forbids him from hiring outsiders. Folks say she's a real humdinger."

Lizzie gripped the steering wheel. She supposed people knew Mama better than she thought. Still, she resented the idea of strangers saying ghastly things about her mother. True, Mama didn't approve of outsiders working on the plantation. But since many of the former field hands had recently moved into the mill village in Geneva to work in the Cotton Mill, perhaps the shortage would cause her daddy to make an exception. She glanced in the mirror.

He rubbed his chin. "Lancaster, you say? You know him?"

"Know him? Of course. Everyone in the South knows him." She shifted her glance toward Bonnie and winked.

"I mean have you ever met him, because I've been wondering . . . are there ruffles on his apron?" He sneered. "I figure he's hen-pecked to let the ol' biddy tell him what to do."

Lizzie bristled. He'd crossed the line. Insulting her mother was one thing, but he had no right to bad-mouth her daddy. She wouldn't stand for it. "That's not so. And I have met him. He's not like that at all. Everyone who knows him will tell you he's the kindest, sweetest man who ever lived. You should hope to be half the man."

"How do you know I'm not? You think money makes a man big?"

She clamped her mouth shut to keep from lashing back. Bonnie was right. He was rude. She felt like giving him the what-for and letting him know it was her family he belittled. She would have, too, if he hadn't been so heart-stoppingly handsome.

He smirked. "I've seen his kind. Squeamish milksops. Not me. I'll never let a dame tell me what to do."

He was good-looking, but was he really *that* good-looking? Unable to resist, she shot back. "Nor do I blame you. I think any man should have the right to remain ignorant, if he so chooses . . . even you." She winced at her words. *Good job, Lizzie. Now, you've blown it.* She glanced back, relieved to see the darkened anger on his face, fade into a sardonic grin.

"Testy, aren't we?" With a gleam in his eyes, he said, "Shall we call a truce?"

Lizzie blew out a soft sigh and nodded, though he seemed to be paying more attention to her car than to her.

"Snazzy automobile. Your father's, I presume."

Bonnie blurted, "Oh, no. This is—"

Lizzie cut her off. Now was not the time to peddle her pedigree. An amusing scheme flashed through her mind. "We don't have a daddy," she said, allowing her shoulders to droop. With a quivering voice, she whimpered, "Sis and I were orphaned at a very early age."

He rubbed his chin and nodded. "I see…so who does the car belong to?"

Lizzie turned toward Bonnie and motioned with her hand. "Go ahead, Sis. . . I believe you were about to reveal the car's owner."

Bonnie's round, freckled face distorted. Her eyes widened. Deception wasn't one of her strong points.

Lizzie cocked her head and waited, trying hard to keep a straight face. "Sis is a wonderful conversationalist—just a little shy sometimes. But once you get her started, she's a real talker."

His lip curled up at one corner. "What do you do to get her started? Maybe I can help. Try filling in the blanks, Miss. The car belongs to—"

Bonnie twisted a shank of her long flaming red hair around her index finger, a nervous habit she'd had for as long as Lizzie could remember. "Uh . . . , the car belongs to . . ."She shot a menacing glance toward her cousin, licked her lips and blurted, "The woman we work for." Her chest rose with every breath.

With a straight face, Lizzie confirmed Bonnie's story with a nod. "That's right. You did us a great favor, kind sir. We could've lost our jobs had you not come along to help."

His brow lifted. "Sisters, huh? Orphans, you say, and you both work in the same household? Now isn't that cozy."

He'd take some persuading but she was up to the challenge. "Sure," she replied, undaunted by his snide remark. "Sis is the cook and I'm the downstairs maid. We went to live in the orphanage after our parents died. Stayed there for three years. Or was it four? It was hard to keep track of the time."

"Oh, that's a most pathetic story. I'm deeply touched. Please go on."

"It was dreadful. We almost starved to death. We had nothing to eat but liver hash and beans three times a day." She made a face and stuck out her tongue. She supposed she should've left off the hash and just named beans. But sitting down to a plate of liver hash three times a day struck her as the most horrid existence imaginable.

He frowned. "Poor girls. No pheasant under glass or baked Alaska? Forgive me. I'm tearing up." He pulled a handkerchief from his pocket and dabbed his eyes.

"You're poking fun, but you should try existing on such meager vittles. A year ago, we ran away to look for work. Being close, we refused to split up. It was very difficult to find someone willing to hire the two of us. There we were, way up north with winter coming on. After weeks of going door-to-door, begging for bread, we jerked the blinds and headed south."

"I'm sure you meant to say you *jumped* the blinds."

Lizzie nodded. "Yes, of course. Like I said, we jumped the blinds and headed south."

He appeared sympathetic enough, with his crinkled forehead and his lips turned downward. He even sucked in a deep breath and uttered a compassionate-sounding "tsk-tsk."

Lizzie was now into character. The drama lessons were paying off. She sniffed. "Yes, those were rough times, all right, until we came to Goat Hill and found a job working for the Goobernut family."

"Goobernuts?" Though he covered his mouth with his hand, the dimples in his cheeks gave him away. "What kind of name is that?"

"Polish, I think." Lizzie replied with a shrug.

"So these Goobernuts whom you work for let you go joy riding in their new car?" He gave a hollow chuckle. "Fascinating. Do you suppose they might need a gardener? I could sure use a new car . . . or even an old one."

"Joy riding? Surely, you jest. We're running errands." Lizzie feigned indignation.

He grinned. "Oh? What kind of errands?"

Lizzie loved the playful banter. She chose to continue the charade and remarked quite seriously, "We're on our way to pick up buttermilk from Mr. Becker. Mrs. Goobernut will be furious if we don't return shortly. She's waiting for Sis to make biscuits for breakfast…that's why we're out so early."

"So early?" He said with a wry grin. "It must be eight-thirty already. Good grief, what time is breakfast?"

"Nine o'clock and we're always very punctual." Lizzie remained straight-faced.

He scratched his head. "Yes ma'am, I'd sure appreciate it if you could help me gain employment with the Goobernuts. Do you think they might let me make the buttermilk run sometime, if I promise to rise early? What other errands do you have to make?"

Lizzie hid her smile behind her hand. "What's with all of the questions? Do you always make it a point to grill people who offer you a ride?"

"I guess I deserved that. Do I get one more question, or have I used my quota?"

"Why not? One more, as long as you allow me one, also." Her heart fluttered. She was making progress. For sure, he'd want to know her name. She'd make up a good one.

"It's a deal—one for one," he agreed.

Lizzie concealed the excitement bubbling inside of her. "So

what's your question?"

"Where exactly were you going when you turned around—before you sailed blindly into the ditch? Did you have a sudden loss of memory and forget where your Mr. Becker lives?"

Disappointed he'd picked the wrong question to ask, yet not defeated, she yelled, "Whoops! So sorry, but I'm afraid you exceeded your limit. I'll answer one, and only one. The answer is 'no,' I didn't forget. Now it's my turn."

Bonnie snickered at her cousin's quick wit.

Lizzie thought for a moment. "You say you're looking for work, but there are other cotton fields, so what brought you to Goat Hill?"

Dimples caved into his tan cheeks. "That's an easy one. The answer is a train."

Lizzie grimaced. "You tricked me." He'd be a hard one to get to know, but Lizzie wasn't a quitter. She could be quite persistent when she wanted to be, and never had she wanted to be, more than now.

A few miles down the road, Lizzie drove slowly and pointed to a field in the distance, "That's the Lancaster fields. If you want work, you should go ask one of the hands for an old man they call Mr. Louie. I hear he does the hiring."

"But I was told I should go to the big house and talk directly to Mr. Will."

"Oh yeah? Maybe some folks do it that way, but I've heard

Mr. Louie is the overseer." She stopped the car. She was taking a chance, bringing him so close to the manor. What if her Mama should ride by? Lizzie chuckled aloud, when she imagined Mama's wide-eyed look of horror if she should catch sight of a hobo perched on the rumble seat. It would almost be worth the consequences to see her mother's face. Poor Bonnie looked as if she'd swallowed a mouse.

He hopped out, slung the bindle over his shoulder and traipsed over to Lizzie's door. Her pulse raced when he leaned in and flashed pearly white teeth. Deep dimples dug into his cheeks like footprints sinking into beach sand. "Thanks for the ride. Have a pleasant day, ladies."

"Yeah, you too. I hope you get the job," she added with sincerity. "Just ask any of the hands to point you to Mr. Louie."

Feeling distraught that he could be walking out of her life forever, Lizzie blurted, "The creek's on the other side of the field. Say . . . would you like to take a cool dip with us, first? I'm sure if there's a job waiting, it'll still be there after we swim." Then with a wink, she added, "Of course, you'll have to promise to keep your eyes shut."

He glared as if she'd spoken in a foreign tongue.

Lizzie covered her lips and snickered—partly because he blushed, and partly because he looked as if he might take her up on the offer.

Bonnie buried her face in her hands.

He said, "Maybe some other time, when you aren't in such a hurry to find a jug of buttermilk." Tipping his cap, he said, "It was a pleasure to meet you, ladies. And please give my regards to Mrs. Goobernut."

Lizzie had a strong urge to reach out and grab his arm. Instead, she attempted to hold him with her words. "But you didn't *meet* us." She supposed if he were truly interested, he would've realized there were no introductions. He hadn't asked her name . . . or the whereabouts of the Goobernut home.

She swallowed her pride and thrust forth her hand, "I'm Jo and this is my sister, Beth." Lizzie glanced over at Bonnie, whose face turned so red her freckles seemed to mesh.

He slung his bindle stick over his shoulder and reached for her hand. His white teeth sparkled when he said, "I'm Kiah Grave."

"Guy Grave?"

He shook his head and spelled it. "K I A H. Short for Hezekiah."

Lizzie's heart hammered out the beat to Mendelssohn's Wedding March, as she gazed into his clear blue eyes. "Interesting. Is it a family name?"

"As a matter of fact—" He bit his lip, and gave a shrug. He lowered his head. "You were kind to bring me here. I'm not usually so crass. If I hurt your feelings, I'm sorry."

"Well, you could make it up to me," she said with a wink.

He stepped back and rubbed a hand across his chin. "Just what did you have in mind, Miss?"

"Get the job and stick around Goat Hill."

"Well, I don't know if I can manage, but I'll sure try. Again, I'm sorry for acting like such a clod today, but you caught me in a lousy mood. I'm not excusing my rudeness, but I'm on a mission—one I'd rather die than carry out—yet I made a promise, which I intend to keep."

"A mission? Here in Goat Hill?" Lizzie sensed an adrenalin rush at the notion that he might stay in the area, even if he didn't get a job in the fields. "A preacher, huh? Well, isn't that a twist—not that I have anything against preachers, understand."

Before he could respond, she said, "Say, if you're planning to stand on the courthouse steps Saturday afternoon to hand out those little tracts, and tell people how to be good and stuff like that—I can help." She hardly slowed down long enough to take a breath. "I'll meet you there every Saturday afternoon, and we'll convert the whole town. It'll be fun."

Kiah threw his head back in a raucous laugh. "No, not that kind of mission, and forgive me for saying so, but I'm afraid I'd need to convert my beautiful assistant first, if that were the case."

Lizzie wanted to say something smart back, but for once, words failed her. *He thinks I'm beautiful.* Her heart throbbed. She longed for him to say he understood what she was feeling because he felt it too. But instead, he turned, jumped a fence and trotted across a vast field of cotton stalks.

"See ya," he yelled.

"Good luck!" She shouted, though he never glanced back. Clutching the steering wheel tightly, she watched him disappear. "Bonnie, did you hear him?" Lizzie slouched down and swooned.

"Yeah, he's on a mission. I wonder what kind?"

"No, not that, silly. I mean when he called me beautiful." Lizzie cranked the car and headed toward Gladstone.

Bonnie smirked. "Like it's the first time a boy ever called you beautiful. But I don't get it. Why didn't you want him to know the car is yours? I'd be telling everyone if it were mine. And why did you make up those names . . . Beth and Jo?"

"Are you serious? Do you think he'd look twice at me if he suspected I'm Will Lancaster's daughter?"

"Why wouldn't he? No other male within a hundred miles has had a problem falling for you."

Lizzie sighed. "But he's different. I can tell. He has principles."

Bonnie giggled. "So you made up those tall tales, because he has principles? I don't follow your reasoning."

"Trust me, Bonnie. I know what I'm doing. I want him to like me."

"Well, you can stop fretting. No doubt about it, he looked smitten . . . but he has nothing to lose, Lizzie. You have your reputation. You can't afford to get mixed up with a hobo."

"Bonnie, I can afford anything I want. But for once, what I

want is not for sale."

Lizzie parked the car in the carriage house behind the manor and nudged her cousin in the ribs. "Okay, what's wrong, kiddo?"

Bonnie twirled a flaming red lock around her index finger. "Jeepers, Lizzie, aren't you worried? Even a little? What if Mr. Louie hires him?"

"Oh, Bonnie, wouldn't that be swell?"

"Swell? You won't think so when Uncle Will hears we picked him up at the tracks. And Aunt Ali will send you off to a girl's school in Siam if she gets wind of such talk from you."

"Oh, stop being such a worry-wart and let's go to my room. I have a two-pound box of chocolates, waiting to be opened."

"From Oliver, I presume?"

Lizzie groaned. "How'd you guess?"

"Face it, cousin. Oliver won't ever give up. Aunt Ali will see that he doesn't. No need fighting it, Lizzie—you know you'll wind up married to him. I'll pick up the Society News one day and read the birth announcement of little Armadillo F. Weinberger, Jr."

Lizzie stuck her finger down her throat and pretended to gag.

The girls scampered up to Lizzie's room and pounced on the feather mattress on the high-poster bed. She picked up a Whitman Sampler box from off the bedside table, and shoved the candy toward Bonnie.

Bonnie paused, eyeing each piece as if she were a candy

inspector, before finally choosing a coconut bon-bon.

At the faint sound of a knock on a door downstairs, Lizzie sprang forward. "Listen! Sounds like someone's at the back door. What if—" She slid off the bed and ran to the top of the stairs. Bonnie followed. The girls ducked down, peered between the balusters and waited.

Lizzie reached over and grabbed Bonnie's hand at the sound of the maid's heavy feet clomping down the marble floors of the antechamber.

Cleoda yelled, "Hold your horses, I'm a coming, fast as I can. This ol' rheumatism makes a body—" When the knocking turned to banging, her voice rose. "Land sakes, you ain't gotta beat the door down. I said I'm coming."

Moments later, Cleoda stomped back down the corridor toward the library, her feet moving more swiftly than before. She hollered, "Mr. Will, there's a young hobo at the back door, insistin' on speaking with you."

"I'm sure he wants something to eat, Cleoda. Fix him a plate and send him on his way."

Lizzie whimpered under her breath, "No, Daddy, no. Please don't send him away." Peeking through the stair rungs, she could plainly see the top of Cleoda's green head rag, as the maid stood in front of the door and shouted toward the open transom.

"But Mr. Will, he won't take no food. Says he's gotta see you. I told him you wuz busy."

"Get rid of him. Tell him if he's looking for work, to see Louie."

Cleoda's voice bounced off the high ceilings. "I told him, Mr. Will, but he's still standin' there with his foot jammed in the door, insisting I announce him. He's a stubborn young stallion. I don't think he has a notion of going nowhere until you go out there. I couldn't even run him off with a broom. What you reckon I ought a do?"

"A hobo, you say? Are you sure?"

"Ain't no doubt about it."

"So you've never seen him before?"

"No, Mr. Will. He ain't from these parts. He said tell you his name is Kite Gravy."

Will shouted, "Is that supposed to mean something to me?"

"Beats me, Mr. Will." Cleoda let out a hearty laugh. "But that's what he calls hisself—Kite Gravy. Ain't that peculiar?"

Lizzie cringed when Cleoda said, "Don't you worry, Mr. Will. I'll get shed of the young rascal, one way or t'other, if I have to beat him over the head with my frying pan."

Will yelled back, "No need, Cleoda. He's already managed to interrupt my day. I may as well see what this is all about. Tell him to wait for me outside on the—"

Before her daddy could finish his sentence, the sound of footsteps pounding swiftly down the long marble hall caused Lizzie to gasp. "Too fast to be Cleoda," she stammered. She clinched her eyelids tightly and squeezed Bonnie's hand. "I can't bear to look. Please tell me Kiah didn't just burst inside."

Bonnie's mouth flew open. "But he *did.* Open your eyes, Lizzie. You've got to see this. Oh my. Now he's beating on the library door, and Cleoda's swatting him with a sage broom. He may not have anything else, but you'll have to admit—he sure has nerve."

Cleoda's voice boomed. "Get out o' here, you young hoodlum. Mr. Will . . . Mr. Will!"

Lizzie moaned, "Oh, I don't have to look to know what comes next. Daddy's fixing to yell, 'What's the meaning of this?'"

The library door swung open, and Will shouted, "For the love of Dixie, young man, are you insane? What's the meaning of this?"

Bonnie giggled. "Jeepers! You must be a mind-reader, Lizzie."

Lizzie opened her eyes. She gazed down to the floor below and strained to hear.

Kiah stood facing her father. He clutched his cap in his hand, and said, "Sir, I only need a few minutes of your time and I'll be on my way. But it's imperative that I speak with you."

"Well, young man, there are proper ways to come calling, and this isn't one of the ways. Tell me—do you make a rude habit of breaking into private homes unannounced?"

"Sorry, sir, but with all the windows up and the back door open, I couldn't help but hear. It seems to me I've already been announced, even though the maid got my name wrong. I'm Hezekiah Grave—I go by Kiah."

"You're a brazen young fellow, I'll say that for you—insolent would be a more appropriate word. But now that you've so rudely pushed your way into my home, I must admit you've sparked my curiosity. Come in and state your business, but be quick. I'm a busy man."

"You'll have no need for the pistol, sir."

Bonnie plopped her hand over her mouth. "Uncle Will pulled a pistol?"

Lizzie whispered, "Daddy's bluffing. He'd never use it." The library door closed. Lizzie groaned. "That does it. He'll never work here. Daddy won't put up with his cockiness."

"I don't mean to bad-mouth Uncle Will, Lizzie, but when he wishes, he can be quite cocky himself. Who knows, maybe the two of them will get along hunky-dory."

"Not a chance. Oh, Bonnie, I could cry. I wanted him to stay—it'll never happen now."

"Lizzie, don't be silly. I'll admit he's good-looking, but what an ignoramus to burst in as if he owns the place, and expect Uncle Will to hire him. You don't want to fall in love with someone so uncivilized."

"But I do, Bonnie. I do," Lizzie whined. "If only he hadn't come barreling through the door with an attitude, who knows . . . one day, he might've owned the place."

"Well, I'm sure it'll take you a good twenty minutes to get over him. Naturally, it takes less time when you aren't quite so serious."

Chapter Three

Will Lancaster closed the door to his study and stared at the mysterious young stranger. He drew a deep breath, filling his lungs, then slowly exhaled. "Please, have a seat."

Kiah shook his head and mumbled, "No, thanks. I'll stand." Darts seemed to shoot from his icy blue eyes as he glowered at Will without another word. He shifted his weight and with his hands clasped together, he popped his knuckles.

The awkward moments of silence caused Will's pulse to race. The boy was just a kid—barely out of his teens. Will rubbed his jaw. Why should he allow a young punk to come into his home and intimidate him? With his gaze fixated on the kid, he trudged over to the mammoth oak desk on the far side of the room, sank down in a plush, leather chair and deposited the pistol in the top drawer. Curiously intrigued by the young man's odd demeanor, he attempted to initiate the conversation. "I suppose you're looking for work. You aren't by chance the stable boy from the Vandergrift Ranch, are you?" Will knew the answer to his question, but he needed a starting point. He waited for a response.

Kiah ignored the question. Instead, he meandered around the room, conspicuously eyeballing every expensive artifact, as if he were an antique dealer come to bid on the contents.

A Ming vase sat on the drum table in the center of the room. Kiah picked it up, turned it upside down, and showing no regard for its fragility, he plunked it firmly back on the table, causing Will to flinch.

When Kiah stalked over to the bookcase, which held Will's prized collection of rare books, Will cringed as he watched the nosey young whippersnapper reach up and carelessly snatch out the 1793 copy of *Leopold's Gilded Glory.*

Will snapped, "Looking for something special?"

"Nope. Nothing special."

Will's breath quickened. Twelve years he searched for a copy of that book and now to watch a kid come in and haphazardly thumb through it as if he were handling a dog-eared copy of Anderson's Fairy Tales made him furious. Will bit the inside of his mouth to keep from scolding. But when Kiah picked up a small what-not and almost dropped it, Will scowled. "Be careful, young man. That's a very valuable figurine."

Kiah smirked. "Who are you trying to kid ol' man? This is a piece of junk." He tossed it into the air, caught it and with a haughty-sounding chuckle he pointed to the vase. "Now *that's* valuable. Yet you said nothing when I held it. I suppose you think

I'm here to rob you and that I'm such a rube I wouldn't know the difference in a dime-store figurine and a Ming vase." He tossed the figurine in the air once again. His eyes widened. "Whoops!" A wry grin swept across his face, when he caught it.

"Young man, you have a lot to learn about the value of things in life."

Kiah chuckled. "Yes, and I suppose you think you're the one who can teach me?"

Will ignored the sarcasm. "The Ming vase, I bought myself. Money can replace it. I have the money. But the figurine is priceless. An identical one is likely to bring no more than two-bits at the Five and Dime. But the one you hold in your hand can never be replaced."

Kiah grinned. "Now, is that a fact?"

Will clinched his teeth. "It's a fact indeed. The figurine is a treasured gift from the family of two colored boys—brothers—in Scottsboro, accused along with others of a crime on a train."

"Yeah? And why would they send *you* a gift?"

Agitated, Will snorted. "Maybe they wanted to."

"So you aren't planning to tell me. Is that it?"

Will couldn't believe he sat there, allowing this little nincompoop to question him as if he were on trial. Still, he had a gut feeling he needed to play along until the boy was ready to reveal the purpose of his visit. Besides, the kid didn't seem dangerous—obnoxious, but not dangerous.

He said, "There was an alleged rape on a train and the boys were accused—"

Kiah grunted. "Forget the current event lesson. I know about the Scottsboro boys' case. I was riding the rails the day it happened. I simply asked why the family sent you the do-dad."

"Call it their way of thanking me for my efforts to locate a reputable lawyer willing to defend them, or appreciation for the letter I sent to Governor Miller on their behalf. Does that answer satisfy you?"

Kiah's face twisted into a smirk. "Well, now aren't you the Big It? Befriending the down-and-out. How touching."

Irritated, Will bellowed, "Stop playing games. What is it you want? Do I know you?"

The boy's chest swelled when he sucked in a deep breath. "You're asking if you know me? That's a rather peculiar question. But I suppose we bindle stiffs all look alike." The corner of his mouth curled in a snarl. "Maybe you think you met me in Hooversville on one of your goodwill missions. You rich dudes strip us of our dignity, and then expect a pat on the back when you toss us a bone." Kiah placed his cap over his heart and gave an exaggerated bow. In a mocking tone, he drawled, "Well, we po' folks sho' thank you, Big Daddy for your alms. Yessiree, I'll have to remember to buy you a do-dad before I go back to the poor farm."

Will's voice rose. "I don't know who you are or why you feel the need to come bursting into my home spewing your venom, but unless you're ready to state your business, you can get out of my house. I don't have time to put up with your tom-foolery."

Kiah pursed his lips. He plodded over to where Will sat and slammed both palms flat on the desk, creating a threatening loud thud. His face reddened as he leaned forward.

Will eased his hand down, allowing his fingers to touch the cold steel in the partially closed drawer. His chest heaved.

Kiah glared at Will and scoffed, "I had you pegged from the get-go. You're no different than I expected."

Will leaped from his chair and stood nose to nose. With clinched fists, he yelled, "Get out of my house, you little nincompoop. I thought I was doing you a favor by giving you my time, but you're the most arrogant young man I've ever met." He stormed over to the door, held it open and ushered the way out with his hand.

Kiah ambled slowly toward the door. He stopped directly in front of Will and sneered.

Will stroked his chin. The boy looked familiar. *If I didn't know better, I'd think . . . no, that's crazy.* Or was it? The same black curly hair, deep dimples, broad shoulders, slender hips, long arms, six feet tall—*the kid looks more like a Lancaster than I do.* He bit his lip. If his hunch was right, Henry was in deep trouble and this would be one time Will wouldn't be able to fix it for him. But why did the kid come to him? Did he think—?

A pain shot between Will's shoulder blades as he stared into piercing blue eyes, which glared back at him. He swallowed hard. Impossible. It couldn't be. Cleoda said his name was . . . Grayvie? Will buried his face in his hands. Grave. No. Oh, dear Lord, no. He reached up and closed the transom. Barely audible, he mumbled. "Please . . . Come back inside and have a seat."

"And why should I do that?"

Will's voice broke. "Because I do know you."

Kiah gave a scoffing snort. "Now the truth comes out. So you do know me?" He paused for a moment, before following Will back into the library.

Will lumbered over to the desk and fell back in his chair. He loosened his tie and unbuttoned the top button of his shirt. With his forefinger he wiped beads of perspiration from his upper lip. He wanted to say something. But what? Speechless, he simply stared.

Veins popped out on the angry young man's neck. He stood tall and flexed his jaw. "I can see my presence makes you sweat. Well, this is probably the first time you've sweated in your life. But don't worry. I'm as stoked about this awkward meeting as you are. I only came to fulfill a promise. Now that I have, we can both forget our shameful little secret. I assure you, I'll find it easy to do—*Dad*." He spat out the last word as if it was bitter, causing his mouth to pucker.

Will hung his head and allowed him to vent. He figured with so much anger boiling inside, it was imperative the boy release it, else the steam would cause him to explode.

Kiah paced back and forth across the room. He stopped with his back toward Will and stared out the window. "You know who I am, yet you remained up here on your throne, dining in luxury while my mother and I lived in squatter camps, and ate mush for breakfast, dinner and supper; that is, on the days we had enough meal to make mush. But I don't expect you have any clue what I'm talking about." He twisted away from the window and stomped toward the desk.

"No, you have it all wrong. You don't understand—"

Kiah hunched over the desk and shoved a finger in Will's face. "Oh, I understand, all right." He straightened and squared his shoulders. "You know . . . I think you're probably the only lie my mother ever told me. But I suppose she had her reasons for not wanting me to believe I was the offspring of some rich fat cat who could allow his own young'un to go to bed hungry, night after night." His chin quivered. "I wonder . . . was there ever a night your belly wasn't full? Of course not. You make me sick, you know that?" His moistened eyes glistened. "What kind of animal are you?" Kiah swatted his face with his hand and turned his back, obviously humiliated when tears trailed down his flushed red cheeks.

Will walked up behind him and grasped his shoulder. Kiah stiffened, though he made no effort to jerk away. "Kiah, I said I knew you, but the only reason I knew was because I looked at you and felt as if I'd traveled back in time, peering into a mirror. Please believe me when I tell you I had no idea Fendora was pregnant when she left." His voice broke. "I know words don't suffice, but I'm sorry. I don't blame you for wanting to punish me. When you go home, tell your mother I plan to see that you both live the remainder of your lives in comfort. You'll never be hungry again. That's a promise."

Kiah slung Will's hand from his shoulder. "You still don't get it, do you? 'Go home,' you say. And where would that be? Where I left Mama? Well, that'd be the bone orchard. She's dead. She worked herself to death to care for a child all alone—no emotional support, and not one dime of financial support." He wiped his cheeks with the back of his hand.

Will trudged back to the desk and fell into his chair. With his head tilted back he clasped his hands over his mouth and moaned. "Why didn't she tell me? Why? Why?"

Kiah sat down on the edge of the desk. His brow shot up. "You're saying you really . . . you didn't know . . . about me, I mean?"

"Not until you marched through the door and I saw my face. Your mother and I worked together at the bank." His lip trembled. "Fennie took ill and up and left one morning without as much as a goodbye—" He closed his eyes and groaned. "How could I have been so stupid?"

Kiah gave a slow nod. "Okay, so maybe Mama was right.

Maybe she didn't tell you. But I still find it hard to believe that you didn't suspect—" He slid off the desk and trekked across the room.

Will lifted his head. "I don't blame you for being bitter. I'll never be able to make up for lost time, but from this day forward, I want you to become a part of my life."

Kiah made an abrupt turnaround and winced. "Not a chance." His words were brusque. "Don't you get it? It's too late to play daddy. Besides, I made Mama a promise before she died. She insisted I meet you, but I vowed not to disrupt your family. Now that I've fulfilled her dying wish, you can forget you ever saw me."

"Not disrupt my family? That's ridiculous. I'll admit this won't be easy to explain to my wife, but because of me, you and your mother suffered a life of shame. Why should my life remain uninterrupted?   I can't erase the pain I've caused, but I'll set up a bank account tomorrow in your name."

Kiah's nostrils flared. He lashed out, "Good grief, man, do you think that's why I'm here? To finagle funds from you? If you really want to help, then you can hire me to work. Jobs are hard to come by."

Will nodded. "I understand. We're living in precarious times, for sure."

"Precarious?" Kiah's temper painted his face. "What a fine word to describe the economic situation at a time when folks are dying of malnutrition every day. Do you have any idea how precarious? Are you in danger of losing your home? Or not being able to feed your family? Have you had to watch loved ones die because you can't afford needed medicine? Have you ever tried to sleep in a cardboard box on a cold night? Or sat down in a restaurant in the early morning and ordered a cup of hot water to make ketchup soup to fill your empty stomach, while the smell of bacon fills your nostrils?"

Will closed his eyes and slowly shook his head.

"I didn't think so. The nation's in the midst of a Depression, in case you haven't heard. You think it's easy leaving Mama buried in Oklahoma with no one to visit her grave? She wanted to be buried in the land where she grew up, so I took her back. But I couldn't survive there. Fields have dried up. There's no work. Those who aren't dying of dust fever are dying of starvation."

Will grimaced. "I'm sorry if I sounded callous. I didn't mean to. Believe me, I know what it means to be poor. My father was a penniless farmer and we lived hand to mouth every month."

"So you think you understand? No!" His voice rose. "You can't understand. Don't you get it? You had a *father*. I wasn't so lucky. You farmed land in the Deep South, where this rich, pancake-flat delta farmland will grow a shirt if you plant a button. Farmers in these parts have food to eat, even if they have nothing else. Not only did we not have land to farm, we had no money with which to rent a parcel. I don't even own the plot where my mama's bones lie. She's in Potter's field, you know."

Will flinched. "I don't know what to say, Kiah."

"I'm not asking for your sympathy. I don't require much, but I'm tired of being hungry. I want to work." He slapped his cap on his head. "But don't feel you owe me anything. I'll be on the next train to nowhere before I'll stand here and beg."

Will reared back in his chair and with a wry grin, said, "You certainly didn't get your bull-headedness from your mother. I wonder where it comes from."

His bright eyes twinkled. "She always said I got it from my father."

"I can see you don't intend to back down. Well, there's no reason we can't find something for you to do. I already have a good gin crew, but I suppose I could let Hiram go and train you for his job. He's getting too feeble, anyway."

"Forget it. I don't want to take someone's job. I want to pick cotton."

Will shook his head. "You can't be serious."

"Of course, I'm serious."

"The fields? But you're my son." His heart raced as the words flowed from his lips. *My son.* He swallowed hard and shook his head. "No, it isn't right. I can't send you to the fields."

"Then I'll continue jumping the blinds until I find work. Thanks for your—"

"Okay, okay. Let me think." Will knew any attempt to dissuade Kiah would be pointless. The boy would walk out the door and never look back—Will knew, because they shared the same stubborn genes. He couldn't risk the chance. He hoped his next statement would suffice. "We'll need to think of something else. The cotton won't be ready to pick for a couple of months."

"But I saw workers in the field. What are they doing?"

"Thinning the stalks."

"Fine. That sounds easy enough. How thin you want them?"

Will grinned. No doubt about it, the boy was cut out of the same burly cloth as his father. "Cotton is usually thinned anywhere from twelve to eighteen inches. I've lost several field hands who've moved into the mill village, leaving me short of workers. So I'm trying something new this year. I ordered six-foot cross beams with small sweeps fastened at twelve-inch intervals. They'll attach to the rear of our cultivators, reducing the amount of work and the number of laborers needed. The hands who aren't running the cultivators will be chopping."

"So I'll chop."

Will scratched the back of his head. "Have you ever chopped cotton?"

Kiah shrugged. "I'm a fast learner. What's to know?"

"It's hard work, Kiah. Weeds and vines have to be chopped from around the stalks. If you don't know how to use a hoe, you'll be chopping down the stalks along with the vines. Your hands will blister and bleed before the calluses develop. And it's hot and dusty out there. You'll get so thirsty your tongue will feel like it's swabbed with a cotton boll, but you have to keep moving. The hands start work at the first signs of daylight and work until almost sundown, stopping only long enough to eat lunch under the nearest shade tree."

As gruesome as Will made it sound, Kiah appeared unfazed by the job description. He made one last attempt. "Kiah, I can't send you to the fields. Let's figure something out."

"We already have. I'll be in the field at daybreak." He held out his hand. "I reckon I've taken enough of your time. Thank you, sir, for seeing me."

Will stood. He grabbed his son's hand and chuckled. "Did I have a choice?"

"I suppose not." Kiah's dimples caved into his cheeks.

Will rang for Cleoda, who came clomping down the hall wielding a sedge broom over her shoulder, as if it were a mighty weapon. She glared at Kiah and scowled. "You rang for me, Mr. Will?"

"Cleo, pack a few jars of vegetables and some of your fig preserves—and if you have any fresh baked bread, stick in a loaf with a pound of butter. Tell Hobart to go to the smokehouse and get a slab of salt pork and tell him to pack everything in a foot tub. Oh yes . . . and stick in a bag of ground coffee beans, and a few jars of pickled peaches."

When Cleoda turned to stalk away, Will added, "Cleo, didn't you have some cat-head biscuits left over from breakfast?"

Kiah frowned. "Cat-head biscuits?"

"Yeah, that's what we call them—Cleo's biscuits are about the size of a cat's head. Smeared with butter and preserves, there's nothing to compare. One's enough to make a meal."

Cleoda stomped back to the kitchen, grumbling aloud. "I Suwannee, if Mr. Will ain't done gone slap loco. I shoulda swept that no-good young rascal out with the rest of the trash 'fore he come in here pollutin' the place."

Will found it hard not to stare at the boy. Amazing. Why didn't he see it the minute he first walked in the door? "Where you staying, Kiah?"

"I spotted an old deserted barn on my way here. I thought I'd check it out."

Will cracked opened the door, stuck his head out and glanced down the hall. "I think I know of a place. There's a little cabin—" His voice trailed off to a whisper.

Chapter Four

When Will and Kiah stepped into the corridor Lizzie cupped her hand over her mouth and whispered, "Well, blow me down, Bonnie. What gives? They were holed up in there for over an hour and both came out smiling. It's a good thing Mama left. She'd have a stomping fit if she got whiff of Daddy entertaining a field hand in the house."

"Well, there's your answer." Bonnie snickered. "He's not a field hand. He's a hobo."

Lizzie's forefinger covered her lips. "Shh! Stay down—don't lct them see us." The girls lay flat on the floor and peered between the railings as they strained to hear the conversation in the antechamber below. Lizzie's heart pounded. "After Kiah said he wouldn't take a hand-out, what did Daddy say? Could you hear?"

"Uncle Will said, 'Nonsense, if you work for me, you'll eat.' Then he mumbled something but I couldn't make it out."

Lizzie clamped down on Bonnie's arm. "For real? You're sure Daddy said those exact words . . . 'If you work for me'?"

"That part was clear."

"Oh, Bonnie. Don't you see what this means? Daddy likes him. Did you hear what he told Cleoda to fix for him?"

"Yeah. Not the usual hobo plate, that's for sure. Uncle Will ordered everything but the fatted calf." She snickered. "Maybe your daddy appreciates a little cockiness."

Lizzie's jaw dropped. "But of course. That's it!"

"It?"

"Sure. Makes perfect sense. Kiah's got spunk. When Mama complains of my bad behavior, Daddy says, 'Leave her be, Ali. The girl's got spunk.' If there's one think Daddy approves of, it's a person with spunk and Kiah's full of it."

"Humph! That's not spunk. Gall—that's what I call it—pure unadulterated gall."

"I declare, Bonnie, you use such weird words sometimes. Come on, let's skedaddle." The girls headed for the barn, where secrets were shared, tears were shed and problems solved. Today, Lizzie had a need to do all three.

Alamanda Lancaster pranced through the kitchen on her way to the car. "Brush me off, Cleoda—this jersey picks up everything."

With the tail of her apron, Cleoda whisked the back of the blouse. "Miz Ali, you sure look nice this morning. Is that a new hat?"

"Yes, thank you, Cleoda, but please hurry. I haven't time to dawdle. Miss Merle and I are going shopping and I'm late."

Shopping was one of Alamanda's favorite pastimes. Tall and slender, her clothes fit her well and she never tired of hearing the compliments she received from wearing nice things. To her dismay, her chestnut hair, which she wore in a bun, had begun to gray at the temples. But a little dab of brown liquid shoe polish on a cotton boll did a fine job of covering the few silver hairs.

She pulled a pair of white gloves from her purse. "Cleo, while I'm gone, I'd like you to gather the laundry and have Hobart take it to Mattie. Send her word to put more starch in Will's shirts. He likes them stiff. She's been stingy on the starch, lately."

"I'll see to it, Miz Ali."

"Oh, and about tonight's dinner—I'd like a sweet potato soufflé, pork chops and collards." Alamanda sighed, as she slipped her hand into a glove. "Cleoda, you know how I hate to complain, but the last sweet potato soufflé was lumpy and you used entirely too much brown sugar. I was quite disappointed."

"I'm sorry, Miz Ali, but how'd you like the mess of turnip greens I fixed with 'em? Oh, my soul, Mr. Will, he sho' did brag. He had me bring him a bowl of pot liquor to sop with his cornbread later that night. He said them was the best greens he ever tasted. I flavored 'em with an extra slab of fatback, a tad more salt and a little more sugar to cut the bitterness." Cleoda wrung her hands. "Was they to your liking, Miz Ali?"

"Much too salty, Cleoda. I don't know why you insist on making everything briny. If I'm not home by suppertime, keep my plate warm, but make sure the bread doesn't dry out. You know how I hate dry bread."

"Yes'm, Miz Ali."

Alamanda tugged at her gloves. "Cleoda, have you seen my husband?"

"Yes'm. Mr. Will's in the library with that scoundrel who come busting in the house like a cat with his tail on fire."

"Cleoda, it behooves me—"Alamanda threw up her hands. "Oh, forget it." She made a mental note to admonish Cleoda for speaking ill of Will's business associates. But later. She had no time to tarry. Besides, no doubt the scoundrel Cleoda referred to was the bookkeeper, John Graton, and Alamanda was none too fond of him, either.

Lizzie plopped down cross-legged on the hay in the loft, closed her eyes and waited. The musty smell always brought on a dozen or more consecutive sneezes. She covered her nose with her hand and tried to catch a breath in between each annoying sneeze. "Oh Bonnie, where do you suppose he's staying? I hope it's not at the horrid hobo jungle near the tracks, where the—"

Bonnie finished the sentence. "Where the hoboes sleep? Jeepers, Lizzie. Why would you think such a thing? Knights and hoboes never share the same quarters."

"You're poking fun. I'm serious. I'm worried about him."

"I wouldn't fret, if I were you. I have a feeling he's capable of taking care of himself."

"Did you hear Daddy mention a cabin? You don't suppose he offered him the shanty, do you? That's a cabin."

"Are you kidding?" Bonnie's brow creased. "Daddy says Uncle Will treats that little bungalow as if it's some sort of shrine."

"It's true. But Daddy keeps it for Cleo's sake. She was born there, you know. She moved into the basement of the big house the day her mammy was buried."

Bonnie shrugged. "Well, I suppose to a hobo, even the shanty might look good. I don't know of another unoccupied cabin in the area—except, of course, Mr. Johnson's fish camp, but I can't see ol' skin flint allowing a hobo to rent it."

Lizzie stuck her head out the loft door and peered down, when Cleo shouted her name.

"Miz Lizzie, git down from there and go wash up. The food's on the table." Cleo grumbled loudly, as she turned away. "I Suwannee, Miz Ali can't do nothin' with that girl—she ain't got no business in a dirty ol' hay loft at her age. It ain't fittin'. Sometimes I think she just tries to act like po' white trash."

Lizzie groaned. "Cleo pretends to be talking to herself, but she means for me to hear every word."

With her hands firmly planted on hefty hips, Cleo stomped toward the manor, her voice rising with each step. "What that girl needs is a razor strap took to her—'at's exactly what she needs—a good whoopin', even if she is grown. She ain't likely to get the strap from Mr. Will though, the way that man dotes on her."

Bonnie crawled toward the ladder. "We'd better go."

"Not yet. We haven't solved my problem. What am I to do, Bonnie? I'm mad about him. I know you think I'm kidding, but I'm as serious as a canker sore." She fell backward on the hay, with her hands clasped over her heart. "I'm in love, I'm in love, I'm in love, and he'll be working here. Right here at Gladstone. Isn't that swell?"

"Lizzie! That sounds so vulgar."

"What, being in love?"

"No, silly. Using such crude words as 'canker sores.'"

"Trust me, Bonnie. If you'd ever been on a hayride with your best beau on a moonlit night and had a canker sore, you'd understand."

"Lizzie, I know you're teasing, but you shouldn't talk like that. It's not lady-like and you're really sweet. I don't know why you like to shock people by pretending to be loose."

"Faddle. Why should I care what people think? Oh, Bonnie, I know you think this is like all the other times, but this time it's real. When he stuck his head in the window of the car and I felt his warm breath on my neck—" She clasped her hands under her chin and swooned. "I declare, it was like a burning fire started in my brain and ran all the way down my body until it reached my toes."

Bonnie brushed hay from Lizzie's hair. "Forgive me, dear cousin, but I think the fire left nothing but charred brain cells."

"Poke fun, but he's the man I'm going to marry."

"Okay, let's suppose it *is* real. And let's suppose he loves you too. Then what? Love leads to marriage. Do you honestly think your parents would let you marry a hobo who hopped a train to find work in the cotton fields? I don't think so. Forget it, Lizzie. He's not your type."

"Oh no? Then who's my type, Bonnie?"

She snickered. "Oliver Weinberger."

Lizzie yanked off her shoe and tossed it toward her cousin. "I declare, Bonnie, you sound more like Mama every day. Sometimes I wonder if we were switched at birth."

Monday afternoon, Will sat alone in his office and strummed his fingers on the desk. Had he acted on sentiment and not logic, when he agreed for Kiah to work at Gladstone? He couldn't deny his first thoughts had been of himself and his son, but there were others to consider.

Wasn't his first obligation to protect his wife and daughter from the scandalous gossip—or was it? What about his obligation to his son?

After the shock had worn off, Will understood he couldn't have it all. If he acknowledged his son, he'd lose his wife and daughter. If he failed to acknowledge his son, he'd never see him again. Could he live with himself, knowing he turned his back on his own flesh and blood? The consequences seemed unfair.

Not in the frame of mind to conduct business, Will moaned when the bookkeeper from the bank dropped by, late Monday afternoon.

Will met him at the door. "Have a seat, John."

"Thanks, but I'll stand. I'm hoping this won't take long. Will, you know why I'm here. Tom's note is past due again. We need to proceed with the foreclosure. If you continue giving him extensions, other farmers will demand equal treatment. Sign the papers and   I'll have them served before dark." He reached into his briefcase and pulled out a manila folder.

Will shifted through the stack of papers and reviewed the transactions, while John Graton stood over him reiterating all the reasons why they couldn't afford to delay proceedings.

Will reared back in the chair with his hands clasped behind his head.

John pursed his lips. "Well? Do you understand now? Tom keeps asking for time, but he won't have a single dime more tomorrow, next week or the next than he has today. We have a buyer, a Mr. Justice from Slocomb who wants that farm but he won't wait forever. We need to push forward." John had kept books for Will for over ten years—a real stickler for details.

Will crammed the papers back into the folder and thrust it toward John. "Give Tom another week and let's see what happens."

"But Will! You said the same thing last week, and nothing's

changed. Why prolong the inevitable?"

Will vaulted from the chair and slammed his fist on the table. "I said give him a week, John. I don't want to argue." Will lowered his head and mumbled. "Sorry. I had no call to yell at you. But let's give him a break—one more week." He sucked in a deep breath. How could he transact a business deal, which could have a devastating effect on a man and his family, at such a time as this? He couldn't think straight.

John's bushy brows seemed to knit together. "I hope you know what you're doing, Will." He stuffed the file into his briefcase and stomped out of the house.

Chapter Five

At the dinner table Monday night, Lizzie swished her spoon around in her tea glass and waited impatiently for her father to mention his encounter with a hobo.

Her mother made a short grunt. "Eliza, please stop that infernal clanging. If you had milk instead of tea, I declare, it would be butter by now."

"Sorry, Mama." She removed her spoon and glanced toward her father.

"Daddy? How was your day?"

He sucked in a deep breath and sighed. "Fine, honey. Eat your supper."

Before Lizzie could respond, her mother chimed in. "Will, are you feeling all right? You've been unusually quiet."

"I'm fine, dear. Just tired."

"You look a mite peaked. I'd like for Doc to take a look at you."

His voice rose. "I'm fine."

"I think I'd feel better if you'd go by his office tomorrow and let him check you out. You're not yourself."

He pounded his fist on the table. "Great thunder, woman, I told you there's nothing wrong with me. Drop it, Alamanda. If I'd wanted a nag for a wife, I would've married Ol' Blue."

Lizzie glanced at her father, and then toward her mother. Except for the occasional jingling sound of eating utensils, an icy silence filled the room.

Will touched his napkin to his pursed lips, leaned over and touched his wife's hand. "I'm sorry, honey. I have a lot on my mind, but I'll be fine. I have to figure some things out—that's all." He tucked the napkin under his shirt collar.

Alamanda looked at him curiously and nodded, without pressing further.

Lizzie could stand it no longer. "Daddy, was there someone in the library with you today?" She hardly had time to finish the question before he spat out the answer.

"Yes. John Graton." His face paled. His hand shook when he lifted a fork.

Alamanda didn't seem to notice the change in his appearance. "Really, Will? What did John want?"

He drew a deep breath, and muttered, "Must we discuss business at the table?"

Her twisted mouth revealed her exasperation. "Good grief, Will. I neither asked for, nor did I want a detailed report. I merely asked what he wanted. It just seems a little irregular that he would come to the house. What's your problem? You're on pins and needles. You've never minded before when we took time at the dinner table to discuss our day."

"You're right, dear. I apologize. Maybe I am a little on edge. John said Tom Becker hasn't made good his promise. It appears we'll be foreclosing soon, unless something bad happens."

Ali gave a mechanical-sounding reply. "That's good, dear."

Lizzie's face burned at her mother's callousness. She blurted, "Don't you mean he'll lose the farm unless something *good* happens, Daddy?"

Will coughed and cleared his throat. "Yes, Princess, that's exactly what I meant to say. I had my mind elsewhere." She watched her parents exchange glances, the way they often did when her mother would throw up her hands, and wail, "What are we going do with her, Will?" But this time, her mother said nothing.

Though she didn't receive the answer she wanted from her father, Kiah Grave was no longer Lizzie's primary concern. With a lump growing in her throat, she took a big swallow of tea. "Daddy, you can't let Mr. Becker lose the farm. Isn't there something you can do?"

He picked up a knife and cut his meat. "I know how you feel, hon. I like him, too."

Lizzie whined. "Then, why can't you help him? He's had at least half-dozen operations on his back. People are saying it was

Papa Gid's fault that Mr. Becker is in the fix he's in. Since our family's responsible, don't you reckon we ought to at least help save the farm?"

Alamanda's eyes grew wide. "Shame on you, Eliza, blaming your grandfather for Tom's accident. Papa was nowhere around the gin when Tom got careless."

Will shot a menacing glance Ali's way and flexed his jaw.

Lizzie couldn't read his mind, but she had a feeling her father agreed with her. She'd heard the talk among the ginners. "Mama, people are saying Papa Gid knew the swivel arm on the vacuum was faulty. Yet, he refused to fix it or to put bars over the opening."

Alamanda's mouth gaped open. "That's simply not true. I declare, Eliza, I'm surprised at you listening to such horrid rumors. Who do you think ordered the bars? Papa, of course."

"That's true, Mama, but it wasn't until after poor Mr. Becker was sucked up the sleeve along with the cotton. If Papa Gid had repaired it when he was told the joints in the swivel arm needed fixing, Mr. Becker would be a whole man today and we wouldn't be having this discussion."

Ali lifted her chin. "Well, I'm appalled at your attitude, Eliza, and I refuse to sit here and let you belittle your beloved grandfather."

"Sorry, Mama. I don't mean any disrespect toward Papa Gid, but I'm just saying the Becker family has had a rough time and I think we owe it to them to help out. I reckon Mrs. Becker has more than a body can stand with six children and no help on the farm."

"Honey, these are tough times. Lots of folks have their troubles. But with that many children, Tom should've had them helping with the harvest."

"But Mama, Harlan's the oldest, and he's only twelve. He's barely tall enough to see above the plough. When his daddy had surgery in March, Harlan dropped out of school to help his Mama plant. Now he's gonna fail another grade. I'm sure with a little time, they'll get straightened out. Please, Daddy. Don't foreclose."

Alamanda blotted her lip with a napkin. "Eliza, your father has a job to do. Papa Gid entrusted him to make wise decisions, when he turned the bank over to him. Will can't afford to be weak. How would you like to run around town, barefooted and dressed in feed sacks like those poor little Loudermilk ragamuffins? If Will gave in to every sob story, that's exactly what you could expect. Naturally, it's sad to see folks like the Beckers lose everything, but we can't let things like that get us down."

Her mother's patronizing tone made Lizzie want to throw up. "Oh, it's difficult for us, but we Lancasters do a real fine job of keeping our chins up, in spite of all of our money, don't we, Mama?" Her eyes clouded as the bitter words rolled off her tongue.

Alamanda glared at Will. Lizzie recognized the look. She knew her mother intended for her father to scold her, but he merely frowned and shook his head, which meant there'd be no more talk of Tom Becker.

She wanted to ask a second time about the other guest in the library, although it seemed far less important now that the Becker family's sad plight occupied her thoughts. But if she let the opportunity pass, she might never know. "Daddy, I heard Mr. Louie say he needed help in the fields. Has he had luck finding workers?" When her father's eye began to twitch, Lizzie knew she'd hit a nerve.

Will stuffed a yeast roll in his mouth.

"Daddy, that *is* what Mr. Louie said, wasn't it? I mean, about needing more field hands?"

Will wiped his mouth and nodded. "That's right, honey. It's hard to find good help these days. Quite a few families, who once worked for us, have moved into the Cotton Mill Village in Geneva to work at the mill."

"Then, I suppose you'll need to search outside the boundaries of Goat Hill to find help. Right, Daddy?"

Alamanda spoke up. "I should hope not. Will, there have been some interesting articles in the Progressive Farmer about the benefits of cotton sledding. Would you need the extra hands if you switched over to sledding?"

He shook his head. "We could get by with fewer hands for sure, but I still hold to the idea that picked cotton is at least two grades better than cotton that's snapped or sledded. But I suppose if Louie can't find enough pickers, I won't have a choice. Lizzie, pass the collards, please."

Lizzie bit her lip and handed the bowl to her father. "Daddy, Bonnie and I went joy-riding earlier and we saw a bedraggled young fellow headed toward the south field. He certainly looked like he could use a job." She swallowed. "I wondered if he might've been searching for work here at Gladstone."

Will laid his napkin on the table. "Well, as a matter of fact, we did hire a young man. He'll start tomorrow." Then he mumbled, "I doubt he'll stay long."

Before Lizzie could ask why he made such a statement, he rang the bell for Cleoda.

"Cleo, bring me a bowl of that banana pudding I saw you making today."

"Will?" Alamanda asked. "Was it one of the Grundy boys?"

"What?"

"The fellow you hired. Was he a Grundy?"

"You can't be serious, Alamanda. Why, I'd work the fields myself before I'd hire one of those foul-mouthed skirt-chasers." Will turned and waved his fork at his daughter. His voice went from quiet and restrained to loud and gruff. "Lizzie, honey, you stay away from those Grundy's. You hear what I'm saying? Stay away from them."

Alamanda sighed. "Well, I'm relieved. I've seen the way Coley Grundy gawks at Eliza. Someone needs to teach that boy his place."

Lizzie rolled her eyes. As much as she detested the Grundy boys, she hated even more the way her mother often referred to one's place as if life were a step-ladder and the Lancasters occupied the top rung. Her father's glare prompted her to respond. "You don't have to worry your head over that one, Daddy. Coley and Grover Grundy make my skin crawl."

"Good! That's what I wanted to hear." Will took his fork and forcefully stabbed at his pork chop.

The skin around Alamanda's eyes tightened. "Will, you never did say who you hired."

Lizzie often criticized her mother for not letting something go, but tonight she felt proud of her tenacity.

"He's not from here, Alamanda. You wouldn't know him." Will changed the subject. "Cleoda sure outdid herself this time. The pudding is delicious."

Alamanda bristled. "An outsider? What's he doing in Goat Hill?"

"He hopped off the train. Would you please pass the iced tea, Lizzie?"

"Oh my stars, Will. You hired a . . . a common hobo?"

"As a matter of fact, Ali, I did. He's young, strong and Louie can use him. Hoboes have to eat too, you know."

"Oh, Will. How could you? You know how I feel about outsiders working at Gladstone. How do you know he's not an escaped convict from the chain gang?"

"Great thunder, Ali, you spend time and energy trying to concoct ridiculous scenarios. You've always said I had an instinct for character." Will's voice reeked of sarcasm. "Well, this kid has breeding and we all know how important breeding is to you."

"Breeding, indeed. He's a homeless vagrant. How can you say he has breeding?"

His voice lowered. "Perhaps, my darling, I don't equate breeding with wealth, as you do."

Lizzie laid down her fork to keep her father from seeing her hands tremble. "Daddy, what makes you think the new hand won't stay long?"

Will frowned. "Eat your dinner, sugar."

"I am, Daddy, but I was thinking you must think right highly of him, since he stayed so long in the librar—" Lizzie swallowed hard. Her daddy had not yet admitted Kiah was in the library. Oops!

Will glared at his daughter. "Lizzie, you seem awfully inquisitive tonight. Is there a reason you should concern yourself with my field hands?"

Now she had done it. "Of course not, Daddy. I was making conversation." Lizzie grabbed her tea glass and took a swig.

"Well, I'd think you could find something more interesting to discuss at the dinner table than my business affairs."

Alamanda pursed her lips. "Will, *was* there someone else in the library—besides John?"

"As a matter of fact, there was, Alamanda." He cut his pork chop, without glancing up.

"Well?"

"Well, what, Ali? You're forever harping at Lizzie for asking a one-word question. What in thunderation do you mean by 'well'?"

"You're right. Forgive me, Will. I'm asking if you brought that vagrant into my house."

Will finished chewing his meat and swallowed. "Yes, dear, I brought him into *your* house."

Alamanda gasped. "Whatever for, Will?"

"Business, Alamanda. I was conducting business, and your house was the only one available, since I don't seem to have one. When did this family become so all-fired interested in how I handle the affairs of Gladstone?" Will picked up his napkin and slammed it on his plate. Apparently, he was finished with dinner, and from his expression, Lizzie feared he was finished with the present conversation.

Alamanda's face turned red. "Why are you being evasive, Will Lancaster? You've always encouraged Eliza to take an interest in the affairs of Gladstone, and when she does, you clam up and refuse to talk."

Will shot back. "That's ridiculous and you know it. Stop meddling and let me handle the fields, Ali. The boy arrived with little more than the clothes on his back. He needed a job and I need pickers. What's so strange about that?"

"Will Lancaster! You know nothing about him, other than he's a common tramp. I don't consider it meddling, to insist you not bring riff-raff into my . . . our home. Why didn't you meet him on the veranda? He could've been scouring the place to see where we keep the silver. For all you know, he could hop a train before morning with our valuables tied up neatly in a rag."

"Aw, Alamanda, you beat all." Will grimaced. "Why do you want to think the worst of folks? Just because he's poor and an outsider is no sign he's a thief. I trust him. That should be good enough for you."

"Paint him any way you want, William Lancaster, but he's still a bum. What makes you think you can trust someone whom you know so little about?"

"I have no reason not to." Will's voice faded.

"Well, I know you think I'm being overly cautious, but you should consider your daughter. Our field hands have always been from the community. I don't like your hiring strangers who mysteriously show up in town. Eliza is forever running around these swamps by herself. A stranger working in the fields could be hiding in the brush, grab her and—" Color rose to her cheeks.

Lizzie squashed the impulse to laugh. "And what, Mama? Grab me and then what?"

When her mother clammed up, Lizzie glanced at her father and shrank down in her chair. She had an eerie feeling he could read her thoughts.

Alamanda cupped her hand over her mouth. "See what I mean, Will? She's naive. Why, I wouldn't have a moment's peace as long as she was out of my sight. I try to keep tabs, but I can't tie her to the bedpost."

Her father groaned. "Land sakes, Ali, the things you conjure up to worry over."

Lizzie closed her eyes and dreamed of the scenario. It was a lovely picture of her tripping down by the creek and Kiah jumping from behind a tree to grab her. She sighed as she imagined them falling to the ground and him pouring out his heart, telling her how he knew she was the one for him from the first moment he laid eyes on her. She drew a deep breath. But he *hadn't* laid eyes on her. Not really. Not yet. He hardly noticed her. But he would. He most certainly would.

"Where is he staying, Will?" Alamanda asked bluntly.

Will shoved back from the table and wiped his mouth with a napkin. He rang for Cleoda.

She clomped in with another big bowl of banana pudding. "I suppose this here is what you wuz wanting Mr. Will?" Cleoda's gold tooth sparkled when she smiled.

"Yep. That's mighty good pudding, Cleo. Mighty good."

Alamanda gave a swift wave of her hand. "No need to dawdle, Cleoda . . . Will, I asked you where the boy is staying."

Lizzie's heart raced. *Yes, Daddy. Where?*

Will's jaw flexed, causing his temples to heave in and out. "What difference does it make where he's staying, woman? He's not sitting at your dinner table, so why should you concern yourself?" Will never called his wife 'woman' unless she stretched her limits. Apparently, she was there, which distressed Lizzie, since she too, was eager to hear the answer to her mother's question.

After dinner, Will retreated to the library. Reared back in his swivel desk chair, he muttered half aloud. "Why, Fendora? Why didn't you tell me?"

He wanted to believe had he known, he would've done the honorable thing—married her and given the boy a name—but how could he be sure? Dared he harbor regrets? If he'd married Fennie, he'd not have his sweet little Lizzie. He swallowed hard. If the aching lump in his throat grew larger, he'd choke to death.

The hours passed. He reached in his pocket and pulled out his watch. Ten minutes past midnight. Relieved that Ali hadn't come searching for him, he saw no need to go to bed at such a late hour and risk waking her. He laid his head on the desk and eventually fell asleep.

Kiah Grave stretched out on the knotty, blue-tic cotton mattress in the shanty and stared through the tiny window at the stars.

His throat closed when he recalled the years of bitterness he harbored toward William Lancaster, in spite of his mother's insistence his father was a good and decent man. Now that he'd met him, he understood. He lay there wishing he could somehow let his mother know how wrong he'd been. If he could talk to her, he knew exactly what he'd say.

Imagining she could hear, he whispered. "Mama, would you believe it if I told you he said, if only he'd known, things would've been different? He loved you, Mama. He didn't say it in so many words, but I could tell. And you know what? He loves me, too. He really does."

Kiah wept. Not one prone to cry, yet from the moment he jumped off the train in Goat Hill it seemed as if the cork had popped on an eighteen-year-old bottle of hot tears. Tonight, they poured out freely on his pillow.

His mother's last words played in his head like a scratched phonograph record. "Hatred doesn't become you, Kiah. Go visit him, and you'll see he's a good man. You're made out of the same cloth." Kiah had resented those words, until today.

His heart lightened when his thoughts turned to the snazzy Model A Ford—and the gorgeous driver of such a fine automobile. He chuckled, recalling the silly banter. "She must take me for a real chump to think I'd fall for that one. A maid? What a laugh." A crazy notion flitted through his head. Was it possible the girl could be his—? Ridiculous. So what if she reeked of money. Surely, Will

Lancaster wasn't the only wealthy man in town.

Her haunting beauty and the mystery surrounding her made it impossible to fall asleep. His breathing hastened as he recalled the image of her shiny blonde locks and the flirty way she flung her hair over her shoulder. Her soft, sun-kissed complexion, the long, thick lashes framing her bright green eyes, her rosy lips, her quirky sense of humor—he drew a deep breath. The girl had the looks of an angel and the devil's wit. She had feelings for him, too. He was sure of it. But whoever she was, she wasn't the poor little waif she tried to portray. The girl had real class.

Kiah glared at the night sky and mulled over the events of the day. Could a classy dame like her really fall for a bindle stiff? "Oh, Mama, I wish you were here. Would you tell me to get my head out of the clouds? I miss you so."

Chapter Six

Will awoke to the sound of footsteps coming down the stairs. He raised his head from the desk and rubbed his aching neck. His eyes squinted at the sunlight streaming in through the library windows.

"Will?" He stiffened at the sound of his wife's voice. How would he explain? Surely, she'd know something troubled him deeply for him to stay in the library all night.

"I'm in the library, dear." He brushed his fingers through his disheveled hair and straightened his shirt. He grabbed a file and pretended to be reading when she walked in.

"Oh there you are." Alamanda peered over his shoulder. "Is that Ken Bullard's file?"

"What?" He glanced down. "Uh . . . yes." He slammed the file shut. "Need something, dear?"

Alamanda ignored the question. She touched the soil in the potted plant sitting on his desk and made a slight grunt. "Dry as a bone. I do declare I have to tell Cleoda every move to make, nowadays. She's getting so forgetful." Then plopping her hands on her hips she frowned.

Will swallowed hard. She'd obviously come in the library for a reason and it had nothing to do with wilted plants. He waited.

"Will, you need to do something about your daughter."

He grinned, relieved that Alamanda hadn't realized he'd spent the night in the library. "What's my little Swamp Angel done now?"

"Cleoda said she refused to eat breakfast again this morning, and her car's gone. I want her sitting down to the table at mealtime."

"Yes, dear."

"I knew this would happen when you bought her a car, but no . . . you insist on spoiling her. Mark my word, Will Lancaster, you'll live to regret it." When he failed to argue the point, Alamanda shrugged. "Put your work aside, Will, and let's eat breakfast. Cleoda has it on the table."

Will nodded and sat down at the table, bowed his head and recited the same words he repeated every morning. "Father, thank you for the bounty set before us. May it bring nourishment to our bodies and make us fit to do thy service. Bless my family and—" He choked. How many times had he prayed those words when he had no idea that his family included Kiah? But God knew.

Alamanda laid her hand on top of his. "Will, what's wrong?"

With his head still bowed, he mumbled, "And guard our hearts. This I ask in Jesus name. Amen."

Ali gave him a strange once-over as she passed the baker of biscuits. "Will, I want you to tell Eliza that we won't stand for her running off in the mornings before breakfast."

He grumbled, "I'm *not* Cleoda, Ali. I haven't forgotten what you said."

"My stars, Will. You've been in a foul mood lately. You're still brooding over having to repossess Ken Bullard's farm equipment, aren't you? Get over it. Ken's young. He can start over. I declare, you take everything so personal. If Papa had fretted over such things, he'd never have been able to get as far as he got."

Will snapped. "He's six-feet under, Ali—that's how far he got. One day, I'll get as far as he got and then maybe you'll be satisfied. You've always wanted me to be like your Papa, but as hard as I try, I won't ever be his equal in your eyes, until I'm lying beside him in Gladstone Cemetery."

"Well, if you don't beat all, Will Lancaster. What's ailing you?"

He swallowed hard. "I'm . . . I'm sorry, Ali. I don't feel well. Excuse me, please."

"Where are you going?"

"Back to the library. I have some important business to attend to."

"Sometimes I don't understand you, Will."

Cleo plodded in as Will stood to leave.

Alamanda said, "Cleo, you can tell Mattie I'm not pleased

with the shoddy ironing job she's been doing lately. Look at Will's shirt. I declare, it couldn't be more crumpled if he'd slept in it."

Will shot a glance toward Cleo, who seemed to understand. She gave Will a wink and said, "Yes'm, I'll pass the word. I sho' will, Miz Ali."

Will sat at his desk and pressed his hands firmly against his throbbing temples. When the phone on the desk blared, he jumped, knocking the receiver off the cradle. He grabbed the dangling phone, held it to his ear and mumbled a weak "Hello."

"Good morning, little brother."

Will's hand shook at the sound of Henry's voice. He opened his mouth, but the words wouldn't come. From the sound of the rapid clicks on the other end of the line, Henry must have thought there was a poor connection. Will gripped the receiver until his knuckles turned white.

Henry repeated his words: "Hey, little brother, I can't hear you—you there?"

Will licked his lips, then mumbled, "I'm here. You know, don't you, Henry?"

"Know what? Will, you okay? You sound weird."

"Nah, you couldn't know. I'm not thinking straight. Odd, though, that you should call. We need to talk, Henry. I'm in trouble. Big trouble—" His voice broke.

"Whoa. What's the problem?"

"Oh, man, you can't imagine." Will sobbed. "I'm in an awful jam. My life is ruined."

"Aw, get hold of yourself, buddy. It can't be that bad."

Will sucked in a deep breath. "It's worse than you can imagine, Henry. I don't know where to start in trying to explain."

"The beginning, maybe?"

"It's a long story."

"I'm listening."

Will sighed. "Henry—" His voice quivered.

"Hey, take it easy. Whatever's troubling you, we'll get through it, you hear? Together. I'm here for you, kiddo. Remember when we contemplated closing the bank doors during the crash? Yet, we made it through, didn't we? Now, suppose you tell me what has you acting as if the world's coming to an end?"

"Henry, I have a son." There. He blurted it out. How else could he say it?

After a long pause, Henry responded. "You have a . . . what?"

"You heard me. I have a son, Henry."

Henry gave a hollow chuckle. "You kidding?"

"It's true. I didn't know until yesterday, but he's only a few months older than Lizzie. Oh, Henry, I'd rather be dead than have Lizzie find out. She thinks her ol' man can do no wrong."

Henry sucked in a breath. "I'm not sure which question to ask first, Will. How is it that you didn't know about the boy until now?"

Will sensed anguish in Henry's voice . . . or was it disgust? "The boy's mother left shortly after he was conceived. Without telling me. I had no idea until today, when he showed up and confronted me in the library."

"Will, don't be foolish—this reeks of a blackmail scheme. The kid probably thinks he can waltz into Goat Hill and claim to be an illegitimate child and scare you into reaching deep into your pockets." Callous-sounding words gushed out. "I'd like to get my hands on the little snit. Just be careful what you say, Will, lest you forfeit the fortune you've created."

"Fortune I've created?" Will scoffed. "You mean the fortune I inherited, don't you, Henry? I'm not proud of the way I acquired my wealth. You and I both know I'm not a self-made man. On the contrary. I'm an Alamanda-made man. No, Henry. I'm afraid I haven't accumulated anything on my own."

"Okay, okay, but the point now is not how you accumulated your wealth, Will, but how you plan to hold on to what you have."

"What I have?" A sarcastic chuckle escaped from his gut. "I have nothing. Everything belongs to Alamanda—even me. From the day we married, she proceeded to mold me into her daddy's image. She employed his tailor to dress me and insisted I use the after-shave Papa Gid preferred, although I hate it. I smell like Granny's rum cake every time I walk out the door. She even had me change the way I parted my hair—from the left side to the center—the way Papa Gid wore his hair. She claims it looks more dignified. Dignity is everything to Alamanda." Will grimaced. Was he taking his frustrations out on his wife? Was it her fault he got himself into such a fix?

"You can't blame her for that, Will. That's how she was raised. She and Merle both are all about impressing people, but you'll have to admit, they've made us old farm boys look pretty good."

"Well, I doubt she'll impress many people with the news that her husband has an illegitimate child."

Henry's tone changed. "I take it Alamanda doesn't know."

"Not yet."

"That's good. No one needs to know. Not even Alamanda. We've got to keep it quiet. You've inherited a legacy and you owe it to those before you to do everything in your power to keep from smearing the family name."

Will's face burned. "Of all people, Henry, I hoped you'd understand."

"But I do understand."

"No. You don't. If you did, you'd realize I've paid my debt to the Gladstones, and we both know that's the family legacy you refer to. It turns my stomach, Henry, when I stop to realize that the Gladstone Empire came about by the blood sweat and tears of former Gladstone slaves. And I can't deny that I've enjoyed a lavish lifestyle with dirty money that came from cheating poor, illiterate white farmers out of their own land. I fear the transformation is now complete, Henry. I walk, talk, and even smell like Mr. Gid. I can't stand to look myself in the mirror."

Henry scoffed. "So your wife had money when you married her. You shouldn't feel ashamed, Will. I came back from the army with nothing but the clothes on my back. I wouldn't be where I am today, had you not chosen to share your good fortune . . . and there are many others in this town whom you've helped in one way or another. You're not like Mr. Gid. You're a generous man. But be careful. Don't be so generous that you hastily hand over money to some little two-bit blackmailer who comes out of the woodwork, claiming he's a long, lost heir. If you do, you can expect many others to follow."

Will mumbled. "There are no more."

"How can you be sure? You obviously didn't know about this one."

Henry didn't sound at all sympathetic. Will wished he'd never said anything.

"Will, this sounds like a bunch of hooey. When the kid realizes you aren't taking the bait, I'll wager he'll disappear and go find another sucker. However, if he persists, tell him to speak to our attorney and let Ramon handle it. But by all means, keep your mouth shut. You don't need to say anything which might incriminate you. We'll boot the little gold-digger back to where he came from."

Will sighed. "No. You have it all wrong, Henry. It's not like that at all. This kid is mine, I'm telling you. I can't deny it, and I don't plan to."

"Don't be stupid, Will. How can you be sure the kid is yours?"

A sharp pain shot between Will's shoulder blades. His voice quaked. "Because I knew his mother."

"You mean in the Biblical sense? So you sewed a few wild oats as a young man. Who didn't? What proof is that? Don't be such an ignoramus, Will. What makes you think you were the only one?"

Resentment swelled. "As I said, Henry, I knew his mother, and not only in the Biblical sense. But I know the kind of person she was. There was no other. She was a sweet kid. She wouldn't have lied to the boy to weasel money out of me, if that's what you're thinking."

"Oh, Will, don't be so naïve. You make her sound morally pure. She was obviously a loose woman—the kind Mama warned us boys to stay away from." He chuckled "She had a kid out of wedlock, didn't she?"

Will's face burned. "You're wrong about her, Henry. I take full responsibility for what happened that night. I can make all kinds of excuses how it happened, but I won't. I'm guilty. But there's another reason I know without a doubt the boy is mine. You'll know too, when you see him."

Henry groaned. "He favors you, huh?"

"Spitting image. She gave him my name. He's my son, Henry.

My own flesh and blood."

Henry's anger spewed over the phone. "He calls himself a Lancaster, does he? We'll see about that. I suppose you consider this sentimental bonding as being gallant, Will, but trust me, it won't seem as valiant to the rest of your family. You can let him take you for a ride, but I'm a Lancaster, too, and he's not coming to Goat Hill and ruin my family's reputation. I'll take him to court, first. He has no proof."

"Calm down, Henry. He's not a Lancaster . . . well, what I mean is, his last name on the birth certificate is not Lancaster. What I meant to say was he has my given name—William Hezekiah. He goes by Kiah Grave."

Henry's tone seemed to suggest a sense of relief, although his words remained harsh. "So after all these years, he shows up on your doorstep to claim his inheritance. Why in the name of Dixie did he wait until now?"

"But that's not why he came. In fact, he seemed offended whenever I offered him money."

Henry groaned loudly. "You offered him money?"

"I did, but he refused."

"Then what in Sam Hill does he want? Part of the estate, I suppose."

"He wants a job. That's all he wants—an opportunity to work, so I hired him."

"You what?" Henry shouted over the phone.

Will held the phone away from his ear, as Henry continued to rant.

"Doing what? Not working at the bank. I'll quit first. You can find yourself another President."

Will burned inside. He wanted to yell, 'Then quit, Henry, and see who's sorry.' But he didn't, and he knew later he'd be glad he resisted the temptation. Instead, he sucked in a deep breath and in a low voice said, "Calm down, Henry. There's no need for rudeness. The boy asked for a job in the fields. That's all. What could I do?"

"Bad decision, Will. Bad, bad decision. I wish you'd conferred with the attorney, first. Ramon could have given you counsel. You're upset, and not in the frame of mind to make these types of judgments. The kid will use it to ruin you. Whatever you do, don't give him a penny. Once you give him a check, you've just admitted paternity. Don't do it, Will. Get rid of him anyway you can. The sooner the better. If you refuse to think of the rest of us, at least think of your daughter. Does having a son mean so much to you, Will, that you'd disregard everyone's feelings but your own?"

Henry's words stung. "You think I like knowing what this will do to Lizzie if she finds out? But he's my own flesh and blood. Don't you get it, Henry? I can't sprinkle him with fairy dust and hope he disappears. He's my son."

Henry scoffed. "So he says, Will. So he says . . . hey, I have to hang up. Someone's coming in. Perhaps it's for the best. Maybe we'll both be a little more rational in our thinking after we've had time to reflect on the situation."

Will seethed. He knew who Henry determined to be the irrational one.

Chapter Seven

Lizzie had waited all day for this moment and now that it was here, she had no idea how to go about finding answers without stirring suspicion. She plopped down at the supper table and hoped her daddy was in a better mood than last evening.

"Daddy, the new field hand you hired . . . I suppose he's staying at the Blanchard's?" There. She'd said it.

Cleoda crouched over Will's shoulder, and filled his cup with coffee.

"Thank you, Cleo." Will picked up the cup and poured a little of the hot coffee into his saucer. He lifted it to his lips and blew a couple of times before taking a sip. "Cleo. Is this a different brand?"

"Nah, sir, its Luzianne, same as always. Why do you ask, Mr. Will . . . somethin' wrong?"

"No. Nothing's wrong, but it doesn't seem to have as much chicory as usual."

"Well, I ain't—"

Alamanda sighed heavily. "That will be all, Cleoda."

Alamanda's brow pinched into a frown. "Will, your daughter asked you a question. I'm curious, also. Where *is* the boy staying? I think Mamie Blanchard would have better sense than to rent a room to a tramp. She runs a respectable boarding house, and I know of no other place he could be staying . . . unless of course, he has relatives in the area. Does he, Will? Do you know his people?"

Will drew a deep breath and sighed. "Land sakes, Ali. When you get a bee in your bonnet, you can't turn loose, can you? Do you know where the other sixty-plus field hands live? Not likely, because you've never taken an interest before. You don't care where they live. But to satisfy your sudden deep and unexplainable concern for my new field hand, the boy is staying at the shanty."

Alamanda's chin quivered.

Will dipped a spoon into the meringue atop the pudding, and rang the bell for Cleoda.

"Yessir?"

"Cleo, the pudding is delicious, but what causes those little golden dots on top?"

"I made it same as always, Mr. Will. It's the weather what's got them sugar droplets collectin' on top. Want I should make some more?"

"No, no. Of course not. It's fine. Really. I wanted to make sure you hadn't changed your recipe. No one can whip up a pudding like you, Cleo."

Cleoda beamed. "Don't you fret, Mr. Will. ol' Cleoda would

never change the recipe. It does a body good to see a fellow enjoy himself the way you do when I set a bowl of my puddin' in front of you."

Alamanda's chin shot up. "That's enough, Cleoda. You can go back to the kitchen now." She glared at her husband. "I declare, I don't know what's happened to you, Will Lancaster. Have you taken leave of your senses?"

"No, dear. The pudding is fine. Delicious, in fact. I was simply curious."

Ali recoiled. "Don't be facetious. You know perfectly well that's not what I'm referring to. You told that . . . that vagabond he could stay at the shanty, after the conversation we had?"

Will's teeth made a grinding noise. "No, I told him before our conversation, though it wouldn't have made a difference. Ali, how 'bout you tending to the house and leave the hands to me. I wouldn't have offered the shanty if he were a threat."

"I don't understand you, Will. By your own admission, the boy's a common hobo. He hops trains, going place to place, bumming hand-outs from hard-working people."

"From folks like us, you mean? Well, dearie, I trust you'll hold on to every morsel of food you've worked so hard for. I'd hate for you to have to part with anything so difficult for you to come by."

"You're being sarcastic, Will, but you know I'm right. He's a no-good, lazy bum, probably thrown off the train, and not only do you parade him around in my house but you put him up in a cabin on the estate. That scares me to death."

"He's barely more than a kid—around eighteen I'd say. And you've no right to judge a young man whom you don't even know. He's a decent human being."

Lizzie squirmed in her chair, as she watched the veins on her daddy's neck protrude. *I think you're wrong, Daddy. He's at least twenty—maybe twenty-one*."

Alamanda threw up her hands. "He's eighteen, and you say he's barely more than a kid? He's a man, Will. A man. We have a daughter to consider and I want that bum on the next train out of here before he decides he wants to sow his wild oats in my backyard."

Will sneered. "Funny, you seem to think Lizzie is a child, and she's the same age."

"Well, it's different with girls—especially girls with breeding. A boy left to wander from pillar to post like a common alley cat has no morals. Sometimes I wonder where your mind is, Will Lancaster. Eliza hikes across the meadow and into those backwoods almost every day of her life during the summer. And to my dismay, she practically lives at the creek."

With a playful wink, he reached over and placed his hand on his daughter's shoulder. "And my little Swamp Angel shall continue to frolic in the woods and swim for as long as she pleases."

Alamanda rolled her eyes. "Will, you know how I detest that crude-sounding nickname. Why do you insist on using such a vulgar term?"

"Nothing vulgar about it, dear. It fits her. My angel is happiest when traipsing around in the swamps or swimming in Sandy Creek. Besides, she likes it when I call her that . . . don't you Swamp Angel?"

Alamanda glared at her husband. "I wish you wouldn't encourage her. You know perfectly well the dangers that exist . . . and now that boy—"

"Oh, Ali, you worry too much. The boy is a perfect gentleman."

"A gentleman? Is that supposed to be a joke? He's a vagrant, for crying out loud. I'm putting my foot down, Will. I want you to get rid of him."

"You've had your say, Alamanda. That's enough."

Alamanda had plenty more to say, but Lizzie heard very little of the conversation that followed. She couldn't wait to tell Bonnie that Kiah would be staying at the shanty. How convenient was that?

After supper, Lizzie went upstairs, took a bath and brushed her teeth. At the sound of loud voices, she eased the bathroom door open and peeked out to see her mother leaning over the stairwell, glaring down toward the antechamber.

Alamanda yelled, "Will, turn out the lights and come on to

bed. It's late."

"Don't coddle me, Ali. I know when I need to go to bed."

"Will Lancaster, how dare you speak to me in that tone. What's your problem? Why are you acting so peculiar?"

"Maybe *you're* my problem. I'm not asking you—I'm telling you—back off, Alamanda. You've been badgering me since breakfast."

The library door slammed with a bang. A split-second later, the door to her parents' bedroom slammed even louder. Never had she heard her father speak so harshly to her mother. For once in her life, she agreed with her mama—her daddy's behavior was most peculiar.

Lizzie couldn't sleep. It was midnight before she heard her daddy trudging up the stairs to his bedroom.

Will opened the bedroom door and tiptoed inside. Alamanda appeared to be sleeping. She looked peaceful, but that would soon change. He'd expect her to divorce him. Last year—last month—or even last week, the possibility of losing Gladstone, the bank, the paper and the gin would've terrified him. Not now. At the moment, none of that mattered. Lizzie concerned him most. Would the news of his indiscretion destroy their relationship? He eased across the room, slipped off his clothes and snuggled under the covers beside his wife. She gave a grunt and rolled over on her side. A knot in his stomach swelled as he tried to imagine life without her. Sure, she was strong-willed and hard to get along with at times, but even so, he loved her.

Wednesday morning, Will arose before daybreak and ambled into the kitchen. The smell of bacon filled the house.

Cleoda stirred a pot of grits. "Mr. Will, you're up mighty early this morning'."

"I've got things to take care of, Cleo. I won't be eating breakfast."

"Nonsense. Old Cleo will have you some flapjacks in no time flat. A man's gotta eat."

"No thanks. I'm not hungry. Tell my wife I went to the fields."

"I'll do it, but she ain't gonna be happy when she hears you didn't wait for breakfast."

He mumbled, "You're right. She won't be happy."

Will drove down the road leading to the cotton field and parked. At the rising of the sun, he saw Kiah approach. He watched his only son swing a hoe in the dusty field. Will's heart couldn't have ached more if someone had reached inside him and ripped it apart. He laid his head on the steering wheel and wept, until there were no tears left.

Alamanda strolled into the dining room. "Cleoda, is there a reason why you failed to set a place at the breakfast table for Mr. Will?"

"Yes'm. Mr. Will claimed he didn't want nothin' to eat. I tried to insist, but his insister was a mite stronger than my insister."

"Did he leave?"

"Yes'm, he did. He said tell you he's checkin' out the fields."

"Whatever for, I wonder." She shrugged. "Thank you, Cleoda. That'll be all."

Lizzie walked in and took her seat at the table. She barely touched her food.

Alamanda threw her hands in the air. "What's happened to this family? First your father starts acting like a rabid dog, snarling and snapping at the ones he cares the most about . . . then you . . . you've stopped eating and sulk for no reason at all. I want to know what's going on. Are you in some sort of trouble, Eliza?"

"Trouble? What kind of trouble can I find at Gladstone? You guard my every move."

"You haven't wrecked your car, have you?"

"No, Mama. I haven't done anything. I'm simply not hungry. Aren't there times when you don't feel like eating?"

Alamanda cocked her head. "If that was all there was to it, I wouldn't be concerned. But you were acting odd at the dinner table last night, asking those peculiar questions."

"But Mama, you explained it to Daddy. Like you said, I was showing an interest."

"Horse feathers! You know I didn't mean it—I wanted to get Will to open up—explain why he's become so volatile. You're using my words as an excuse for your bizarre behavior, but Eliza Lancaster, trust me, I'll get to the bottom of this. You can count on it. Something's upset your father, and I know of no one other than his little pride and joy who could cause him such anguish. It would serve you well to confess before I find the truth for myself."

"Mama, I don't know what's bothering Daddy. Maybe it's Mr. Becker."

"Tom? For crying out loud, child. Why would you think such a thing?"

"Because Daddy is a big softy at heart. He doesn't like to take people's land away from them. He only does it because you expect him to. He thinks he'll be letting you down if he fails to foreclose."

"Well, if that's not fine and dandy. Your father fires off on you like a stick of dynamite but somehow it's supposed to be my fault? He does no wrong in your sight, does he, Eliza? Well, you might want to get it into your little naive mind that your father is not as perfect as you've been led to believe."

Her jaw tightened. "Mama, may I be excused?"

"No, you may not. I haven't finished." Ali rang the bell for Cleoda and shouted, "Where is that woman when I need her?"

"I'm coming, Miz Ali. Ol' Cleoda's slow, but I'm coming. Whatcha need?"

"I don't have all day. I'm volunteering at the Charity Bazaar and I want you to kill a hen and prepare chicken and dumplings for supper . . . and pick some butterbeans."

"Oh, me and my grand young'un took care of the picking at sunup. I've got a hamper nigh full on the back porch, waiting to be shelled."

"Fine." Ali turned and pointed a finger toward her daughter. "And Eliza, you stay near the house today. I don't want you roaming around the estate. It isn't safe, anymore with that . . . that—" She shuddered and hurried out the door.

Chapter Eight

The sight of a dead chicken hanging from a low branch on the magnolia tree caused Lizzie to shriek.

"Land sakes, you act like you seen a ghost. What's all that carrying on about, Miz Lizzie?" Cleoda's teen-age granddaughter, Comfort, sat shelling butterbeans under a Live Oak tree.

Lizzie pointed to the upside-down fowl, with its neck hanging limp. "That is *so* atrocious."

Comfort frowned. "What? Drawing blood out of a chicken? You'd rather eat the blood?"

Lizzie grimaced and plopped down on a stump. She picked up a stick and wrote initials in the sandy soil—LL + KG. She sighed and sent the stick sailing through the humid air. "I'm bored."

Comfort hissed. "You bragging or complaining? I done picked a hamper of beans, shelled a mess and rung a chicken's neck. I ain't bored. Wishin' I was."

Lizzie ducked behind the well when Cleoda stuck her head out the window and yelled.

"Comfort McRawlins stop yo' piddling and tote a pale of water to the field hands, afore I take a strap to you. It's gonna get hot early, and Mr. Louie don't need no workers falling out with heat stroke because of your lazy bones."

Comfort held up a wicker basket. "I ain't piddling, Big Mama. I'm half-way finished with this hamper of beans."

"Well, you can finish shelling after you tote the water . . . and Miz Lizzie you ain't hiding'. I done seen you, so you can jest come on out. Comfort's got a heap of chores to do and she ain't got time to dilly-dally with the likes of you. Now go find you somethin' to do."

Cleoda started bringing her granddaughter to work with her from the day she was born. The two girls were near the same age and spent hours together when they were younger, playing with doodlebugs under the smokehouse. When Comfort turned ten, she had to help with the chores and Lizzie lost her playmate.

Lizzie glanced at the window to make sure Cleoda wasn't looking. She moseyed out from behind the well and whispered, "Comfort, I'll take the water for you."

Comfort covered her mouth. "You crazy? You saying you wanna go to the field?"

Lizzie nodded. "Yeah, hurry and fill the bucket before your Big Mama catches us."

"No, Miz Lizzie. Your' mama will have a conniption fit if she catches you out there and Big Mama would beat the living daylights out of me for allowing you to go."

"Fiddle faddle. Mama doesn't care, and Cleo is too busy to notice."

"But Big Mama told me—"

"Aw, shucks, Comfort, all she cares about is making sure the hands get water. What difference does it make who goes, as long as the water gets there? Now give me your apron."

Comfort's brows arched. "Whatcha want my apron for?"

Lizzie didn't have time to answer Comfort's many questions. She yanked at the apron sash, untying it and then jerked it over Comfort's head in spite of the girl's objections. After pulling it over her own head, she said, "Now, let's swap shoes."

"Nah, Miz Lizzie, I can't oblige you on that. What if your mama come a walking out?"

"She won't. She's gone. And stop calling me 'Miz Lizzie.' You only do it to irritate me."

Comfort grinned and slipped the shoes from her feet. "Well, I reckon they'll fit, since these was yours before they wuz mine."

Lizzie plopped down on the back steps and buckled the worn patent-leather Mary Jane's.

Comfort giggled. "I Suwannee, if you ain't a sight for sore eyes."

"You think I'll pass?"

"Pass? You're funny. Here you are wanting to look like hired help, and I want to look like a rich gal, but no matter how hard we try, we ain't neither one gonna fool nobody. Not really."

"Sure we can, and I aim to prove it. The only difference between Alice Loudermilk and me is our clothes, and she's a cook for Doc Griffin. Alice is quite pretty in a plain sort of way. If she was dolled up, she'd look like a Princess."

Comfort snickered. "Miz Alice *is* kinda pretty. Well, now that I think about it, I reckon she might look like a Princess if she had somethin' besides that ratty ol' feed sack dress to wear."

Lizzie quickly pulled her long blonde hair into a bun and secured it with a comb. Then, jerking down several strands, she attempted to make herself look a mite haggard—not ugly—just haggard in an attractive sort of way. She still had her pride. Whirling around, she asked, "How do I look, Comfort?"

"Like a rich gal who's done gone slap loco, Miz . . . I mean, Lizzie."

Lizzie dropped the bucket down into the well and pulled it back up. "Help me, Comfort."

"Land sakes, white girl, don't you know nothing? You ain't got to unhook the well bucket. Just dump the water into the pail hanging over the side."

Lizzie sloshed water into the pail, grabbed the dipper and headed for the field. Her heart raced when she spotted Kiah, halfway down a row on the north side.

One of the field hands, hollered. "Miz Lizzie? That you?"

She glanced toward Kiah, who didn't appear to hear. Sucking in a deep breath, she yelled back. "Hold your taters, Charlie, yo' time's a'coming." The comical words flowing from her lips almost made her laugh out loud. *At least I sound like Comfort.*

She wormed her way toward the back row and watched the muscles in Kiah's arms bulge when he dug the hoe into the ground. His bib overhauls clung to his body by one strap. The other strap trailed behind his back. Her heart pounded as her eyes shifted to his sweaty chest and broad shoulders. Though she supposed there was nothing indecent in the way he was dressed, yet Lizzie felt it almost sinful to look. She sucked in a deep breath, before shoving the dipper under his nose and asking, "Want a drink?" Her face burned. Maybe it was the hot sun. Maybe not.

Without missing a swing, he continued to chop without taking his eyes off the cotton stalks. "I'm fine. Give it to the ol' man."

Lizzie followed him as he made his way down the row. "Aw, go ahead. Take a drink. There's over half a bucket here, and more where this came from."

"The ol' man needs it worse than I do." He jerked on a vine that wrapped around the hoe.

Lizzie made a last attempt. "One could easily become dehydrated in this heat. You may as well take a sip."

He ignored her and never missed a swing.

Anger boiled inside her. For all he cared, she could be a ninety-year-old woman standing there. But she wasn't. She was

Eliza Lancaster, daughter of one of the wealthiest men in the Deep South. Folks were forever telling her she was the prettiest girl in Geneva County. She could have her pick of beaus, and she chose him. *What do I have to do to make you take notice of me, Kiah Grave?*

In spite of the urge to pour the pail of water over his head, she trudged over and handed the bucket and dipper to old man Louie and suggested he pass it around when he had his fill.

Louie furrowed his leathery brow and frowned. Lizzie wasn't worried. He had no way of knowing why she was there and he wouldn't give her away, even if he did. He took a slurp from the dipper and with his head lowered, he raised an eyebrow and whispered, "You ought to be ashamed of yo'self, young'un. Whatever it is you up to, it ain't gonna work."

Lizzie frowned. "Shh! Maybe . . . maybe not, but we won't know until I try."

"Yo' daddy just drove off. What do you suppose he'd say if he knew you wuz out here acting like a hired hand?"

She swallowed hard. "What was Daddy doing out here in the field?"

"I might ask the same question of you, missy."

Lizzie shrugged and walked away.

When everyone had a drink—everyone except Kiah—she took the bucket and dipper and turned to walk back to the house. Her lip quivered as she trudged down a long row of cotton stalks. *Be that way, Kiah Grave, and see if I care. I wish I'd never given you a ride. You're nothing but a—*

She stopped in her tracks at the sound of his voice. Maybe she only imagined it.

"Wait!" He yelled.

When she turned, Kiah motioned for her. Water sloshed as she ran through the rows, scratching her legs and coating her with dust as she wound her way through the green stalks.

Kiah reached in his back pocket, pulled out a handkerchief and swiped across his sweaty face. In a soft voice, he said, "I'll take a swallow now, if there's any left."

Lizzie peered into the bucket, glad she hadn't spilled it all in her haste to reach him.

His gaze stayed focused on the dipper and not once did he look her in the eyes. When he finished drinking, he splashed the last bit of water in his face.

She sighed. He was thirsty. She had water. Simple as that. He returned the dipper to the bucket, mumbled what she supposed was a 'thank-you', and picked up his hoe and began chopping. Never had she encountered such an arrogant chump. Judging from the cool reception, she concluded he'd already heard she was the Lancaster's spoiled daughter. He completely ignored her and acted as if he'd never seen her before. Lizzie didn't know which emotion to dwell on first: humiliation, anger or heartbreak. *I'm not through with you, Kiah Grave. As Cleo says, 'there's more than one way to skin a polecat.'*

Lizzie kicked dirt as she ambled back to the manor, consumed by anguish that went far beyond humiliation. No boy had ever shunned her. Kiah Grave would live to regret it. She'd see to it.

Comfort's eyes widened at the sight of Lizzie's smudged face. "Well, blow me down, if you didn't pull it off. You sure look like hired help, now."

Lizzie jerked her hair down and shook her locks into place. She reached up and wiped the sweat gathered around her temples. "Oh, shush, I'm in no mood." She handed the apron to Comfort and exchanged shoes.

"Sorry, Miz Lizzie. Somethin' go wrong?"

"Everything's gone wrong, Comfort. Everything!"

Lizzie moped around the remainder of the day, wishing Bonnie were there. Aunt Merle had insisted Bonnie go with her to Dothan to attend a relative's funeral. Aunt Merle had always referred to her Cousin Baxter as being a cousin, twice removed. She supposed this time was his third. Three times and you're out.

Chapter Nine

Will trudged into the smoke-filled restaurant on Main and rubbed his burning eyes. His nose turned up at the unmistakable odor of Wednesday's special—corned beef and cabbage—normally a favorite, but today the smell nauseated him. Stifled, he pulled at his tie. Rivulets of sweat collected around his collar.

When his brother called earlier and suggested they meet for lunch, it sounded like a good idea. Now, he wanted to renege. The place was packed. Henry waved from a table against the far wall. Will fanned the smoky blue haze with his hand and sauntered across the room, questioning his sanity with every step. He hoped the tables were far enough apart that no one could hear their conversation. One overheard word out of context could ruin him. He swallowed hard. What was he thinking? Taken within the context could become even more of a problem.

If he knew Henry—and he did—there'd be only one subject of conversation. Will sighed, knowing he had no one to blame but himself. He never should've said anything. Not to Henry. Not to anyone. Alamanda was his wife. If anyone had a right to know, wouldn't it be his life partner? Will ached inside. Life partner indeed. His partner would send him packing if she knew. She must never know.

Henry shoved his chair out, stood and greeted his brother with a handshake. After exchanging short pleasantries, Henry sat down and cupped his hand over his mouth. "Will, I've been thinking this over. I wish you hadn't hired the boy but what's done is done. Firing him now might upset him and make things worse. But we've got to figure the best way to keep it quiet. Will . . . are you hearing me?"

Will nodded and mumbled. "I hear you, Henry."

Henry seemed annoyed. "You look like you're in another world. I'll admit we have a mess on our hands, but we'll figure something out. I'm sorry, but I don't trust the kid. I hope you won't let a false guilt trip rob you of your senses. That's probably what he's counting on." Henry lowered his voice to a whisper when two men took seats at a nearby table. "I'm confused. You say he and Lizzie are the same age—which means you were having—"

Although Henry failed to finish his sentence, Will knew what his brother was implying, but he was wrong. But why bother to clarify? What was done was done, as Henry had pointed out. "Henry, I won't sit here and try to excuse my sin, but there are some things I can't explain. I need you to help me—not condone or condemn—but help me figure out what I should do." Will's eyes clouded.

Henry frowned. "Get hold of yourself, Will. You ask me to help, but you say there are things you can't explain. I can't help unless I understand how you got yourself into this mess. Either you trust me or you don't."

Will sucked in a breath. "Okay, so what do you want to know?"

"I've been wondering why she didn't tell you."

"I don't suppose she found the right opportunity, Henry." He covered his nose with his hand. The smell coming from the kitchen was nauseating—or was it the present conversation that turned his stomach?

"What do you mean she couldn't find the opportunity? How long does it take to say, 'I'm pregnant'?"

The question didn't deserve an answer. Will rubbed the back of his neck to relax the tight muscles. His shoulders ached. A deep pain ran from his right temple, to his neck, down his spine, reaching all the way to the small of his back.

Henry cocked his head. "Let me get this straight. So you were working for Mr. Gid at the bank when you sowed your wild oats in a public field. I get that—but I'm having problems with the timeline."

Will cringed at Henry's choice of words. Fennie was too innocent to be referred to as a public field. She wasn't like that. She was pure. Sweet as honey. That is, until— Will bit his trembling lip.

Henry rubbed his chin. "Help me, here, Will. When did you first realize you were in love with Alamanda?"

"Today, I suppose—"

Henry looked puzzled. "What are you saying?"

"I'm saying Ali hasn't been an easy woman to love, but now the thought of losing her scares me to death. She has her high-hat ways, but it's not as if that little trait caught me by surprise. I knew what she was like when I married her."

When the waitress brought the food to the table, Will glanced down at his plate and pushed it aside. "I can't eat. Coming here was a bad idea."

"Well, I'm hungry." Henry picked up his knife and cut a piece of corned beef. "Level with me, Will. I want to know everything. Start from the beginning. When I left for the service you were living on the farm with Mama and Papa. The next thing I knew, Mama wrote saying you were a banker. How did you pull it off?"

His brother showed no signs of dropping the subject. Will drew a deep breath. "That was the year of the drought, Henry, and the corn burned up in the fields. We didn't have enough to feed the hogs. We were on the brink of losing everything. I went to the bank to see if I could borrow a little money on the farm, though I didn't expect much. I was stunned when Mr. Gid approved the loan, but not nearly as shocked as I was when he turned around and asked how I'd like to work at the bank. I couldn't imagine why he picked me to train for the job but I didn't ask questions."

"You lucky stiff. But then you've always had a certain charisma that seems to draw the right kind of people."

Will shook his head. "No, Henry, charisma had nothing to do with me getting the job."

"Call it what you may, but you were the pick of the Lancaster litter. I'm sure Mr. Gid saw the potential. Clyde was too much like daddy, and as much as I hate to admit it, I suppose I was, also. But you took after mama. You were the good son."

"It seems I had you fooled."

Henry smiled. "I won't deny that learning of your little romp with a chippy took me by surprise. I didn't know you had it in you, little brother. I could almost be proud of you, if I wasn't so afraid your little tryst has come back to haunt us. Until today, I thought you could do no wrong."

"Henry, I'm sorry to disappoint you, but it's never good to put your faith in a man . . . not even if he's your little brother."

Henry's jaw jutted forward. "Get off the pulpit, Will."

Will pushed his chair back. "You know, Henry, I'd hoped you'd be a little more supportive but apparently I made a mistake when I involved you."

"Aw, don't get sore. Give me time to get over the shock. I want to help you. Honest I do. Now, tell me—how did you meet this—this woman?"

Will bristled. He resented the way his brother referred to Fennie as 'this woman.' He pulled at his collar. "Whenever I took the job at the bank, I moved into Mrs. Blanchard's Boarding House and that's when I learned the bank bookkeeper also roomed there. She was a sweet young thing by the name of Fendora Grave. We ate breakfast downstairs every morning and walked to work together."

"I think I'm ahead of you. One thing led to another and then when you found out your co-worker was pregnant, you proposed to Ali because you were afraid of losing your job at the bank. Smart move."

Will's brow creased. He shoved his chair away from the table and stood.

Henry jerked on the tail of his coat. "Sit back down, Will. I'm not judging you, understand. A man's got to eat—and I reckon Mr. Gid would've fired you and the woman both, if he'd found out his employees were having a little hanky-panky after hours."

Will glanced around the room and saw a couple of people staring. He eased back into his chair. "It wasn't like that, Henry. I can't believe you'd honestly think I could've walked out on any woman, had I known she was carrying my child. But not once did it cross my mind she could be pregnant. One night . . . that's all it was, Henry. One night . . ."

"Yeah, yeah." Henry's lip curled. "And every convict on the chain-gang is innocent. It's me you're talking to little brother."

Will bristled. "I've never claimed innocence. I merely made the point that I had no inkling that Fennie was pregnant."

Henry nodded. "I gotcha. But Will, I've always thought it strange that you and Ali wound up together. You're leather and she's silk, if you know what I mean."

Will's tight face relaxed in a thin smile. "You're asking what she saw in me?"

"No, but you'll have to admit—you two are as different as grits and greens. But I guess love is strange, huh?"

"Love? Surely, you know by now it wasn't love that brought us together, Henry. Our marriage was nothing more than a well-calculated business deal. The plan was to lure the snake out of the box."

"I don't get it."

Will frowned. "Forget it. I shouldn't have said it."

"But you did. Now I want to know what you meant."

"Henry, I guess I want to blame Ali for what happened the night of the party, but I didn't have to yield to her luring. Underneath the good ol' boy façade, I was a snake. I knew the little scheme was wrong from the beginning."

"Hold on!" Henry waved his arms. "You're talking in riddles. Wrong? What was wrong? What night? What party?"

"Mr. Gid's annual Christmas party at Roseland, the night Alamanda proposed to me." A shiver ran down his spine. He'd never mentioned the proposal to anyone until now.

Henry chuckled. "So you're saying Alamanda made you an offer you couldn't refuse?"

Will nodded. "I guess you could say that, but I didn't know she was serious. I barely knew her. As you can imagine, we didn't travel in the same circles, and I'd only worked at the bank less than two weeks. The night of the party, she escorted me into the parlor to show me her new piano. I sat down beside her on the bench—and that's when she asked if I'd like to marry her. I didn't take her serious. I said, 'Of course, sweetheart, and we'll live happily ever after on your father's mullah.'"

Henry chuckled. "No one ever accused Mama of raising dumb young'uns. Go on—"

Will gazed into space. "She laughed. I assumed that was the end of her little joke, until we strolled back into the ballroom. Minutes later, Mr. Gid stood above the crowd on the first landing of the winding staircase. He motioned for Ali and then called for me. Ali ran down the stairs, grabbed me by the hand and pulled me up there with them. I was a new employee and hadn't expected a bonus but it didn't keep me from hoping for a little something in an envelope."

Henry chuckled. "I hear you."

"Well, Mr. Gid glared at me, peculiar like, and then slapped me on the back. My knees shook. I didn't take to being in the limelight."

Henry scratched his head. "Forgive me for jumping ahead but I think you're about to tell me the bonus you received that night wasn't the one you hoped for."

"You're absolutely right. Mr. Gid said he had a couple of announcements to make. The first one left me numb, when he put his arm around my shoulder and looked out over the crowd staring up at us. And that's when the shocker came. He said, "I'd like to announce my daughter's engagement to William H. Lancaster IV. I waited for the punch line, but it soon became apparent there wasn't one. The man was serious.""

Henry jerked his head back and cackled. "You've got to be kidding."

"Nope. It was no joke. The guests applauded as Ali flung herself into my arms. It soon became apparent to me the whole scenario had been prearranged without my knowledge. Ali and her father knew of my impending marriage way before I had any clue what was taking place."

"I see . . . so what did you do after enjoying the accolades? Did you protest?"

"That was my first impulse. I wanted to yell out that I had no plans to wed a girl I wasn't in love with. I hardly knew her."

Henry chuckled. "But I'm guessing you didn't go with your first impulse."

Will shook his head. "Before I could think how to phrase it without being offensive, Mr. Gid said he had another announcement."

"Nothing quite as surprising as the first one, I'm sure."

"You wouldn't think, would you? To tell the truth, Henry, if I could relive that moment, there are a lot of things I'd do differently." Will drew a deep breath. "But I won't deny my marriage has worked. She loves her family, and nobody in this community works harder in the church than Ali. She practically runs it." He mumbled, "She's . . . she's a good wife."

Henry pretended to choke. "Hey, it's me, you're talking to. I know her. Remember?"

Will stiffened. "None of us are perfect, Henry. I'm saying she runs the household well. Sure, Ali and I have our differences." He rubbed the back of his neck. "But Henry, I don't want to hurt her. Deep down, she's a good woman. This could devastate her and she doesn't deserve it."

Henry stuck his tongue in his cheek. "Will . . . I don't know if you're trying to convince me or yourself that Ali's some sort of saint, but you don't have to pretend with me. I don't mean to demean your wife, little brother, but you and I both know if she does find out, the only wounds she'll suffer will be her wounded pride."

Will propped his elbows on the table and rested his chin on his fists. "So she has her faults, Henry. It's not as if I don't have a few of my own. How many times did you hear Mama tell us, 'Boys, be sure your sins will find you out?' Well, Mama was right. The consequence of one of my sins—a bitter, half-starved kid with my blood running through his veins came bursting into my library, Monday morning. My sin has found me out. Oh, Henry, I'm so ashamed. What have I done?"

Chapter Ten

Lizzie grimaced at the sound of the front door opening. "Eeks! It's Mama." No need to get up. She was caught. Red-handed. Or more to the point, barefooted. Her shoes lay on the floor on the opposite side of the parlor.

Alamanda gasped. "Eliza, you are trying my patience. I'm sick and tired of seeing you run around the house looking like a little street urchin. Don't let me catch you in your bare feet again. I wish you'd remember who you are."

"How can I forget, Mama? A day doesn't go by that you don't say, 'Don't forget who you are, Eliza Lancaster . . . you're acting like a Loudermilk, Eliza Lancaster.' I wonder if Mrs. Loudermilk stands over Alice, constantly harping, 'Pull off your shoes, Alice Loudermilk . . . you're acting like a Lancaster, Alice Loudermilk.'"

Her mother's face distorted. "Shame on you, Eliza. Those unfortunate children can't help it if their father died and left them at the mercy of the world, but you don't have to act like one of them."

"Mr. Loudermilk died? I didn't know. When, Mama?"

Alamanda turned away. "Does it matter when? He's gone. Driven to the grave no doubt by the woman he married. She has no shame. She doesn't seem to care what people think about her little runny-nose, barefoot ragamuffins. But you're a Lancaster, and people expect more of you. A lady doesn't traipse around in her stocking feet."

Lizzie crossed the room and picked up her shoes and grumbled, "I sometimes wish my name *was* Lizzie Loudermilk."

The words barely escaped her lips when the back of her mother's hand whacked her across the side of her face. Lizzie screamed and jerked back. Her face stung—her eyes widened, yet from the troubled expression in her mother's eyes, one would've guessed that Lizzie had struck the startling blow.

Alamanda screamed, "Don't you ever say such a thing again. Never!" She clamped her hands on Lizzie's shoulders and shook. "Do you understand?"

Lizzie clinched her teeth together. She watched in wonder as the color drained from her mother's face.

Alamanda clasped her hand over her mouth and shrieked. "I'm sorry, Eliza. I'm so sorry. I've had a very exhausting day, and I lost my temper. Please don't mention this to your father. I promise it will never happen again, but you drove me to it."

Lizzie's jaw tightened. Her mother often threatened to slap her, but until today it never went further than empty threats. Lizzie wanted to lash back with spiteful words but she could tell her mama was truly remorseful—a rare emotion for Alamanda Lancaster. Besides, it didn't hurt. Not really. Something upsetting might've happened at the Bazaar to rile her mother, but this didn't seem the proper time to inquire—at least not while standing at arm's length.

Her mother cleared her throat and in a firm voice said, "Sit down, Eliza."

Lizzie moaned. "If it's about your little temper tantrum, Mama, forget it, because I have."

Alamanda's face turned crimson. "For both our sakes, that's a wise idea. I've already apologized and I don't intend to dwell on it, but I declare, Eliza, you drive me crazy with your insolence. I think you purposely jerk off your shoes when you hear me coming, for no other reason than to irritate. Eliza Virginia, are you listening to me?"

Lizzie nodded. She bent down to slip on her shoes and lifted her head when her father entered.

"Hi, Daddy," she said, buckling the ankle strap.

Will looked first at Lizzie, then at his wife. The chill in the room must have given hint that mother and daughter were at it again, because his first words were, "Hi, Swamp Angel. What's going on?"

Lizzie turned her eyes toward her mother and lifted her shoulders. "Ask Mama. I think she can make it sound much worse than if I try to tell it."

Alamanda huffed. "Your daughter is trying my patience, Will. I declare, it's a wonder she doesn't get ground itch, the way she traipses all over God's creation in her bare feet."

Lizzie studied her father's face. Something heavy seemed to be weighing on his mind but she was confident it had nothing to do with the present conversation.

Will glanced at his wife and chuckled, but it wasn't a ha-ha sound. To Lizzie, it sounded rather hollow. Even remorseful. What sadness lay behind those serious blue eyes?

Alamanda slammed her hands on her hips. "Will Lancaster, do you intend to stand there and say nothing? She doesn't listen to me."

His mouth gaped open. "I declare, Ali, you beat all. You stay on her back constantly. She's in the privacy of her own home, for crying out loud. Who cares if she runs around barefooted? She's bright and she's beautiful, and she can't help either of those traits." He winked at his daughter. "She takes after her old man. Lizzie doesn't need you hammering on her all the time, just because she has my genes." A rueful grin on Will's face vanished as quickly as it appeared.

Before Alamanda could offer further objections, Cleoda clomped into the parlor. "Mr. Will, Hobart wants to know how much meat you want him to barbecue on Saturday?"

"Tell him we'll smoke a whole hog . . . and Cleoda, make a

couple of gallons of your mashed potato salad."

Alamanda frowned. "Whatever for, Will? Please tell me you aren't planning to—"

Will interrupted. "Yep. I'm planning to . . . I went by the field this morning and told Louie to send the hands over about four o'clock Saturday and we'll have a big barbecue."

Lizzie swallowed hard. Her cover was about to be blown before she had an opportunity to carry out her plan. It wasn't uncommon for her daddy to plan a barbecue for field hands on a Saturday afternoon, but she hadn't counted on it happening quite so soon. He usually waited until mid-season. Kiah would be coming to the house. If he didn't know already, he'd soon learn she was a Lancaster.

Lizzie's thoughts were interrupted when her mother screamed, "You should have discussed your plans with me, Will, before planning to bring those people here. What if I'd already invited guests to Gladstone?"

"The more the merrier. I invited Henry and Merle, but of course, we both know as much as Merle enjoys Hobart's barbecue served on china in the dining room, it's beneath her to rub shoulders with common folk in the yard. So I don't expect she'll be coming with Henry and Bonnie. But you're invited, my dear. I can promise you an experience like you've never had."

"I declare, Will, you make it sound as if Merle and I are committing some great sin, because we aren't comfortable mixing.

We weren't raised that way."

"I know how you were raised, honey bun. How well I know—but sometimes folks change their ways—even after they're raised. Take me, for example."

Lizzie wanted to ask her father what he meant by his remark. She considered him to be the kindest, smartest, most wonderful man in the whole world. Was he saying he wasn't always a good person? If that were the case, then she assumed she *did* get his genes, because sometimes she didn't consider herself to be very nice. Occasionally, she entertained wicked thoughts that proper young ladies should never have. Still, it was hard to imagine her daddy ever being anything but perfect.

Alamanda's head shot back, thrusting her chin in the air. "Well, I wouldn't think anyone would object to changing for the better, and you can't deny that both you and your brother live better than you did before we married. If it hadn't been for Papa, you'd still be a dirt farmer, trying to eke out a living on a two-horse farm—and as for Henry . . . well, there's no telling where he'd be. Likely a starving sharecropper, married to some wash woman like Nancy Loudermilk."

Will muttered, "You hate her, don't you, Ali. You think I don't know why?"

Lizzie's interest peaked at her father's words. Lizzie had always known why her mother objected to her associating with the Loudermilks. They were poor. Pure and simple. What other reason would she have? Had her father just now figured it out?

Alamanda crossed her arms. "You twist everything I say, Will. I merely made a point you should be grateful for what my father did for you."

Will sneered. "Yeah, it was my lucky day for sure, when I married you and got to ride into the elitist circle on your coattail. But you know, sweetheart, I didn't realize how dizzy I was until I decided to step off. I'm tired, Ali . . . tired of what I've become."

His confession seemed to jar her. "You're not making sense. You sound as if you resent what Papa did for you."

"No, honey. I only resent what it turned me into. Lately, I've begun to search for the real Will Lancaster and I can't find him. I regret to say I fear the man died years ago."

Alamanda shot her chin in the air. "And you should be thankful he did . . . a much more affluent William Lancaster was born in his stead, thanks to Papa. Good grief! Look around you, Will. My father left everything—including the bank, the gin, the paper, the house and the land to us."

"No, my dear. He left it all to you. Not that it matters at this point in my life, but my name appears on nothing."

She smirked. "What's the difference? You're my husband. I suppose you'd prefer to sit on the curb and sell vegetables."

Will couldn't deny he led a comfortable life, or that he didn't enjoy what he did, though it didn't start out that way.

For too many years, he cowered under the thumb of his late father-in-law. Lizzie was right when she said her grandfather knew about the faulty vacuum arm. Will had begged him to have it repaired. The old man sacrificed lives to save a dollar, though his coffers were full. Tom's accident still haunted Will. Was that why he found it difficult to foreclose on the man's farm, in spite of Alamanda and John's assertions? Will dreaded falling asleep at night for fear the horrifying nightmare would return. Night after night, Tom's piercing screams would awaken him and he'd see the mangled arm in a grisly scenario that continued to torment him.

After Papa Gid's death, Will turned the gin into a safer environment by upgrading the equipment and teaching safety rules. He took comfort in knowing there hadn't been a single serious accident since he'd taken over. But all of his efforts did nothing to help Tom become whole again. And in Will's troubled mind, though he wasn't directly responsible for the horrid accident, he believed it to be a cross he'd forever bear.

Alamanda stopped midway up the stairs, turned and shook a finger at her husband. "Will, I'll leave you with this tidbit: If it weren't for Papa, you'd be among the field hands instead of planning this . . . this—"

"Barbecue, honey. It's called a barbecue."

She threw up her hands. "For the life of me, I can't understand your ungrateful attitude. I'm warning you, Will. You've made a grave mistake by allowing your daughter to attend your little hootenannies and mingle with the help. Mark my word—the mixing will come back to bite you."

Will nodded. "You're right, my astute wife. I have indeed made a grave mistake—but teaching Lizzie to love all people may be the only wise thing I've ever done."

Chapter Eleven

Lizzie paced back and forth in front of the manor, Saturday, waiting for Bonnie and Uncle Henry to arrive for the Barbecue.

"Hey, what's the hurry?" Henry shouted, when Lizzie jumped on the running board before the vehicle came to a full stop.

"Sorry, Unk. Bonnie and I have urgent business to discuss."

Henry chuckled. "Honey, with you, everything is always urgent."

Lizzie grabbed her cousin by the hand, pulling her toward the barn. "Bonnie, we need to talk. I'm so nervous—he'll be here, you know—Kiah will be coming to the Barbecue." They climbed the ladder to the loft.

"Uh-oh. I see the problem. How can we be orphans, if Uncle Will is your father?"

"Oh Faddle. You never see past your nose, Bonnie. That isn't the problem."

Bonnie's brow arched. "No?"

"No. But you were right about one thing—he's not my type." She flung her head back. "I hope he doesn't come here and expect me to fall for the likes of him . . . a hobo with airs. Who does he think he is?" She flipped her hair to one side. "You should've seen him in the field Wednesday. The soles on his old brogans flop when he walks, and those ragged overhauls are six inches too short. He's pathetic." Lizzie shuddered. "Black, sweaty curls kept falling in his face. Grimy fingernails on his calloused hands looked as if he'd been digging a well with them. He's not only crude, he's also rude."

"I agree, Lizzie. I told you the day we met him, he wasn't right for you. I'm glad you've come to your senses."

"Yeah, me too . . . I think."

Bonnie rolled her eyes. "You think?"

"Yes, I'm furious with him—but Bonnie, what can I do? He's the best looking fellow I've ever seen. And he's funny, too. Don't you think he's funny?"

Bonnie's jaw fell. "About as funny as typhoid. You were right when you called him a hobo with airs. That's exactly what he is."

Lizzie shrugged. "I know. He's terribly pompous to be so poor. But, hey, who's perfect? I watched him swing a hoe, and you should have seen the muscles in his arms bulge. I declare, Bonnie, he reminded me of a cross between the strong man in the Barnum & Bailey Circus and Clark Gable. One side of his overhauls was unstrapped, and—" She grabbed her throat and swooned. "His left torso was bare as a slick pig. He's so handsome, it's a pure sin."

Bonnie did nothing to hide her disgust. "I reckon you're right about that. It *is* a sin. You had no business gawking at him, and him half-dressed. And you liked it, too, I can tell. Lizzie, you don't make sense. One minute, you say you're over him and the next minute you're gushing and acting like a . . . like a shameless chippy."

"You weren't listening. I never said I was over him. I said he's not my type. And he isn't. I said he's crude and rude. And he is. I said I'm furious with him—which I am. But I never once said I was over him. Not once."

Bonnie shrugged. "So you didn't. But Lizzie, I'm puzzled. How could you see dirt under his nails, as you rode by?"

She grinned. "I didn't ride by."

"I didn't think so. You parked the car in the road and took in an eyeful, didn't you?"

"Nope. I did better than that. I went into the fields, and stood beside him. I could've reached out and touched his sweaty chest." She covered her mouth with her hand.

Bonnie's face distorted. "You didn't!"

Lizzie giggled at her cousin's shocked expression. "Didn't what? Go to the fields or touch his chest? I'll have to admit, rubbing my fingers across his wet skin was tempting, though I restrained myself. I did go to the field, though, and it was so much fun, Bonnie. Of course, I could've had more fun if he'd paid me a little attention, but he didn't."

Bonnie's mouth turned down. "Lizzie, you scare me."

"Faddle. Everything scares you, Bonnie."

"But you know nothing about him, Lizzie. I heard Mama tell Daddy that Aunt Ali is afraid of the new boy—meaning Kiah, of course. She said your mama is fearful he might make advances toward you. Doesn't it frighten you, even a little?"

"Yeah, it does, Bonnie." Lizzie's jaw dropped as she feigned a look of horror. She whispered, "On the way to the field, I glanced behind every tree—terrified Mama's fears might be in vain. I kept hoping he'd jump out and grab me . . . like this." Lizzie lunged toward Bonnie, and playfully grabbed her around the neck. She fell back laughing, pulling Bonnie down on the hay.

"Stop it!" Bonnie jerked up and brushed hay from her hair. "You're trying to shock me, but I know you don't mean it, Eliza Lancaster."

"I mean every word of it." Lizzie lay staring at the beams in the top of the loft. She sighed heavily and lowered her voice. "But alas, Mama can relax—he acts as if I have the Blue Bonnet Plague."

Bonnie chuckled. "Bubonic, silly. Bubonic Plague. Lizzie, you make me dizzy. I feel as if I've stepped off a merry-go-round. First you agree he's not your type. And then you say you wish he would . . . kiss you?" Bonnie shuddered and made a face.

Lizzie lifted a brow. "Did I say that? You're putting words in my mouth."

"Well, that's what you were implying, wasn't it?"

Lizzie shrugged. "So what if I was? Plenty of girls have been kissed by the time they're sixteen, Bonnie."

"Yes and there's a name for those kinds of girls. I don't intend to let a boy kiss me until I'm married . . . or at least until I'm spoken for. I certainly wouldn't kiss a hobo. And I don't think you would either, Eliza Lancaster."

"Double-dog-dare me?"

Bonnie blurted, "No!"

"You're afraid, because you know how I hate to lose. But with or without your dare, I'll show you. I'll have him wrapped around my little finger before summer's end. I'll let you know what it feels like to be kissed by the best-looking fellow in the whole world."

"You're crazy, Lizzie. You'd best forget such silly notions. If Aunt Ali finds out you have your sights set on a hobo, she'll lock you in your room and you'll die a withered up old maid at Gladstone."

"Whatever will be, will be, but I have no intentions of giving up until he realizes he's mad about me. When that happens, I'll shun him like cow-itch for a week or so and show him what it feels like to be in love and have your heart shattered into a million tiny bits."

Bonnie smirked. "Are you sure your heart's been shattered, Lizzie? I think it's more like a hair-line crack."

"Okay, so maybe shattered is an exaggeration, but I was

wounded. Who does he think he is, snubbing me?"

"Maybe he thinks he's a hobo, snubbing a Goobernut maid." Bonnie's expression turned serious. "Lizzie, you don't think he believed we were poor, do you? I mean it's not just the clothes, which makes the difference, is it? Can't you just tell when a person has class?"

"Oh, I don't think class is so much how we look, as how we act. When we see him at the Barbecue, let your shoulders droop a bit, and glance at your feet when he talks to us. You don't want to appear confident. Act the part and he'll have no cause to suspect we're not the help. Why would he?"

"Our clothes for one thing. How many days does Comfort come to work wearing store-bought dresses?"

"More than you might think. Mama gives her my hand-me-downs, but they don't look old. I simply get tired of wearing the same old thing. Comfort is quite exotic looking, but she acts and talks like she's the hired help, so no one really notices how pretty she really is. Bonnie, you must do this for me. Please? I'm not ready for him to learn I'm a Lancaster. Not yet."

"I'm scared. What if he calls you Jo and me Beth?"

"What's wrong with that . . . *Beth*?"

"What will Daddy and Uncle Will say?"

"Think about it, Bonnie. Do you honestly think our fathers will be paying attention? But avoid Cleo like a dose of Castor Oil. If you see her coming, head the other way."

The girls peered in the distance and saw the field hands heading toward the house. Bonnie's eyes widened. "Lizzie, this is crazy. Won't he wonder why the Goobernut maids are hanging out at Gladstone?"

"Bonnie, Bonnie, Bonnie. Must I walk you through everything? Use your imagination. If we're at Gladstone, then obviously we no longer work for the Goobernuts."

"What if he asks why?"

Lizzie rolled her eyes. "Don't you remember, dear Beth? We didn't get back in time with the buttermilk the day the car slid into the ditch. Mrs. Goobernut was furious because there were no biscuits for breakfast. She fired us on the spot."

Bonnie chewed her thumbnail. "I declare, I sometimes think lying comes easier for you than the truth, and I don't like being a party to it. Lizzie. Lying is a sin and you know it is."

Lizzie shrugged. "You can't think of it as lying, cuz—it's pretend. We're play-acting. Think of it as your script. Watch Comfort and mimic her actions. Grab the bread baskets and take them back to the kitchen for refills, and when he looks our way, we'll stir the beans and toss the salad . . . things like that."

"Why do we have to stir food, which is already prepared?"

"I don't know why, Bonnie, but I've seen Comfort stand there and stir, so that's what we'll do." She squinted her eyes as the field hands drew nearer. "Do you see him?"

Bonnie shielded her eyes from the sun. "Not yet."

The last group of field hands passed by, but there was no sign of Kiah. Lizzie grabbed Bonnie's arm. "Oh, Bonnie, I'll die if he doesn't come."

Bonnie cocked her head slightly. "Aww . . . what a grim thought. I'd miss you terribly, Lizzie—but if it should happen, can I have your car?"

Chapter Twelve

Will Lancaster swallowed the growing lump in his throat. He gazed out the window over the vast fields planted in cotton.

The Great Depression—at a time when people all over the country were starving, his barns were full . . . yet his heart was empty. His eyes clouded, when he reflected on the words of Jesus in the book of Matthew: "What doth it profit a man if he owns the whole world and loses his soul?"

Henry cracked open the door and stuck his head in. "Hey, little brother . . . Hobart says the hog is fully cooked and the food will be set out shortly. Cleoda caught me sneaking a peach tart and chased me out of the kitchen, so I came to bother you. Mind if I come in?" He didn't wait for an answer before entering.

"Hi Henry." Will's voice sounded strange, even to himself. He continued to stare blankly at the open fields.

Henry plopped down in a swivel chair near the desk. "I've been quite curious since last Wednesday," he said with a sly grin. "I was sorry Robert came over to our table before I had a chance to hear the second announcement. What happened the night of the party?"

Will winced. A queasiness rose from the pit of his stomach. As far as his eyes could see, were acres and acres of cotton coming into bloom. He pursed his lips. "Henry, for these fields, I sold my self-respect and yet, I still have nothing to call my own. No land, no house, no gin, no paper, no bank . . . it's not mine. Never has been. It all belongs to Alamanda. But you know, big brother, the thing I miss most of all is my self-respect. What's that verse . . . the love of money is the root of all evil?"

Henry seemed impatient. "Will, would you please stop the morbid philosophizing and finish the story? We haven't much time."

Will ambled slowly back to his desk and took a seat. Though as different as a bull and a Billy goat, he and Henry had always been close. "The story? You act like we're discussing a fairy-tale, Henry. We're talking about people's lives. Real people. And if I sound morbid, I feel I have cause."

"Okay, sorry. But get on with it before they come looking for us. The second announcement, Will."

Will sucked in a breath and exhaled slowly. "Henry, it was Mr. Gid's second announcement that kept me from backing down from the marriage proposal, even though I knew I wasn't in love with his daughter."

"I suppose whatever Ali wanted, Mr. Gid intended for her to

have, and apparently she had her sights set on you. So how'd the ol' geezer buy you, Will?"

Will bristled. He couldn't deny Henry was right. He *was* bought, but somehow it sounded differently when the words came from someone other than himself. "Mr. Gid said for a wedding gift he was promoting me to Bank President. He stood in front of a ballroom full of people and said, 'William, I'm to the age I need to retire, so I'm handing the reins over to you, *son.*' Those were his words. Son, he called me. He claimed I'd proven I could handle the job—a rather strange statement to make to a young man fresh off the farm who'd only worked two weeks. I was stunned. Then, the old man pulled out a set of keys to the bank and handed them to me."

Henry's eyes widened. "Wow! Did you pinch yourself to see if you were dreaming? Truthfully, how did you feel when you took the keys in your hand?"

"How do you suppose? Flabbergasted. The crowd applauded once more. Men of means surrounded me and slapped me on the back to offer their congratulations. In a split second, I went from being the invisible son of a poor farmer to the future son-in-law of the wealthiest man in Alabama."

Henry shook his head, slowly. "Unbelievable."

"I won't deny, Henry, it felt good to envision myself as a big wig. One brief announcement from the leader of the pack and I immediately joined their ranks. At that moment, I dismissed any notions of canceling the engagement. I liked Ali. She was a beautiful young woman—very desirable. But I didn't love her. Nevertheless, I couldn't deny that I loved the idea of being bank president, and it was a package deal. I made up my mind I'd learn to love her. Why not? I asked myself. She was gorgeous and rich. What more could a man ask? Tell me, Henry. What would you have done?"

Henry tilted the chair back and guffawed. "Exactly what you did little brother—except I would've found me a preacher that same night before the old man had opportunity to back out. Forgive me for laughing, but for a farm boy growing up in the backwoods, you sure rose above your raising."

Comfort knocked on the door. "Mr. Will, Hobart said tell you everything's all set."

"Thanks, Comfort. Tell him we're coming." As she turned to leave, Will said, "Wait. Turn around, Comfort."

"What's the matter, Mr. Will?"

"Nothing's wrong. You look different. Is it your hair?"

"Nahsir, I ain't changed my hairdo. Not lately, no how."

"Well, I can't put my finger on it, but you seem . . . well, maybe a little more sophisticated. I like it. You have a look of confidence that I've not noticed before. It's becoming."

Comfort blushed. "Thank you, Mr. Will. That's mighty nice of you to say so." She pranced away with her shoulders slung back and a bounce in her step.

Henry's jaw dropped. "Will, you need to be careful how you talk to the help. It's that kind of familiarity that breeds trouble—as if you aren't up to your neck already."

"Don't be ridiculous. Comfort grew up here. Why, she's almost like a daughter to me."

Henry threw his arm around Will and with a raucous laugh, said, "Good grief, please tell me she's *not* your daughter. We've got to figure out what to do with your illegitimate son before you come forth with any more admissions."

Will clamped his lips together and prayed he could keep his mouth shut.

Will walked out the back door and listened as the soothing sound of Spirituals wafted through the warm afternoon air. The hands work hard all morning for a pittance, yet look at them . . . songs in their hearts and smiles on their faces. I want what they have. His eyes moistened. If it were mine to give, I'd swap every acre of this vast estate for a fraction of the peace these workers enjoy.

Hobart started serving plates as soon as the line formed.

Will glanced about. "Louie, Where's the new kid? Didn't he work today?"

"Yessir, Mr. Will, and I'll have to say, the boy's good with a hoe—I wish I had a dozen like him. I thought he was trailing behind me when I left." Louie shrugged. "Reckon he changed his mind about coming."

Will attempted to hide his disappointment.

"Mr. Will, I been aiming to ask you—I hear tell the town of Enterprise has a monument to the boll weevil, set up right in the middle of town. You seen it?"

Will nodded. "Yes, there's a large statue atop the fountain."

"I don't get it. Why in tarnation would a town wanna glorify a boll weevil?"

"Well, Louie, when the boll weevil destroyed so many cotton crops in Alabama, many farmers turned to peanuts and found it to be a much more profitable venture. For that reason, they feel they owe a lot to the boll weevil."

"Well, I reckon that makes sense." Louie rubbed his chin. "Mr. Will, you think spraying with calcium nitrate is why we ain't having no problems with them critters? A lot of folks say it don't do no good, but seems to me the proof's in the pudding, as Mattie would say."

But Will wasn't in the mood to discuss boll weevils or ways to rid them. Something more important occupied his thoughts. He scratched his head. *Where are you, Kiah?*

Lizzie eased over toward her daddy and Mr. Louie, when she overheard a discussion about the new field hand.

Will said, "Louie, you did tell him about the Barbecue, didn't you?"

"Sure, but he's a peculiar sort. He didn't say yea nor nay when I mentioned it. He's a quiet one, for sure. I can't weasel two words out of him. But I like the kid. Yessir, that Kiah, he's all right."

Lizzie whispered to Bonnie. "Oh, drats. I guess he stayed at the shanty." She developed a strong urge to go swimming. "Daddy, Bonnie and I'd like to take a dip in the creek. It's dreadfully hot, today."

"Okay, sugar, but don't you want to eat a bite first?"

"No thanks. I don't want to get cramps. I'll pack us a picnic and we'll eat after we swim."

After stuffing a basket, Lizzie said, "Let's skedaddle, Bonnie."

Bonnie whispered, "Are we going swimming—for real?"

"Of course. But if by a strange coincidence we should get sidetracked, we can't be faulted, now can we?"

"What about bathing suits?"

"Who needs them?"

"Lizzie!" Bonnie shrieked. She crossed her arms over her chest. "I won't go."

"Silly, you know I'm joking. I have a couple of suits on the clothes line. We'll dress in the barn."

The girls grabbed two of Mr. Will's long sleeve white shirts from the line to use as cover-ups, before heading toward the meadow with the basket.

"You're so bad, Lizzie Lancaster. I never know what to expect next from you. Like now—I have no idea what you're up to, but I don't think we're going on a picnic. Are we?"

"Nope. That's not the plan. Kiah didn't come to the barbecue, so we'll take the barbecue to him. What better way to get acquainted than to pay a visit with a basket of food?"

"But Lizzie, aren't you even a little bit scared? What if he grabs us, like Aunt Ali said?"

Lizzie bit her lip. "Then I choose to be first."

"You're so silly, Lizzie Lancaster. You'd die of fright if he so much as laid a hand on you. You aren't fooling me."

The girls giggled all the way up the path as they made their way to the log cabin. After knocking repeatedly, Lizzie cupped her hand over her eyes and stared toward the cotton fields. "Where could he be?" Her stomach wrenched. "Why do you suppose he didn't come to the picnic with everyone else? Unless—" She clasped her hand over her mouth and gasped. "What if he's gone? Oh, Bonnie I could die."

"Poor baby. One guy fails to bow at your feet and you fall apart. Trust me, you'll survive. It happens to me all the time. Are we going to swim or not?"

Lizzie slipped off her cover-up and hung it on a blueberry bush. "May as well," she said with a pout.

"Oh, look, the blueberries are beginning to ripen," Bonnie squealed. She picked a few of the juicy ripe berries and popped a couple in her mouth. "Want one?"

Lizzie turned up her nose, took a running start and dove into the creek.

Bonnie jumped in, went under and bobbed up screaming. "Lizzie! I think I saw an alligator."

Lizzie would've laughed at such an absurd statement, but she was still pouting over Bonnie's unsympathetic attitude.

"I'm telling you, I saw it," Bonnie screamed. "I'm getting out."

When a mass of black hair sprung up out of the blue, Lizzie's eyes widened. "Kiah?"

He blushed and quickly turned his head.

Lizzie giggled. "No need to turn around. We're decent."

"Sorry. I . . . I didn't expect anyone to be here. There's a Barbecue at Gladstone and I wanted to clean up before going. If you'll kindly close your eyes, I'll get out and be on my way. I apologize. Never would I have come if I'd known this was your bathing spot."

She swallowed to keep from laughing. "Oh, don't mind us. You come here anytime you like." With closed eyes, the girls waited while Kiah scurried out of the water and dressed.

Lizzie could hold back no longer. She laughed until she could hardly catch her breath. She yelled, "Sis and I have been hired to help with the Barbecue. Slaving over a hot stove all day is tiresome but a quick dip in the creek has proven to be even more refreshing than I could've imagined. I suppose we'll see you at Mr. Will's."

Bonnie stood in the water with her arms crossed over her

midsection and sniffled. Lizzie could never manage to squeeze out more than a couple of teardrops, even in the most trying of circumstances. Laughing inappropriately had gotten her in trouble more times than she cared to remember. However, she viewed the immediate situation as terribly funny—and though it might be inappropriate, she made no attempt to squash the laughter.

Kiah said, "Okay, you can open your eyes. Please accept my apologies, and I promise no one will ever know what happened here."

"But nothing *did* happen," Lizzie yelled back as he scurried down the path, leading to Gladstone. "We closed our eyes . . . or at least one of us did."

"Lizzie Lancaster." Bonnie screamed. "Tell him you didn't peek."

"Bonnie wants you to know I'm the one who didn't peek." She studied her cousin's red, pouty face and knew she'd taken her teasing too far. She whispered, "I'm kidding, Bonnie. Don't be so sensitive."

"Lizzie you aren't funny. You embarrassed me. I hate it when you do that."

"I'm sorry," she said, biting her lip. "I got carried away. I can't help myself. Come on. Let's head back to the manor."

"No, Lizzie, we can't. Not now. You heard him—he'll be there."

"So will we." Lizzie's squished her brow. "Why are you still crying?"

"I'm scared, Lizzie. You know how opposed Mama and Aunt Ali are to mixed bathing, and if they get wind were in the creek with a boy, they'll never let us out of their sight again. Besides, our reputation is ruined if folks find out we swam in the creek with a hobo who . . . you know."

Lizzie cackled. "Who skinny dips?"

Bonnie's face glowed. "Please, don't tell anyone, Lizzie. You know how gossip travels in this town."

"Fiddle faddle. You're worrying over nothing."

"Lizzie, he wouldn't have said he wouldn't tell, if there was nothing to tell." Bonnie covered her face with her hands. "I can't face him. I'll die if he so much as looks at me."

"Well, cuz, seems one of us will need to plan a funeral, because I'll die if he *doesn't* look at me. Let's go."

They changed back into their clothes at the barn and followed the wonderful aroma of Hobart's barbecue. Servants wearing aprons were busy bringing food from the kitchen, taking turns tending the meat, and fanning flies away from the table. Lizzie spotted Comfort standing over a number two washtub filled with a large block of ice and sweet tea. The young colored girl held a tin dipper in her hand, which she used to swish the ice.

Lizzie eyed the crowd and soon spotted Kiah standing under an oak tree. She whispered, "Comfort, give me the dipper."

"No. You'll get me in trouble."

"Comfort. Please?"

Comfort shook her head furiously. "No, Lizzie. Big Mama will get my goat if she catches me standing idle. Anyhow, I'd rather be doing this than stuck inside washing dishes. Now git! Your pappy's been calling for you."

Lizzie turned and swallowed hard when she saw her father talking to Kiah "Uh-oh." When her daddy shifted his glance in her direction, she quickly slammed the dipper back in Comfort's hands.

Chapter Thirteen

Caught!

When Lizzie's father made a large sweeping motion with his hand, beckoning the girls, she swallowed hard.

"Come, girls. I'd like to introduce you to our newest employee. This is Kiah. Kiah Grave."

Baffled, Lizzie could understand why Kiah's good looks had her foaming at the mouth like a rabid dog—she was shallow and didn't deny it. But what kind of spell did he hold over her father?

"Kiah, this is my beautiful daughter Eliza, and my sweet little niece, Bonnie."

Lizzie bit her lip.

"Your daughter, sir? Well, I see my intuitions were correct. I'd already guessed as much."

"Oh?" Will gave a questioning look.

Lizzie grimaced.

"Yes sir. On my way to Gladstone, I saw these two young ladies taking a joy-ride on a brand-spanking new automobile. I looked at the driver—that is, after taking a long gander at the swell-looking vehicle, of course—and it was then I said to myself, 'Now, that little filly looks like a thoroughbred. She must be a Lancaster.' By June, I see I was right."

A game player, Lizzie grinned. She now had a partner. This could prove fun. She tapped her temple with her finger. "Oh, yes. I do recall seeing you. I believe you were carrying a small bundle of clothes."

"Clothes? Are you referring to the rags tied on a stick?"

"Call it what you may. Actually, I've heard it referred to as a bindle. Tell me, Mr. Kite, what brought you to these parts?" She flinched. "Let me rephrase. What I meant to ask was do you happen to know someone who lives in Goat Hill?"

"Maybe. But the name is Kiah, not Kite. And I have something to ask you, Miss Jo, if you'll allow me one question."

Will made the correction and smiled. "It's Eliza."

Kiah arched his brow. "I beg your pardon, sir?"

Lizzie squeezed her lips together and clinched her eyes tightly.

Her daddy repeated himself. "I'm sorry. Perhaps I didn't make myself clear. My daughter's name is Eliza."

Kiah nodded. "Well, of course. Forgive me. I meant to say Eliza."

Will said, "Actually, she prefers to go by Lizzie."

"Does she, now?" He looked bewildered, although the girls knew he wasn't nearly as confused as he pretended. "Well, Lizzie is a lovely name, but you look so much like a girl I met once—I suppose that's why I called you Jo. That was the name she preferred to go by." He squinted his eyes, as if to scrutinize her. "Ah, yes, there's a remarkable resemblance. Of course, she didn't have your class. She was a sweet little milk-maid . . . or buttermilk-maid, I'm not sure I ever understood her title. Such a sad little wench. A mite on the skinny side."

Lizzie chewed the inside of her jaw. Not only was Kiah Grave dashingly handsome, he was quick-witted and she suspected extremely intelligent, too. She supposed with his looks, she could have fallen in love with him even if he'd been a dimwit, but his keen sense of humor adorned him like a red comb on a rooster's head. She glanced over at Bonnie, whose face resembled a ripened pomegranate.

Lizzie cocked her head. "Kayak? Am I pronouncing your name correctly, now?"

He grinned. "Kiah. My name is Kiah. Would you like me to spell it for you?"

"No need. I presume it's short for Hezekiah."

"Well, aren't you the perceptive one. I have to explain that to most folks."

"I was at the top of my class, so I suppose I'm quicker than the people you hang with."

"Lizzie!" Her father reprimanded. "I'm sure you didn't intend to sound so impetuous. Perhaps you'd wish to apologize?"

Kiah held up his hand. "Whoa, Mr. Will. There's no need for

apologies. The lovely lady is correct. I could tell right away you weren't slow, Miss Lizzie. You don't strike me as slow at all. In fact, I'd venture to say you're probably one of the fastest girls I've ever had the pleasure of meeting. But then I suppose lots of fellows tell you that."

Will Lancaster watched with interest, realizing his daughter had met her match. Whether good or bad, Lizzie seemed to enjoy the catty remarks—both Kiah's and her own.

Will sensed a mutual admiration between the two, which made him sweat beneath his collar. He prayed Lizzie and Kiah didn't become carried away with their little word-games. After all, he'd be in enough trouble when Alamanda discovered the boy's true identity. He certainly didn't need the situation complicated.

Will stepped over to the spit for another helping of barbecue. Though he couldn't hear the banter, he watched his daughter out of the corner of his eye.

Lizzie walked slowly around Kiah, sizing him up from head to toe. She chewed on her lower lip and shook her head.

"Miss Lizzie, if you're planning on buying me, perhaps you'd like to check my teeth. That's the first thing to look at when purchasing a stud."

"Stud?" She laughed. "Why would I want to buy you? I wouldn't know what to do with you. You're a bit scrawny to put in front of a plow . . . besides, ol' Blue still has plenty of life left in her before she's a candidate for the glue factory. But I'm amazed at how spotless you are, after working in the field all morning. Look at those squeaky-clean locks, Bonnie." She reached up and tousled his inky black curls. "However do you do it—hoe all day, and not a speck of dirt on you?" She slapped her hand against her cheek. "Oh, but perhaps you took a dip in the creek before coming over?" She pressed a finger to her lips and scrunched her brow. "No, you couldn't have, because we were in the creek. Weren't we Bonnie? We would've seen you, for sure. Did you see him, Bonnie?"

Bonnie clinched her eyes shut and shook her head. When she opened her eyes, she appeared to be gazing toward the heavens. Maybe waiting for lightning to strike. Or perhaps she was sending up prayers—pleading for forgiveness.

With his back pressed against a Live Oak tree, Kiah fiddled with a leaf. "As a matter of fact, I did bathe before coming over. How astute of you to notice. If I understood your father correctly, creek privileges come with the job. Here he comes now. I'll make sure."

Kiah scratched his head. "Mr. Will, you did say I could use the creek for bathing, didn't you sir?"

Lizzie eyed her father. He didn't appear to be listening. In fact, he hadn't paid attention to much of anything lately. Lizzie tugged on her father's shirtsleeve. "Daddy, he asked you a question."

"What's that?" Will asked.

Kiah said, "I asked if you had objections to my bathing in the creek behind the little cabin."

"Of course not. Why should I mind? I would expect it . . . you know what they say about cleanliness being next to Godliness. Besides, I'd think it'd be quite refreshing after a hard day's work in the fields."

"Well, thank you, sir. I wanted to make sure I wasn't out of line this afternoon when I took a dip."

Lizzie bit her lip, but a chuckle escaped in spite of her efforts. Regaining her composure, she said, "Just be careful and watch out for strange creatures around the creek. You can never tell what might be lurking under water, peering at you when you think you're all alone."

"Oh trust me. I make a habit of being familiar with everything around me before I jump in. And at the slightest sound of bushes rustling, I always pop up to check it out. One can certainly see some weird sights by keeping alert."

Will appeared to have one ear tuned in to their conversation. "Oh, no need for worry—there may be a snake or two, but they won't bother you if you don't bother them"

Kiah snapped his fingers. "As a matter of fact, sir, that's exactly what I saw—two peculiar-looking snakes in the grass. I watched them closely, as they slithered into the water."

Lizzie giggled. "So you kept your eye on them, did you?"

"Of course. I first saw them over near a blueberry bush. Mr. Will, do snakes eat blueberries, because I'm thinking that's what I saw."

Bonnie's red face distorted.

Will shook his head. Not likely eating the berries. It's possible the snake was searching for tiny bugs, which creep on the fruit.

Lizzie mused and nodded. "Daddy's right. Snakes have an uncanny ability to spot creeps." Her father looked befuddled, but perhaps he understood this was one time he wasn't supposed to understand.

Bonnie bent over, holding her stomach. She moaned. "Uncle Will, do you know where Daddy went? I don't feel well. I want to go home."

"Sure, baby. Stay put and I'll go find Henry."

Kiah said, "I'll admit I have a lot to learn about snakes. Why, I had no idea they shed their skins this time of year." He pretended to shudder. "What a wicked sight."

"Oh, fiddle-faddle, Daddy left. I'm sure you wanted him to hear all about your observations of snakes in the raw. But I'm curious—were the creatures as beautiful as you imagined?"

"You mean when the shedding took place?"

Lizzie bit her bottom lip and nodded.

"Oh, my no. I was horrified." Kiah made a gasping sound. "It was not a pretty sight. As a matter of fact, the longest one looked frightfully skinny, once the outer layer peeled off." He wrinkled his nose and grimaced. "To tell the truth, I wanted to rush over and cover the hideous creature."

Her mouth gaped open.

"What's wrong? Cat got your tongue?"

"You should be horse-whipped, Kiah Grave. You're awful, but you don't scare me. We had our suits on before we left the barn. You didn't see a thing. And if you had, you'd know I'm not skinny. Meet me at the creek tomorrow and I'll prove it."

Bonnie gasped. "Lizzie, stop it."

Henry and Will came walking up. Henry took one look at his daughter, and said, "You're right, she does look a little green."

Kiah cocked his head to the side and looking quite concerned said, "Goodbye, Miss Bonnie. Meeting you was indeed a pleasure. I can't imagine what caused such a peculiar malady. Do you suppose it was the barbecue, or something in the water—at the creek, I mean. I believe you mentioned you went swimming?"

Bonnie glared at him, without uttering a word.

Will put his hand on Kiah's shoulder and said, "Kiah this is my brother, Henry Lancaster. Henry, I'll like to introduce you to—"

Kiah extended his hand, but dropped it when Henry turned sharply without waiting for Will to complete his sentence.

Henry mumbled, "My daughter isn't feeling well. I'd like to get her home."

"Bye Bonnie." Lizzie reached over to give her cousin a hug. "I hope you feel better, soon." She whispered in her ear. "Isn't he wickedly funny?"

Bonnie whispered back, "No, he's not funny, and neither are you. It's stupid, Lizzie Lancaster, and I'd feel much better if you'd stop this idiotic game you're playing. You'll get both of us in trouble. He's crude. I hate him."

Henry motioned for his daughter. "Coming, honey?"

"I'm ready, Daddy."

Will excused himself to mingle with his guests.

Lizzie whirled around at the sound of a deep male voice piercing the air. Three-hundred pounds of solid muscle stood near the pit, waving a dark brown hand at Kiah.

"Yo! Peckerwood, you still think you're faster than me? I can take two rows to your one, any old day."

Kiah yelled back. "It's a crying shame you can't hoe as fast as you talk, Rodolph. If you could, we'd be through by now."

Lizzie's neck stiffened. "What did he call you?"

"Peckerwood."

"Well, of all the nerve. Why?"

"Because I'm a poor whitey."

She cringed. "How rude. Doesn't it offend you?"

He shrugged. "Should it?" Kiah held out his palms and stared. He turned them over and shrugged. "They look white to me." He pulled his pockets wrong-side out. "Hmm. . . Nothing there. I must be poor. Yep, no doubt about it, I'm a Peckerwood, all right. I suppose you think being a poor white field hand is shameful."

"But that term. It's derogatory."

"Only when the intention is to degrade. Rodolph's a good egg. I couldn't ask for a better friend. I have no doubt he'd have my back if the need ever arose. Just don't let the wrong fellow think he can get off with calling me a Peckerwood, or I might show him how much harm a Peckerwood can do."

"You're an odd sort of fellow, Kiah Grave. Did anyone ever tell you that?"

"As a matter of fact, I believe you're the first to notice."

When Will walked up, Kiah reached out his hand and said, "Thanks for the invitation, sir. The barbecue was delicious. If you'll excuse me, I think I'll mosey on down to the shanty."

"I'm glad you came, Kiah, but don't go yet," Will said, clamping down on Kiah's hand. "I have something to discuss with you before you leave. Meet me in the library, where we'll have privacy."

Lizzie grabbed her stomach when a sickening feeling swept over her. Until now, everything seemed ha-ha funny but her intuition told her something wasn't right.

What could be of such importance that her daddy chose not to discuss it outside? Had her father sensed she was romantically interested in the new field hand? *Daddy will fire him for sure.* She grimaced. If only she'd been more discreet instead of drooling over him like a pig eyeing a mud hole.

Will thanked everyone for coming. When he said he hoped they all had plenty to eat, the field hands understood it to mean the party was over.

Lizzie slipped into the house ahead of her daddy and ducked into the music room. Minutes later, the sound of footsteps in the hall caused her pulse to race. She left the door cracked, hoping to hear.

The first voice was Kiah's. "What did you need to see me about, sir?"

Lizzie's heart pounded, as she strained to hear her father's reply.

"Wait until we get into the library. I don't mean to sound mysterious, but I'm sure you understand my position."

Lizzie's heart pounded when the door closed. Her imagination ran askew. When Lizzie peered out the window and saw her mother's car pull up, she plopped a record on the Victrola and fell across the divan, with the pretense of enjoying the music. The front door opened, and the clicking of her mother's high heels coming down the hall grew faster as they approached.

Alamanda stuck her head in the door. "Eliza, please turn down that awful noise you call music. I could hear it from the yard." Her face distorted. "What is that horrid song you're playing?"

"It's called *Making Whoopee*." She giggled, when her prim and proper mother dropped her jaw and gasped.

"Eliza, I'll not have the devil's music played in my house, nor do I want to hear those vulgar words escape from your lips again. Where is your father?"

"I think he's conducting business in the library. Someone's with him at the moment." Lizzie held her breath, hoping her daddy would stay behind closed doors until her mother walked away. "Mama, should I give him a message when he comes out?"

"No, I'll speak with him later. Tell him I had to run out again. I only stopped by to pick up my gray chemise to take to Ola Mae for alterations. I'll be back shortly."

"Sure, Mama." As soon as Alamanda closed the door behind her, Lizzie ran across the hall to the parlor, adjacent to the library and pressed her ear against the wall. Her heart pounded at the sound of her Daddy's voice.

He said, "I can't sleep, Kiah. I can't think. I don't know what to do. What do you want me to do? Tell me."

Lizzie bit her nails as she waited for Kiah's response.

"Sir, I came looking for a job. You gave me one. You don't owe me anything."

"That's not true. You know it, and I know it. We have to settle this."

Lizzie swallowed hard.

"It *is* settled sir. Thank you for your time," Kiah replied.

Then her daddy made a peculiar sounding statement. He said, "I wish you'd let me do more."

Surely, there was a simple explanation. Lizzie wanted to come flat out and ask her father—privately, of course—what was going on, but she dared not. Not yet.

She peeked out the keyhole at the sound of Kiah's brogans clopping down the hall. She only caught a glimpse and then the back door slammed. He was gone. Had he left for good, or would he be back in the fields tomorrow?

Maybe she was making too much of the whole situation. She mulled over the strange conversation. Kiah had thanked her daddy for his time and then Will had said he would've given him more. Did he mean more time? More food? But Kiah said he'd already given him what he came for. He came looking for work, and her daddy gave him a job. That wasn't so mysterious. Was it? Perhaps her active imagination had clicked into overtime.

Relieved that the little clandestine meeting between her father and Kiah had nothing to do with her picking up a stranger along the side of the road or swimming with him at the creek, the tense muscles in her neck relaxed. Apparently, Kiah kept his word and didn't mention either incident.

Saturday evening at sunset, Will looked out the library window in time to see Henry drive up.

"Come on in, Henry. How's Bonnie?"

"Oh, she's much better, thanks. I keep telling her mama Bonnie doesn't need to wear that confounded waist pincher, clincher or whatever those confounded undergarments are called that squeeze the very breath out of young girls. It's inhumane. I think that—and the heat got to her. But she was fine after I got her home and she cooled off."

"Good. I'm glad it was nothing serious." Will stroked his chin. "What brought you back? Did you come for another plate of barbecue?"

Henry hung his hat on the rack and took a seat. "No, I had plenty, thanks." Rubbing his stomach, he said, "Hobart sure knows how to roast a pig." His smile faded. "Will, you're right about the boy. Uncanny resemblance. It's sure gonna be hard for you to deny he's yours."

"Well, for once, I was glad Alamanda refused to attend the shindig. If she ever gets a glimpse of him, she's bound to see it. That's a chance I'll have to take, but Henry, *if* and when she does find out, I'll never deny he's mine. I can't send him away. He's a good kid."

Henry gave a short chuckle. "Well, we'll soon know how good he is, when we find out what he's come for, won't we? But I'm not here to argue." He pulled a toothpick from his shirt pocket and chewed on it. "You threw out a cliff-hanger earlier, and left me dangling in the air like a Saturday afternoon serial. So what happened?"

Will lifted his shoulders. "What do you mean?"

"I want to hear the rest of the saga. I'm eager to know what your poor, pregnant little girlfriend said when you broke the news to her that you were betrothed to the boss's daughter?"

Will drew a deep breath and settled back in his chair.

"Well?" Henry waited and then prompted. "After the party, what happened?"

Now that he'd gone this far, there was no turning back. Henry wouldn't rest until he was satisfied he knew all the details and for some reason unbeknownst to Will, he felt an urgent need to tell someone after all these years. Will wet his lips. "Where was I? Oh, yeah . . . it was late when I left the Christmas party. When I arrived back at the boarding house, I almost knocked on her door to tell her the news. But since she hadn't been feeling well, I decided not to disturb her. The next morning, when she didn't come down for breakfast, I assumed she left for work early. I walked into the bank and when I saw her, suddenly what I had to say seemed insignificant."

Henry seemed captivated. "Big belly, huh?"

"No . . . well, as a matter of fact, I do remember thinking she'd put on a little weight, but the idea of her being pregnant never crossed my mind."

"Go on—"

"She had a pasty look . . . pale-like. I said, 'Fennie, I'm worried. You don't look so good,' but she lifted sad-looking eyes and said, 'Congratulations, Will,' real soft like. Naturally, I felt disappointed to find out Mr. Gid had told her. I wanted to share the news and see the surprise on her face—me, Will Lancaster, the new Bank President. Who would've ever suspected? I wanted Fennie to be proud for me. But she didn't seem proud. She didn't seem proud at all."

Henry scoffed. "You don't know much about women, do you Will?"

"What do you mean?"

"I mean the girl was in love with you, ignoramus, and you expected her to be thrilled that you were willing to trade her love and affection for the Gladstone's fame and fortune? As a man, trust me, I get why you jumped at the opportunity, but when there's a choice between logic and love, women will choose love every time."

Will caught his bottom lip between his teeth and groaned. "I'm such a hare brain. I must have hurt her deeply. If only—"

Henry shrugged. "Get on with the story. What did she do next?"

"She stood, picked up her purse and mumbled something about leaving. Of course, I assumed she meant she was sick and planned to go back to the boarding house." He paused.

When Henry shifted in his chair, looking impatient, Will swallowed the lump in his throat and continued. "Her eyes looked swollen. I told her to get some rest and after work I'd ask Mrs. Blanchard to fix a bowl of soup for supper and I'd take it up to her."

"What did she say to that?"

"She told me not to bother—but then it was her nature not to want to put anyone out—so I responded it was no bother at all." Will swallowed. He'd come this far—he may as well finish. "That evening, I asked Mrs. Blanchard if she'd fix Fennie a bowl of soup. She frowned and looked bumfuzzled. She said, "You don't know, Will? She's gone. Paid her rent, packed up and caught a bus out of town.""

Henry snorted. "Ol' boy, looks to me like she did you a big favor."

Will pulled a handkerchief from his pocket and blotted his eyes.

Henry said, "Hey, get hold of yourself. You'll get through this. No one knows about your infidelity except me and the boy. You know I won't tell, and there are ways to deal with the kid. Let the attorney handle the details. You need to stay out of it."

Will bristled. "No, Henry. *You* need to stay out of it." Will stood. "I think you'd better go before I say something we may both regret."

"Oh, Will, don't get your dander up. I'm simply trying to get you to understand the ramifications if this sort of news gets out. I'm not about to let some rag-tag young whippersnapper waltz into town and ruin the family name."

Will clamped his teeth together. He and his brother had always shared their problems. Why was Henry being so intolerable now, at a time when Will desperately needed his support?

Sunday after church, Lizzie took her seat at the dining table and eyed the bounty—baked ham, string beans, squash casserole, fried okra, fresh tomatoes and fried corn pones. Cleo had starched and ironed the fine linen tablecloth, which Will brought back from England last fall. A colorful arrangement of gladiolas graced the table. It seemed the perfect setting for an enjoyable meal. Yet, a coldness in the room caused Lizzie to shiver as she watched her mother and father politely pass food in frigid silence.

Alamanda spoke first. "That was a good sermon today." Thick silence hung in the air like a heavy fog. She cleared her throat and gave it another try. "Pastor Hawkins delivered a fine message, even though he left out the most important point. I had included a passage from Ephesians in his notes. In the fourth chapter, if I can quote it correctly, it begins, 'I beseech you that ye walk worthy of the vocation wherewith ye are called, with all lowliness and meekness, with longsuffering, forbearing one another in love.'" She shrugged. "I don't understand why the pastor didn't stress the point. If you ask me, that's the problem with the church today . . . people just don't love like they ought to."

Will glared at his wife. "Pass the okra, please."

Alamanda handed him the platter. "Folks aren't tolerant of others. The church is filled with ignorant, ornery people who come and plop down on a pew, wearing the same ratty clothes they wear to the fields, having absolutely no regard for the house of the Lord."

Will took a bite of corn bread.

"Didn't you enjoy the sermon, Will?"

"What dear?"

"Never mind. I declare, you don't listen to half of what I say." She rolled her eyes. "Will, who were you talking with in the library last evening? Was it John?"

"No." He directed his gaze toward Lizzie. She squirmed. Had he known she was in the next room listening?

She lifted her shoulders, as if to say, "I know nothing."

Alamanda continued to probe. "Was it Tom Becker?"

Lizzie swallowed hard. "Daddy, pass the okra, please."

Will passed the platter to his daughter. His wife continued to glare. He picked up his tea glass. Then without taking a swallow, he sat it back on the table. "No, Alamanda, it was not Tom."

Ali laid her fork down and blotted her mouth with a napkin. "I declare, Will, getting you to talk is like pulling hen's teeth. I asked you a simple question, and you're turning it into multiple choice. Well, I'm running out of choices. You act as if you have something to hide."

Will frowned. "For the love of Dixie, Alamanda, can't I eat without listening to you nag?" He spat out the words. "If you must know, it was the new kid."

"Who?" Alamanda asked. "Will, you didn't say—"

"Yes, Ali, I did. I said the new kid." He picked up a knife and cut his ham.

"Will Lancaster! The field hand? That hobo?"

"Yep." Will replied curtly. Will took a swig of sweet tea and allowed her to rant.

"Have you completely lost your senses? We still don't know anything about the boy."

"Ali, there's nothing you need to know, and I know enough."

"Well, would you please explain to me why he had to come inside?"

"He didn't have to. I invited him in. But don't worry, hon. I checked his pockets before he left to make sure he didn't leave with the silver chalice."

Lizzie perked up. She rather enjoyed the conversation. From the way her father defended Kiah, it appeared he approved of him.

Cleoda walked in and placed a big bowl of Will's favorite banana pudding in front of him. He shook his head. "No thanks, Cleo."

"Land sakes, Mr. Will, you ailing? You ain't never turned down my banana pudding."

Alamanda's brow furrowed. "Well are you, Will?"

He grimaced. "Am I what? Going to turn down banana pudding? I think I just did."

"Don't be facetious. I'm asking if you're sick. You're acting mighty peculiar."

"I'm fine, Ali. Just leave me be."

"If you're sick, I'll call Doc Griffin."

Will raised his voice and told her again he was fine. But Lizzie knew he wasn't. She knew it, just like her mother and Cleo must have known. When her daddy refused banana pudding, there was ample cause to worry.

Chapter Fourteen

Monday was a gorgeous day. The sun had never seemed brighter, the grass never greener and the fragrance of honeysuckles in the air had never smelled sweeter. It was a perfect day for swimming.

At last, the moment Lizzie had waited for all day had come. "Listen, Bonnie." The sound of singing in the distance indicated the field hands had come to the end of a workday and were leaving the fields. Kiah would soon be heading toward the shanty.

She pounced out of the creek and grabbed her cover-up from off the blueberry bush. "Let's go meet him." Bonnie trailed behind, muttering her objections.

Kiah came hiking up the trail, hot and sweaty with the laces of his brogans tied together and thrown over his shoulder.

Lizzie flashed her biggest smile. "Hello, Kiah. Want to swim? The water's great. We're decent, if you call this decent." She snatched open her cover-up, revealing the new polka-dot bathing suit she ordered from the Sears and Roebuck catalog.

He ran his fingers through his hair and then fixed his focus on a turtle crawling nearby.

Lizzie grabbed him by the hand. "You aren't afraid of two innocent little girls, are you? Come on, we'll have fun."

"I don't know. Maybe I shouldn't. You go ahead and enjoy your swim. I'll come back later."

"Later? Why later? You *are* afraid of us. You are!" She giggled, pulling on his arm.

"That's silly. I'm not afraid. But . . . your daddy . . . he doesn't object to mixed bathing?"

"Daddy? Of course not. He believes in keeping up with the times. He's not some fuddy-duddy. I've been swimming with boys for as long as I can remember."

"You're sure Mr. Will doesn't mind?"

"Don't be silly. Didn't he say you could swim here anytime?"

"Well . . . yes, he did say that."

"And he told you that Bonnie and I often swim in the creek."

Kiah nodded. "Yeah, he said that, too."

"Then that should be proof enough." She knew it never crossed her daddy's mind that she and Kiah might both swim in the same water-hole at the same time, but even if he found out, she could explain it away to her doting father. In his sight, she could do no wrong.

"What about your orphaned sister? Is she not speaking to me because I embarrassed her at the picnic?"

Bonnie blushed. "I may speak to you but it doesn't mean I've forgiven you. You and Lizzie are one-of-a-kind. You're both dreadful. You could've been twins."

Kiah's face turned ashen. "What do you mean by that snide remark?"

Lizzie saw no reason why he should appear offended. As far as she was concerned, Bonnie had just paid them both a compliment.

Bonnie snickered. "Hey, I was joking. I don't really think you're dreadful. Maybe I did earlier, but I'm over it. Honest."

Lizzie yelled, "Let's hurry. It'll soon be dark."

He threw his shoes on the ground. Lizzie grabbed him by the hand and they ran down together and jumped in the creek. The water made his overhauls balloon, causing him to look as if he'd gained two hundred pounds. Lizzie cackled and pointed. He splashed her and then playfully ducked her for poking fun. Squeals of laughter echoed through the woods. Bonnie lightened up and seemed to enjoy it as much as Lizzie.

When the sun sank out of sight, they swam to the edge and trudged up the embankment.

Bonnie blushed as she hurried over to grab her shirt. Lizzie moseyed over to the bush and picked up her cover-up. Dragging it behind her, she strolled alongside Kiah, giving him ample time to admire her beauty, even if he did try hard not to notice.

With tongue-in-cheek, Kiah said, "Thanks for inviting me to swim. It was very refreshing, *Jo*."

Lizzie giggled and threw her hands over her face. "How was I to know Daddy would plan a barbecue so soon and unravel my little plot?"

"So you thought I swallowed that bunch of baloney you fed me?" He let out a sarcastic-sounding chuckle. "Did you honestly think I was surprised to find out your name wasn't Jo, and I was hoodwinked into believing the car wasn't yours?"

"Okay, so what gave me away?"

"You're a lousy liar, Miss Lizzie Lancaster. But I suppose that's better than being a good liar. I'm hoping it means you haven't had much practice."

Bonnie's eyes widened. "Oh, she's had more than you might think." She grabbed her shoes. "Lizzie, we'd better get back. It's getting dark."

"You can run on if you like. If Mama should ask, tell her I'll be there in a jiff."

"All right, but you know Aunt Ali will be furious with you."

"She'll get over it, Bonnie. She always does." Bonnie ran across the field, while Lizzie lingered behind.

Kiah said, "You must take me for a real sap to think I was fooled into thinking that two beautiful young girls dressed in those fancy glad-rags were maids, on the way to pick up . . . what was it? Buttermilk? An errand for the lady you *both* happened to work for." He rolled his eyes. "When you made the vain attempt to pass yourselves off as Beth and Jo, I almost asked about your other sisters, Meg and Amy, but I decided to wait and see how far you'd go with your little charade."

Lizzie admitted defeat. "Well, who'd expect a hobo to be familiar with *Little Women*?" She crossed her arms and pretended to sulk. *Did he call me beautiful? He did.*

"Miss Lizzie, normally I'd take offense to being labeled a hobo. But somehow, you manage to take such pleasure in constantly repeating the title as if it's admirable to be one, that I almost feel unworthy of the honor. It's true—I'm poor, homeless, and I've been known to hop a train or two. But there are things you need to learn about your underlings. I take it you think we were all born in a cotton patch, and have the IQ of a boll weevil."

Lizzie frowned. "That's ridiculous. I never said that."

"Yes, you did. You phrased it differently, but you said it in so many snooty words. You didn't think I had the intelligence to maneuver an automobile. And you thought I was such a dumb cluck, that I'd fall for your little stunt when you pranced around the fields pretending to be hired help. Forgive me for saying, but that was a pathetic performance."

When Lizzie attempted to interject, he held a flat palm inches from her face.

"Excuse me, but I'm not through. It never crossed your mind that I might recognize the characters in Louisa May Alcott's *Little Women*. Why? Because you had me pegged as a hobo, and in your little world, hoboes are dumb Palookas who can't read. It may surprise you, but reading is my favorite pastime. When my mother became ill, I sat by her bed every night and read to her. *Little Women* was one of the books she requested, and to tell the truth, I rather enjoyed it myself, since I find both the female species to be a fascinating study."

Lizzie grinned. "Okay. I'll admit I was wrong. I did assume you were illiterate—so go ahead and give me thirty lashes with a corn silk."

"And I suspect no doubt that'd be the most painful discipline you've ever experienced."

"Are you saying I'm spoiled?"

"And would I be wrong?"

"Indeed! I'm not spoiled. I'm just—"

"Do you need help in finding the right word? I have a few spares I keep tied up in my hobo rag, in case I have a need to communicate with rich girls and wish to hide my ignorance. Shall I pull one out for you?"

"No. I know what you'd say."

"And what would that be, Miss Lizzie?"

"Stop with the Miss Lizzie! You're irritating me."

"I'd think you'd be accustomed to it."

"Well, not from a—"

"I think the word you're searching for is 'tramp.' My, Miss Lizzie, you should work on your vocabulary. You seem to have a problem in that area."

"No, I normally don't. It's you."

"Me? And why would that be, Miss Lizzie."

"You get me all flusterated."

Kiah laughed. "Flusterated? Now, it seems *my* vocabulary is the one lacking, for that's a new word for me. But I'm guessing flusteration is simply an unhappy mix of being both frustrated and flustered. What a predicament to be in. My deepest apologies for causing you such undue anguish."

Lizzie feigned a look of anger, which would've been much easier to pull off, if only he were less handsome.

Kiah smiled and shook his head. "You're a funny girl, Lizzie Lancaster."

"Thanks."

"For saying you're funny?"

"No. For dropping the 'Miss.'"

"I must admit—it was easy. It was beginning to stick in my craw." His smile faded. "Lizzie, I'm puzzled. Why did you go to such great lengths, to keep me from knowing the real you?"

Lizzie had a ready answer, but it would keep. The time wasn't right. Not yet. Not until he could admit his love for her. He tried hard to conceal it, but he couldn't hide the way his eyes lit up and he fidgeted whenever she came near. Yep, he was in love, all right. She was sure of it.

When Lizzie reached the house, she found her mother in a tizzy. "Where in the world have you been, Eliza Virginia? Do you realize what time it is?"

Will chimed in. "Now, now, Ali, no need to get on your high-horse. She's safe and sound. You should be grateful instead of jumping on her with all four feet."

Lizzie knew better than to laugh. "Sorry, Mama. Before I realized it, it was dark."

"Well, that's strange. Your cousin Bonnie didn't seem to have a problem noticing night was drawing nigh. She returned an hour ago. What were you doing out there all alone?"

"Think what you will, Mama. You always think the worse." Lizzie tried desperately to squeeze out a few fake tears, but found it impossible. How could she cry when things were going so good?

"I'm sorry, Eliza, but I worry when you're out this late by yourself. Maybe I am a bit overprotective."

"Does that mean you'll give me a little slack from now on?"

"Don't press me, Eliza. Now, go tell Cleoda you'll take your supper in your room."

Lizzie was glad her Mama and Daddy had already eaten. Alone in her room she replayed the conversation between her and Kiah over and again in her thoughts. The more she thought about it, the more convinced she became that she wasn't the only one falling in love.

Chapter Fifteen

The summer had gone much too quickly to suit Kiah. His hands were sore and his back ached from leaning over and dragging the heavy burlap bag. He was tired. Yet not too tired to run all the way from the field to the creek.

The sun would soon set, and he didn't want to waste a single minute. He swallowed hard. *Why do I torture myself by meeting her every evening? If she knew the truth, she'd hate me—and him too, I suppose.* He wanted to turn and run the other way as fast as he could. Though he'd never lay a hand on her, he was no imbecile. It had to end. Yet for months, he'd looked forward to the close of the day when she'd be waiting for him at the creek. These longings churning inside him were wrong. Terribly wrong. But life without her was too painful to imagine. Yet, he'd have to get accustomed to the idea, because one thing was certain—there could never be a life *with* her.

For the sake of all concerned, there was only one thing he could do. Leave Goat Hill. He had no choice.

The sound of water splashing told him she was waiting.

Lizzie yelled, "Come on in, slow poke. I'll race you to the bend."

He bit down on his bottom lip, and shook his head. "Not today, Liz."

She giggled. "Scaredy-cat. You're afraid I'll win."

"Yeah. That's it." He took a seat on the rock and rubbed his hand across his mouth, to hide the quivering.

Lizzie's smile could light up a dark cave. When she stepped out of the water, his heart hammered as he gazed at her stunning silhouette. His eyes wanted to linger, yet he dared not appease them. The leaves crackled beneath her feet as she scurried up the bank. He grabbed her cover-up from off a bush and threw it in her direction.

She shook her head and plopped down beside him. "No thanks, I don't need it. I'm not cold."

"Put it on."

"But I told you. I'm not cold."

His pulse raced. "It's not a jacket, Liz. It's a cover-up. I said put it on. We need to talk."

With her head tilted to the side, she said, "Snippy, snippy! Did Rodolph beat you picking today?" She stuck her arms in the long-sleeved shirt and snuggled up close. She put an arm around his shoulder and playfully tousled his curly hair.

"Stop, it Liz." He bolted from the rock, and stumbled down the embankment to the creek's edge. He crouched down, picked up a pebble and slung it into the water.

Bewildered, she followed, stooped down in front of him, and placed her hands on top of his. "Kiah, I think I know what's wrong."

His eyes looked past her. "You . . . you know?"

"Yes. And I don't mind. I want you to."

He shifted his gaze and stared into her eyes. His brow creased. "What are you saying?"

"I'm saying I know you want to kiss me, and it's okay. I want you to." She closed her eyes and leaned in his face.

Kiah leaped to his feet and yelled. "Stop it!"

Without a word, she jumped up, darted up the steep embankment and was running through the meadow when he caught her.

"Oh, Liz. I'm sorry if I hurt you."

Sobbing, she screamed, "I feel like such an ignoramus."

He kicked up dust with his foot. "Liz, please, don't take it this way."

"How can I take it, Kiah? I keep getting mixed messages from you."

His eyes glistened.

"Kiah, talk to me. Please. What's wrong?"

"Everything."

"What do you mean by everything?"

He closed his eyes to hold in the moisture. He had to be firm and make her believe she meant nothing to him. "I mean it's all wrong. I don't want to hurt you, Liz, but you keep pretending there's something between us, and I've told you over and over there's not. Sure, you're a swell kid, but my purpose for coming to the creek is to bathe. I'm hot and tired after a long day's work. I'd appreciate it if you wouldn't be waiting here for me every day." His voice quaked. Drats! It sounded like puberty all over again.

Liz's pulse raced when she felt a strange sensation on her cheek. A tear? Her voice trembled when she said, "Okay, so you don't love me. If I say I believe you, can we swim tomorrow?"

"But you don't believe me, do you?"

"Sure, Kiah. Why wouldn't I? Just because you get all google-eyed when I'm near you is no sign you love me." She giggled and grabbed him by the hand. "Now, come on, let's swim. We don't have time for a lover's spat. Summer's practically over. We won't have many weeks left to enjoy the creek."

He knew he shouldn't, but for months he'd been telling himself he shouldn't. Yet, here he was again. Perhaps tomorrow he could find the strength to resist her confounding charms.

Chapter Sixteen

Lizzie rushed to the creek at four-thirty, Tuesday afternoon—just as she'd done every day all summer. Yet today she had an uncanny feeling something was about to go wrong.

Kiah was late. The sun lowered, and he was nowhere in sight. What if he should decide not to come? *He'll come . . . he knows I'm waiting. He loves me, even if he tries to deny it.*

She held her breath and listened. The singing in the distance stopped, which meant the pickers had left for the day. Except for the cooing of doves, and water babbling over the rocks, there were no other sounds. And then, whistling. Her heart beat faster. Kiah. "He's coming."

She positioned her slender body on the rock and pondered her best pose. What difference did it make? He never looked at her. Not really. She certainly wasn't afraid to look at him. Was it his pride—because he was a field hand, and she was heir to a fortune? Didn't he know she'd give up everything for him? The bushes rustled as he made his way down the path.

She called out, "Hey, you're late."

"Late? Did we have an appointment?" His voice sounded gruff.

"Of course we did. Don't act so naïve, Kiah Grave. You knew perfectly well I'd be waiting, and I knew you'd come as soon as you could get here. Why do you keep pretending?" She ran and grabbed his hand.

He jerked away from her grasp. "Stop it, Liz. Why are you so pig-headed? I've told you how I feel. You think every guy who sees you is ready to fall in love. Well, for your information, I'm here for three reasons, and you aren't one of them."

"No?" She stuck her tongue in her cheek. "And why are you here?"

His voice sounded edgy. "I'm hot, I'm tired and I'm dirty. A dip in a cold creek will eliminate all three problems. I don't need a fourth one. I'll admit I enjoy your company, but if I were to fall in love, it wouldn't be with a girl as pushy as you."

"Ooh. You must be crazy about me, to get so twisted out of sorts. You're stammering."

With a wry twist of his mouth, he said, "So you think I'm flusterated, do you?"

"Well?"

They both laughed. "I'm only flusterated, as you call it, when I suspect you view my intentions as anything but honorable. I have no intention of—"

She finished his sentence. "Of allowing yourself to fall in love with me? Oh my, but it's too late to worry over something that's already happened, now, isn't it?"

"Do you make a practice of finishing people's sentences?"

"Only for those who are afraid to say what they feel."

His upper lip shot up in a snarl. "Would you stop it? I've told you I'm not in love with you. It's all in your head."

If Lizzie's heart hadn't told her differently, she could've almost believed him. She snickered when he said, "You're too arrogant to consider that you might not be my cup of tea."

Lizzie sucked on a pine needle. "Hmm . . . arrogant? Is that what you find most attractive about me, or could it be my legs?" She lifted her left leg slightly and pointed her toes in the air.

"You're crazy, Liz. I've never noticed your legs." His red face lit up like a ghost firefly on a dark night.

"Oh? Then I suppose it's my eyes that you like . . . or is it my lips?" Lizzie enjoyed watching Kiah squirm. He seemed easily embarrassed, which she considered quite charming.

He frowned. "Why can't you believe there might be at least one guy in the universe who doesn't drool on himself when he looks at you?"

"Oh, I suppose there could be one—but his name doesn't happen to be Kiah Grave."

Kiah threw up his hands. "You have no idea what you're doing. It's shameless the way you flirt. You're gonna get yourself in big trouble, one of these days."

"You promise?"

"It's not funny, Lizzie. I'm serious. A fellow doesn't want a girl who throws herself at him. Haven't you heard it said that the fruit you reach for is better than the fruit that falls at your feet?"

"Oh, now I've made you angry. I was toying with you, Kiah. Don't be mad. You like me. I know you do."

"I'm not angry . . . but I don't want to lead you on, and it seems no matter how hard I try to avoid it, you think I'm like all the others—that I'm madly in love with you. Well, I'm not. Can't you get it through your head?"

"Are you trying to say you don't find me attractive? Even a little?" She giggled.

"Of course I find you extremely attractive . . . you're—"

"Beautiful?"

"There you go finishing my sentences. Just because I have eyes doesn't mean I'm in love with you. I think Myrna Loy is extremely attractive too, but I'm not in love with her."

"But she's a movie star. She's off-limits."

He bit his lip and dropped his head. "As far as I'm concerned, you are too."

Lizzie stuck her lips out in a little pout. "Isn't there anything about me you like?"

"I didn't say I didn't like you. I said I don't love you. I don't deny I enjoy your quirky sense of humor, even though you irritate me with it sometimes. I like—"

Lizzie broke out in a big smile. "I'm glad you like me. I think every relationship should begin that way."

Kiah groaned. "Relationship? There's no relationship. You're fun . . . you amuse me. But I'm not romantically interested, and never will be, I assure you."

"You tell me I'm beautiful, funny and you enjoy my company, yet you don't want me to believe you're in love with me?"

"There you go again, stretching my words. I merely said you were attractive. I didn't say you were beautiful. Those were your words. Come on, stop the silly yammering. It'll be dark soon. I'll race you to the bend." The words barely escaped his lips when water splashed. "Hey, you cheated. I wasn't ready."

Lizzie's head bobbed out of the water. "Oh, didn't I tell you? Honesty isn't among my virtues," she yelled, paddling furiously.

"Virtues? What virtues? Are you hiding something?" Kiah took a running start and leaped into the water. With the resilience of an Olympic swimmer, he drew close enough to grab Lizzie's heel.

"Gotcha!"

Her heart leaped within her chest. *Don't let go, Kiah. Don't ever let go.*

But he did. He glided past her and rounded the bend. "And the 'winnah' is Hezekiah Grave," he shouted, thrusting a fist into the air.

No, dear Kiah. I'm the winner. Things were going according to plan. He was in love—Lizzie had no doubt. She saw it in his eyes. How could she get him to admit it?

After swimming back, Kiah emerged from the water and with an outstretched hand, reached down and lifted Lizzie to the bank. Wet ringlets framed her beautiful face. Her blonde locks glistened in the moonlight, as she bent over and shook water from her hair.

He watched as she blotted her lips with her fingertips. Her cheeks were rosy—the shade of a newly ripened peach. Her skin appeared soft and unblemished, like that of a baby. Her slender body was—his heart hammered. He wet his lips and turned away. *Watch it, Kiah. This is a battle you can't afford to lose.*

They ran to the rock, where Kiah picked up her cover-up and gently laid it across her shoulders.

She ran her fingers through her long blonde locks, and snickered when she caught him looking. She reached up and with the back of her hand, stroked his cheek. "Kiah Grave, I do believe you're blushing."

"You'd better go, Liz. Your folks will be worried."

Lizzie ambled slowly down the moon-lit path leading to Gladstone, sensing his gaze following her as she walked away. *I saw the way he looked at me when he called me Liz.* She'd always felt the name Eliza sounded cold and formal, and Lizzie—well, Lizzie had begun to sound a bit childish. But Liz—it sounded so mature—so romantic, when it came from Kiah's lips. In the distance she could see light shining through the windows at the manor. Mama would be angry, and maintain it was 'dark'. Any other time, Lizzie would insist it was 'dusk'. But tonight she was in no mood to argue.

Chapter Seventeen

Lizzie pulled the bedspread over her head and moaned.

"Wake up Sleepy Head." Her mother raised the window shades and pulled back the white Priscilla curtains, allowing the sun to shine through.

"Oh, Mama," she whined, "Why do I have to get up so early?"

"It isn't early, Eliza. The morning is half spent already. Cleoda has breakfast waiting, and you and I have lots to do today."

"We do? What? I don't remember seeing 'bonding time with Mama' listed on my itinerary."

Alamanda jerked back the white crocheted bedspread and tugged on Lizzie's arm. "It's Wednesday and the party is tomorrow night. You and I are going to Dothan, young lady."

Lizzie groaned. "Aww . . . not me, Mama. I don't want to go. Get Aunt Merle to go with you. I hate shopping."

"Aunt Merle can't try on dresses for you. I need you with me."

"But I have plenty of clothes."

"Stop being contrary, Eliza, and get up. We'll be leaving after breakfast."

"Why do I need a new dress?"

"You know perfectly well Lula Weinberger is planning Oliver a surprise Going Away Party before he leaves for Harvard, and naturally he expects you to be there. Lula plans to give him a big send-off."

"Well, I can't fault her for that." Lizzie smirked. "If he lived with me, I'd want to send him off also."

"Eliza, I don't know where you got your smart mouth, but I find your impishness to be deplorable. You aren't the least bit funny."

"Nor am I trying to be. I was as serious as a . . . never mind. But seriously, I'd rather be married to a mule—though I don't suppose there'd be a thimble's worth of difference."

"Shame on you. Now get up and get dressed."

After a miserable day shopping, Lizzie returned home loaded down with shopping bags and hatboxes.

Alamanda pulled a sheer white negligee from a shopping bag and held it up. "Oh when I saw this in Blumberg's today, I knew you had to have it. This is imported lace, you know. Here, honey, put it in your hope chest for your wedding night."

"That's a good place for it, since I hope I never have to wear it. It's disgusting, Mama."

Alamanda threw up her hands. "I declare, you're impossible,

child. I give you everything, and you appreciate nothing."

"Oh, but you're wrong. I'd appreciate it if you'd forget about Oliver's party."

"Well, *that* my dear will not happen. I promised Lula you'd be there, and you're going. Ali opened a large box and pulled out two exquisite evening gowns. She laid them on the bed, side by side. With her index finger pressed against her cheek, she mumbled, "I can't decide—they're both gorgeous. Personally, I prefer the red one—it's so vibrant." Ali bit her lip. "On the other hand, with your bold personality, I'm not sure you need anything quite so daring. Pink is feminine, and the pastel might help give you a sense of softness which you lack." She shook her head. "I don't know . . . the red one *does* accent your cute little figure and the color looks fabulous with your blonde hair. Ali held them up again, one at the time. What do you think, Eliza?"

"It doesn't matter, Mama. I don't think I'm going. Why don't you go in my place, and wear the one that accents your cute little figure."

"Stop being sarcastic, Eliza. You *are* going, and you'll act civil. I know how much you like to swim, but if you give me a hard time, your swimming days are over for the season."

Lizzie flinched. Of all things her mother could take away from her, the creek was the one thing she couldn't afford to give up. "You win, Mama. I'll go to Oliver's boring party if you'll agree to let me swim as long as I like, and stop badgering me about coming home late. I'm eighteen, but you treat me as if I'm a child." She watched tiny lines form on her mother's forehead.

"Honey, I do declare, you must be part fish. I wish you'd spend as much time practicing your piano lessons as you do romping around in the backwoods and swimming in the creek."

"Well, Mama—is it a deal?" Lizzie concluded she could endure one boring night with Oliver, in exchange for countless romantic evenings at the creek with Kiah.

Alamanda threw up her hands. "Eliza, Lancaster I may as well agree to your terms, though you know I don't approve."

"And you know I don't approve of Oliver, but that doesn't keep you from trying to force me into an arranged marriage, which would end my life."

"You could do much worse, my dear."

"If you're still thinking of the mule, I honestly don't think it would be considered worse."

Alamanda frowned. "You're so hard to understand. Sometimes I wonder how we could have the same genes."

"I'm like my daddy. He understands me, Mama. You never have."

Ali glared at her daughter. "You're right in saying that I can't understand you. You're impossible. But if you think—" She drew a deep breath—then clamped her lips together.

"What?" Lizzie lifted open palms.

"You know how I detest it when you ask a one-word question,

Eliza. Exactly what do you mean when you ask 'what'?"

"I could tell you wanted to say something. So say it, Mama."

Ali frowned. "You can tell when I want to say something, can you? And now among your other abilities, I suppose you're a mind-reader? You should know me better than that, Eliza. I have no problem speaking my mind."

Lizzie couldn't argue the point.

"I'd like for you to try on the red dress, Eliza. I've decided that's the one you'll wear to the party."

"Mama, I haven't grown since we left the store. Why should I keep trying it on?"

"For me. Do it for me, Eliza. Please?"

Lizzie shrugged. "Okay, Mama. But after I try it on, I want to put on my bathing suit and run down to the creek."

"But Eliza, it'll soon be sundown. You'll hardly have time to get in the water before it'll be time to come home. Besides, it's getting too cool to swim. You'll catch pneumonia."

"Mama, we made a pact together, remember? I'll go to the party for you, and you'll stop treating me like a child."

Alamanda sighed. "You win, as usual. Slip into the dress, and I promise I'll try to be less restrictive on your activities. But please do be careful when you go to the creek, and don't get too far from the house. That hobo Will hired is staying in the shanty. Who knows what he might try if he should see you down there. You can never be too careful."

"Don't worry, Mama. I'd like to see him try to make a pass at me. I promise you I'd know how to handle him." Lizzie managed the words with a straight face.

She put on the dress and feigned a curtsy, which seemed to delight her mother.

"Oh my, you look lovely, Darling!" Alamanda clasped her hands under her chin. "Oliver Weinberger's eyes are going to pop out."

Lizzie lifted her shoulders. "Well, I'm for anything that might improve his looks, Mama."

"Eliza, that's mean. I wish you'd give him a chance. Lula says he talks of you all the time."

"Oh? And did you mention to Mrs. Weinberger you talk of *him* all the time too? What a shame you were born too soon—you two would make a charming couple."

"Eliza, I find that kind of talk very vulgar. Get out of the dress and hang it in the armoire." Alamanda huffed out of the room, slamming the door behind her.

Lizzie cherished every moment she and Kiah spent at the creek. There were times she sensed he wanted to kiss her, though he never made an attempt nor verbally suggested having such a thought. He could at least try, and give her the option of refusing his advances—the way he'd refused hers.

She imagined the scenario. He'd be sitting on the rock beside her, gazing into her eyes. He'd slowly lean forward and kiss her—and she would let him. Then she'd pretend to be shocked, and slap him—not hard enough to make him angry—but with enough force to let him know she was not 'that kind' of girl. *I suppose it's too late to pull that one off since I've practically tried to seduce him.* Besides, even she found it hard to imagine herself as anything but a loose goose if he ever dared tempt her. Lizzie swallowed hard. Where were these thoughts coming from? Sure, he was good-looking and she was crazy about him, but she'd never—or would she?

Kiah was waiting on the rock when she arrived at the creek. His downtrodden face caused her concern, but she assumed he was tired from a hard day's work, and would lighten up after a few laps.

She grabbed him by the hand and ran down the embankment, pulling him into the water—but he didn't swim after her, the way he always did. She stopped at the bend and turned around. He'd climbed out of the creek and sat on the rock, skipping pebbles across the top of the water. She swam back to the bank, ran and snuggled close beside him. "Ooh, I can tell summer's ending. I'm freezing."

He edged over, making room between them.

"What's wrong, Kiah? You look worried."

He'd barely finished his first sentence, before Lizzie tried to tune him out. She didn't want to hear. *He can't mean what he's saying. Is he trying to find out how much I care? Doesn't he know?* Had she been wrong about his feelings? Perhaps she only imagined what she wanted to be true. She shivered as the cool autumn breeze dried her wet skin. Tears welled in her eyes as he talked of leaving Goat Hill.

Kiah's words were void of emotion, as he attempted to say goodbye.

"Why, Kiah? Why?" Her voice broke. "Look at me. Why won't you look at me?"

Kiah drew a deep breath. He stared at the rippling water. "I'm done here. We sent the last bale of cotton to the gin today. Mr. Louie asked if I thought I'd be back next summer."

"Next summer?" Lizzie's words were barely audible. "No, Kiah. You can't leave."

"There's no reason to stay, Liz. I came looking for work in the cotton fields, and Mr. Will gave me a job. The job has ended. It's now time to move on."

"So where will you go?" Her lips trembled.

He stood. "I think I'll hop a train to South Florida, and work in the orange groves." Kiah's heart broke, listening to her quiet sobs. If only he could tell her the truth. "Hey, now, stop the blubbering, kiddo." His arms ached for her. He wanted to comfort her but words wouldn't suffice. What could he say? He didn't want to leave her—he wanted it to go on forever—but like every other good thing in his life, it was doomed from the beginning.

"You can't leave, Kiah. I love you. You must know that."

Kiah swallowed hard and turned his back toward her. "Don't say that, Liz. Don't ever say it."

"But I do . . . and . . . and I had begun to believe you loved me too. But if you did, you wouldn't leave."

"Oh, Liz. You don't understand. I can't stay."

"You're right. I don't understand. It doesn't make sense." She stood and reached for his hand. "Kiah, I've never loved anyone but you. I never will." Her brow furrowed. "Have you? I mean have you ever loved anyone besides me?" The color left her face. "Is . . . is there someone else in your life? Is that it?"

Kiah swallowed hard and pushed her away. He had to end it. He never should have allowed things to progress this far. "It's wrong, Liz."

"What do you mean, wrong?"

"Some things aren't meant to be. I . . . I like you, Liz, but I don't love you. Do you understand? I don't love you." His words were harsh, but he feared his eyes would betray him.

Liz shook her head in disbelief. "You didn't answer my question. I want to know, Kiah."

"Okay, if you must know, I did love someone before you. I loved her very much."

She snickered. "I thought so."

"What do you mean?"

"You said you loved her before me. So you've just admitted that you do love me."

"No, you're twisting my words. I don't love you, Liz, so get over it, okay? You said I wouldn't leave if I really loved you—yet I'm standing here, telling you that I'm going. That should prove something."

Lizzie eased back down. Kiah couldn't have hurt more if a knife had jabbed him in the heart. He reached down and wiped away her tears with the tips of his fingers. She grabbed his wrist and pulled his hand to her lips.

He jerked away and shouted. "Stop it, Liz. Leave me alone. Get it through your head. I don't love you." He bit the inside of his mouth until he tasted blood. He ached to tell her the truth . . . but he couldn't for Will's sake as well as for hers. He dropped his head. His voice was barely above a whisper. "Go home, Liz."

"Look at me, Kiah Grave."

Kiah slowly raised his head until their gaze locked. He flexed his jaw.

The lump in his throat swelled as he watched the tears trail down her cheeks. Everything he wanted to tell her—the love, the joy, the excitement he felt when she was near, could only serve to cause her more pain. "I have a job to do before I go, and then I'll be on my way."

Confused, she mumbled, "A job? Here in Goat Hill?"

"Oh, not a paying job. Mr. Louie's been busy tending the

cotton and now he's behind in the chores on his own little plot of ground. I plan to help him before I leave. I'll plow up his corn field so the stalk stubs can rot over winter. His hay is still stacked in the field, so I'll get it in the loft for him. Then there's the matter with the leaking roof, and after that I'll be on my way."

"That's good of you, Kiah," she said, her voice trembling.

"His place is small. It shouldn't take long. Mr. Louie and Miz Mattie are good people. It's a shame more folks can't be like those two. I'll sure miss them."

"When do you plan to leave?"

Kiah squinted. "Let's see . . . this is Wednesday. Come Monday, and I reckon I'll vamoose."

"Why, Kiah? Why do you have to leave? Please stay. I need you."

He swallowed hard and hoped he could sound convincing. "Liz, it's been swell knowing you. But I'm a traveling man and I get itchy if I stay in one place too long." He reasoned if he could make her hate him, it'd be less painful for her to see him leave. "I can hardly wait to jump the blinds and see the world. America, here I come." He cringed at how lame his words sounded. He tried once again. "As much as I look forward to moving on, I suppose the one thing I'll miss more than anything, will be Miz Mattie's cooking. Ah, what a cook. More days than not, Mr. Louie would come to the patch with something in a syrup bucket. Inside would be a big slice of fresh baked pecan pie. Mr. Louie would hand me the bucket and say Miz Mattie wanted me to try a sampling. Yes ma'am, I reckon more'n anything, I'll miss her samplings."

Lizzie fell for it. Her reaction didn't take him by surprise. But her stinging words cut deeper than he'd anticipated. He tried to swallow the pain.

"Kiah Grave, you're the most heartless human being on this planet." She grabbed her shoes and vaulted from the rock, sobbing as if her heart would never mend.

Kiah drew a deep breath. He had to be strong and carry through. He shrugged and feigned surprise. "What's with you? Have you gone loco, Liz? All I said was I'll miss Miz Mattie's cooking. Have you ever tasted her dumplings?"

"Forget it," she screamed.

"What did I do?"

"I said forget it. If I have to tell you, it doesn't matter anyway."

Kiah had accomplished his goal, so why did he feel so lousy? He wanted to hold her—comfort her and tell her there was nothing in the world he'd ever miss more than he'd miss her. The pain on her face devastated him. He grabbed her in his arms before he realized what he was doing. A sick feeling of horror swept over him. His heart pounded. He quickly shoved her away and turned his face, as if she were covered with lepers' sores.

Unaccustomed to seeing her cry, his throat swelled when giant tears streamed down her rosy cheeks.

"Goodbye, Kiah," she whispered.

"Hey, I haven't left yet." His lip quivered. "I'm sure I'll see you before I go."

She screamed. "I hope not. I never want to see you again. I . . . I hate you." She turned and ran toward the manor.

Through clouded eyes, Kiah watched until she was out of site.

Lizzie ran up the stairs and fell across her bed. She sobbed. *I thought he loved me. The thing he'll miss most of all is Mattie's cooking?* She hated him for that. He made her fall in love and left her feeling like a dumb Dora. For years, she'd tried to cry. Now, she tried to stop. She didn't need him. There were plenty of fellows who'd be happy to share her affections. She could marry Oliver Weinberger if she wanted to. Of course! That was exactly what she'd do. Why not?

Lizzie had tried for weeks to think of an excuse to avoid Oliver's party—but not anymore. She'd go to the stupid party and inform Oliver of their nuptial plans. Then she'd take an announcement of their forthcoming marriage to Robert Loch and have him print it in the Tribune the morning after the party. Naturally, the wedding would have to wait until after Oliver finished law school. That was the most appealing part of the whole scenario. Waiting suited her just fine, but the announcement couldn't wait. She wanted Kiah to read it before he left town. He'd be sorry he let her go.

If she couldn't have the one she wanted, she might as well settle for the one who wanted her.

Chapter Eighteen

Thursday morning, Lizzie opened her eyes and groaned at the sight of her mother standing over her bed.

Alamanda jerked the sheet back and tugged at her arm. "Get up, Eliza. You have a nine o'clock appointment at the beauty shop. I've instructed Louise to pin your hair under the silk turban with just a few tendrils peeking out." Alamanda clasped her hands under her chin and gushed, "You'll be the Belle of the ball. I wish I could see Oliver's face when you walk in that room tonight. Won't he be surprised?"

Lizzie's head throbbed. You can't imagine how surprised, Mother, dear.

"Eliza, you look pale. Do you feel well? Maybe a dose of chill tonic might do you good. I certainly don't want you coming down with something, after we've waited so long for this night."

"I'm fine, Mama. I know you think Grove's Chill Tonic is a cure-all, but it won't cure my problems."

Alamanda chuckled. "Your problems? If there's one girl in this universe who has no problems, it's you, my dear. You know you've always been able to have anything you want."

"Sure, Mama. And whenever I can't have what I want, I simply give up and take whatever *you* want."

"Sometimes you talk in riddles, Eliza. I often wonder if you even know what you're saying."

Lizzie trudged down the stairs at six o'clock in the evening, wearing a red dress and a frown.

Alamanda's jaw dropped. "Oh, honey you're a sight to behold. I love the ruby brooch on the white turban. What a classy touch. You look like a Princess."

"Well, I suppose that's appropriate, since I'm on my way to kiss a frog." She mumbled, knowing her mother would fail to understand.

"Your father will drive you. Here, take my wrap."

Lizzie refused the fox stole, and shook her head. "Ugh! I'm not wrapping a dead animal around my neck." She flung the fur toward the settee. "Mama, I don't need Daddy to drive me. I plan to take my car."

"Now, that's nonsense, Eliza. Your father needs to escort you to the door. It's only proper. Besides, what if Oliver wants to bring you home?"

Lizzie grimaced. "I give up, Mama. You win. Whatever you say. I don't care anymore. I don't care about anything."

"Eliza, I don't think I like your attitude."

"Oh, but you will, Mama. I promise you, you will."

Will Lancaster entered the room and whistled. "Wow, look at my little Swamp Angel. You look beautiful, darling."

Alamanda said, "Will, I need you to escort her to the party."

"But I'm running late, Ali. I need to be in Dothan by seven for the seminar. Lizzie has a car. She can drive."

"Don't be ridiculous. She needs an escort. You won't be staying with her, Will. You'll simply walk her to the door and wait for her to be announced. You don't seem to realize the importance."

At six-thirty, Will escorted his daughter to the door of the Weinberger home, and kissed her on the cheek. "Have a good time, Honey."

"Daddy?"

"Yes, angel?"

"Daddy, I love you." She threw her arms around her father, tears welling in her eyes.

"Hey, little Swamp Angel, what's wrong?"

"I don't know. I suppose I'm feeling a little weepy." She replied.

"For no reason? It's not like you."

"We girls don't have to have a reason, do we?"

Her father pulled a handkerchief from his back pocket and dabbed at her moistened eyes. With his head tilted down, he whispered in her ear. "It isn't too late to back out, sweetheart. You don't have to attend this stuffy old party if you don't want to."

Lizzie dropped her head. "Apparently, you haven't met my mother."

His nose crinkled. "I happen to know the lady and trust me, her bark's worse than her bite. She'll get over it."

"I could prove you wrong, daddy, if I skipped this party. Mama's heart has been set on this night for months. I'll be fine."

"Is Bonnie coming?" Will asked.

She shook her head. "She's visiting her Granny in Slocomb and won't be back until next week. I'd gladly swap places with her."

Will frowned. "Honey, let me take you home."

She rose to her toes and kissed her father on the cheek. "No, Daddy. There's something I need to do and I must do it tonight."

The front door swung open, and the butler stood with his hand extended toward Lizzie.

"Bye, Daddy," Lizzie whispered, before she made her grand entrance. She wanted to tell her father of her plan, but she couldn't. He wouldn't approve. He'd try to stop her because he knew—he knew how much she detested Oliver Weinberger.

Will turned and trudged away, shaking his head.

The butler clicked his heels together. With his nose in the air, he bellowed each syllable separately, "Miss E-li-za Vir-gin-i-a Lan-cas-ter." Lizzie resisted the urge to roll her eyes. With a fake smile, she nodded politely as she entered the room. Mama would've been proud.

The Weinberger mansion had the earmarks of a fine museum with all the magnificent antiques and priceless artifacts strategically placed in the elegant rooms. Lizzie had visited here many times in the past, but not until tonight did she realize how stuffy and austere the house felt.

She shivered as she gazed at the humongous moldings and thick velvet drapes which covered the windows. Oil paintings of grumpy-looking ancestors hung on the walls. Certainly, the décor was not unlike anything to which she was accustomed—but somehow she'd never considered how cold and uninviting the furnishings seemed. Her knees weakened as she glanced from wall to wall. This was the way of life she was born into and Lizzie knew it was the way of life she'd be expected to maintain. *Falling in love with a hobo was a stupid, immature fantasy. I'm a Lancaster. A year from now, I won't even remember Kiah Grave's name.*

She eased around the ballroom, mingling with friends the Weinberger's had purchased for their son through the years. Most of them were from Dothan, but all of them were from well-to-do families. Lizzie wondered how many people attended because of their fondness for Oliver. He was boring, a braggart, and a genuine milksop. His peers, who for the most part, shared the same traits, had come because his last name was Weinberger.

She didn't want to entertain such horrid thoughts. She'd never known Oliver to be mean—like Kiah. Oliver gushed over her looks. Called her beautiful. Gorgeous. Lizzie couldn't remember a single time Oliver had ever used such a broad, unromantic term such as 'attractive' to describe her. When he sailed to Bermuda last summer he sniffled and told her he couldn't bear to leave her. Bertha Adams was the Weinberger cook and a fine one indeed. But not once did Oliver mention he'd miss Bertha's cooking when he was ready to depart. *I hate Kiah Grave. I hate him.*

She seethed, as she lumbered across the room. When Sallie Belle Sellers sashayed over to Lizzie's corner, she groaned under her breath.

In a sing-song voice, Sallie gushed, "Eliza Lancaster. It's been eons since I've seen you."

The Sellers' family lived across the line in Chancey, Georgia, and it was a known fact that Sallie's grandfather made the family fortune by selling moonshine. Of course, the people who criticized him most were the ones who made him wealthy.

"Hi, Sallie. Yes, it's been awhile. You don't come to town much anymore."

"No, since Grandpa retired, we don't get down as often. But I've looked forward to the party all summer. Oliver and I keep in touch on a regular basis. He writes me faithfully, you know. He's such an interesting character, don't you think?"

"Oh, you said a mouthful. He's a character, for sure."

"I can't wait for him to arrive. He has such a swell sense of humor. He cracks my ribs."

Lizzie nodded. "I know what you mean. I suffer similar pains when I'm around him."

"Some lucky girl will hit the jackpot when he gets around to proposing." Sallie pulled a small compact from her evening bag and powdered her nose. "How do I look?"

Lizzie raised her brow and grinned. "Attractive."

Apparently, Sallie took it as a compliment, though Lizzie had no idea why. An arrangement of fruit could be attractive, but what girl in her right mind wants to look like a banana? Lizzie sipped a swallow of punch and placed the cup on the silent butler. "Excuse me, Sallie, I think I'll mosey over to the cake table." She could walk out the side entrance and . . . and then what? Walk home? Face her mama, who'd be furious with her for not staying the duration of the party? Lizzie caught her lip between her teeth. She had no choice but to stay.

Before she had time to reconsider her decision, the French doors flew open and Oliver strode in. Exuberant shouts of "surprise," greeted him. Sallie ran and threw her arms around his neck. He crouched over and whispered something in Sallie's ear, which caused her to giggle and cover her face.

When he spotted Lizzie, he rushed across the ballroom floor in her direction. She swallowed hard. She stared as if she were seeing him for the first time. *Armadillo Face . . . my husband.* His hair, parted in the middle and slicked down with Vitalis, made his face look gaunt. His soft white skin appeared too delicate to touch—not that she had any such desires. It was merely an observation that verified what she knew to be fact. Oliver wasn't an outdoorsman. He reminded her of the 'before pictures' on the back of comic books, where the skinny guy is standing on the beach watching all the girls swoon over the muscular fellow. She'd never thought to ask, but judging from his pale skin, she assumed he didn't swim. Though she'd known him forever, the thought never occurred to her before, how little she knew about his likes or dislikes. *And this is the man I plan to marry?*

Oliver rushed toward her with outstretched arms. "Well, blow my socks off, if it's not the prettiest girl in all of Alabama. Hello, Eliza. Honey-Bun, I'm delighted to see you." Oliver reached down, gave her a big hug, then held her at arm's length and looked her over. "Va-va-voom! You look smashing, my dear. I've missed you this summer. You've kept yourself hidden, but all is forgiven, now that you're here."

"Hi Oliver. I don't know the proper salutation for a Going Away Party. Toodle-doo, maybe?"

"I think 'hasta la vista' might sound a tad more appropriate," Oliver said with a condescending smile. "But who cares about protocol when the words proceed from the lips of such a cute little tomato."

Lizzie rolled her eyes. "Thanks. I think."

"Would you like some punch?"

"No, thanks," she muttered. "I've had about all I can take."

Oliver poured him a cup. He took a sip and then pointed to his feet. "How do you like my new wingtips, doll-face?"

Lizzie glared at his pointed finger and winced. Did he think she might have a problem knowing on which end he wore his shoes?

"I'm still trying to break them in. What do you think?"

He expected her to brag on dumb shoes? This was even harder than she imagined. She sighed. "They're very nice, Oliver."

"Thanks. I have a pair of brown ones, exactly like these. Mother picked them out for me to take to college this fall. She says all the young men at Harvard will be wearing wingtips."

Lizzie bit her tongue to keep her first smart-aleck thoughts from escaping through her mouth. When it was safe to respond, she replied, politely, "Well, I declare, isn't that fascinating?"

"Why, thank you, dear. Not only are you beautiful but you've proven you have discriminating tastes." Oliver raised his brow, as if he expected a reply . . . but what was the question?

Unable to read his signal, Lizzie shrugged.

"Well?" He lifted his palms.

At least she now understood what Mama meant when she said one-word questions were hard to decipher. "I'm sorry?"

"Wouldn't you care to return the compliment?" He pretended to tease, although Lizzie knew he was quite serious.

"Oh! Forgive me. You too."

"Me too? I'm not sure I grasp your meaning, dear." He winked. "Could you expound on that little phrase, please?"

Lizzie silently recited poetry . . . a simple trick she learned to keep from spouting off whenever her temper flared. Sometimes, it worked. *Peter, Peter, pumpkin eater, had a wife and—*

His smile seemed to wrap all the way around his face as he appeared to expect a flattering remark to be forthcoming.

"Oh, Oliver, can we please skip the compliments. Let's make a deal. If you promise not to say anything nice about me, I promise not to say anything nice about you."

With a sinister grin, he said, "You're a very complex individual, Eliza Lancaster."

"Oliver! I asked you not to—"

"That was not intended as a compliment, Sweetheart. It behooves me to understand why a fairly intelligent, beautiful and vivacious lady would object to a beau-hopeful admiring her outstanding qualities."

Lizzie mulled his words. "Beau-hopeful" sailed right over her head, for it was no secret he'd spent years hoping to be her beau. The word that stuck in her craw was "fairly." What did he mean by fairly intelligent? He didn't feel the need to say fairly beautiful or fairly vivacious. *Why does he think I'm only fairly intelligent?* "You just can't stop, can you, Oliver?"

"Sorry, my darling, but you're right. It's nigh impossible for me to keep from extolling your praises when in your presence. You must know how I feel. I've admired you since the first day I saw you. We were in the sixth grade, and I sat behind you in class. Do you remember?"

"Oh, I remember all right." She hung her head to hide her smile. "And I'm sorry I called you a nasty name. That was very rude." *Some things shouldn't be said aloud, even when they're true.*

Oliver smiled, as if recalling a tender moment. "I'll have to admit at first my little heart felt wounded, but when I shared with Mother what you said, I'll never forget how thrilled I was when she explained. She said, 'Oliver, sweetheart that means she likes you. Like her father, Eliza has trouble expressing herself.' According to Mother, it's a flawed gene, but it's nothing to be ashamed of. You certainly have your strengths."

"But Oliver, I—"

Oliver gently placed his hand in front of her mouth. "Love, I haven't finished. There's something I've wanted to say for a long time. Eliza Virginia, I've loved you every minute of every day since sixth grade. Believe me, I don't mind when you sometimes use words inappropriately. None of us are perfect. I'm sure I have my own faults." He smiled. "But you mustn't expect my mother to confirm them."

Lizzie's jaw dropped. He tapped her on the shoulder. "That was a little joke, dear. I was being witty."

"Yes, I think I got it." *Little Boy Blue come blow your horn, the sheep's in the—* "Oliver, now that we've aired my flaws, do you want to marry me?" She blurted the words.

Pineapple punch spewed from his nose. He choked. His eyes opened wide, as he heaved. Lizzie pounded his back. People turned to stare.

Sallie Belle ran over and wrapped her arm around his waist. "Are you all right, love? What happened?"

"I think I just got engaged." His Adam's apple bobbled.

Sallie gasped. "What are you saying, Oliver?"

Oliver pulled a handkerchief from his back pocket and wiped his face. "I'm not sure. Ask Eliza."

Sallie glared at Lizzie. "Well . . . what does he mean?"

"I'm his fiancé. That's what he's trying to tell you."

Without another word, Sallie Belle jerked her long dress up in her hands and scurried across the room toward the exit.

Lizzie shrugged. "Excuse me, Oliver, but now that we've come to an understanding, I'd like for you to drive me home. Do you mind?"

"Okeydokey, sugar plum, but first we'll share the good news with Mother. She'll be ecstatic. She's dreamed of this day, even longer than I have."

Lizzie shook her head. "I'd rather not announce it tonight, Oliver. I don't feel well. You can tell her after you take me home."

"Oh, contraire. This can't wait. We'll break the wonderful

news together. Come, tootsie. It will only take a moment to turn this party into a real wingding.

Lizzie jerked on his coat sleeve. "No, Oliver, please—"

"Mother," he yelled, ignoring Lizzie's objections. "I have an announcement to make. Come stand with us, as we invite our friends to celebrate." With his left palm extended in the air, he reached up and gave three quick claps with his right hand. "Listen up, everyone," he shouted. "I have some exciting news." His voice quaked. "Pardon me, but I'm overwhelmed with emotion. Eliza Lancaster has asked me to marry her and I couldn't be more proud than I am at this moment."

Silence filled the room as bewildered-looking guests stared with mouths gaped open.

Lizzie muttered under her breath, "I can't believe you just told everyone I proposed."

Oliver bent down and pecked her on her forehead. "But darling, what difference does it make which one popped the question. The important thing is that we both desire to spend the rest of our lives together. Oh, my dear, you've made me the happiest man on the planet."

Lizzie bit her tongue to keep from shouting, "What's wrong with you people? I just got engaged to Oliver Weinberger and you look as if you're waiting for the punch line. Don't you get it? The engagement is the punch line and the joke is on me."

A slow clap . . . clap. . . clap, and then more hands joined in, and in minutes the applause gained momentum, although Lizzie didn't detect the enthusiasm that normally accompanies such announcements.

Lula Weinberger stepped forward. With deep creases between her eyes and her lip slightly curled, the woman seemed to have the unique ability to simultaneously form both a frown and a smile. Her strong jutting nose appeared to grow when her head lowered and she peered over the tops of her spectacles at her future daughter-in-law. She stiffened, drew a deep breath and demonstrating the same sort of misplaced fondness a fox might have when hugging a hen, she wrapped her arms around Lizzie and squeezed.

"A daughter at last. I'm thrilled." Lula's stabbing gray eyes contradicted the message flowing from her lips. "This is the second happiest day of my life. The first, being the day my precious little Oliver was born. He's a good boy, Eliza. If you two ever have problems, I'll know where the fault lies, because my Oliver gets along with everyone. You'll be good to him, won't you?"

Lizzie felt faint. She shifted her eyes toward Oliver and gasped when enormous teeth looked as if they'd stolen his face. *What have I done?*

Lula said, "I know you can sometimes be a bit overbearing, dear. But I've never blamed you for being spoiled. That's William Lancaster's doings. I've always said the man dotes on you entirely too much."

Oliver yelled, "Hey, Lehman, strike up the band and play some schmaltzy tune. I want to dance with my little muffin." He sounded like a pig snorting when he laughed. "Shoot the juice, Bruce," he yelled to the orchestra. "Let's get this party swinging. The little lady and I'll take the first dance."

Lizzie shook her head with all the vigor she could muster, though Oliver didn't appear to notice. The crowd backed away when the music began.

Oliver bowed and extended his hand. "May I have this dance, my love?"

"No, Oliver," she whispered, "I need to leave."

"But, tootsie. Don't be shy. Everyone's waiting for us to dance."

"Let them wait. I'm not going to make an idiot of myself." *At least not twice in one night.*

Oliver motioned for the band to stop playing. "Sorry to disappoint you folks, but the little lady has the jitters. To tell the truth, my knees are knocking, also. You understand our excitement."

The guests nodded politely. Oliver appeared to savor the moment, as he shook hands with all the men and hugged the ladies.

Uncomfortable with the attention, Lizzie stood on tip-toes and whispered, "Oliver, I want to go. Now!"

"But, tootsie. We can't make such an important announcement and deny our friends the opportunity to express their sentiments.

This is a very big moment. We owe it to our guests to stay."

She raised her voice. "Oliver Weinberger, take me home this instant."

"Lower your voice, dear. People are staring."

"Let them stare. I want to go home. And don't ever, *ever* call me 'tootsie.' My name is Lizzie."

Oliver glanced at his mother and nodded when Lula nudged him. "That's something we might wish to discuss, my dear." He glanced at his mother as if seeking approval.

Lula smiled and nodded.

"Sweetheart, I don't wish to hurt your feelings, but the pet name Lizzie sounds so . . . so simple-minded. Mother agrees. Do you not, Mother?"

Oliver's mother hadn't left their side since the big announcement. "Well, I'm not one to butt in, but since you're both asking my opinion—he's right, darling. You're a big girl now. Your mother is so proper, I can't imagine why she allowed your father to call you such a common name, when she's given you a lovely one. Eliza Virginia suits you."

"But I happen to prefer Lizzie."

Oliver placed his hand on her shoulder and with a smile that appeared more condescending than affectionate, he patted her. "Frankly, sweetheart, neither Mother nor I approve of diminutives. We consider the only acceptable nicknames to be the endearing ones. Eliza is a fine name, and I shall call you by your proper name, unless of course I'm choosing to use an affectionate term."

Lizzie's face grew hot. "I'm leaving here, Ollie Boy. If you don't take me, I'll walk."

Lula bristled. "Eliza, my son's name is not Ollie Boy. I named him Oliver after my father, his father, and his father before him. One day, he shall father a son, who will follow the tradition. No one has ever called him anything but Oliver since the day he was born."

Lizzie pursed her lips. "Oh, did I forget to mention that I prefer nicknames. Now, for the last time, Ollie—are you coming, or do I walk?"

Lula clutched her hands across her chest and though she whispered, her voice was loud enough for anyone within six feet to overhear. "Oliver, dear, she'll blush tomorrow when she realizes how she spoke to you tonight, but we must make exceptions for her. This has been a big day. She's understandably excited that you've accepted her proposal. Likely, she's fretted over it all day. Why don't you take her home? I'll let everyone know she's overcome with emotion and you'll return after settling her down. If you happen to speak with Alamanda, tell her I'll get with her tomorrow to discuss the wedding plans. One can never start too soon when planning such a large celebration."

Lizzie turned and headed toward the door. *I have a feeling there's a reckoning day coming for one of us. No husband of mine will be a Mama's boy.* "Oliver," Lizzie yelled. "You can stand here all night if you want to, but I'm leaving. With or without you."

Lula Weinberger fanned her face. "Calm down, Eliza. You're making a scene," she whispered. "Do something with her Oliver. Her behavior is embarrassing."

"And what do you propose, Mother?"

"Take her home. But you need to be firm and let her know you'll not tolerate such ill manners."

Lizzie was a quarter-of-a-mile down the dirt road before Oliver could crank the car. He pulled up beside her and opened the door.

"Get in, sweetheart. I'm sorry you're upset. I take full responsibility. I should've been more . . . more—" He paused, and searched for the right word.

"More what, Oliver? Tell me. Do you even know what went on?"

"Well, perhaps I don't. But we can work these things out, precious. I know we can. Now get in the car."

"No."

"No? And I suppose you intend to walk five miles?"

"I most certainly do." With her shoes in her hand, Lizzie upped the pace. Oliver's car eased along beside her.

"Don't be ridiculous, darling. Why would you want to walk, when you can ride?"

"You haven't a clue, do you Oliver? You didn't ask me to get in the car. You ordered me. I don't take orders—Precious!" She spat the last word with all the sarcasm she could muster.

Oliver pleaded. "Eliza, please get in."

Lizzie hoped he'd not give up. Her feet ached.

"Come on, Eliza. Please?" Oliver drove slowly beside her.

She stopped. Oliver put on brakes. Lizzie threw her shoes on the front seat, and stepped up on the running board. "Let's go."

"But honey, you look silly riding on the running board in your lovely gown."

"Not as silly as I'd feel sitting beside you—after the shameful way you treated me."

"Please don't be angry, toots . . . I mean Eliza. I shall make it up to you, I promise. Whatever I did to upset you, I'll refrain from ever doing again."

She wanted to say, "You agreed to marry me, Oliver. That's why I'm upset. You know I don't love you. I could respect you more, if you'd turned me down. Sally loves you and I've blown it for you. You should hate me. It would be easier for us both if you did.

When Oliver pulled up in front of Gladstone, Lizzie ran to the front door.

He turned off the ignition and ran after her. He grasped her upper arms with both his hands, and panted. "Wait! Dearest, I'm sorry you're upset, but no doubt your reaction is due to nerves. I'm nervous, also. But you've made me the happiest man on earth.

Eliza, I'd like nothing more than to hold you in my arms and plant a kiss on your lovely lips but I shant. Mother didn't bring me up to be an animal. I've resolved to restrain myself until we become man and wife. Goodnight, my dear."

Lizzie hoped she wouldn't upchuck on the marble porch, but never had she experienced such extreme nausea. "Yes, I think putting it off as long as we can is a terrific idea."

Oliver patted her hand as she reached for the doorknob. "Love, I understand what you meant to say. But we'll have a lifetime to work on verbalization after we're married."

"Goodnight, Oliver."

"Goodnight, sweetheart. I'll bring Mother over tomorrow. She's eager to get together with your—" He blushed. "I suppose I should begin calling her, Mama Alamanda." You and I can sit on the veranda and discuss things which concern us, while our mothers make preparations for our wedding."

"And what may I ask concerns us, Oliver?"

He grinned. "For one thing, we should discuss how many children we want."

Lizzie's mouth flew open. She ran toward the door, reciting every verse of Little Boy Blue in an effort to clear her head of the horrid thought. The door slammed behind her.

When Lizzie walked into the parlor, Alamanda shrieked. "Eliza Virginia Lancaster, what are you doing with your shoes in your hand? And look at your feet. They're filthy. I should have known you'd bungle things up."

Alamanda's voice reached the screaming stage. "I do declare you're such an imbecile. It seems you delight in disgracing this family. I trust you have a good excuse for leaving the party early?"

Lizzie glared without speaking.

Alamanda shouted. "You've probably ruined the chance of a lifetime. What were you thinking? Answer me, Eliza."

"I suppose I thought at last I had done something to meet with your approval, Mama."

"I've had it with your insolence. You've brought shame to the family name. My mother warned me long ago that you can't cross a morning glory with a kudzu vine."

Eliza rolled her eyes. "And what's that supposed to mean, Mama?"

"You wouldn't understand. I've tried to smooth over your rough edges, but as the saying goes, what's in the well comes up in the bucket. You're a disgrace. You act more like a Loudermilk than Alice does. Perhaps Mrs. Bea's Finishing School can help in the areas where I've failed."

"No need to send me there, Mama. I'm finished already. I took care of that for you, tonight. *My* life is over. From now on, I'll be living your life for you."

"Eliza, you talk nonsense."

"I'm saying you won, Mama. You don't have to push Oliver on me. I proposed at the party, and he accepted. We're getting married as soon as he graduates from Harvard. Happy?"

"If you think you're being funny, let me assure you, you're not."

"Am I laughing? No ma'am, I find nothing humorous about the situation. You should jump for joy, though. Mrs. Weinberger is coming tomorrow to plan my wedding with you."

Alamanda's jaw dropped. She stammered, "Wh . . . what? Eliza Virginia, are you telling me the truth? Did . . . Oliver propose? Really?"

"No, Mama. You weren't listening. I proposed."

"You? Please tell me this is your idea of a joke." Alamanda gasped. "Eliza, you didn't!"

"But I did. Isn't this what you wanted? Oliver for a son-in-law? Relax, Mama. He accepted."

Alamanda squealed. "How utterly humiliating. Can't you do anything right? You know the boy is crazy about you. He was only waiting for you to show an interest in him. He would've gladly asked you to marry him if you'd given him any inkling you were interested. Oh, my stars, you'll be the laughing stock of Geneva County—the girl who had to propose. We can't let this get out."

"Oh, it's out all right. Oliver made a point to announce that he accepted my offer of marriage. Everyone knows. But why should you care, as long as I wind up with Senator Weinberger's only heir? Be happy for me, Mama. I did it for you." Lizzie snickered as she screamed the words. The snickering soon evolved into weeping. She swatted furiously at the unwelcomed tears.

"Now, now, dear. I didn't mean to come down hard on you. Naturally, I'm thrilled. But you went about it all wrong. I wish you'd spoken to me first." Her face paled, as her eyes conspicuously shifted to Lizzie's waist. "You aren't—" She couldn't finish the sentence, but Lizzie had no difficulty reading her mother's thoughts.

"In the family way? Is that what you're thinking, Mama? Not unless you get that way by eating muscadines. I've consumed my share lately. Of course, I'd much prefer having little muscadines running around my house than little Olivers, any day. No ma'am, Mama, you need not worry—not now, and not ever, ever, ever." She shuddered. "You'd better find someone else's little darlings to call you 'Granny', because unless you have a love child hidden away that I know nothing of, you'll never have grandchildren of your own."

Ali patted her shoulder and smiled. "I understand your qualms, dear, I'm a woman too, you know. We all go through those same fears, but you'll change your mind about having children . . . just as you changed your mind about Oliver."

Lizzie scoffed. "Horse feathers. I haven't changed my mind about Oliver. I was doomed to marry him. I simply proposed to keep from dreading it later. I expected you to be ecstatic, Mama."

"Oh, honey, I'm very happy for you, but this has been such an unexpected shock. I'm still puzzled. But then you've never been an easy child to understand."

"I'm going to bed while you figure it out, Mama. Maybe we'll wake up in the morning and discover tonight never happened. Goodnight."

Alamanda seemed lost in her thoughts. "Oh! Did you say you're retiring? Goodnight, dear. I wish your father were here. He won't be back until Saturday, but won't he be surprised? Our baby, engaged to a Weinberger. I knew all along you two were destined to be together. It was meant to be."

Lizzie retired to her room, and cried herself to sleep. What had she done?

Chapter Nineteen

When Will showed up at the gin a day early, Louie expressed surprise. "Mr. Will, we weren't expecting you 'til tomorrow but I'm sure glad to see ya."

"The lectures were extremely boring, and I had more important things to attend to at home, Louie. I passed by the fields on the way over. The pickers are gone?"

"Yessir. The cotton's all ginned except for the starter bale over yonder, which we'll use to start the machines to rolling next season. We done real good this year. Finished up earlier than I expected—the weather being in our favor—and young Kiah was a real help. He's a go-getter, that boy. I sure hope he finds his way back next summer. I hated to think about him leaving."

Will's heart raced. "What do you mean—leaving?"

"He took his wages and said he was planning to hop a train and head south. Did I do somethin' wrong, Mr. Will?"

Will patted his shoulder. "No. No, you had no instructions,

Louie. Where's the boy now?"

"Dunno. I s'pose he could've left on the morning train." He scratched his head. "Mattie's gonna miss the kid. She took a real liking to him. I was kinda hoping he'd run by to see her before he left."

"Excuse me, Louie, but I've got to find him." Will jumped in his automobile and drove across the clearing toward the shanty. He parked at the edge of the woods and ran the remainder of the way.

He grabbed his chest, stopped and attempted to draw a breath. A sharp, excruciating pain shot through his left arm. *I think I'm having . . .* "Kiah! Kiah, help me," he yelled, stumbling toward the cottage.

Will awoke in the hospital with wires attached to his body and his son staring down at him. "Kiah? How did I get here? What happened?"

Kiah drew a deep breath. "You gave me quite a scare. I was scrubbing clothes in the creek when I heard you yell. I ran and found you crumpled on the ground in front of the door to the shanty."

"How did I get here?"

"I carried you to your vehicle." He chuckled. "You're heavier than you look. I drove your car—hope you don't mind, sir."

"Mind?" Will tried to smile.

Doc Griffin entered the room, holding a clipboard. "Will, you can thank this young man for saving your life. He acted swiftly, and therefore we were able to get you stabilized."

"How long do I have to stay here, Doc?"

"You only have one ticker. When that one blows, it's all she wrote, so don't push me, Will."

"But Henry needs me at the bank. John Graton is moving to be near his wife, while she's in the sanatorium.

The doctor scratched his head. "Nita? Nita Graton? Are you saying she has tuberculosis? Are you sure?"

"Yes, I'm surprised you didn't know. I was in Pensacola when Henry called with the news that we're without a bookkeeper. I promised I'd help out until we can find a replacement. That's why I've got to get out of here."

Doc Griffin shook his head. "Will, you can whoop and holler all you want, but I'm not sending you home. Not yet. Henry will have to figure something out. You're staying here if I have to keep you sedated."

Will groaned. "Oh, Doc. You don't understand."

"No, my friend, you're the one who doesn't seem to understand. We've been friends a long time, and I need all the friends I can get. I'm not ready to lose one."

Will blew out a heavy breath. "Does Ali know I'm here?"

"No, but I'll go call her."

Will shook his head. "Not yet, Doc. I need to talk with Kiah. Oh . . . forgive me, have you two met?"

"Not formally. We didn't take time for introductions when he rushed in with you." The doctor extended his hand. "I'm Jake Griffin. Folks in these parts just call me Doc."

"Glad to make your acquaintance, sir. The name's Kiah . . . Kiah Grave."

"Grave, did you say?"

"Yes sir."

"Seems I recall a young woman many years ago who lived in Goat Hill by that name."

Kiah answered quickly. "I suppose it's a rather common name. But I'm not from these parts."

"Common? Perhaps in some areas of the country—but not around here." He turned his attention toward the patient. "Will, are you sure you don't want me to call Alamanda? Won't she be worried?"

"No, she doesn't know I'm back in town. Wait until Kiah leaves."

"Whatever you say. I'll check on you before I go home tonight. You take it easy." He turned to Kiah. "Son, make sure he doesn't get overly excited. He's a coconut head, for sure."

When Doc Griffin left the room, Kiah pulled a chair closer to the bed. "What did you want to talk to me about, sir?"

"First things first. I want to thank you for saving my life."

"Sir, don't paint me as some sort of hero. I did what anyone would do."

"Well, I can't discount the fact, had you not been there, I would've died. When Louie told me you were leaving Goat Hill, I can't tell you how the news affected me. I don't want you to leave, Kiah."

Kiah popped his knuckles. "I appreciate the kind words, but with all due respect, I can't eat words. The cotton is ginned. I need to move on and find a job. I s'pose Miz Mattie thought I left without telling her goodbye, but I'd never do that."

Will's eyes moistened. "But Kiah, I can't let you—"

"Let's discuss another subject. You know what the doctor said."

"Then say you'll stay."

Kiah made a thin smile. "Begging your pardon, sir, but stay and do what? I didn't come here looking for charity. I worked hard in the fields and I feel I earned my wages. And forgive me if I sound harsh, but I'll not hang around for hand-outs in order for you to appease your conscience."

Will heaved a sigh. "You have every right to loathe me. Your mother was a very special person, and I hurt her deeply. I wish I could go back in time and change things, but I can't. Surely, she hated me."

"You're wrong. She loved you until the day she died. Your name was the last one she uttered before taking her last breath. You can't imagine how I resented it—until I met you."

"Kiah, If only I had known . . . about you, I mean . . . I would never have allowed her to leave. You believe that, don't you?"

"But it was for the best. You didn't love her."

Will swallowed hard. "Is that what she told you?"

"No." Kiah gazed at the floor. "She chose to believe you were weak and chose an extravagant lifestyle over love. But Mama was a romantic. I guess she couldn't bring herself to believe that you didn't really love her, so she concocted a fairy-tale romance."

"But she was right. I *was* weak . . . and I did love her, even though I didn't realize it until it was too late." A tear made its way down his cheek.

"Sir, I don't believe this is the time to discuss the past. You need your rest. You're getting emotional."

"Kiah, if you knew you were needed here—I mean really needed—would you stay?"

Kiah glanced toward the floor and bit his lip. "Needed, sir?"

"Yes. You heard the doc. I can't leave and Henry's counting on me. Would you be willing to help at the bank until we can find someone? I realize it may sound overwhelming, and I don't expect you to be able to keep the books—not at first, anyway, but Henry can teach you. While you're learning, you can help in other ways. John also acted as courier."

"It sounds tempting, sir, but I can't. I'm thinking of Liz . . . zie. Lizzie, sir. I think it would devastate her to learn the truth . . . about your past, I mean." He glanced down at the floor. "We have to protect her."

"She never goes into the bank. Has no reason to. I have a safety deposit box at the house, and she has ready cash. Please, Kiah. Say you'll stay. We'll both benefit."

Kiah lifted his head. "Are you sure, Sir?"

"Quite sure. So you'll stay?"

Kiah smiled. "Accounting was my best subject in school. I'm very good with figures."

Will blew out a grateful sigh. "That's wonderful. I'll have Doc call Morrison's Mercantile and have Luther choose an appropriate suit, shirt, tie, shoes . . . the works. You can't work at a bank dressed like a farmhand. I'll call the widow Blanchard and reserve you a room in the Boarding House, beginning Monday morning. You'll be able to walk to work."

Will let out a sigh and closed his eyes. "I can rest now. On your way out, would you tell Doc to call my wife and let her know I'm here?"

Kiah nodded. "Goodnight, Mr. Will. I hope you rest well."

"Would you do me one last favor before leaving?"

"Of course, sir."

"My heart aches each time you address me as 'Mr. Will.' Can you call me Dad—just once?"

He smiled. "I think I can handle that, Dad. Get some rest."

Will's lip trembled. "Good night, my son."

Alamanda hung up the phone and raced to the hospital.

She met Doc Griffin in the parking lot as he prepared to leave. "Doc, what happened? How did he get here? Did he come in an ambulance?" She placed her hand across her chest. "Please forgive me, I'm terribly nervous. He will live, won't he, Doc?"

"Whoa! First things first. Yes, barring further complications, he should pull through with minimal damage—but he must start taking care of himself. I'm glad I was still here when the young man brought him in."

Alamanda's brow lifted. "What young man?"

"Grave, I believe. Yes. That's it, I remember now, because I mentioned a young woman, a patient of mine, who once lived in Goat Hill by the name of Grave. It's a rather unusual name for these parts."

"Grave? That sounds familiar. Oh, yes." She sucked on her bottom lip and nodded. "Yes, I remember the girl. She worked for my father at the bank. I was even a bit jealous of her." Alamanda rolled her eyes and smiled. "Of course, Will would never have been interested in her, romantically, but I was jealous of their friendship. He probably pitied her. You know what a softy he is. You could look at the girl and tell she was dirt poor. I don't know why Daddy hired her. I suppose she had a head for figures. Isn't it funny the trivial things we remember?"

"Yes, and sad the important things we forget." He placed his hand on her shoulder. "Alamanda, Will is highly medicated and should sleep, so why don't you go home. There's nothing you can do for him tonight."

Chapter Twenty

Kiah finished plowing Mr. Louie's corn field, pitched the hay and was busy repairing the tin roof on the house. As long as he remained busy, he had less time to think. Less time to miss her. Less time to crucify himself for having feelings he seemed unable to control.

Mr. Louie stepped up on the bottom rung of the ladder. "Mattie said tell you dinner's about done, so come on down and wash up."

Kiah's eyes grew wide when he looked at the table and saw the platter of Southern fried chicken, bowls of poke salat, field peas and an iron skillet filled with hot crackling bread.

When he'd finished eating, he rubbed his stomach and sighed. "It's a shame you don't have a daughter. I'd sure like to find me a wife who could cook like this. You're a lucky man, Mr. Louie."

Louie cackled. "Yep. I think I'll keep her."

Mattie didn't appear to be listening. She picked up her napkin and blotted her mouth. "Kiah, I've been thinking . . . oh, never mind. It wouldn't work."

"What wouldn't work, ma'am?"

"Nothing. It was a foolish idea."

Louie spoke up. "Now, Mattie, go ahead and speak your mind and let the boy be the judge of whether or not it's foolish."

"Well, I was wondering . . . no, I don't think so."

"Sugarfoot, you're driving me crazy. Spit it out."

"Louie, it was just an idea, but I don't want to put Kiah on the spot."

"What spot?" Louie asked. "What in tarnation are you talking about, Mattie?"

Mattie chuckled. "I declare, if that man wuz a cat, he would've killed over years ago. I've never seen a body so curious. All right, if you must know, I was thinkin' of asking Kiah if he'd like to go to church with us tomorrow night, since it's our time to have the preacher. But then I thought better."

Kiah wiped his mouth with the edge of his napkin. "Why, Miz Mattie, I'd be delighted to go with you to your church. Thank you for asking. But what do you mean, 'it's your time to get the preacher?' Is Mr. Louie gonna preach?"

Louie held his head back and guffawed. "Ain't no way that'll ever happen."

His wife gave him a stern look. "Kiah, we share a preacher with three other churches in the county. Bro. Rufus will be at our church tomorrow. When he ain't there, we just all testify."

Kiah nodded. "What time should I be here?"

"Honey, maybe I shouldn't have asked. You'd be the only white face in the room, and although I know folks would welcome you with open arms, I wouldn't want you to feel uncomfortable."

"What time, Miz Mattie?"

"You mean you'll go?"

"Of course, I'll go. I'll look forward to it. Mama and I didn't attend church regularly. The fact is, I'm what they call—well, what I'm trying to say is I'm illegitimate. Folks where I grew up looked down their noses at us because of it. The stares and whispers were painful, so we stayed home."

"Well, bless your heart, sugar, you won't have to worry 'bout no whispers at St. Stephens on the River Church. Won't nobody point fingers. We're reaching toward the mark of the high calling, but ain't none of us there yet."

"That sounds like the church I've been looking for."

"Be here about five o'clock tomorrow evening and don't fret about your clothes. I know them overhauls is the best you've got, and that's good enough for the Lord. Folks'll come dressed all sorts o' ways. Some will be dressed to kill with zoot suits and fancy ties and some will be in their bare feet with wore-out overhauls. But the Lord looks on our innards, not our outterds, as the preacher says."

Kiah said, "Oh, but didn't I tell you? I've got some new glad rags to wear to church. I picked them up last evening at the mercantile. Mr. Will has asked me to fill in at the bank until they find another bookkeeper. I've never had a desk job before, so I'm seesawing between extreme excitement and gut-wrenching nervousness."

Mattie's face lit up. "A bank job? Well, ain't that nice? I'm proud for you, Kiah. I reckon that means you'll be sticking around. I'm tickled."

Kiah smiled. "Thank you. And thanks for the delicious meal, Miz Mattie. Now if you'll excuse me, I need to finish the roof."

When he reached the door, Kiah turned and looked back. "Mr. Louie, I know Mr. Will's daughter thinks highly of you, but if you happen to see her and my name comes up—not that I think it will, mind you—but if it does, I'd appreciate it if you wouldn't mention I'm staying in town."

Louie looked puzzled. "I ain't got no problem with that, but why—"

Mattie swatted her husband's upper arm. "It ain't ours to wonder why, Louie. Just do as the boy asks."

After Kiah left the room, Mattie asked, "Louie—does he remind you of someone?"

"You mean Kiah?"

"Yes. Does he favor someone you know?"

"Funny you should ask. The first day he showed up in the fields, I almost asked him if he was a relative of Mr. Will's—but the notion was crazy. The boy was a hobo. Came here with nothin' but a changing of clothes tied on a stick. But I can't deny it's eerie how much he looks like Will Lancaster looked at his age."

"Spittin' image, if you ask me, Louie. You don't suppose?"

"Now, don't go jumping to conclusions, sugar. It's pure coincidence. That's what it is."

Mattie looked at her husband. She knew—and what's more, she knew Louie knew.

Chapter Twenty-One

"You call that breakfast?" Will grumbled and shoved the hospital tray aside, almost knocking over the small glass of watered-down orange juice.

The nurse glanced at Alamanda and smiled. "I don't think he likes our cuisine. Maybe you can coax him to eat."

She nodded, then bent over and kissed her husband on the forehead. "You really should eat, dear. Did you sleep well last night?"

"Quite well. I don't know what was in that syringe but I feel better this morning. Get me my clothes. I'm going home."

"Not yet. I spoke with Doc on my way in, and he's not ready to discharge you this soon."

"He's being overly cautious. I feel fine. I need to get out of here."

"Will Lancaster, you need to relax and let Doc Griffin do his job. There's nothing you need to oversee that someone can't take care of for you. You aren't indispensable, you know."

He felt light-headed and rested his head on the pillow.

"Will, where did it happen? How did the young man find

you?"

He hesitated and took a deep breath. "I was on our property when I had the attack. I yelled before I collapsed. He heard me, brought me here and saved my life, Ali."

"Well, thank the Lord. Doc Griffin said his last name was Grave. Do you remember the young girl who worked for Daddy at the bank before you and I married? She was a Grave—Endora, I think her name was."

Will squirmed in the bed. He picked up his pillow, fluffed it and put it back under his head.

"Will? Do you remember? She was right pretty in a plain sort of way. Oh my lands, I remember her clothes. I don't think the girl owned more than two dresses and both were made from chicken feed sacks. You remember her, don't you?"

Will gazed out the window.

"Will, I asked you a question."

"I'm sorry, Ali. I'm not feeling up to par. What is it you want to know?"

"Oh, it wasn't terribly important. I simply asked if you remembered a girl by the name of Endora Grave—she worked at the bank for father."

"Yes, I . . . I do remember."

"You don't suppose the young man could be her child, do you?" Before Will could answer, she retracted. "No, I don't suppose so, since Grave was her maiden name."

Will drew a deep breath. "Honey would you mind asking the nurse to bring me a glass of water? My throat feels parched."

Alamanda picked up the pitcher. "You have water, dear." She poured a full glass and handed to him. "Now, what was I saying? Oh yes, about Mr. Grave. How fortunate for you that he came along when he did. But how did he happen to find you?"

"Providence, Ali. God sent him. Did I mention he's our new bookkeeper at the bank?"

"No, you didn't. But what about John?"

"John resigned."

"Resigned?"

"Yes, according to Henry, Nita's been diagnosed with TB."

Alamanda pulled an emery board from her clutch bag and proceeded to file her nails. "That's too bad."

"Yes, I thought so, too. I was shocked when I heard the news."

"How old is the new bookkeeper? Is he married?"

"He's quite young, and no he isn't married."

"How young? Do you think he's qualified?"

"I have no doubt that he'll be able to handle the job. The boy's exceptionally smart. Accounting is the subject he excelled in, in school."

"That's good. I hope he works out. I've never been particularly fond of John, anyway. I declare the man was so set in his ways. Young blood may be just what the bank needs."

Will breathed a soft sigh.

Alamanda bit her lip and snickered. "Dear, I'm about to burst to share something with you, but I'm not sure this is the right time."

Will found it difficult to concentrate on the conversation. What if Ali should walk into the bank? Would she see the resemblance?

Her eyes squinted. "Will Lancaster, are you listening?"

"Yes, honey." He smiled slightly and dropped his gaze. "Sorry, I don't suppose I was. I seem to have trouble staying focused."

"I understand, dear. I shouldn't have been so sharp. I'm sure the medication makes it difficult to concentrate. I was saying that Eliza and I have some very exciting news for you. I don't know if I can keep it bottled up much longer. It's wonderful. I'd planned to let her tell you, but I can't wait. You'll never believe what happened while you were away."

He smiled, relieved the subject changed and there was no more talk about Kiah or the boy's mother.

"So what's the good news, Ali?"

"I really should let Eliza tell you, I suppose. But I'm sure she won't mind if I share it."

Will smiled. "I can hardly wait to hear. What has my little Swamp Angle done that you find pleasing?"

Alamanda clasped her hands over her heart. "Will, our daughter is engaged to be married."

Will waited for the punch line. Confused, he stammered, "What . . . what are you talking about, Ali? She isn't even courting anyone."

"I could hardly believe it myself, but it's true. She and Oliver Weinberger are planning to be married. Can you believe it?"

Through clinched teeth, he responded, "No, Alamanda. I certainly can't. And if this is supposed to be a joke, it isn't funny. Lizzie can't stand to be in the same room with the boy."

"Oh, Will. Need anyone remind you that love is strange? Our little girl, engaged. Isn't it wonderful? Don't let her know I told you, in case she plans to surprise you. For months, she balked at the idea of attending Oliver's party—so you can imagine my shock when she came home last night and told me the thrilling news."

He shook his head. "No. It isn't true. I don't believe you."

"I had the same reaction at first—our Eliza, a Weinberger."

Will grunted. "Something's not right, Ali. Surely, you must know it."

"Now, honey, if you're thinking she's in the family way, I'll assure you she isn't."

Will shouted, "For crying out loud, Alamanda, that's the last thing that would've crossed my mind."

Alamanda huffed. "Well, I don't know why. It wouldn't have surprised me at all as brazen as she is. I'll have to admit, that was the first thought that popped in my mind when she told me she was getting married. It's disgraceful the way she prances around in her bare feet and practically lives in skimpy little bathing suits. But I should have known better. Oliver is such a gentleman. I think they realized at the party they were right for one another and were eager to announce their engagement before Oliver leaves for Harvard. I applaud them for their decision. The formal engagement will help them remain faithful during the separation. Be happy for her, Will. She thrives on your approval."

Will felt a knot growing in his stomach. "But Oliver Weinberger? The boy she once called Armadillo Face? No. Impossible. I can't believe she changed that quickly."

"Quickly? Be serious, Will. They were kids when she persisted in calling Oliver that ridiculous name. But our little girl grew up, and I imagine when she looked at him last night dressed in formal attire, she realized he wasn't the same funny looking kid she compared to an armadillo. She saw the change and liked what she saw."

"But Ali, honey, the only thing about the boy that's changed is his pants are longer and his head is larger. That's all."

Alamanda made a slight shrug. "Granted, he may not be the best looking boy in town, but what girl wouldn't rather spend her life with a homely rich man than with a handsome pauper? Oliver Weinberger certainly has more going for him than any other young suitors in the South. He'll be Governor one day. You mark my word. He has plenty of pull in all the right places. Our daughter will be an asset for him. Why, he could even be President of the

United States, one day."

Will sucked in a deep breath. "Where's Lizzie? I'd like to talk to her."

"She'll be here around noon. But remember—act surprised."

Will turned over in the bed, and faced the wall. "Ali, Honey, I'm extremely tired. Would you mind terribly if I told you I'd like to be left alone?"

"I understand, dear. I'm sure I've worn you to a frazzle with my chatter. If I don't make it back tonight, I'll see you in the morning." Alamanda pecked him on the cheek and left the room.

The next thing he remembered were the nurses standing over him, poking him with needles. The medicine made him drowsy. He wanted to stay awake long enough for Lizzie to come tell him it wasn't so—that her mother dreamed it.

Sunday evening Kiah Grave headed down the dusty road, leading to Mr. Louie and Miz Mattie's tidy little home.

Mattie gushed when she saw him. "Well, if you ain't a sight for sore eyes in that fancy worsted wool suit. Look, Louie, don't he look like a man of means?"

"Yep, he does clean up real good, I'll have to admit." Louie slapped Kiah on the back and chuckled. "But Mattie, I do believe I've seen suits a lot worsted than this one."

Mattie swatted at her husband and gave Kiah a hug. "Don't you pay no mind to that ol' man, sugar. I have me a Sears and

Roebuck catalog, and for years, I've admired them kind of suits. If I live long enough to make enough money, I'm gonna buy Louie a suit just like the one you got on. He'd look mighty fine in a wool suit."

Louie threw up his palm. "Me in a suit? Over my dead body."

"That's exactly where I plan to put it, and I don't reckon you'll rise up to do no protesting, neither." Mattie placed her hands on Kiah's shoulders and held him at arm's length. "My, my sugar, you wuz already a handsome young fellow, but that suit really does something for you. Why, with your good looks, you could be in moving pictures."

Kiah bent forward and kissed her on the cheek. "My, how you do go on, Miz Mattie." He grinned. He pulled a rolled appendage from his coat pocket. "Mr. Louie, I brought a tie, but I've never had one before. Do you think you might be able to show me how to wear this thingamabob?"

Mattie seemed tickled. "Hon, you come let ol' Mattie show you how. I'm the one who taught Louie. Just stand in front of this looking glass and watch how I do it. It ain't nothin' to it, sugar. You'll get the hang of it."

After three tries, Kiah mastered the Windsor knot. He nodded at his reflection in the mirror, and straightened the knot. With a wink and a grin, he said, "I do look like a banker, don't you think?"

"As fine a banker as I've ever seen." Mattie's face beamed.

When she walked into the adjoining room to don her hat and gloves, Louie placed his hand on Kiah's shoulder. "Kiah," he whispered, "thank you for coming. Mama's been beside herself ever since you agreed to go to church with us."

"Sir, I'm the grateful one. But Mr. Louie, I'm puzzled."

"Puzzled?"

"Yes. I've noticed you sometimes refer to Miz Mattie as 'Mama'yet you have no children. I couldn't help wonder—"

Louie dropped his head. "It's a habit I started years ago, and sometimes still catch myself doing it. She *was* a mama once, and a good one."

"Was? I don't understand. You mean—?"

The old man nodded. "We once had three young'uns—two girls and a boy—lost all three of the sweet little boogers to the flu, the winter of 1892." Louie's lip trembled. "Only the Good Lord knows how Mattie's mourned for them babies. She told me the other night if Ralphy had lived, he might've had a son your age 'bout now. She likes the idea of having you around—I think she sees you as the grandson she never had. I told her you was a mite pale for me to think about as being Ralphy's boy, but frankly I don't think the woman's noticed your skin ain't the color of hers." He reared his head back and cackled. "She thinks mighty highly of you."

"She's a jewel. I'm touched that she'd think of me as a grandson, because if I could've picked a grandmother, I would've picked Miz Mattie and that's the honest truth. And since you come with the package, I reckon I could even learn to call you Grandpa, ol' man."

Louie smiled. "Well, that'll tickle Mattie when I tell her."

Mattie walked in and asked, "Tell me what?"

"Now if I was to tell you before church, you'd have to race down to the altar and confess the sin of pride, and far be it from me to cause my little woman to transgress." Louie winked.

Kiah put his arms around her. "I don't think it's possible for her to sin. She's perfect."

Mattie shook her head. "Oh, honey, I thank you, but there's only one who's perfect, and it certainly ain't ol' Mattie. No siree, I'm a far cry from being perfect, but one day, praise God, I'll be made perfect and what a glorious day that'll be. I'll be singing with the angels, 'Glory to God in the highest.' Hallelujah!" She shouted.

"Let's go before Mama starts to preach." Louie said with a twinkle in his eye.

The tiny log church was nestled in the woods. Kiah could hear jubilant singing long before they neared the building. "Sounds like they're having a good time," he whispered, when Mr. Louie opened the door. Two oil lamps lit up the small room.

"You ain't heard nothin' yet," Louie said. "Just wait 'til they get wound up."

Mattie smiled. "Oh, honey, ain't no way we can hold it in. If we shouted our praises from now to eternity, it wouldn't be loud enough nor long enough to express our gratitude for God's goodness."

Kiah trailed slowly behind the elderly couple. He slid across the slatted wooden pew and sat beside Mattie when she and Louie took a seat near the center of the church. The flickering light from the Aladdin oil lamps gave the room a warm, soft glow. Beads of perspiration lined his upper lip when he noticed people lean over to get a better look at their white-faced guest—but the curiosity was short lived. He knew he'd found a safe haven when the curious stares turned into friendly smiles.

A little girl with two missing front teeth and tiny red bows on all her braids walked over and stopped on the pew directly in front of Kiah. Looking quite timid, she held out a hand fan. "This is for you," she said, then pointed to the picture on the front. "That's Jesus. And that's the little children." Kiah smiled and thanked her. She ran back to her pew, grinning.

With his head held down, he lifted his gaze and peered about the room. His thoughts carried him back to his childhood—the day three pious ladies from a church visited his unmarried mother to inform her that neither she nor her illegitimate son were welcome in their fellowship. He'd once looked up the meaning of "legitimate" in a dictionary and the definition was "genuine or valid." He figured a scarecrow, though made in the image of a man, could rightfully be considered illegitimate. A scarecrow can't hear, feel, smell, taste or see. It doesn't bleed when cut. Kiah could do all those things, just like any other genuine human being. Yet, when he and his mother sought refuge in a church, he'd been made to feel as invalid as a brainless man of straw. Would the sting never go away?

He felt his shoulders relax as his eyes searched the faces in the room. He settled back into the pew. From the kind expressions, he concluded that neither his skin nor his parentage was up for review. What a great feeling.

Kiah searched the back of the pews for a hymnal when the congregation joined the choir in singing 'There's a Great Day Coming.' But the racks were empty. Folks sang from the heart, not from the printed page. Occasionally someone would trail off in a different direction, yet it never interrupted the harmony. Feet stomped, hands clapped, and it was evident to Kiah that these joyous people had something he didn't have. They were different, yet it had nothing to do with the color of their skin. There was an indescribable peace abounding in the little log church.

Three men sat in high-back chairs on a platform in front of the congregation. When the music stopped, the tall, skinny man sitting in the center sprang from his seat. He stroked his salt and pepper goatee and with a warm smile, said, "Good evening, all you saints and sinners, I'm here to tell you God loves you." He jumped from the platform, and waved his arms. "Tell me brothers and sisters, do you know it's so?" Arms waved in the air.

Kiah jumped when an elderly fellow sitting at the back of the church shouted something that sounded more like a hog-calling than an affirmation. When the people responded by clapping, Kiah felt his face burn. Should he join them, even though he had no idea why anyone would applaud such an outburst? But before he could decide, the clapping ceased. All eyes fixed on the feeble old man, who hobbled down the aisle and made his way to the front.

The old fellow propped against the piano and waved his cane in the air. His voice broke when he said, "I know it's so, Brother Dave, because God said it, and God don't lie." The crowd cheered. The old man pulled a handkerchief from his overhauls and wiped his balding head, before shuffling back to his seat.

The preacher paced down the center aisle. Back and forth, back and forth, he gazed into the eyes of various individuals, without uttering a sound. Kiah watched with wonder. Grown men cried. People crossed the aisles and hugged those who wept.

A large woman sitting on the second pew stood and started humming. Others joined in. Kiah didn't recognize the tune, but it seemed to have a calming effect. When the woman sat down, an eerie silence filled the room for several minutes.

"I'm not gonna preach today. You are," the preacher said, flailing his arms at the congregation. "Let's hear some preaching. Somebody testify. Tell us how you know God loves you." He continued to traipse back and forth, peering into faces in the crowd, as if he were looking for someone special. Kiah's heart hammered. He dropped his head, and slightly lifted his eyes, watching Bro. Dave's feet moving rapidly across the plank floor. Kiah caught his breath when the feet stopped in front of a beautiful young girl who appeared to be no more than sixteen years old. "What about you, Tillie. Does God love you?"

"He does, Bro. Dave. He sure does love me."

"How do you know, precious?"

"He saved my life when I tried to end it."

"And why did you try to end it, Tillie?"

"Because I found out I got pregnant the night my step-daddy raped me. I didn't see no way I could raise a baby when I couldn't even feed myself. But God used Mr. Louie and Miz Mattie to rescue us. They gave us food to eat and clothes to wear when I didn't know where my next meal was comin' from. Now I've got me a good job working for a Christian family who loves my little Felicia and lets me bring her to work with me. Ain't God good, Bro. Dave?"

"He's good, all right, sugar. But tell me, Tillie, does God love that baby, even though she ain't got no pappy?"

Kiah squirmed.

Tillie smiled and nodded. "You know He does, Bro. Dave. Ain't her fault. T'weren't my fault neither, but there ain't no sin too big for God to forgive. Even if it hadda been my fault, it ain't too big for God. That's right, ain't it, Preacher?"

"That's right, sugar." Bro. Dave pulled out a handkerchief and wiped his mouth.

"Hallelujah, Praise God." Shouts echoed throughout the room.

"Church dismissed." Pastor Dave yelled. "I can't top what Almighty God's done here tonight. Go home and keep on praising Him. No matter where you've come from, where you're going, who you are or what you've done, God is a forgiving God. He loves you, and that's a fact."

Kiah was quiet on the walk back to Louie and Mattie's house. He had a lot on his mind. Strange, but Louie and Mattie seemed to understand he needed time to reflect. As they walked down the long, dusty road, the only sounds were coming from the whippoorwills.

"Miz Mattie," Kiah spoke softly.

"Yes, honey, what is it?"

"Miz Mattie, is it true, what the preacher said? No matter who we are, where we come from, or what we've done, there's nothing too big for God to forgive? Do you think God really loves me?"

Mattie threw her arms around him. "Well, sure He does, honey. What's not to love about you?" They stood in the moonlight, arms wrapped around one another. Kiah swatted the tears trailing down his face.

Louie walked up the steps to their humble dwelling made of logs and chinked clay. He held the door open wide.

Mattie said, "Kiah, come on inside, and we'll talk to the Lord about what's got you all tore up inside."

He shook his head and swallowed hard. He supposed she'd expect him to pray. He wanted to—but not where anyone could hear. "No ma'am, I reckon not. The hour is late and tomorrow is my first day at work. I won't go in. But if I can ask a favor—"

"Anything, honey. You just ask."

"Would you and Mr. Louie approach God in my behalf? You know—tell him I'm sorry. I didn't mean for things to turn out this way. I can't explain but I think He'll know what I'm talking about."

"You can count on us, sugar. Here, I want to give you something," she held out her Bible.

Kiah shook his head. "No, Miz Mattie, I can't take your Bible. I know how much it means to you."

"Indeed it does, but I want you to have it." She pounded her palm on the back of the Bible and shoved it toward him.

Kiah reluctantly took it from her hands and kissed her wrinkled brow. "Thank you, Miz Mattie."

Kiah returned to the shanty and lit an oil lamp. When he opened the dog-eared Bible, the pages fell open to the book of Ruth. He read a gripping love story, about a wealthy landowner who fell in love with a poor, lonely widow. He closed the Bible and lay awake looking at the ceiling. "God forgive me, for I fear . . ." He sobbed. "I fear that I've fallen . . . in love." The agonizing confession coming from his lips made him sick on his stomach. "I'm so ashamed. I fought the fight and lost. But why? Why did she have to be my . . . my sister?" The bitter taste of bile rushed to his throat. Nauseated, he reached under his cot and grabbed a porcelain chamber pot and heaved. Minutes later, he blew out the lamp and prayed for sleep to come.

Chapter Twenty-Two

Will Lancaster awoke to find his beloved daughter dozing in a chair near the window.

What joy this precious girl had brought into his life. He remembered the day she was born, when Cleoda handed her over, all wrapped up in a soft, pink blanket, looking like a porcelain baby-doll.

Was it wrong to keep the truth from her? Doc Griffin said barring complications, Will would live, but might not be so fortunate the next time. Who was to say when the next time might be? Will's temples throbbed. What if he died? Would anyone ever tell? There were people in Goat Hill who knew, but who would ever tell? Didn't she deserve to know?

When she looked up, he smiled. "Hello, Swamp Angel. When did you get here?"

Lizzie blinked her eyes. "I came yesterday afternoon, but the doctor said he'd given you a sedative and you needed rest. I've been here for a couple of hours. How do you feel?"

"Oh, I'm fit as a fiddle. Pull your chair closer to the bed and let me look at you."

"I'll do better than that." She leaned over, kissed her father and sat on the side of the bed.

"You look beautiful, as always, Lizzie. Is that a new dress?"

"It is. Do you like it?"

"It's very becoming. You're the prettiest girl in all of Alabama. You could have your pick of beaus. You realize that, don't you?"

Lizzie shifted her eyes toward the floor. "Mama told you, didn't she?"

Will's lip trembled. "Lizzie, tell me it isn't so."

"Why Daddy? Why shouldn't I marry Oliver? Mama can tell you a dozen reasons why I should."

"Well, baby, I can give you only one reason why you shouldn't."

"And why would that be?"

"Because you don't love him."

"Really? And how would you know that?"

"Because I know you, Lizzie. What possessed you to accept his proposal?"

She snipped. "Oh, but haven't you heard, Daddy? He didn't propose. I did. I'm sure it's all over town by now—not that I care. Why should I?"

Will groaned, "Lizzie, Lizzie. I'm worried. This is not you. Where's that smile I love—the bubbly personality that always lifts me when you walk into a room? Something dreadful has happened to break your spirit. Tell, Daddy what's going on, baby."

Lizzie's lips trembled. She laid her head on his outstretched arm. "I don't want to talk about me. Let's concentrate on getting you well. I don't know what I'd do if anything happened to you." She lifted her head and looked at her father. "Mama said your new accountant saved your life. I'm so thankful he was there for you. I'll be sure to thank him, personally. I love you, Daddy."

"And I love you, darling, but I'll convey your thanks to the young man. He's humble, and appears embarrassed by suggestions that he did anything heroic. But you're avoiding the subject—what's this nonsense about you and Oliver Weinberger."

Lizzie dropped her head and sobbed. "I'm sorry. I didn't want to come here and cry. I don't want to upset you, Daddy."

"Now, now, angel, let's get to the bottom of this. Tell me everything."

"There's nothing more to tell. Oliver and I are engaged. It's official. He announced it at the Ball." Lizzie tried to blink away the tears.

Will's voice boomed. "Well, he can un-announce it. You aren't going to marry someone you can't stand to be in the room with, and frankly my dear, I don't blame you."

"Daddy, he's not so bad—and for once I've done something to make Mama proud of me. This is what she's always wanted."

"Oh, angel, you can't marry someone just to please your mother. She's not the one who'll have to live with Armadillo Face."

Stunned by her father's response, Lizzie raised her head and dropped her jaw. She looked into his twinkling eyes and together they laughed—and laughed until the tears were gone.

"That's better," Will said. "Now, you're sounding like my little girl."

"Your *bad* little girl, you mean. How did you remember that, Daddy? I was in the sixth grade. You punished me and made me go without dessert for a whole week and I think Cleo made dewberry tarts every night just to torment me."

"Maybe I remembered because it seemed an appropriate name for him." He smiled. "Yet, I had to punish you because it was rude."

"He does slightly resemble an armadillo, doesn't he?"

"Slightly? If the boy were to lay on his back in the middle of the road with his hands and feet in the air, he'd be swooped up for road-kill."

Lizzie feigned a frown. "Okay, no dessert for you this week, mister. You're bad."

Will held his head back and laughed, and Lizzie joined in the laughter. He said, "Now that my Lizzie is back, sit up and talk to me. Tell me from the beginning how this mess started, and then we'll decide what to do about it."

As if someone flipped a switch, the laughter halted and Lizzie's face distorted. She wet her lips. Her voice had a sad ring to it, when she said, "Daddy, you'll not do anything about it. He wants to marry me, and I intend to go through with it."

Will reached for her hand. "Oh, honey, you can't be serious. Marrying someone you don't love would be like building a fireplace in a room with no chimney and then stoking the fire and expecting it to bring comfort. You might stand the heat for a short while, but it wouldn't take long before you'd begin to suffocate, and soon the very life would be stifled from you. You're a sweet girl, full of life. Don't let your mama stoke this marriage until she suffocates you." His voice broke. "Please, Lizzie—"

A nurse opened the door. "Mr. Lancaster, I could hear your voice booming from the far end of the hall. Is something wrong?"

He heaved a loud sigh and shook his head. "Nothing you can fix."

The nurse took his blood pressure and frowned. She scribbled something on his chart.

He craned his neck in an attempt to read what she wrote. "I don't know what you're writing, but I hope it's my discharge papers. I need to go home."

"I'm sorry, Mr. Lancaster, but I don't think you'll be leaving today." She ambled out the door, paying little attention to Will's grumbling.

"Daddy, please don't let this worry you—you'll have another

heart attack. Everything will work out, I promise. You'll see."

"Does that mean you intend to break the engagement?"

"I can't do that. Daddy. As I told you, Oliver didn't propose. I did."

"Are you trying to tell me this is what you want? I find it hard to believe. Look me in the eyes and tell me you love the boy."

"Love? What's love got to do with it? I can point out plenty of couples who are married who can't stand one another. They call it a marriage of convenience. Don't force me to point fingers," she urged. "That might make us both uncomfortable."

"That's absurd. Who put such nonsense in your pretty little head?"

"Mama's been prepping me for this day for a long time, Daddy, and I've come to realize that it makes sense. Love's nothing more than a beautiful fairytale. Life is real. Surely, I don't have to tell you that."

"And what's that supposed to mean?"

"Tell me that you love my mama."

Will bristled. He shot back, "Of course, I love your mama. Why would you even ask such a thing?"

"Because I want you to see that I love Oliver in the same way that you love Mama. He's dependable, smart, rich, and he wants to marry me. The union will be convenient for us both. How do your feelings for mama differ? Tell me, Daddy. How is it different?"

Will had a faraway look.

Lizzie gave a thin smile. "You can't answer, can you? I didn't think so. I've made my point. You and mama have had a long and successful life together, and Oliver and I will follow in your footsteps. Wish me well, Daddy." Lizzie bent over and kissed her father on his forehead, after gently blotting a lone tear from his rugged face. "Bye, Daddy. You listen to Doc Griffin and don't give him a hard time—I want you to stick around. I need you to walk me down the aisle."

"Lizzie, honey you know I'd do most anything for you. Anything but that. Don't count on me walking you down the aisle if you marry Armadillo Face. I can't."

She waited until she was outside the door of the hospital, before she broke down in uncontrollable sobbing.

Chapter Twenty-Three

Where is he? Where's my daddy?" Lizzie ran from her father's empty hospital room, Tuesday morning, screaming.

A heavy-set nurse with red-frizzy hair glared over her spectacles, and snorted. "Calm down, Miss Lancaster. Your daddy's been moved."

Lizzie snubbed. "Moved? I was afraid . . . afraid he'd—"

An older nurse walked up and wrapped compassionate arms around her. "I understand, child. I'm sorry you had such a fright."

"I want to see him."

The sympathetic nurse patted Lizzie's back. "Honey, I'm afraid that isn't possible. You'll need to come back around two o'clock."

"Why? Why can't I see him now?"

"He's been moved to ICU. His brother is with him."

Lizzie held her hand over her mouth. "Oh, my, stars! ICU? Can I go in when Uncle Henry comes out?"

"I'm afraid not. Doctor's orders. Only one visitor during

visiting hours. And no longer than fifteen minutes. But don't worry. Your father's doing much better. Before long, he'll be in a room and you can have a nice long visit."

Lizzie peered at her watch and groaned. Six more hours. She might as well leave. Perhaps Bonnie would be home by now.

Will couldn't believe it—didn't want to believe it. He ran his fingers through his hair and groaned. "But Henry, it doesn't make sense. Why would Kiah demand money from you? I offered him money. He refused."

Henry rubbed his chin, and shifted in his chair. "It's left me baffled, also, Will. I'm telling you the way it happened. I took him back to my office yesterday to inform him of his duties, and that's when he floored me with his outlandish demand."

"Tell me word for word what he said, Henry."

"Good grief, Will, how many times do I have to go over it— I've told you what happened. Are you calling me a liar?"

"Of course not, but I keep thinking that I'm missing something. I want to hear it again, Henry."

"Like I said, he told me he was your son—a Lancaster. I didn't let on that I knew. He insisted the Lancaster family owed him for all the years he and his mother kept out of sight. He said for twelve-thousand dollars, he'd remain quiet. I told him if I got the money for him, he'd have to leave town. He refused. He said he liked the prestige of being able to work at the bank and he had no intention of leaving. He insisted I get the cash and that you should never know. He said if you found out, that neither Lizzie nor Bonnie would be able to hold their heads up in this town again.' And that's exactly what he said, Will. I don't know how many times I have to repeat it."

"But it doesn't make sense, Henry. I've got to see him."

Henry bristled. "Are you crazy? No, Will. Weren't you listening? He made threats, and I took them very seriously. He claimed twelve-thousand dollars was a meager amount to save your reputation. I suppose he thought since I'm the Bank President that I possessed your kind of money. I warned you, Will, the boy was up to no good but you wouldn't listen. I think the best thing now is to meet his demands. Will, you know I don't have that kind of money. You got us into this mess. It's up to you to get us out."

"Henry, there has to be an explanation."

"Of course, there is. He came here wanting a piece of the pie. I told you in the beginning this would happen. He'll ruin us, Will. Give me the money, and I'll get rid of him." Henry pulled a handkerchief from his back pocket and swiped beads of sweat from his forehead.

"And how do you propose to get rid of him, if he said he didn't plan to leave?"

Henry shook his fist. "He will, whenever I finish with him. Before the month is over, he'll decide being a banker is not as glamorous as he might've imagined. He'll leave, all right. You can bank on it, pun intended. Let me handle him."

Will lay on his back and stared at the ceiling. His jaw flexed.

Henry twisted his hat in his hands. "Hey, I know it's a lot of money, and I don't blame you for being upset, but we're in no position to barter."

Will winced. "You keep saying, 'we'. This isn't about you, Henry."

"Sure it is. I'm a Lancaster. If you allow him to bring shame on our family name, my wife and daughter will never forgive you. And must I remind you—neither will yours."

"I need time to think."

Henry's voice quivered. "Get serious, Will. There's nothing to think about. Pay him off, and get him off our backs."

Will drew a deep breath. "Maybe you're right. I don't care about the money—but it doesn't make sense. He knows I would've given him money. Why this way?" My checkbook is in the briefcase in the closet. Write him a check."

Henry shook his head. "The boy wants cash."

"Then I'll have to wait until I'm out of the hospital."

"You can't reason with a lunatic, Will. He's not willing to wait. Don't you keep that much cash in your home safe?"

Will nodded. He picked up a pencil and a pad of paper from the bedside table, and scribbled some numbers on the pad. "This is the combination to the safe. Make sure Ali is not home when you get the money."

A nurse poked her head in the door and announced visiting hours were over. Henry crammed the paper in his pocket and hurried out the door.

Lizzie cried all the way from the hospital to Bonnie's house. She honked the horn and Bonnie rushed out the door, holding her cat.

"Oh, Bonnie, I'm so glad you're back. I've missed you. I need to talk. Can we go to the loft?"

"Lizzie, I wish I could, but I have music lessons in ten minutes. Your eyes are swollen. I understand they put Uncle Will in ICU. Did he take a turn for the worse?"

Lizzie shook her head. "I didn't get to see him. I'm going back this afternoon."

"Then what's wrong?" The cat jumped out of her arms and scampered up a tree.

"Everything's wrong. Oh, Bonnie, my life is ruined." She told Bonnie about the spat with Kiah.

Bonnie ran around to the passenger side of the car and slid in. "Oh, you poor dear. You're saying he's gone?"

Lizzie nodded. "Yes. He was to leave on the train, yesterday."

"You didn't see him off? How do you know he didn't change his mind?"

"I couldn't bear to see him leave, but he left all right. He was eager to leave. Bonnie, I can't bear to think I'll never see him again."

"Well, Lizzie, I know it hurts, but face it—it wasn't meant to be. You and I both know Aunt Ali would've stopped it eventually."

"Bonnie, I'm afraid that—" She dropped her head.

"What were you about to say, Lizzie? Afraid of what?"

"Well, I remember what you said about my . . . my lying. You said my sins will find me out, or something like that. Bonnie, do you think God's punishing me for telling Kiah those dumb stories about being poor? Maybe God sent him away. I wish I'd listened to you and told the truth. Maybe things would've turned out differently."

Bonnie threw her arms around her cousin. "Oh, Lizzie, I lied too, remember? But we don't have to live with the guilt. The Bible says if we confess our sins, God will forgive us. For sure, lying is wrong, and it's true that sin has consequences. But the answer to your question is 'no.' I don't believe God sent Kiah away as a means to punish you. Don't you know how much God loves you, Lizzie? I believe Kiah loves you, too, but he knew Aunt Ali didn't approve of him. Maybe he loves you so much that he left because he didn't want to alienate you from your family."

"Bonnie, if he loved me the way I love him, nothing could have stood in our way. Not even Mama. But it doesn't matter now, anyway. I'm engaged."

Bonnie chirped, "Yeah, and I'm the mother of triplets."

"You think I'm joking. Haven't you heard what happened at

the party?"

Bonnie shook her head.

"I may as well tell you." Lizzie threw her head back and closed her eyes. "Bonnie, I proposed to Oliver."

"Oh, you did, did you? Hmm . . . Mrs. Eliza Face. It has a nice ring to it." Bonnie's smile faded when she saw the tears. "Lizzie, you . . . you're crying? What's going on?"

She dropped her head. "I told you, already. I proposed."

"No. It can't be true. You can't stand Oliver. That's a sick joke."

"It's no joke. I was so angry with Kiah for rejecting me, that I wanted revenge. So I proposed to Oliver. I planned to announce it in the paper, hoping Kiah would read it before he left and be sorry he rejected my love."

"Are you serious?"

"As serious as a . . ."

Bonnie popped her hands over her ears. "Don't say it. I get the picture. But it wasn't in the paper, was it?"

"No. Mr. Loch said the type was already set." Tears trickled down her face.

Bonnie slid down in the seat and moaned. "Tell me, Lizzie, what have you accomplished? This isn't revenge—it's stupidity."

"Maybe so, but the only man I'll ever love, left town on a train. Between you and me, I wish I'd not been so hasty and proposed—but I did, and the whole town knows it by now."

"Lizzie, you can't go through with this."

"I can and I must. I could never hold my head up in this town if I backed down. To add to my woes, Oliver has suggested he may wait until winter quarter to start school. He thinks we need to spend time together before he leaves. Ugh! But I suppose there's a silver lining. The longer he waits to enroll, the longer it'll take for him to graduate. The wedding follows graduation."

"Oh, here comes my music teacher. Try not to worry, Lizzie. We'll think of something. I won't sit by and let you ruin your life."

"My life is already ruined and there's nothing anyone can do."

At two o'clock, Lizzie tiptoed into her father's hospital room. Her heart wrenched at the sight of his tear-stained pillow. "Oh, Daddy, I can see you're in pain. I'll call for the nurse to give you something to relieve you."

Will shook his head. "No." His voice was low. "There's no pill to cure what ails me. Forgive me, angel, but I need to be alone. Can you understand? Please, just leave me be, honey."

Lizzie wiped her eyes. "Sure, Daddy. I'll come back later when you're feeling better."

Outside his door, she braced her back against the cold block wall and wept. She'd broken his heart. Her father knew she didn't love Oliver and it was killing him. He couldn't even look at her. "Oh, Daddy, Daddy, please don't die."

Lizzie groaned when her mother greeted her at the front door by pushing a bridal catalog in her face.

"Mama, Daddy's in the hospital, very ill. I don't think this is the proper time to plan a wedding that won't take place for years."

"That's foolish. Our planning your wedding will have no effect on your father's health. Eliza, I presume Oliver will graduate in the month of May. Roses will be beautiful in May. We'll have plenty of time to plant new bushes. Yellow ones, maybe—yes, that should be your color. We'll take up all the red ones and replace them with yellow. How does that sound?" As usual, Alamanda didn't wait for Lizzie's opinion. "Yellow denotes friendship, and by using yellow you'll be making a bold statement that the love between you and Oliver grew from a lifetime of friendship. Isn't that lovely? I'm thinking we can use mint green as the secondary color. Would you like that, Eliza?"

"Perfect, Mama, since green denotes a feeling of nausea, which is how I feel about the lifetime friendship."

"Eliza, Honey, your dry wit is seldom as funny as you seem to think. There's a time and place for humor, and this is neither the time nor place. You're now betrothed to a very sensible, sincere young man—and there are certain expectations that will now be required of you. Dispensing with that sarcastic sense of humor is one of those expectations."

"No need to worry, Mama. The sense of humor will be the first thing to go, after I'm married."

Chapter Twenty-Four

After spending ten days in the hospital, Will was glad to be home. The medication made him drowsy. He drifted in and out of consciousness. He seemed unable to sort nightmares from reality. *Did Henry really say*—? *He did.* A hard knot formed in his gut. *But how could it be?*

Lizzie knocked on his bedroom door. He rubbed his eyes. "Yes?"

She stuck her head in the door. "Daddy, Mr. Graton wants to see you. Is it all right if I send him in?"

Will stretched and pulled up the chenille spread "Sure, Honey."

John entered, holding his hat in his hands. "Hi, Will. I was sorry to hear of your setback. You're doing better, I hope?"

"Yeah. Much better. Thanks for stopping by. Have a seat."

"I . . . I don't plan to stay. I only stopped by to see how you're doing." He stood by the bed, wringing his hands.

Will cocked his head. "Who you trying to fool, John? What's up?"

"What do you mean?"

"I mean you're nervous. You can't look me in the eyes."

John walked over and pulled up a chair near the bed. "You know me well, don't you, Will. You're right. I'm not here on a social visit, but now that I'm here, I'm not sure I should unload on you. I don't want to cause you a set-back."

"Hogwash. Nothing you say will have a bearing on my condition. Tell me you aren't still upset over our differences about Tom Becker."

"No. I'd give my eye-teeth to be here discussing Tom Becker's woes."

"John, what do you have against the man?"

"Nothing, Will. I didn't mean it the way it sounded. I meant I'd rather be discussing Tom than the subject I came to discuss."

"Well, now that you have my attention, suppose you tell me what you mean by such a bizarre statement."

John wiped the perspiration from his upper lip. "I don't suppose it's any of my business, now that I'm no longer employed by the bank . . . but."

Will threw his head back. "Do you plan to tell me, or not?"

John nodded. "Will, I want to, but I'm not sure how you'll take it."

"Tell me and find out. I'm tired of playing games."

"It's Henry."

Will let out a snort. "So that's it. Well, you and I both know my brother can be a bit overbearing at times, but don't let his remarks bother you, John."

"That's not it, Will."

"What do you mean?" Will slid up in bed and fluffed his pillow.

"I can overlook his sarcasm . . . but he's been—" His chin lowered. "There's no gentle way to say this, Will. Henry's been tampering with the books." John's brow furrowed. "I'm sorry to have bothered you. I can see you don't believe me."

"Oh, John, I believe that you believe it. But you're mistaken."

John shook his head. "I wish I were. I didn't want to bother you with this, but I felt you should know the truth. I don't want anything pinned on me after I'm gone."

"John, think about what you're saying. You're accusing Henry of embezzling." Will squirmed.

"Will, please listen. I've kept books for you for years, and every audit has proven me to be proficient."

Will smiled. "I've never had a problem with the way you keep books, John. You were an excellent employee. I wish we weren't losing you."

John's face distorted. He tilted his head to the side.

Will tried to read him. John and Henry had never gotten along but this seemed more than a personality clash. Will threw his legs off the side of the bed and sat upright. "Now suppose you start from the beginning. I'm listening."

John drew a deep breath. "For weeks I've had reason to suspect Henry of juggling."

Will restrained himself to keep from revealing his emotions. He bit down on his lower lip. "Go on."

"On more than one occasion, Henry asked me for the ledger. Each time, he took it to his office and kept it for hours before bringing it back. At first, it made me nervous because I assumed the only reason he'd spend hours going over the books would be because he suspected me of mismanagement of the funds. But I've always given you both a detailed accounting every trimester. And never has my integrity been questioned in the nine years I've worked at the bank."

Will knew John believed himself to be telling the truth but he was mistaken. Henry could be accused of a lot of things, but embezzlement? No way. Still, Will needed to allow John the opportunity to present his case. "Did you look to see if any changes were made, after he brought the ledger back?"

"No, I suppose I should have. But at the time, it never crossed my mind that Henry might be changing the figures. My only thought was that he suspected me of wrongdoing. I didn't care for him reviewing the books—it wasn't that. I knew he wouldn't find any money missing. But I didn't like feeling as if I couldn't be trusted." John pulled at his tie and glanced around as if he were afraid someone might be listening. His voice sounded raspy. "Will, three days before you went into the hospital, I got a call from the

State Auditor saying an audit was due. They set the date for Friday, October 2nd. Of course, I wanted to go over the books to make sure things were in order before the audit, as I always have. That's when I discovered twelve-thousand dollars missing."

Will swallowed. His throat felt parched. He reached for a glass of water sitting on the bedside table and took a sip. "Twelve-thousand? Are you sure that was the amount?"

"Are you okay, Will?"

Will nodded. "Yeah. Go on . . ."

"Are you sure? This can wait. I'll come back later."

Will stammered. "I said I'm okay. You started this, now finish."

The color drained from John's face. He swallowed. "Well . . ." He paused. "When I discovered the money missing I was in shock. I went to Henry and suggested we consult with you, but he said you were ill and I wasn't to bother you. He said he'd handle it."

Will nodded. "I see. So what steps did Henry take?"

"None. That's just it. I can tell you, Will, I was terrified. I went over and over the books, but the money wasn't there. I stayed at the bank until four o'clock Wednesday morning and that's when I found the changes—changes that I hadn't made."

"So you assumed Henry had made the changes?"

"Who else? He was the only person with access to the books. I lock up the ledger every night. Will, I don't want to go down for something I didn't do, so when Henry came in later that morning I confronted him. He was furious. He called me a liar, and yelled, 'You'll see I'm no thief whenever the auditor gets here.'"

Will tried not to sound alarmed. "You had nerve to accuse him without proof, John. It's good you already had plans to leave or he probably would've fired you."

John scratched his head. "What do you mean, he *would* have fired me?"

Will swallowed hard. "You're not saying—"

"I assumed you knew. In fact, I thought you went along with the idea. I was afraid Henry had led you to believe I was the one with a hand in the pot. That's why I had to talk to you."

"No, I thought . . . never mind what I thought. I'm just surprised."

John said, "Wednesday night, I was on my way to Prayer Meeting. I passed by the bank and the light was on. Henry's car was parked out front. I drove back by after church and he was still there. Tell me, Will. What reason would Henry have to be at the bank at that time of night?"

Will pursed his lips. "Isn't it possible he was trying to find the mistake?"

John shook his head. "There was no mistake, Will. It was deliberate. Money was gone, and the figures were changed. Simple as that."

"So what happened when the auditors got there?"

Henry came to work Thursday morning, unlocked my drawer,

grabbed the ledger and took it to his car. He left and didn't come back to the office until Friday morning when he personally handed the ledger to the auditors. Strangely enough, everything checked out."

Will sighed. "So didn't that prove you were wrong?"

"No. It only proved Henry is good at covering his tracks."

"Maybe you miscalculated."

"No, Will. I think we both know I didn't miscalculate."

Will rubbed his chin. "I don't know what to think, John."

"Well, I know what to think. I know we were twelve-thousand dollars short one day, and the next day, the books balanced. I suppose when he found out the auditors were coming, he put the money he took back into the account to keep from getting caught. But I figured if he did it once, he could do it again and pin it on me."

Will had to stay calm. He pulled his legs up on the bed, and laid his head against the pillow.

John reached over and touched his forehead. "You okay?"

"Yeah. Just a little warm."

"You look fevered. Are you sure you're up to this?"

"I'll be okay when I cool off. Would you mind letting in some air?"

John walked across the room and opened the window. The sheers fluttered.

"Much better," Will said, sucking in a deep breath. "I can feel the breeze already."

"Will, I hate to keep badgering you with bad news, but I think you should know, and I don't think anyone else will tell you."

Will gasped. "There's more?"

"I heard from the grapevine that Henry's giving the new kid a hard time. The word I got is that he's trying to run him off. They say the kid's very bright. I suppose that's why he frightens Henry. I feel sorry for the boy."

Will needed time to sort out the information. "Thanks, John. I'm sure it wasn't easy for you to come and tell me these things."

"No it wasn't. But I like you, Will, and I don't want to see anyone rob you blind—not even your brother." John stood. "Well, I've stayed much too long. I hope I didn't upset you."

Will made a faint smile. "I'll be okay. By the way, how's your wife?"

"Oh, Nita's great. She's excited. You know our daughter is expecting twins any day now and Nita plans to go to Dothan to help with the new babies."

Will sat upright. "But what about Nita's tuberculosis?"

"Nita? My Nita with TB? That's ridiculous. Where'd that notion come from?"

Will lifted his shoulders. "Who knows how rumors get started in Goat Hill, but I'm relieved that she's okay."

"Thanks. Nita's been after me to go in business for myself for a long time, but I liked working for you, Will. Your brother is a different story. Maybe Henry did me a favor. I don't know if I would've had the nerve to quit but I'm excited to be starting my own accounting firm. We'll be moving to Dothan, where we'll be near the grandchildren."

"I'll miss you, John. Stop by and visit from time to time and let me know how you're doing."

John reached out his hand.

Will grasped it with both of his. "I don't know what to say, except I'm sorry. You've been an excellent employee."

"Hey, I don't blame you for anything, Will. You've been nothing but kind. In fact, the only problem I've ever had with you was a result of your kindness. You can't stand to foreclose on anyone. I'm a stickler for details—to a fault—but I had to admire your compassion. If more people were like you, the world would be a better place in which to live." His lip turned up. "And I think Tom Becker would agree."

"Thanks. Take care, buddy."

From his bed, Will watched through the window as John drove away—the haunting questions gnawing at his confidence, bits at the time, like termites on rotten wood. Someone was lying. But who? Kiah? Henry? John? *Who can I trust? I tend to believe the one I'm with at the time.*

Will pretended to be reading a book when Ali stuck her head in the door.

"How do you feel, dear?"

"Fine." His eyes stayed focused on the pages.

She walked over, straightened the chenille spread, then picked up a magazine which had fallen to the floor and laid it on the bed. "Can I have Cleoda bring you anything?"

"No, thanks."

"Your face looks flushed. I think I should give Doc Griffin a call."

"Ali, for crying out loud, can't you hear? I said I'm fine."

"In that case, I see no need for you to be so grumpy." The door slammed.

Will laid the book down. John's story certainly sounded plausible. Could it be true? He said twelve-thousand dollars was involved. Not ten, not fifteen, but twelve. Will tried to make sense of it all. He knew John didn't pull that figure out of the sky. And what about Nita? No wonder Doc seemed surprised to learn Nita had TB. *But why would Henry lie to me?* Will mulled over several scenarios in a desperate effort to direct his suspicion away from his brother.

His theory was a feeble one, but it was all he could come up with.

John didn't like Henry—and for good reason—yet, he appeared to be fond of Kiah. Maybe after overhearing Kiah approach Henry for the twelve-thousand, John concocted the story. But would John go so far as to conceal Kiah's guilt, in order to implicate Henry? Was it possible that John may have told Henry that Nita had TB as part of the plot? When Henry repeated the story and the truth came out, it would appear he lied.

Will felt the gears turning in his head. Yes, that's it. John quit on his own accord, but decided to get revenge before leaving town, by making it appear that Henry was a liar and a thief.

Will knew it was more conjecture than sound reasoning, but for the moment it was the best he could do. He and Henry often rammed heads, but his brother had never lied to him. Why should he let a rumor from a disgruntled employee spoil his trust? The more he pondered, the more he realized there was no 'best' scenario.

Suppose John was telling the truth—it would mean Kiah was innocent of any wrongdoings. Yet, if Henry's story was true, Will would have to conclude his son was a blackmailer. He rubbed the tense muscles in the back of his neck.

At a quarter past three, Will slid out of bed and dressed. He reasoned if he was going to die, he'd do it on his feet. He had to know the truth. He picked up his keys from the top of the bureau. His knees were weaker than he anticipated. Gripping the railing, he descended the winding staircase. When he entered the library, he heaved and fell into his chair. He picked up the telephone to call the bank. He owed Henry the opportunity to clear his name. Will sighed. He knew his brother had a rotten temper and would be furious when he learned of John's accusations. Henry would insist on suing John for defamation of character but it would be Will's job to convince his brother to let it go. Although Will couldn't justify John's motives, a lawsuit might unravel family secrets. He couldn't take the chance.

The telephone operator came on the line.

"Lucy, get me the bank please . . . I'm fine, thank you. Yes, Lucy, I am home. No, I didn't know . . . I don't wish to appear rude, but I'm in a bit of a hurry. No, I haven't tried vinegar and honey, Lucy, but would you please ring the bank for me? No, I'm not angry. I'd appreciate that, thank you."

The phone rang twice when a man answered.

"May I speak to Henry Lancaster, please?"

"I'm sorry, sir, but Mr. Lancaster is not in. May I take a message?"

"No." Will slammed down the phone. *Kiah. I'm sure he recognized my voice.* A dull ache formed in the pit of his stomach.

He looked out the window. Ali's car was gone. He reached for his hat and headed out the door. Cleoda caught sight of him. She threw down a wet dishrag and ran as fast as her bowed, arthritic legs would go, yelling his name. "Mr. Will? Mr. Will, where do you think you're going?"

"Out, Cleo. I'm going out."

"Oh, no you ain't. Miz Ali will have a duck fit if I let you leave this house in your condition."

"Well, it won't be her first, now will it, Cleo."

Cleoda chuckled. "I reckon you're right there, Mr. Will. It

sho' won't be her first. But are you sure you're well enough to be driving around?"

"If I'm not, Cleo, will you promise to plant daisies on my grave?"

"You're josting with ol' Cleoda. But Mr. Will, I don't know what I'd do if anything happened to you and that's the Gospel truth."

"Don't you worry, Cleo. You have the pudding ready when I get back and that'll cure anything that's wrong with me."

"You beat all, Mr. Will. You sure beat all."

Chapter Twenty-Five

Lizzie trekked downstairs and cringed at the sound of a familiar voice coming from the parlor. Holding her breath, she tiptoed past the door.

"There you are, dear," her mother chirped.

Lizzie gushed. "Oh, I didn't realize you were home, Mama. Excuse me, please, but I'm in a bit of a hurry."

Before she could take another step, her mother sprang up and grabbed her by the arm. "I'm sure it can wait, darling. We have company. Do come in and say hello to Mrs. Weinberger."

Lizzie feigned a smile and muttered, "Hello, Mrs. Weinberger."

"Come, come, dear." Lula Weinberger patted the seat beside her, though Lizzie pretended not to notice. "Let's dispense with the formalities. You may as well get accustomed to calling me Mama Lula." She held her head back and with her prune-like mouth in a puckered position, she clicked her tongue. "Tsk, tsk. Eliza, you do look weary, my dear. But I suppose you've been unable to sleep, due to the excitement."

"Oh, it's definitely more excitement than I can stomach," Lizzie remarked as Lula reached up and grabbed her by the hand, pulling her into the adjoining seat.

Alamanda said, "Eliza, darling, Lula and I have been discussing the wedding plans."

"Why so soon, Mama?"

Lula chimed in. "It isn't at all too soon, my dear. You've no idea the preparation involved in such a lavish affair, but no need to fret. Your mother and I will handle all the details."

Alamanda gave a curt nod. "She's right, dear. That's what mothers are for. Eliza, Lula tells me she has a surprise for you."

Lizzie raised a brow. "Oh?"

"Well, I shan't keep you in suspense." Lula reached in her purse and pulled out a dainty handkerchief. Lizzie could see she had something tied in the linen cloth.

"Close your eyes, dear, and don't peek. Hold out your hand."

Lizzie held up her right hand, palm out.

Lula giggled. "No, no . . . your left hand . . . and turn it over."

Eliza felt something slide across her knuckles. She opened her eyes and stared at a gaudy gold-tone ring with fake emeralds adorning her third finger.

"What do you think?" Lula asked, flashing lipstick-smudged buck teeth.

Lizzie grunted. "I hardly know what to think. I suppose you and I just became engaged."

Lula snickered and pinched Lizzie's cheek. "You're such a little tease. Oliver asked what we should do about an engagement ring, and I suggested this little bauble that Oliver's father won for me at the County Fair before we married. It has such sentimental value. Frankly, it isn't my tastes, but I told Oliver it looked like something you might like. It could even become a family heirloom."

Lizzie stared at her hand and flinched. "I'm sure it breaks your heart to part with it. Trust me, I feel your pain, Mama Lu Lu."

Alamanda tilted her head and discreetly whispered in Lizzie's ear. "The name's Lula, Eliza. Not Lu Lu."

Lula stiffened. "Eliza, perhaps I'm misreading you, but you don't appear to be appreciative, my dear. I'm sorely disappointed in your attitude. But this engagement happened so . . . so sudden. I think my Oliver was as surprised as I, when you proposed. I'm sure when my son felt the time was right, he would've done the asking if you hadn't been in such a hurry to announce it."

Lizzie watched her mother bristle.

Alamanda gave her head a little jerk. "Lula, I'm sure you didn't mean it the way it sounded when you insinuated Eliza had a reason for being in such a hurry, as you so bluntly put it. If you're wondering if she's in trouble, we'll clear that up, here and now. She's not!"

"Well, my stars, Alamanda, I didn't mean to ruffle your feathers. I never entertained such a thing. My Oliver would never allow a girl to take advantage of him. I brought him up to have scruples."

Lizzie stuck her tongue in her cheek. *Two weeks before they'll go for the jugular.*

An uncomfortable chill filled the air. Lula stood. "My, how the time has flown. I really must go."

Lizzie and her mother escorted their guest to the porch, where Lula motioned for her waiting chauffeur.

Alamanda said, "I'm so glad you came, Lula. We'll have to get together again real soon." Her icy tone betrayed her warm words.

"Oh, indeed. My house, next time. Between now and then, Oliver and I will meet with Senator Horton's wife—she'll be our wedding coordinator. We'll try to have the major details nailed down to present to you and Eliza upon your visit."

Alamanda sucked in a deep breath. "Well, aren't you sweet to want to help? Eliza and I will be happy to consider your suggestions to see if there's any we might care to use. Of course, I have a million ideas of my own." Her jaw trembled. "And though I don't doubt Mrs. Horton's abilities, my sister-in-law, Merle, is quite capable of coordinating this wedding."

The chauffeur opened the door to the automobile and helped Mrs. Weinberger into the back seat. She poked her head out the open window. "Alamanda, I'm sure you recognize that my responsibility is not only to my son, but to my husband. A senator, you know. Don't misunderstand. I'm not saying I don't invite your input. It's just that we have friends in high places, and it's imperative that this wedding be done right."

The car pulled slowly out of the driveway. "Ta ta." Lula waved a handkerchief out the window.

Alamanda threw up a hand and wiggled her fingers. "Bye, bye now," she yelled through clinched teeth.

Lizzie sat in the old porch swing on the veranda, and rocked slowly back and forth.

Her mother plopped down in a wicker chair beside the swing, and threw her arms up. "That woman is hollow as a gourd if she thinks I'll sit idly by while she plans my daughter's wedding. Well, we'll see about that. She invited herself over—it was certainly not my idea for her to come here today."

Lizzie giggled.

"So what do you find humorous, Eliza? Do you not see what's happening? You should be as upset over this as I. The woman wants to take control of your wedding plans."

"Oh, I'm not worried, Mama. I'm sure you'll find a way to keep her in her place."

Lizzie sighed, watching her mother thumb through the latest bridal catalog. Alamanda Lancaster would waste no time. Everything down to the last detail would be set in stone before they saw Mama Lula again.

"Eliza, we'll have the wedding in the rose garden—although

Lula seems set on having it at Oakdale church, since her daddy's name is on brass plaques on every stained glass window and the back of every pew. She's such a narcissist. There's only one bride in this wedding and she happens to be *my* daughter. The Weinberger's have no say-so concerning where this wedding will be held. And furthermore, I'm appalled that she didn't bring you one of her diamonds. That dime store ring is atrocious."

Lizzie held her hand out and gazed at the garish stone. "Why, Mama, I think it's quite appropriate. It makes a loud statement, don't you think?"

Alamanda grumbled. "Well, no ring should use such vulgar language."

Chapter Twenty-Six

Will parked his maroon Nash in front of the bank, stepped up on the curb and put a penny in the parking meter. His eyes caught sight of Kiah through the plate glass window, causing his stomach to churn. He supposed Henry was right all along. Kiah had every reason to want to ruin him. *He's played me for a fool, but I guess I made it easy for him.*

When he opened the door, his heart raced. Everything looked the same as the day Papa Gid handed him the keys: the same dark pine paneling stretching from the polished oak floor to the fifteen foot ceiling; three huge ceiling fans making the same annoying clicking sound as the blades turned; the same oak desks, same swivel chairs, same teller windows. Everything was just the way the old man had left it and far be it from anyone to dare suggest changing anything that Papa Gid laid his hands on. Alamanda wouldn't hear of it. He swallowed hard. *Papa Gid didn't die—I did.*

The bank employees—all but one—swarmed him with hugs

and warm welcomes. Kiah stayed seated at his desk and appeared to be fumbling through files.

After the other employees had ample time to greet Will and returned to their stations, Kiah rose, walked over and extended his hand. "Welcome back to the land of the living, Mr. Will. I understand it was touch and go for a while. I'm glad to see you're up and about."

What gall. Glaring into eyes that reminded him of his own reflection, Will made a point to ignore the outstretched hand. "Thank you, Mr. Grave. I'm touched by your concern." His voice reeked with the intended sarcasm.

Kiah's shoulders drooped. Slowly, he brought his hand down by his side and said, "If you'll excuse me, sir, I have work to do."

Will's knees wobbled. He turned his back to Kiah and spoke directly to the teller. "When Henry gets back, tell him I dropped in to see him. I'll catch him later." He walked across the street to the City Cafe and took a seat in a back booth.

The waitress came over to his table with a glass of water. "Hi Mr. Will. It's good to see you."

"Thanks, Lottie."

"What can I get for you?"

"Coffee. Black, please."

Lottie came back with the coffee and placed the mug in front of him. "Is that all?"

Will nodded. The café was empty, except for a couple of out-of-town salesmen. Will was glad. He needed time to sort things out, without interruptions. He took a sip of coffee, sat it down, and held his head in his hands. *Why do I refuse to believe John? Everything fits. But Henry's my brother. He couldn't . . . he wouldn't.*

He lifted his head when Lottie walked up.

"Can I bring you another cup of coffee, Mr. Will? I'm afraid you've let that one get cold."

"No, thank you." Will glanced up and saw Kiah Grave coming across the street.

Kiah slung open the door and stalked straight back to his father's booth. "Mind if I sit down?"

Will had the distinct feeling it didn't matter whether he minded or not. "Have a seat," he muttered.

Lottie didn't take her focus off Kiah from the moment he came through the door. She walked over to the booth and smiled. "You're new in town, aren't you?" she asked, sounding more than casually interested.

"Yes. I work for Mr. Will and Mr. Henry . . . at the bank."

"I thought so. What would you like?"

"Nothing, thank you. I'm here to discuss business with Mr. Will."

Will's temples throbbed. "And what kind of business do you wish to discuss?"

Kiah's jaw jutted forward when he slammed his fist on the

table. His face turned red. He glanced around the room and then whispered, "I want someone to please tell me what's going on."

"Maybe you should tell me."

Kiah bellowed, "How should I know?" He closed his eyes and blew out a heavy breath. "Sorry, I didn't mean to yell, but I'll be June if I'm gonna sit back and take the heat for whatever's happened—and I know something dreadful has happened. Your brother treats me like a leper . . . and now you're acting most peculiar. When you entered the bank, you were very congenial to the other employees, but you refused to shake my hand. I understand you don't want people to know our connection. I'm fine with that, but I got the distinct impression today that you feel you made a mistake by hiring me. If that's the case, tell me, and I'll move on. All I ask is that you level with me."

Will rubbed his chin. "Kiah, maybe giving you the job at the bank *was* a mistake."

Kiah sucked in a breath. "I understand, Mr. Will. If you wanted me to go, all you had to do was tell me. But I hold no hard feelings. You've been good to me and I appreciate your giving me a chance." He held out his hand. "I'm sorry I didn't meet your expectations, but there's a train leaving tomorrow evening, and I'll be on it." A crooked little smile crossed his lips. "I'll even be able to pay for a seat. I got paid Friday. Man, I'll have to say that was the easiest twelve dollars I've ever made. Sure beats hoeing cotton."

Will frowned. "Did you say twelve dollars?"

Kiah nodded. "I know we didn't have an understanding when I started, but that's how much Mr. Henry gave me." His eyes widened. "Oh, but if you think it's too much—"

Will scratched the back of his head. "No, Kiah. To the contrary. I was thinking it wasn't enough. Forget buying the ticket. You aren't going anywhere."

"I don't understand, sir."

Drawing air into his lungs, Will blew out a heavy breath and said. "I didn't understand, either. But I think I'm beginning to."

Kiah stood. "I'd better get back to work before Mr. Henry comes back and catches me slacking. I feel like road-kill and the old buzzard is constantly hovering over me, waiting for the proper moment to swoop down. But I had to talk to you, even if it means the death of my job."

Will said, "I'm sorry, Kiah, that you've been put in such an uncomfortable position." He squinted. "How do you like staying at the Boarding House?"

"It works. " He shrugged. "But frankly I enjoyed the solitude at the shanty. I miss it."

"Really? Well, feel free to go back, anytime. You might like to spend the week-ends there. Fish in the creek if you like. I've caught some nice-sized crappy in times past. I haven't had much time to fish lately."

Kiah shook his head. "I'd like that . . . but I can't."

"You can't? And why not?"

"I'm thinking of your daughter."

Will's brow furrowed. "I don't understand."

"Well, sir, I hear she likes to swim in the creek. Suppose she discovers one of your pickers is now a banker. She seems smart. She might ask questions."

Will took a swig of cold coffee and grimaced. "I hadn't considered that possibility. You're right." He twisted a napkin in his hands and lowered his voice. "But evidently she isn't as smart as I thought, or she wouldn't be making such an idiotic mistake."

"Mistake, sir?"

"Yes, and it's killing me. She's foolishly agreed to an arranged marriage."

Kiah's eyes widened. "Liz . . . uh, Lizzie? I don't understand. To whom?"

"Senator Weinberger's son. The boy's mother and my wife, for their own selfish reasons have pushed this union since the two kids were in grade school."

Kiah seemed to have trouble breathing. He mumbled. "I hope she'll be happy."

"Happy? How can she be happy?" Will raised his voice. "She loathes the guy. But when Lizzie makes up her mind, she can be stubborn like her mother. If only she'd talk to me about it, but she seems determined to ruin her life. If only I knew why."

Kiah rubbed his hand across his face. "I'm sorry, sir. I'm so sorry."

"I'm the one who needs to apologize. Forgive me for unloading on you. But this has me stumped. I can't imagine what she hopes to prove."

Will watched Kiah walk out and wondered how he could've suspected him of such a heinous act. *He's a good kid—compassionate. I could see he felt my pain. His eyes moistened as I shared my anguish over Lizzie's situation. Someone lied to me, but it wasn't my son.* Will threw change on the table and stalked out. He had a job to do that he didn't relish.

He headed across the street to the bank and waited in Henry's office, for him to return. His eyes fell on the bulky bank ledger lying atop the desk.

Henry stormed into the office and slammed the door behind him. His face reddened. He bellowed, "I saw your car out front when I pulled up. Aren't you supposed to be home in bed? What are you doing here?"

Will frowned. "Slow down and take a breath, Henry. What's your problem? I own this bank, remember? I have a right to show up any time I feel like it."

The veins on Henry's neck ballooned. "I'm quite aware who owns the bank and everything else in this town. You don't have to throw it in my face. I happen to know the real reason Gideon Gladstone chose to make you the proud proprietor. The *real* reason, Will. You're so smug, you thought you fooled me with your condensed version. Well, I'm not the only one who knows. Everyone in Goat Hill knows." Henry moved toward the window and stared outside.

Will thrust his jaw and clinched his fists. He sucked in a breath, and slowly exhaled. *Why, Henry? Why?*

Henry stomped across the room to his desk, picked up the heavy leather-bound ledger and slammed it back down. "You don't have to come snooping while I'm gone. Tell me what you want to see, and I'll show it to you." He scooped up a stack of papers from off the desk, held them high in the air and let them scatter to the floor. "I suppose you've already plundered through the files. Did you find what you're looking for?"

Will could never remember a time when he wanted to slug his brother, but today he came frightfully close to laying him out. Henry's words stung.

Henry paced the floor and ranted. "You may think I don't know what's going on behind my back, Will, but I'm not stupid. Whenever I dropped Bonnie off at your house today, I saw John Graton's car parked there. What kind of lies did he tell you? He's sore because I fired him."

Will smirked. "Fired him, Henry?"

Henry seemed flustered. "Yes, yes . . . I didn't tell you because I knew you wouldn't understand. I suppose you'll choose to believe him over your own flesh and blood."

"Flesh and blood? Don't make me go there, Henry." Will

grabbed his hat, and stood to leave.

Henry shouted. "Why don't you get it off your chest, now that you're here? Go ahead, Will. Say what you came to say."

Will shook his head. *I've got to get hold of myself, before I have another heart attack.* In a low voice, he said, "I'm in no hurry, Henry. You come by the house whenever you calm down and are ready to talk."

Henry plodded over to his desk and plopped down. His hands shook when he reached for a glass of water.

Will's feet drug as he shuffled toward the door. Henry held up his hand and in a calm voice, said, "Wait, Will. Don't leave."

"Why? So you can unleash your fury on me? No thanks, big brother. I think I've heard enough."

Henry pulled a handkerchief from his pocket, and swiped his eyes. "Sit down, Will . . . Please?"

Will dropped his hand from the doorknob. He walked over to the leather chair near the window, sat and waited for an explanation.

"Will, I told you I was no good. I'm just like Clyde and Daddy. I'm rotten to the core." When Henry broke down in sobs, Will didn't know how to react. He'd never seen a grown man exhibit such intense anguish. Part of him wanted to put his arms around his brother, while the other part wanted to smash his face.

Henry snubbed. "I've done a terrible thing. I know what John told you. It's true. Nothing you do to me will be more than I deserve."

Will's temples throbbed. "But why, Henry? Help me understand."

"I don't expect you to understand."

"Try me."

Henry lifted his head and Will could see water filling his brother's eyes. A broken and contrite man was now sitting in the same chair where a raving maniac sat, only moments before. What brought about Henry's sudden transformation? But even more difficult to understand was the transformation in his own heart. He had a strange compulsion to hug his brother and tell him he was forgiven. He winced, silently chastening himself for being soft. He had every right to be angry—a terrible injustice had taken place. He couldn't pretend nothing happened. "Just tell me why, Henry? Why did you do it?"

Henry twisted the handkerchief in his hands. "Will, when Alamanda goes to Dothan on one of her big shopping sprees, you hand her a blank checkbook."

Will's muscles tightened. "And you fault me for that, Henry? You hold it against me because my wife likes to shop?"

"No, you don't understand, Will. But it seems at some point, Merle thought she had to keep up with Ali's spending habits—and she did a good job trying. I started getting calls from all the major department stores in Dothan, saying they were cutting off her credit because she charged hundreds—some places, thousands—of dollars' worth of merchandise. I had creditors threatening me with a jail sentence if I didn't come up with the money. What I did was stupid and inexcusable, Will. I know that. But I felt desperate. I couldn't think straight. I didn't know what else to do."

Will felt a migraine coming on. "But why didn't you come to me, Henry? We could have worked something out."

"I couldn't. I was too embarrassed."

Will stood and walked over to Henry's chair. He gently laid his hand on his brother's shoulder and smiled slightly. "So how do you feel now, big brother?"

Henry's lip quivered. "I feel like scum. Will, after seeing John's car at your house today, I knew my sins had caught up with me. I rode around all afternoon, so ashamed. I knew I'd rather die than face you with the truth. I don't expect you to forgive me—I can't forgive myself."

Will glared at his brother from across the desk. "Henry do you wonder why Christ died?"

Henry seemed offended by the question. "No. I don't wonder. I know. I admit I need preaching to, but I think you've picked the wrong time and the wrong sermon, preacher."

"I simply want you to tell me why Christ died."

Henry winced and let a few memorized-sounding words roll from his lips. "To pay the penalty for . . ." He stopped.

"Finish, Henry."

Henry's voice broke. "For my sins."

"Your sins? Which sins, Henry? The little white lies or the great big, ugly sins?"

"But Will, what I did was inexcusable. I did it with both malice and forethought. I not only deceived you, stole from you, lied to you about your son, fired a man without just cause—"

"So you're telling me Christ died for excusable sins? What sins would that be, Henry? Are you saying your sins are too big, too black or too horrible to be covered by the blood?"

"Well no, but . . ."

"There are no buts, Henry. If Christ was willing to die for the forgiveness of your sins, then surely I can find it in my heart to forgive you, also. We're brothers, remember?"

Henry reached in his back pocket for a handkerchief and blotted his eyes. "Will, I hurt you, I hurt John, and I hurt Kiah, and none of you deserved it. I'll never be able to make amends. What I did to Kiah is despicable. He's a good kid, Will. You should be proud of the boy."

"I am, Henry. I truly am."

"Will, I don't understand how you could sit there and say you forgive me, but I'm grateful. I'll pay back every penny, if it takes the rest of my life."

"Henry, with me, it was never about the money. I hope you know that."

"I know, but I want to make up for what I've done. Merle promised to help me."

Will grunted. "Merle? Excuse me if I sound surprised."

"I understand." Henry shrugged. "Sometimes the little lady surprises even me. Will, when I saw John's car at your house, I knew I was entrapped by my own vicious web. I panicked and drove home. I went back to our bedroom, opened the dresser drawer and pulled out a pistol. Merle happened to walk in as I loaded it. I quickly threw the gun on the bed and hoped she wouldn't see it. She could tell I'd been crying, and until today, she'd never seen me shed a tear. When she sat on the bed, she spotted the gun. She went berserk and demanded I tell her everything."

"What did she say when you told her?"

"Her response took me by surprise. She cried and held me in her arms like a baby. She's a real piece of work, Will, but I love the woman, warts and all." He bit his lip. "I guess I love her too much. She had no idea our finances were in such a fix. That was my first mistake. I should have said something. I kept hoping every month that things would get better, but instead, things grew progressively worse." Henry's voice cracked. "Will, I wanted to die."

Will threw his hands in the air. "Of all the stupid stunts you've already pulled, Henry that would've topped them all. You wanted to kill yourself and leave us with the guilt? Didn't you realize each one of us would've agonized over the part we might've played in driving you to such a low point?"

"When you're there, Will, you don't think rationally. I expected you all to hate me, so in my mind, I thought I'd be doing everyone a favor."

Will nodded. "I understand."

Henry sucked in a deep breath. "No, Will, you can't possibly understand. You're rational, and suicide is not a rational decision. Only someone who has reached that depth of despair could possibly understand the tricks the mind can play at such a time. It all started with one tiny lie. Soon, I needed to tell just one more . . . and then one more . . . and each time I told another, I had to tell one more, until I was in such a mess I could see no way out. No one drove me to that point. I was my own jury and judge."

Will reared back and clasped his hands together. "Henry, sweet Mattie told me something once, which I've never forgotten. She said 'sin carries us ten times further than we want to go, keeps us a hundred times longer than we intend to stay and costs us a thousand times more than we're willing to pay.' I'm not sure where she heard it, but there's a lot of wisdom in those words."

Henry nodded. "I'm living proof." He walked over to Will. The two brothers embraced. "Will, I was so despondent when I came in here today and had to face you. I wasn't prepared for your forgiveness. I don't know why it caught me by surprise, though." He formed a soft smile. "You always were the pick of the litter."

Kiah's pulse raced when Mr. Henry called him into his office.

"Have a seat, Kiah."

Kiah eased to the edge of the chair with his hands clasped together. "Mr. Henry, I realize I've been a disappointment to you, but I want you to—"

Henry held his hand up. "Whoa!" Their gaze locked. "Kiah, you've been an excellent employee; yet, I've treated you terribly. If you can find it in your heart to forgive me, I promise the working conditions at the bank will improve greatly."

Kiah rubbed the back of his neck. "I'm not sure I understand, Mr. Henry, but if the improved working conditions hinge on my forgiveness, you betcha I can forgive." He blew out a sigh. "When you called me in here, I expected to get the boot."

Henry reached in his pocket and pulled out a gold fob watch. "No, boot, but I do have something, which belongs to you." He handed him the watch.

Kiah shook his head. "Oh, no sir. That's not mine. It is beautiful though, isn't it? I don't own a timepiece. "

"You do now. Take it."

Stunned, Kiah said, "But sir—it's gold."

"You're right. It's gold. Now you'll never have an excuse for being late to work," Henry said with a wink.

Kiah didn't understand, but thanked him, with no idea what had taken place.

Will parked in front of the manor and ambled slowly up the steps to the veranda. Lizzie curled her legs beneath her in the wicker swing.

"Hi, Daddy. It's good to see you up and about. 'Feeling better?"

"Hello, Swamp Angel. Yes, I do feel much better, thank you." He glanced at his wife, sitting nearby.

Alamanda let the magazine fall to her lap. "Will Lancaster, I couldn't believe it when Cleoda told me you had gone out. Whatever were you thinking? You know Doc Griffin said you shouldn't drive."

He turned toward Lizzie and winked. "What's this? A Mother-Daughter Pow-Wow on the porch?"

Ali answered. "We're planning her wedding, Will."

Lizzie held out her hand. "Look, Daddy—my ring."

Will's eyes bulged. "Grieving granny! I'm sorry, sweetie, but that's undoubtedly the ugliest excuse for a ring that I've ever seen. It *is* a joke, right?"

Lizzie's mouth gaped open. "Isn't it, horrid? It's my engagement ring—but it isn't from Oliver, Daddy, if that's what you think."

Will reached for her hand and took a second look. "Ah! I like it much better, already, angel. If not Oliver, then who?"

"Mrs. Weinberger." She giggled.

Will gnawed his bottom lip. "Who?"

"Congratulate me, Daddy. Mrs. Weinberger and I are

officially engaged. She picked out the ring especially for me and placed it on my finger, all by herself. What a shame you weren't here to share our romantic moment."

Will threw his head back and groaned.

Ali didn't appear to be listening. She was too busy writing a to-do list. "Will, do you think you could talk Merv Pittman into sculpting two life-sized cupid statues for the rose garden? A male and a female?"

Will rolled his eyes and took a seat on the marble steps. Lizzie left the swing, walked over and plopped down beside her daddy. He drew his daughter close and gently swept a blonde lock of hair from between her eyes. He shook his head and moaned, "Oh, my precious, Lizzie. If only I could get inside your pretty little head."

Ali said, "Will, tell Merv there's no hurry. I'd rather he take his time and do them well."

"Do what, well, Ali?"

"Oh, you never listen," she grumbled. "Picture this, Eliza." Alamanda made a dramatic sweeping motion with her hand. "I envision a large fountain, surrounded by yellow rose bushes. Two cupids perched in the center, sitting on a mushroom-like pedestal. I'll have the florist make a crown of roses to adorn the head of the female angel, and construct a black top hat for the male. What do you think, dear? Sound elegant?"

Lizzie grinned. "Ah, I think I'm getting the picture, Mama. We'll have water spewing from the female cupid's mouth. What do you think? Wouldn't that be keen?"

"Sweetheart, I'm glad you've decided to participate in the planning process. Give me a moment . . . I'm trying to get a mental picture. I'm sure it will come—"

Will clinched his eyes shut. "Hey, let me try." A deep furrow split his brow and then he snapped his fingers. "I think I've got it. Would you ladies like for me to share my mental picture?"

Lizzie glanced at her father's silly expression and giggled.

Ali seemed annoyed. "Would you two like to explain what you find so amusing?"

Will feigned a smile. "No, dear."

"Then if you've nothing to add, Will Lancaster, you might wish to excuse yourself and leave. You should be upstairs resting, instead of sitting here, interfering."

"Yes, dear."

Ali's body language matched the exasperation in her voice, when she slammed her hands on her hips and said, "Would you stop saying, 'no dear . . . yes, dear?' You're beginning to annoy me with your patronizing attitude."

Will stood and stretched. "Yes, dear."

Alamanda flexed her jaw. "Now, Eliza, let's get back to the cupids . . . help me see what you're seeing. I'm thrilled you seem to be taking an interest."

Lizzie nodded. "Okay, Mama, picture this: Mrs. Cupid will be facing Mr. Cupid. Get it?"

Ali clinched her lips and nodded. "Ah, yes, honey. That's sweet . . . they'll be gazing into one another's eyes."

"Right. Someone will be standing nearby, playing soft violin music while water shoots in rhythmic spurts from Mrs. Cupid's mouth. What do you think?"

Ali closed her eyes, as if to meditate on Lizzie's words. "Hmm." She tapped her cheek with her forefinger. "I don't know, Eliza. I like the idea of them facing one another and the violin would be a nice touch . . . but I'm afraid it might look as if she's—"

"Spitting on him?" Lizzie giggled.

Ali threw her hands in the air. "Oh, Eliza, why do you insist on being so flippant? You are too old to be acting so childish"

Chapter Twenty-Seven

Lizzie woke early, ran down the stairs and made a quick dash for the door. Cleoda caught her by the tail of her dress. "Where do you think you're going, Mizzy Lizzie?"

"Let go, Cleo. I'm taking a walk."

"Not until after breakfast, you ain't. You gonna sit down at the table and eat with yo' folks. Now go take a seat. Yo' daddy is already seated, and Miz Ali will be down shortly."

"But I'm not hungry."

"Well, you gonna eat, whether you're hungry or not. You been moping around for days, all droopy-eyed, looking sadder than an ol' hound dog. Now go sit."

"I'm eighteen, Cleoda. I'm not a child, and you aren't my mother."

"Huh! Well ain't that the truth. If I was yo' mama, you wouldn't have been traipsing off to the creek and hanging out in them woods 'til after sundown every night. Ol' Cleo's got eyes. You was down there chasing after somebody who you ain't got no business chasing. Folks like to talk, and you seem to delight in giving 'em fodder." Cleo shook her finger in Lizzie's face. "I know what you wuz doing."

"You don't know what you're talking about, Cleo. You know I like to swim. You used to call me your little tadpole when I was little. Remember?"

"It's true, I ain't never seen a baby who could swim like you." Cleoda shook her head and frowned. "But you ain't no tadpole no more, and that's what troubles me."

Lizzie peeked into the dining room and saw her daddy reading the morning paper. "Not so loud, Cleo," she whispered. "But in case you haven't noticed, I haven't been to the creek lately."

Cleoda wiped her hands on her apron. "And I know why. The pickers left. You was chasing after that young fellow what ain't got no manners. Well it's a good thing he left. You don't need to be hanging out with riff-raff and you know it's the truth—especially down there in them swamps. You gonna get yo'self in a heap o' trouble one of these days and break yo' daddy's heart. Now get to the table. The biscuits are ready to come out of the oven."

"No need for the lecture, Cleo. I'm an engaged woman." She held up her left hand.

"Shaw. You ain't no more planning to marry that feller than I am."

"That's what you think." Lizzie moseyed into the adjoining room and plopped down in the high-back velvet dining chair.

When Alamanda walked down the stairs, Cleo followed her into the dining room and moved the ham platter to make room for a baker of biscuits.

Will put down his newspaper and greeted his wife and daughter. "Good morning my two beauties."

"Morning, Daddy."

He had a twinkle in his eyes when he reached up and touched Cleoda's arm. "Ah! This is my favorite breakfast, Cleoda. Fried ham, red-eye gravy, grits, eggs, biscuits and your famous fig preserves. It doesn't get any better than this."

Ali mumbled something.

"You talking to me, Miz Ali?" Cleoda asked.

"I said I wish you wouldn't put so much soda in the biscuits. I could smell it from upstairs."

"Sorry, Miz Ali. Could I make you some toast?"

"No. I'll manage. That will be all."

Cleoda clomped back into the kitchen.

Will pursed his lips. "Ali, do you think you might be able to say something nice to Cleoda, sometime? She tries hard to please you and all you ever do is complain. We're blessed that she chose to stay with us—especially the way you treat her."

"Will Lancaster, it seems to me you have enough to do, seeing after the farm, the paper, the bank and the mill. I'll handle the household help. If I need your advice, I'll ask for it." She turned to Lizzie and said, "Eliza, I'd like you to go with me today."

"Oh, Mama. I don't want to go anywhere. Do I have to?"

"I'm afraid so."

"Where are we going?"

"We'll be making a day-trip to Dothan."

Lizzie sighed. "Not another shopping trip."

"You might be interested to know that Bonnie will be going with us."

"Really? And Aunt Merle, I suppose?"

"No, Merle said she had other things she needed to do. It must be terribly important, because I've never known Merle to turn down a trip to Blumberg's. I told her I wanted to have you fitted with proper foundation garments. I thought Bonnie might like to ride up there with us."

Lizzie held her head back and groaned. "Foundation garments? You mean you want to tie me up in one of those awful corsets like you wear? Don't punish me that way, Mama—just take me out to the woodshed and shoot me."

"You are so dramatic, Eliza. I don't intend to buy you a corset—not yet, anyway. But there are certain unmentionables which all well-dressed young women should include in their wardrobe. I intend to see that you're properly harnessed."

Will frowned. "You make her sound like a horse, Ali."

"Keep your thoughts to yourself, Will. I have enough trouble with her without your interference."

Lizzie groaned. "She wants me to look like Sallie Belle

Sellers. She wears a waist-clincher, but all that fat has to go somewhere, so it balloons out on either end. If God wanted us to have a sixteen inch waist, He wouldn't have invented pastries."

Will gave a short laugh. "I don't think you should blame pastries on the Good Lord, Lizzie. I'm guessing Eve may have been the one responsible for the first apple turnovers."

Lizzie could think of nothing more excruciating than a shopping trip, but since Bonnie agreed to go, the suffering would be less painful.

The giggling in the backseat stopped when Alamanda drove through town in Goat Hill and parked.

"Why are we stopping at the bank, Mama?"

"I just remembered I left the checkbook in my other purse. I'll run in and pick up a few counter checks."

Ali was at the teller's window with Lizzie and Bonnie trailing behind, when Kiah Grave stepped out of Henry's office.

"Kiah!" Bonnie squealed. "What are you doing here?"

Ali turned at the sound of Bonnie's voice. She glanced over at the smartly-dressed young man.

Kiah didn't respond to Bonnie's question. He turned his back, lowered his head and scrambled through a file drawer.

Lizzie's knees grew weak. She grabbed the back of a chair and held tightly. "Kiah?" She whispered his name. *What's he doing here? A suit?*

Ali had the checks in her hand and headed toward the door, when she stopped and whirled around. She turned and stared at Kiah—then stomped out to the car without a word. Lizzie and Bonnie followed in silence.

As they rode away, the girls shot hushed glances at one another.

Alamanda peered into the rear view mirror. "Who was that young man in the bank?"

Lizzie was aware her mother was watching for her reaction. Too emotional to speak, she nudged Bonnie.

Bonnie said, "I think he may be the new bookkeeper, Aunt Ali. Daddy said Mr. Graton is not working at the bank any longer."

"So I've heard." Ali bit her nails. "The young man looks familiar." Her brow furrowed. "I can't place him, but I'm sure I've seen his face before. Do you girls know him?"

Lizzie nudged Bonnie once again—this time, a little harder.

Bonnie gave Lizzie a quick kick, which Lizzie took to mean that her cousin didn't wish to answer any further questions.

Alamanda glanced in the mirror. "I asked you girls a question."

Lizzie swallowed. "I think Bonnie knows him."

"Oh?" Alamanda's brow lifted. "A friend of yours, Bonnie?"

"Not exactly. I've seen him before—on a few occasions." Bonnie held her hand with fingers crossed, firmly against her knocking knees.

"Well it sounded to me like you knew him quite well." Ali smiled. "He's handsome, I'll have to say that for him. Of course, Lizzie is engaged, but he might be someone for you to set your sights on, Bonnie. If I were a little younger, I might give you some competition." With tongue-in-cheek, she said, "Who knows, if you treat him right, it's possible we can keep the bank in the family, after your father retires."

Bonnie glared at Lizzie. "Yes ma'am."

Lizzie's head whirled. Why did he want me to believe he was leaving town? And what is he doing working at the bank? Aware of her mother's watchful eye, Lizzie remained composed.

Lizzie peered cautiously in the mirror and swallowed hard when her mother suddenly screeched. "Bonnie, what did you call him?"

"Call him?" Bonnie shifted her glance toward Lizzie.

"Yes. I seem to remember you called him by his name. I know you did. What did you call him?"

Bonnie hesitated. When she spoke, her voice quivered. "Kiah."

"That's what I thought." Ali slammed her foot to the floorboard, bringing the car to an abrupt halt. She turned a sharp right and circled the block.

Lizzie sucked in a deep breath. "Why are you going back, Mama? Did you forget something?"

"Oh, yes, my darling. I forgot something, all right." Ali pulled up in front of the bank so fast the car ran up on the curb. "You girls wait here." Her red face twisted into a scowl. "This will only take a minute."

Lizzie trembled as she watched her mother storm into the bank.

"Why do you think your Mama came back?" Bonnie asked.

"Oh, Bonnie, she recognized his name. Mama was upset when Daddy hired Kiah to work the fields, him being an outsider—I suppose she's doubly mad to find out he's given him a job at the bank. But why would Kiah tell me he was leaving town?"

"What do you think she'll do?" Bonnie asked.

"With Mama, one never knows." Lizzie chewed her nails. "Maybe he was planning to surprise me." She threw her hand over her heart. "I know he loves me, Bonnie. Maybe he talked Daddy into giving him the job, so he could support me and wouldn't be ashamed to ask me to marry him. Of course! That has to be it. Daddy likes Kiah."

Bonnie stuck her head out the window to get a better look. "Oh, my. Aunt Ali looks madder than a wet setting hen. She's shaking her finger and giving Kiah the what-for. Reckon what she's saying?"

"I have no idea, but I can't stand the suspense. I love him, Bonnie. Let's go find out what Mama's up to."

Alamanda turned around when the girls walked through the door. "Get back in the car, Eliza," she yelled.

"No, Mama." Lizzie's knees stiffened. She couldn't remember ever blatantly defying her mother, but knowing how vicious and unpredictable Alamanda could be, when on one of her tirades, Lizzie was determined to stay.

Venom seemed to spew from Alamanda's lips, when she grabbed a shank of Lizzie's hair and screamed, "Don't sass me, girl. I'm beginning to understand a few things. You like to swim, do you? You've been slipping around behind my back with this no-good drifter, haven't you?"

Kiah stepped between them, and grabbed Ali's arm. "Ma'am, you have no right to—"

Ali jerked from his grasp and screamed, "Don't tell me my rights, you two-bit bum. I'll teach you about rights. I happen to know your dirty little secret. It took a few minutes to figure it out, but it's as plain as an Amish bride. You mess with me, and the whole town will know. Eliza, I told you to get in the car."

Lizzie sobbed. "Secret? What secret, Mama? What are you talking about? There's no secret. I love him."

Henry grabbed Ali and held her hands behind her. "Come on, Ali. Let's go to my office and talk this out, privately."

Alamanda screamed. "If you value your job, Henry Lancaster, you'll turn me loose this instant. This is none of your business."

Henry lifted his hands and tried to coerce her into going into his office. She turned back and yelled, "Eliza, get in the car. Now!"

"But Mama. I want to know—"

Henry whispered to Bonnie.

Bonnie tugged on Eliza's arm. "Do as she says, Lizzie. It'll make it easier on everyone."

Kiah whispered, "Go Liz. Please. For me."

Lizzie burst into tears as she ran out the door.

Ten minutes later, Ali stormed back to the car—her tight-lipped silence told Lizzie this wasn't the time to ask questions. It became obvious the shopping trip would be postponed. When Alamanda pulled up in front of Bonnie's house, Bonnie jerked open the door, scurried out and ran. Neither Lizzie nor her mother exchanged words on the way home.

After arriving at Gladstone, Lizzie ran up the stairs to her room, fell on her bed and sobbed.

At ten-thirty, Henry called his brother on the phone.

"Will, get over here, quick. Something terrible has happened."

Henry was pacing the floor when Will arrived.

"What's wrong, Henry?"

"It's Kiah."

"Kiah? What do you mean? Where is he?" Will's voice trembled.

"Will, Ali was here."

Will buried his face in his hands. He drew a deep breath. "Well, I think I knew it was coming. She was bound to find out."

"There's more to it, than her finding out, Will."

"I don't follow you."

"She took leave of her senses. She stormed in here, looking madder than a run-over dog, flinging her arms and yelling like a wild woman. She ran up to Kiah's desk and screamed, 'I know who you are, and you'd better stay away from my daughter.' Then she hollered, 'Get out. Get out of my bank.'"

Will's pulse raced. "What did he say, Henry?"

"Nothing at first. Kiah turned pale as a corpse. I could tell the kid was terrified. I tried to calm Ali, but she was furious."

Will bit his lip. "Were customers in the bank at time?"

"No and that was a blessing. Ralph stood like a stature behind the teller's window. He looked frightened and I could relate. I didn't know what Alamanda was capable of doing in her frame of mind. She acted crazy, Will."

Will's heart beat furiously against his chest. "So where's Kiah now?"

"He left. I felt for the boy. I called you from my office while she was here, but your line was busy. That's when I stepped out and attempted to reason with her, but I couldn't handle her."

"Do you have an idea where he might be?"

"He told me he had to leave town—that his staying could only bring heartache."

"I've got to find him, Henry." Will rushed out the door and spent the remainder of the afternoon looking, without success.

When Will arrived home that evening, Hobart met him in the

yard. "Mr. Will . . . Mr. Will." He called out. "Louie's been looking for you. He said tell you he'd be waiting behind the barn—said what he had to say, couldn't be said in front of folks. I don't know what it's all about, but Louie sounded fretful."

Will knew Kiah felt close to Louie. He sprinted to the back of the barn and found the old man sitting on an overturned #2 washtub.

Will tried to catch his breath. "Louie, you know where he is, don't you? Where's Kiah, Louie?"

Louie stood. "Slow down, Mr. Will. You're a sick man. You sit here on this ol' tub and try to calm yourself, and I'll tell you everything I know."

"Then you do know? You know where he is?"

"I know. Take it easy, now." Louie propped against a fence post. "Kiah said he left the bank, and went to the big house, hoping Miz Alamanda's car would be gone so he could tell you goodbye. Seems she beat him back, but you weren't here no how. He said he went by the shanty, and stayed awhile, reading a Bible Mattie gave him. Said he was praying you'd show up."

Will slapped at his forehead. "The shanty. Of course. Thanks, Louie, I'll go talk to him."

"No need in going. He ain't there. He came by our place to tell Mattie bye. Said he forgot to put Mattie's Bible in his bag and asked me to get it and give it back to her. But Mattie insisted I leave it be. Bless her heart, deep down Mattie knows better, but she wants to believe one day the boy'll come back for it."

Will blew out a breath. "You know where he is, don't you, Louie? I have to talk to him."

"Now that would be the part I can't tell you, Mr. Will."

Will caught Louie by the arm. "What do you mean, you can't tell me? You must, Louie. I have to know where the boy went."

"No sir, I made the young'un a promise, and I ain't got much in this world except my word. But I will tell you he's a mite upset, but he'll be all right. That boy is as fine a young fellow as I've ever known. As tore up as he was, he took time to come and say goodbye to me and Mattie. Mattie's at the house right now, squalling her eyes out. Oh, my how she loves that boy. He left a message for you."

Will swallowed. "What did he say, Louie?"

"His exact words?"

"Yes, Louie. His exact words."

"Well, he said it like this. 'Tell my daddy I love him and I'm sorry I brought him shame, but I'm not sorry I got to know him.'" Louie drew in the dirt with his foot. "Mr. Will, he didn't tell us nothin' we didn't already know. Mattie had done figured out the boy was yours. He's a fine boy."

"Yes, he is." Will scratched his head. "Is that all he said?"

"Well, he did promise Mattie he'd keep in touch and let her know where he was. She made him promise to write. Mattie got the coffee can out from the cupboard and made him take the money she'd been saving up to buy a new stove. He put up a fuss but she wouldn't turn him lose until he agreed to take it."

Will wiped his eyes. "Thank her for me, Louie. You tell Mattie she has a brand-spanking new stove coming real soon."

"No, no, Mr. Will. Ain't no need. We're doing just fine with that ol' wood stove. Mattie won't forgive me if she knows I told you about her giving him that money. She don't want no crowns in this world . . . says she wants to save hers up for when she gets to Glory."

"She's a jewel, Louie."

"Yessir, she sure is. You know, Mr. Will, me and Mattie lost a boy many years ago. I think Kiah sort of filled that empty space in Mattie's heart." Louie's eyes twinkled. "She was so proud of Kiah, when he got all dressed up in that pretty new suit you bought for him. Looked like a real gentleman, he did. He went to church with us, and to tell the truth, I think the boy got religion. Ain't no wonder, though, the way Mattie's been praying for him. Sometimes I think that woman has a direct line to the Almighty. Kiah come away from church with a head full of questions. I couldn't answer 'em, but Mattie knows her Bible. She knew what to say to him."

Will swallowed the pain. "I'm glad she was there for him."

"I asked what he was gonna do, and he said he's gonna find him another one of them countin' jobs now that he's got proper clothes. He's a smart boy, ain't he, Mr. Will. Our boy is real smart."

Will patted Louie on the back. "You bet, Louie. Our boy is real smart. He'll make a great accountant. I won't insist that you break your promise, but will you make me a promise, as well?"

"If I can."

"Promise me you'll let me know when you hear from him . . . just tell me how he's doing and tell him his daddy loves him. That's all I'm asking."

"I reckon I can do that, Mr. Will."

Lizzie cried herself to sleep, and slept through supper. Aroused by loud noises coming from down the hall, she glanced up at the clock above the fireplace. Ten-thirty. She eased out of bed, tiptoed over to the door and cracked it slightly. The commotion was coming from her parents' room.

Her mother screamed, "Will Lancaster, I should have suspected something fishy whenever you hired that no-good foundling and let him stay in our own backyard, over my objections."

Will shouted back, "You have no right to call him names, Alamanda. What has he ever done to you? Nothing. If you want someone to blame, here I am, but don't go blaming the boy. None of this is his fault. Times are hard. He came looking for a job, and I gave him one."

Lizzie eased outside the door and plopped her hand over her

mouth when Alamanda said, "You think I don't know? I know, Will."

"You think you know everything, don't you, Ali? If you'd only give me a chance to explain—"

"Maybe there's a few things I should explain to *you*. Did you know he's in love with your daughter?" She cackled. "Ah, yes, I can see that tidbit of news catches you by surprise. But he is."

Lizzie's heart beat faster. Did he say it, Mama? Did he? How would you know?

Will countered. "That's absurd, Ali. You're making up things."

"Oh, am I? You should've seen him gawking at her today. I should've suspected something peculiar when she insisted on swimming every afternoon until dark. Today, it all made sense. She's been sneaking off in the swamps with that no-account rascal. I wouldn't be surprised to find out she's pregnant."

Lizzie held her breath, waiting for her daddy's reaction. Then, her mama yelled, "Don't you even think about it, Will Lancaster. I'll leave with her if you ever lay a hand on me." Then the voices lowered and all she could make out was when her father said, "What did you tell the boy, Alamanda? Tell me what you said."

"Among other things, I told him he was fired—to get his things and get out of town immediately." She let out a hideous cackle. "He had the gall to tell me he wanted to talk to you, since you owned the bank and had hired him."

Lizzie strained her ear, but failed to hear her father's response. Her mother said, "I gave him an ultimatum. Lucky for you, Will, he took it."

Never had Lizzie known her parents to engage in such a heated argument. But what was the big secret that caused such an uproar? She braced against the door jam and held her breath, in an attempt to hear every word.

Her mother said, "I'm tired of this conversation. But let me warn you, Will Lancaster. This matter will lay buried. We're never to discuss it again. Do you understand? You can sleep in the guest room. I'm going to bed."

Lizzie eased her door shut and crawled into bed. Since you know everything, Mama, why didn't you tell him the rest? Why didn't you tell Daddy that not only is Kiah in love with me, but I'm in love with him? Lizzie found it impossible to fall asleep. She lay awake listening to loud claps of thunder, and watching streaks of lightning flash across the room. Oh, Kiah. Where are you?

Chapter Twenty-Eight

October 1932

Kiah sat on the beach in a little Florida town, watching the tide ebb. The ocean water rolled in with a force and just as quickly, flowed back out. Love had come splashing into his life in much the same way, but before he could grab hold, it washed away. He remembered his first love—a beautiful teenager named Zann in Pivan Falls, Mississippi. When she died, he felt he'd lost everything—that he could never love anyone the way he loved her.

Then Lizzie came along and as hard as he fought against it, he fell totally and irreversibly in love, all over again. He swallowed hard. His admission made him sick, yet to deny it only served to make him a liar. Never again would he put himself through such torment. Having his heart ripped from his chest twice was more than enough.

He pulled a pencil and small pad from his jacket pocket and composed a letter, as he listened to the waves pounding against the shore.

Dear Mr. Louie and Mrs. Mattie,

I'm in northwest Florida in a little ocean town called Palm City. I've rented a room over a storefront, and I have a window facing the water. The sunsets are breath-taking, and I love to hear the waves splashing against the dunes and watching the tide ebb. It's peaceful. I think I'll like it here.

He paused and mused over his words. Peaceful? True. So why couldn't he find peace in such a serene setting? He chewed his bottom lip, and continued to write:

The people seem friendly, but I'll sure miss you folks. I applied for a job at the bank as soon as I got off the train this afternoon. The bank president seems interested in hiring me, but they require a recommendation from my previous employer. Since I don't want anyone to know where I am, could you talk to Mr. Will privately, and ask for a letter of recommendation and forward it to me? I'd be grateful.

Please don't divulge my whereabouts, but thank Mr. Will for the nice suit of clothes. I couldn't have landed the job without them. And thank you again for the money. I'm praying for God to bless you ten-fold.

Your loving Grandson,

Kiah

Tuesday morning at the first signs of light, Lizzie leaped out of bed and jerked on her clothes. She yanked the gaudy ring from her finger and crammed it in a coin purse, before running down the stairs, skipping every other one.

Cleoda yelled after her as she ran out the door, but Lizzie didn't stop. She had to find him. She wouldn't let him leave without her. All the unanswered questions swirled in her head, but there was one thing she knew for certain—she loved him and he loved her. Even her mother had seen it.

She drove as close to the shanty as she could get. The recent rains made the two-rut dirt road leading to the meadow, impassable. She dashed out of the car and ran the remainder of the way, yelling his name. The little cottage was empty. She was drenched. Her shoes caked with red clay. She left and drove to Mrs. Blanchard's Boarding House, but Lizzie's hopes faded when Mamie Blanchard said yes, Kiah had stayed there, but he packed his things and she had no idea where he went.

Lizzie rode around for hours before returning to Gladstone. Kiah Grave was gone and she'd never see him again. *I'll never forgive you, Mama. Never.* She was packing a suitcase when her mother entered her bedroom.

Alamanda plopped her hands on her hips. "And where do you think you're going, young lady?"

"I'm not sure, Mama. At the moment, all I know for certain is that I'm going."

Ali threw up her hands. "It's that boy, isn't it? I knew it. Eliza don't be foolish. You have a long and wonderful future ahead of you as Mrs. Oliver Weinberger. You'll be Alabama's First Lady one day. Wake up from this childish dream of yours. Oliver wants to marry you."

"But I don't want to marry him, Mama. If you don't mind, I'd like a few minutes alone. I need to finish packing."

"You're being ridiculous. I'll get your father. Maybe he can talk sense into you."

"You do that, Mama. Go tell Daddy what to do. He'll do it. He always does. You lead him around like a puppy on a leash. If you say heel, he heels. If you say roll over, he does it. Well, I'm not your pet. I'm your daughter."

Alamanda stomped downstairs, yelling, "Will, get up here and talk to your daughter. You're responsible for these foolhardy notions. Will? Will!" Ali screamed. "Where are you?"

Lizzie pulled back the Priscillas and peered outside. Her daddy's Nash was gone. *Just as well—I don't think I could stand to say goodbye.* She scribbled a note.

She ran outside and threw her suitcase on the rumble seat, in time to see the taillights of her mother's Rolls, rounding the long driveway.

Cleoda, Comfort and Hobart came running toward the car. Lizzie supposed they'd kept an ear to the wall, hearing all the commotion.

With a trembling voice, Cleo said, "Honey, get back in that

house where you belong."

Lizzie shook her head, "I can't, Cleo." She handed her an envelope. "Cleo, will you see Daddy gets this letter?"

Cleo cried. "But honey, why don't you wait and tell 'im yourself what it is you want him to know. Mr. Will's gonna be all tore up inside when he finds out his baby's gone. Please wait, sugar, jest 'til your Daddy gets back."

Lizzie hugged Cleo. "I can't. Tell him I love him—and Cleo, I love you, too. You've been more of a mama to me than she has. I can't understand why you've stayed around to be her slave. She treats you awful."

Cleo grabbed Lizzie by the shoulders. "Honey, you're more of a slave than I've ever been."

Lizzie grimaced. "Oh, Cleo, whatever are you talking about?"

"I'm talking about that bitterness what's got you bound with chains that the eyes can't see. Turn it loose, sugar. Give it to the Lord."

Lizzie smiled faintly. "That's crazy talk, Cleo. I'm not a slave. I'll prove my freedom. I'm leaving Goat Hill and I'm never coming back. You should've done the same years ago."

Cleo threw her arms around her and held tightly. "Well, just do ol' Cleo a favor. "Member when you was a wee thing and learned how to say The Lord's Prayer in Bible School? Would you start prayin' it every night when you crawl in bed? That's all I is asking. Would you do that for me, child?"

Lizzie shrugged. "But I wouldn't mean it."

"Then pray it until you do mean it."

"Cleo, ask me to do anything, but don't ask me to call on God—not yet. Not the way I feel. Besides, I'm not sure He wants to hear from me." She cranked the car and was ready to leave, when she saw her mother's car speeding back toward the house. The servants quickly scurried around to the back.

Ali pulled up in the yard, with Oliver sitting in the front seat. Ali slung the door open and clomped into the house, without a word. Oliver dashed over to Lizzie's vehicle and jerked open the door.

He reached for her hand. She pulled away. "Eliza, my sweet, what's the meaning of this? Your mother says you're overwrought and I should calm you down."

Lizzie slumped down in the seat and turned off the ignition. "Great idea, Oliver. So get to it."

Oliver's eyes opened wide. "What . . . what do you mean, doll face?"

"Mama told you to calm me down. Now do it." Lizzie screamed the words. "I want to be calm, Oliver, and Mama told you what to do."

"But Eliza, I . . . I don't know what it will take."

Lizzie shrugged. "Oh well, if you can't take orders from my mother, then I can see a marriage between you and I could never work. Everyone in our family must be subjective to the higher authority—Queen Mama."

"Tootsie, you're not being rational."

Lizzie cringed. "Oliver, Tootsie has something for you." She reached across the seat and picked up a small clutch bag. She took out a coin purse, opened it and pulled out a ring. "Oliver, please return this to Mama Lu Lu and tell her I'm sorry but she's not my type."

Lizzie drove away, splattering mud on Oliver's wingtips. She rode by the Tribune to give Robert Loch an announcement for the morning paper.

The kind, elderly gentleman had worked for her father and her grandfather before him. Some said he was married to his work, which Lizzie found terribly depressing.

He greeted her warmly. "Well, hello Miss Eliza. What do I owe this pleasure?"

Lizzie reached in her coin purse and pulled out a folded piece of paper. She wet her lips. "I have an announcement, which I'd like for you to print in the morning paper."

"You say you have an announcement you'd like me to print?" Lizzie hoped he hadn't noticed her eyes rolling, but she wondered why he always had to repeat everything anyone said. She watched as he carefully unfolded the piece of paper.

Lizzie flinched. "Uh . . . yes, thank you, Mr. Loch. 'Be seeing you." She waved and rushed toward the door.

"Not so fast, young lady. Wait until I have a chance to read it—in case I have questions."

"I'm really in a bit of hurry. I think you'll find it self-explanatory."

Robert Loch peered through the spectacles which rested on the tip of his red bulbous nose.

Lizzie's eyes squinted as she observed his expression changing from curious to shock. She fidgeted and swallowed. "Now that you've read it, I'd best be on my way. Thanks Mr. Loch."

"Not so fast, my dear." He held it at arm's length, as if the words would change if he didn't look at it quite so closely. Slowly, he shook his head. "I can't print this."

Lizzie's brow shot up. "And why not, may I ask?"

"Because we don't have a comic section in The Tribune."

Lizzie thought she detected a slight chuckle, but if she did, likely it was a first for the stoic Mr. Loch.

Rubbing his chin, he said, "This is quite humorous, but I'm afraid I can't go along with your little joke."

Lizzie stiffened. "I assure you, it's not meant as a joke. And I don't doubt that you don't understand, but my father doesn't hire you to understand everything you print, does he? Doesn't he hire you to print the news?"

Robert Loch removed his visor and scratched his bald head. "But . . . but Miss Eliza, this isn't news."

"Tell me something, sir. Did you know it before you read it

just now?"

He pursed his lips. "Well no . . . but this reads like an obituary and you aren't dead."

Lizzie pulled at her collar. "That's your *opinion*. Please print it in the obituaries, where it belongs. That will be all, Mr. Loch. I'll put in a good word for you to my father. Thank you, sir, and have a good day."

Lizzie drove home and decided to wait until morning before leaving. Cleo was right. She shouldn't leave without letting her father know. She'd tell him at dinner.

Before Lizzie had a chance to turn off the ignition, Cleo was hanging onto the door handle. "Glory be, child, I was so glad when Hobart yelled and told me he saw you coming down the road. But I knowed you'd come back, sugar. I just knowed you couldn't leave your daddy. I'm so glad you changed your mind. I ain't quit squalling since you left."

Lizzie got out of the car and trudged up the steps with Cleo hugging her all the way. "But Cleo, I haven't changed my mind. I just decided to wait until morning."

Cleo's eyes took on the shape of saucers. "Why, honey, you can't mean that. You sit down with your daddy tonight and tell him where it hurts. Mr. Will would do anything in the world for you, sugar. Whatever it is that's laying heavy on you, he'll take care of it. Just don't leave. You ain't ready to be on your own, child. The world's a big place and you've been sheltered. You don't know what it's like out there."

"I don't want to talk about it, Cleo. I'm tired. I'm going to my room."

That night when the dinner bell rang, Lizzie walked into the dining room to find her father's place empty. She looked at her mother. "Where's Daddy?"

"You'll have to save your questions for your father. I have no idea. I've been in my room all afternoon. Eliza, I hope you've had time to think about what a dunce you made of yourself in front of Oliver. It wouldn't surprise me if he never wanted to see you again. But he's such a gentleman. He said he's willing to forgive you, but I advise you not to wait too long before apologizing."

Cleo served fried chicken with mashed potatoes and gravy— Lizzie's favorite foods. And to top it off, there was a platter full of hot, crispy, dewberry tarts. But Lizzie couldn't eat. She laid her napkin on the table, asked to be excused and went to her room, where she stayed the remainder of the night.

Chapter Twenty-Nine

A piercing scream—not just a mere shout or a yell, but an ear-tingling, crystal shattering, heaven-help-me kind of scream—woke Lizzie the next morning.

Seconds later, a shout of fewer decimals than the previous but still not one to be easily ignored resounded from the floor below. Then something hit the wall. She rolled her eyes. *I guess Mama loves me after all. Seems the news of my recent death has caused her great anguish.* She sat up in bed, yawned and stretched.

Her mother's voice bellowed. "Eliza Virginia Lancaster, get downstairs immediately."

Lizzie tied a robe around her and ambled slowly down the long staircase and into the dining room. "Why, Good morning, Mama. Sleep well?"

Alamanda's face resembled a pomegranate—all red and hard looking. "What is the meaning of this," she shrieked, waving the obituary column in Lizzie's face.

Lizzie took her place at the table. She winked at Cleo, who was peeking out from behind the kitchen door. Lizzie unfolded her napkin, placed it in her lap and poured a cup of hot cocoa from the chocolate set.

Alamanda waved the paper in Lizzie's face. "I'm talking to you, girl. What is this?"

"Oh!" Lizzie feigned surprise. "Are you referring to my obituary, Mama?"

"Obituary, my foot. Eliza Virginia, I declare, I don't know what to do with you. You-re going to be the death of me yet."

Lizzie reached for a biscuit. "Is that a fact? The death of you? Well, if you need help wording your obit, feel free to call on me. I've had practice."

Alamanda screamed. "I'm fed up with you and your smart mouth. You've humiliated me. Everyone in town will read this. What were you thinking? You've made a fool of yourself. And as for Robert Loch—he'll lose his job because of this. I'll see to it. He may as well pack his bags, because he's history."

Lizzie swallowed the lump in her throat. "No, Mama. You can't do that. It wasn't his fault. I made him do it."

"He's a grown man. He knew better than to print such foolishness."

Lizzie pleaded, "You can't fire him, Mama. The Tribune is his life. Everyone in town knows how much the job means to him. Daddy won't let you fire him."

"Ha! That's what you think, little lady. Your father doesn't happen to own the paper. I do. I can fire and hire who I will, and he had no business printing this without speaking to me first." Alamanda glared at her daughter, before shouting, "Get out of my sight! Get out!"

Lizzie jumped up from the table and ran upstairs. She packed her bags and rang for Hobart.

When she walked outside, Hobart had loaded her belongings and was standing beside her car, holding a paper sack. "Here, Miss Lizzie. Cleo sent you some left-over chicken from last night and some of her dewberry tarts. She's too tore up to see you off, but she wanted me to tell you she loves you and she'll be praying for you."

"Bye Hobart. You tell her I love her, too."

Lizzie stopped to fill the gas tank and saw her daddy's maroon Nash turning into the filling station.

Will honked his horn and pulled up beside her.

A lump formed in her throat when he got out of his car and trudged over to her vehicle. His brow creased. "Hello, Swamp Angel." He stuck his head in the window and with his thumb and forefinger, he gently lifted a curl, covering her eye.

Lizzie gazed into her father's eyes and burst out crying. "Oh, Daddy, Daddy."

"Hey, hey, angel, dry those tears. May I get in?"

Lizzie dabbed at her eyes and nodded.

"Going somewhere?"

"I've got to get away, Daddy. I can't stay here another day."

Will hung his head. "I know, baby. I know."

"Daddy, I'm in love with Kiah Grave, but I know I'll never see him again. I don't know what Mama said to make him leave, but she had no right. He's never done anything to her, except be born poor. I wish I were poor, then maybe we could be together." Lizzie gripped the steering wheel. "Daddy, why did he leave?"

Will lifted a shoulder. "Maybe it's for the best, angel."

"The best? How can you say that, Daddy?"

"Honey, you say you loved him, but did he—" Will stopped and stared at the sky as if he'd lost something in the clouds.

"Daddy, if you're asking if he loved me too, the answer is yes."

Will's face turned red.

"Don't look so shocked. Maybe you think of me as your little girl, but in case you haven't noticed, I'm all grown up now, Daddy. You shouldn't find it too surprising that a young man might fall in love with me. Some fellows even think I'm pretty."

"Oh, my precious Swamp Angel, I don't find it strange at all that a young man would fall in love with you. You're beautiful. But . . . did he—" His Adam's apple bobbled.

Lizzie grinned. "Oh, my sweet, sweet daddy. If you're trying to ask if he took liberties with me, the answer is no. Never. And I'd be lying if I said I didn't encourage him to take me in his arms and kiss me." She paused and smiled when her father's expression didn't change. "It's harder to shock you, than it is Mama. She would've had a conniption fit if she heard me say I wanted him to kiss me. But I did, Daddy. Is that horribly wicked?"

Will pulled at his tie. "But he didn't . . . did he?"

"No. In fact, he never even admitted that he loved me. But I knew. I could see it in his eyes. He loved me all right. I'm as sure of that as I am of my name being Eliza Lancaster."

The color slowly seeped back into Will's face. "Where are you headed, angel?"

"I'm not sure, but Daddy, please don't try to stop me."

Will shook his head. "What about Oliver?"

Lizzie frowned. "You know I don't love Oliver."

"So you won't be getting married?"

"No, Daddy."

"I'm glad. Lizzie, sweetheart, may I make a suggestion?"

"Sure."

"You talked of enrolling at Agnes Scott Institute and Training Center, before you became engaged to what's-his-name." The corner of his lip lifted. "I was thinking—since you're insistent on leaving, and you've nowhere in mind to go—I thought maybe—"

"Maybe I might consider going to college?"

Will nodded. "Honey, you could be furthering your education and I wouldn't worry so much if I knew you were in a safe environment. You're packed, already. What do you think?"

"Why not? I have nothing better to do. But I think it's too late to enroll." Lizzie saw a flicker in her father's eyes, as his face split into a crooked little grin.

"I don't think there'll be a problem," Will said with a wink. "I'll drive you there and get you settled. Why don't you wait for me at the City Café? I'll run to the house and pack my overnight bag, and meet you at the restaurant. I'll leave my car parked behind the bank. We'll drive to Georgia in yours, so you'll have wheels while you're there."

"But how will you get home?"

Will smiled. "That's what buses are for."

Lizzie reached over and hugged her father. "Thank you, Daddy. You're the greatest. Just between the two of us—I was scared to death. I had no idea where I'd go. I only knew I couldn't stay at Gladstone."

Twenty minutes later, Lizzie was sipping a malt through a straw, when she glanced up and saw her daddy tapping on the plate glass window. She grabbed her sweater, and ran outside.

"Do you think your ol' man might be able to drive such a fine automobile as yours?"

Lizzie slid over. "Be my guest." Tears welled in her eyes, when her daddy wrapped his strong arm around her and pulled her close as they drove out of Goat Hill.

Chapter Thirty

Gladstone Cemetery, 1939

"Ah, yes, I remember it well."

Unaware of the lapse of time, Eliza had no idea how long she'd sat in the cemetery. Ten minutes? Or an hour and ten minutes? She composed her face, refreshed her lip rouge and dabbed powder from her compact over damp cheeks.

She winced and cranked her Packard when she saw two men walk toward her mother's grave with shovels.

As she drove away, she recalled the weather was cool that October day, seven years ago when she and her father drove out of Goat Hill on their way to Agnes Scott. He helped her settle in and that evening they had dinner at a little restaurant near the college. She remembered waving goodbye as he rode away in a cab the following morning—wondering if she'd ever see him again.

But she did see him. Her father visited her often at school, but not once did her mother come with him. Alamanda did, however, write letters occasionally, although most of them were about Oliver and how well he was doing at Harvard, and to let Eliza know that he had forgiven her for having "cold feet."

According to her mother's letter, Oliver vowed he'd never love another woman the way he loved her. Eliza thought it sad. Oliver was a good man—a bore, and certainly not the kind of man she'd choose to share her life with—but still, he was a decent, upright sort of fellow. Too bad he was stuck on her. Eliza knew the agonizing pain of not being with the one you love.

Her mother's letters always ended with, "It would be nice if you weren't so stubborn and could see fit to come visit your family once in a while."

Eliza always ended hers with, "You know where I am. Anytime you decide to visit, I'm sure Daddy will let you ride with him. He comes often." Eliza had missed her mother. As much as she disliked her, she still missed her, though she couldn't imagine why.

"If Mama had really loved me, she would've come to visit me at Agnes Scott. All I wanted was for her to come just once—and if she had, I would've gone home. But she was too mule-headed."

But six years after leaving Goat Hill, the visits from her father and the letters from her mother ceased.

Only two weeks before receiving word that her mother had died, Eliza received a letter from Aunt Merle, telling her that both her mother and father were gravely ill. But the illnesses didn't seem to be Aunt Merle's greatest concern. It was the gossip, which re-circulated in Goat Hill that seemed to bother her most. She wrote:

Dear Eliza,

I'm sorry to inform you that your father is gravely ill. Heart disease is now taking its toll. Your mother has been diagnosed with consumption and her remaining days on this earth will be few.

Eliza, I think it's high time for you to come home and clear the family name. I'm greatly concerned about the rumors that continue to circulate in Goat Hill. I'm sure there's absolutely nothing to the gossip, but folks have been saying the reason you left home back in '31 was because a young hooligan took liberties with you. Some even say you encouraged it. I'm sure that's a fabrication, but I'm tired of trying to defend our good name. Please consider returning home to squash the rumors that seem to have resurfaced since your parents became ill

Sincerely,

Aunt Merle

Eliza found the rumors humorous. "If only I could find the handsome hooligan, I'd give the folks in Goat Hill reason to gossip." She regretted not coming back sooner, but not for the purpose of answering false rumors. She only wished she'd returned earlier for her daddy's sake. He hadn't been able to make the trip to the college in over a year. She should've come back sooner to see him. It would've meant a lot to him. Why didn't she?

Why did she allow the rift between her and her mother to

devour her, stealing her joy and turning her into such a wretched, spiteful creature? It was all Mama's fault, she reasoned.

By the time Eliza arrived at Gladstone Manor, the rain had ceased.

The oyster-shells covering the long driveway crackled under the wheels as she drove slowly, weaving to keep from running over children who scurried about the estate in a game of hide-and-seek.

Eliza glanced around the manicured grounds of Gladstone and winced. She muttered, "Look at this mob. One would think the World's Fair is being held on the premises." Her mother's death provided an excuse for the curious public to roam the lavish manor in the pretense of being there to mourn the dead.

Eliza parked in the carriage house and trudged up the stone steps in the back leading to the kitchen. She hoped to avoid Oliver as long as possible. When she opened the screen door, suppressed tears unleashed at the sight of Hobart, a long-time family servant. He threw his arms around her and held tightly, as she sobbed against his broad chest.

"Now, now, child. It's all gonna be all right. You'll see. Everything's gonna work out."

Eliza peered into his kind, black face and said, "It's good to see you, Hobart. How've you been?"

"Some of us good, some of us not so good, sugar. I'm fine, but Cleo's havin' a rough time. She just ain't at herself. She refuses to leave Mr. Will's bedside for more'n a few minutes at the time. I reckon she blames herself for Miz Ali's passin'. I ain't never heard such carryings on as she done the night it all happened. Poor ol' Mr. Will. I wish . . ." Hobart stopped in mid-sentence. "Welcome back to Gladstone, Miz Lizzie."

"Ah, yes. Gladstone." It was the name her mother christened the Tudor-style mansion, when Papa Gid purchased it for his only daughter as a wedding present, January 10, 1914. Built by slave labor of marble from the North Alabama quarries, the pink veins gave the house an iridescent glow on a sunny day.

Hobart wrung his hands. "We've missed you Miz Lizzie. We've all missed you."

"Thanks, Hobart. I've missed you too, but I plan to stay awhile. We'll talk later."

"Yes'm. I'd like that. I sure would."

When Eliza walked from the kitchen and passed through the butler's pantry, she could almost smell the wonderful aroma of dewberry tarts. She smiled at childhood memories of tarts cooling on the top shelf—purposely positioned out of her reach.

She strolled down the colossal hall, ignoring the hordes of people milling around. The Gladstone family crest was inlaid in the marble tile in the antechamber. She gazed at the mammoth oil portrait of Papa Gid, hanging near the winding staircase. A brass plaque attached to the frame acknowledged his many accomplishments, lest anyone dared forget. Eliza suspected there were a few notable deeds listed, which weren't rightfully due him.

Nevertheless, she conceded the lengthy inscription looked quite impressive to anyone interested in such things.

Aunt Merle spotted Eliza, traipsed over and with a hand fan held over her mouth to disguise lip movements, she whispered, "Honey, you need to get out of that wet dress. It's scandalous the way it clings to your figure. I ran home and slipped on dry clothes. You need to do the same, sugar."

Eliza lifted her shoulders. "Oh, but I'm afraid there isn't a second funeral dress in my trunk, Aunt Merle. But I do have a red organza with a lovely halter neck. Shall I put it on?"

Merle's mouth dropped. She fanned her face. "No, Honey. Don't fret. I suppose silk dries quickly."

"I hope so. Excuse me, Aunt Merle."

Merle grabbed her arm. "Don't leave, sugar. You need to acknowledge the guests."

"Make my apologies, Aunt Merle. I want to go upstairs to see Daddy."

"Of course you do, dear, but the doctor has him sedated for a purpose. There'll be plenty of time to spend with Will when he's lucid, and the guests are gone. Your father would want you down here among Ali's friends. Did you speak to the Vandergrifts? Mingle, sugar. Mingle."

Chapter Thirty-One

In spite of Merle's protests, Eliza slipped upstairs, and cracked open the door to her daddy's room.

She glanced about, disappointed not to find Cleoda by his side. She tiptoed up to the bed and gasped when she saw her father's emaciated figure, partially concealed under a white cotton sheet. The ruggedly handsome face, which she remembered so well, appeared pale and gaunt. His eye sockets looked sunken. Strong arms that held her tightly in front of Buttrick Hall at Agnes Scott College only seven years ago, now looked bony and weak. He appeared twenty years older. His thick, black hair had become thin and gray. She sat on the edge of the bed and sobbed as she held her daddy's withered hand while he slept.

Knowing he couldn't hear, didn't stop her from pouring out her heart.

"Why, Daddy? Why did Mama make him leave? Sure, Kiah was poor, but I've always known there was something more . . . like a dark, dreadful secret that he was trying to run away from. And I believe Mama found out and used it to get him out of my life. If only I knew the answer, perhaps I could put the past to rest."

Eliza sobbed, and laid her head upon his chest. She jerked when the bedroom door swung open.

Cleoda walked in with a bowl in one hand, and the other arm held high. "Glory," she wailed. "Thank you Sweet Jesus for answered prayers." Her lip trembled. "Oh, sugar, I never doubted. I said to Hobart 'she'll be back, you wait and see.' I just wish Mr. Will could see you, looking like a princess out of a fairytale book. You're a sight for sore eyes, Miz Lizzie, but you always was a pretty little thing. Oh, sugar, forgive me for squalling, but I'm so glad to see you."

"Hi Cleo." Eliza rose to her feet, took the bowl from Cleoda's hands and sat it on the dresser. She held out her arms and whispered, "I need a hug, Cleo."

"Well, ol' Cleo's been saving one just for you, Miz Lizzie." The elderly black lady wrapped Eliza in a tight hug and wept uncontrollably. "For seven long years, I've been prayin' for you to come home, sugar, but I wish yo' mama could've lived to see it. Oh, I've missed you, child."

"I've missed you, too, Cleo."

Cleoda pulled away and wiped her eyes with the tail of her apron. "Things at Gladstone ain't never gonna be the same no more. First you leave, and now Miz Ali's gone, and just look." She pointed toward the bed. "Ain't that a pitiful sight? Yo' poor ol' daddy's lying here not knowing daylight from dark. No, Miz Lizzie, things won't never be the same, and that's sad, but it's the honest-to-goodness truth."

The truth of Cleoda's words stung like a prickly pear. *She's right. Things will never be the same. So what if I discover why he left? Will it change anything?*

In a deliberate effort to lighten the mood, Eliza made a thin smile, and said, "I see you're still making Daddy his favorite banana pudding."

"Indeed, I am. There ain't much I can do for him, but I keep hoping he'll be able to eat a bite when he wakes up. I figure this is what he likes most of all." Cleoda shook her head slowly. "I ain't never seen nobody what loves anything like Mr. Will loves my puddin'."

Eliza nodded. "Where's Comfort?"

Cleoda's smile faded. "Why she took off shortly after you did, hon. Seems somebody put foolish notions in her head about New Orleans and she just upped and left without a word. I reckon it was for the best, though, 'cause she found her a husband. Calls him a Creole, and I ain't quite sure what that is, but I don't think it's catching. I Suwannee, the man sho' must love her, though, to take care of her the way he does. She's been after me to go live with 'em, and I reckon when I ain't needed here no more, I'll pull up and go." Her lip quivered. "I miss my baby."

"I'm sure she misses you, too, Cleo."

"Well, enough talk about us. Miz Lizzie, why don't you go downstairs to the dining room and get you a plate, while I sit here with Mr. Will?"

"I'm not hungry. I want to be with Daddy, Cleo. He's the reason I returned—the only reason." She drew a deep breath and dabbed at her wet cheeks.

Cleoda lifted her head. "You don't mean that, child. You woulda come home for your Mama's funeral. I know you woulda. Now you go on downstairs and talk to folks and eat a bite. Doc Griffin says he don't 'spect your daddy will wake up no time soon."

"But I want to be here if he does, Cleo. I want him to know I came back."

"Miss Lizzie, I'm gonna be right here by his side. If he rouses, I promise to tell him you're here. I'll send somebody to fetch you the minute it happens. You go on now—sitting up with sick folks can plumb wear you out. Your daddy wouldn't want you tiring yourself out like this. You know if he could speak to us right now, he'd be saying, 'Cleoda, you take care of my baby.'"

Eliza trudged half-way down the stairs, when the sounds of laughter and children running through the house caused her to retreat back into her daddy's room.

Cleoda looked up. "What's wrong, honey?"

"I don't want to be with those people downstairs, Cleo. They're strangers. I want to be with you. I want you to tell me everything."

"Like what, sugar?"

"Like what happened to Mama and Daddy? I got a brief telegram from Aunt Merle telling me Mama died, and Daddy collapsed . . . but . . . why? I . . . I mean how?"

"I reckon that's pretty much what happened, all right, but you'll have to ask the Good Lord the hows and the whys. There are some things we won't understand this side of the pearly gates. But in spite of the terrible heaviness pressin' on your heartstrings, I do know the Lord loves you, honey, even more than Mr. Will does, and that's a heap o' loving."

Eliza glanced down. "How long was Mama sick? What happened, Cleo?"

"Well, I had a notion your Mama was sicker than she was letting on, but she never was one to slow down. She and Miz Merle went to Dothan on the bus the day before it happened. She said they was going on a shopping spree, and planned to take in a picture show. You know how crazy your mama was about Clark Gable. They stayed overnight in one of them fancy motels. The next evening when she got home, I could tell she was ailing. She was green as a gourd, and she went straight to her room and went to bed."

"Did you give her anything?"

"I tried, but she said leave her be, she just wanted to sleep. She wouldn't let me tend to her, Miz Lizzie. You know I woulda done anything for that woman. I tried, honest, I did."

"I know, Cleo. I'm not blaming you. You were always good to her. Go on—"

"Well, in the middle of the night, Mr. Will stormed down to the basement and woke me, yelling my name. He told me to fix a poultice for Miz Alamanda . . . said she needed some relief." Cleoda sucked in a deep breath and fanned her face. Her eyes widened. "Oh, Miz Lizzie, Miz Lizzie—"

"Don't stop, Cleo. What happened?"

"When I walked in the room and laid that poultice bag on her chest, I could tell she was burning up with a fever. I ain't ashamed to tell you, I was scared. She had the color of death all over her. You can tell when a body's dying by the color . . . did you know that? It's the truth." Cleoda stopped and shook her head slowly. "I ran down to the basement and told Hobart to go fetch Doc Griffin, but before the doctor could get here, she was gone. I mean it happened just that fast, Miz Lizzie. Just that fast."

Eliza spoke softly. "I see. So tell me about Daddy. When did he collapse?"

"I don't know nothing 'bout time, but I'll tell you it happened quicker than it takes to boil a hard egg. I was bathing Miz Ali's face with cold water when she sorta went limp like a wet dishrag and I started to holler, 'She's gone, she's gone.' Now Miss Lizzie, I've seen folks die before, but it was doubly hard, being it was Miz Alamanda. Why, I took care o' her when she weren't no bigger than a wharf rat."

Eliza pulled a neatly folded handkerchief from her jacket pocket and handed to Cleoda.

Cleo shook her head. "No thanks, Miz Lizzie, I can't wipe my ol' salty tears on your pretty little hanky," she said, as she reached for the tail of her apron.

"Don't be silly." Eliza reached up and dabbed Cleo's face with the dainty linen cloth. "Now. Finish your story. What happened to Daddy?"

Cleo drew a deep breath. "Well, it was like this, Miz Lizzie. Mr. Will was sitting on the faintin' couch, and when I saw the life leaving Miz Ali and I hollered, then Mr. Will, he jumped up and started yelling at me, like it was my fault she was gone. Scared me, 'cause you know that man ain't never raised his voice at me. But he yelled, 'Do something, Cleoda, do something.' I was screaming back that I didn't know what to do. That's when Mr. Will grabbed his chest with both hands and slumped over. Oh, my soul, Miss Lizzie, I just knew there was gonna be three corpses in that room 'fore Doc Griffin could get here. I went over and splashed what water I had left in the dishpan in Mr. Will's face, trying to bring him around. And that's when Hobart and the doctor came bustin' in. They said they could hear me carrying on all the way to the end of the road. I didn't know what to do, Miz Lizzie."

"I'm sure you did all you could, Cleo."

"Well, I did all I knowed to do. I was mighty glad to see Doc

Griffin walk through that door. And that's just the way it happened. I'm so sorry, honey. I wish I coulda done more, but I didn't know what else to do." Cleoda's body shook in full-blown sobs. "Miz Ali was like my own young'un."

Eliza rose and wrapped her arms around the faithful servant. "I'm so sorry. I know you loved her in spite of her short-comings, and we both know Mama had a few."

"You're good as gold, Miz Lizzie. You always was. A mite high-strung sometimes," she chuckled. "Well, what I'm trying to say is you possess a deep-down goodness like Mr. Will. If I didn't know better, I'd think . . . never you mind. Ol' Cleo talks too much sometimes."

"I wish I were more like Daddy." Liz mumbled. "Oh, Cleo. What if he doesn't wake up? He must, Cleo. He must!"

"Now, now. Fretting don't change things, honey, so you try and get hold of yourself. Doc says the best thing for Mr. Will is rest, so I'll be stayin' up here to run folks off. Hobart and Ludie Mae are taking care of the kitchen duties. Occasionally someone meanders up this way, and I have to shoo 'em back down. I don't think Mr. Will would want me to let folks come up here gawking at him, with him in such a fix. Doc Griffin keeps pumping stuff in him to keep him knocked out so's he'll get some rest. But I'll be sittin' right here if he should arouse. If he does, I'll be sure and tell him you're here, Miz Lizzie. I sho' will. So you run on, now."

Eliza took time to change into dry clothes. Knowing the red halter-neck dress could send Aunt Merle to a quick grave, Eliza reached in the suitcase and pulled out a white bolero, which she slipped over her arms. She swallowed hard, then trudged down the long corridor. A knot formed in her stomach when she walked over to the banister and peered down toward the library door. She remembered a day long ago, when she and Bonnie hid in that very spot and watched in amusement as Kiah Grave burst into the house like a madman. *Bonnie didn't believe me, but I knew from the moment I saw him, I was in love. I was a kid, but I knew what I wanted.*

She walked downstairs and gasped at the mass of people roaming around—strangers who wouldn't have known Alamanda Lancaster from Hobart's house cat, but here they were— multitudes, with pretenses of paying their respects. People she'd never seen before milled about the mansion as if they belonged. A dozen or more perched in rocking chairs lining the veranda while hundreds wandered around the palatial grounds. It reminded Eliza of a circus with far too many clowns.

She had to go somewhere—anywhere—to get away from the smothering crowd. She slipped back into the kitchen and darted out the back door, hoping to elude Oliver. Eliza's emotions reeled. She needed time alone. Time to think. Time to figure out where to start digging for answers.

Now that her mother was gone, no one would know what

really happened that fateful October day, back in 1932. No one except her daddy, and unless he received a miracle, he wouldn't be telling anyone anything. Did she believe in miracles? She wasn't sure. She believed in God. She could look at the world around her and know He existed—but she found it hard to believe He would concern Himself with a family who gained their wealth off the misfortunes of others. Surely, God couldn't reward a family steeped for generations in such greedy, evil deeds.

She thought that sad, for she hated to think her daddy could miss a much-needed miracle, when he was such a good man at heart. Eliza wanted to believe he'd simply been misguided, but perhaps she was making excuses for him. Why blame it all on her mother and Papa Gid? Her father was an intelligent man. He didn't have to give in to their every whim and allow them to turn him into a puppet.

Chapter Thirty-Two

Eliza wandered aimlessly around the grounds of the massive estate, attempting to avoid as many people as possible.

As she walked past the old red barn, her mind drifted back to the summer she turned eighteen, when she and Bonnie would sneak up to the loft and share their hopes and dreams.

Eliza knew exactly who had shattered her beautiful dream, although she knew neither how nor why. One little word played over in her head like a scratched record. *Forgive . . . forgive . . . forgive.*

How could she forgive the one who purposely and deliberately set out to ruin her life? What did her mother dig up from Kiah's past to force him to disappear? Murder? If so, it was self-defense. If robbery, he was framed. He was a good man—a little spirited at times, but he was no criminal. *I miss you, Kiah. Oh, how I miss you.*

With no forethought to where she was going, Eliza strolled through the meadow, her heels sinking into the wet mud. She stopped to pull off her shoes and stockings and walked across the tall wet grass in her bare feet. She followed an overgrown path and soon found herself standing in front of a little log cabin. For as long as Eliza could remember, everyone referred to the one-room shack as the shanty. After priming a nearby pump, she washed her feet and rinsed the mud from her shoes.

She didn't intentionally set out for the shanty—she supposed her subconscious led her there. Made of split logs, the one-room shack had a lone window on the east side. The chimney, constructed from fieldstones and chinked with red clay, had holes where bees bored through the clay. She held her hand on the doorknob. Did she dare enter and open old wounds? She had no choice. There'd never be closure if she left Goat Hill without learning the truth. If finding the answer meant reliving the pain, so be it.

As she jerked open the door, a creature ran past. She supposed it to be a raccoon, but it happened so fast, she couldn't be sure. Her heart raced when she stepped inside. Everything looked exactly the way it did, the day he left. Shoved against the wall was a small iron bed frame with a cotton mattress.

The rusty old springs creaked and then sank as she slowly lowered her body down. A bed slat fell to the floor, causing her to jump. She caught her breath and snickered. *I'm acting like Bonnie. What's wrong with me? I'm as skittish as a rabbit in a foxhole.* She dropped her shoes and stretched out on the bed. Her pulse raced as she lay there, knowing her head rested on the same pillow where Kiah's had once lain.

A wooden apple crate, standing upright served as a bedside table. On the far side of the room, a bowl and pitcher sat atop an oak washstand. A small mirror hung on a nail above the dry sink, where he must have shaved in the early mornings. Eliza had an eerie feeling, as she imagined his reflection staring back at her. The image was so vivid, she felt she could almost reach out and touch him. She envisioned a lock of black, curly hair falling loosely over his forehead—his clear blue eyes shining brightly against his sun-drenched skin—dimples sinking into his cheeks, and his funny little crooked smile. She imagined him dipping a shaving brush into a mug, and lathering his face. Then, as quickly as the image appeared, it vanished.

Eliza's eyes moved slowly across the room, searching for clues. A small porcelain-top table and two cane-bottom chairs were in the center of the room. The fireplace was on the north side. A black iron kettle rested on the hearth—hanging on the spit was an empty iron pot. It was then she spotted a red flannel shirt, hanging on a nail on the back of the door. Eliza grabbed it, held it to her nose and sniffed, hoping his scent lingered. Too many years had passed. Hugging the shirt to her breast, she walked over to the tiny window that faced the creek. She pulled a glove from her suit pocket and attempted to wipe away years of dirt, dust and grime from the windowpane.

Eliza blinked, and then blinked again. She threw the glove down and quickly ran her fingers over the glass. Etched on the window pane was a small heart with the initials, K.G. and L.L inscribed in the center. She pressed her palm against the glass and sobbed. *He did love me. I knew it.* As she peered out the window, she could see an old washtub sitting on a stump. Eliza could almost see him, standing under the mulberry tree in his overhauls and brogans, sipping water from the tin ladle.

The one-room shanty and nearby creek were links to a romantic past she chose to remember. Forty acres away sat a grand mansion, filled with memories Eliza longed to forget.

She ambled across the room and fell on the cot. She picked up Kiah's flannel shirt, held it close to her heart and reminisced of what is, what was, and what might have been. To her dismay, what *was*, was not what *is*, and what might have been, turned into what never will be. As the sole heir to Gladstone, she could rightfully expect to inherit the vast wealth of those who came before her.

"I'd swap it all to have what might have been." She buried her face in the pillow and groaned. "Oh, Kiah, my love. If only I could move on. I'm turning into a bitter, resentful old maid. What have I to live for?"

When she turned over on the cot, and something hit the floor with a loud thud. Eliza reached down and picked it up. A Bible? Strange, she didn't see it earlier. She flipped it open and on the inside flap in bold print were the words, "To Mattie Brunson, from her beloved husband, Louie. December 25, 1920."

"Miz Mattie's Bible? But how did it get here?" She laid it

back on the apple crate.

Though she didn't want to leave, she supposed she should amble back to the manor. Surely, the crowd was thinning by now. She was sorry Bonnie had to leave so soon after the funeral, but she understood. "Bonnie—married to a pilot—I'll bet he'll never get her on an airplane. She's the world's biggest scaredy-cat." Eliza smiled.

When she sat up on the bed, her knee hit the apple crate, and once again, the Bible hit the floor. She reached down to pick it up. Thumbing through the pages, her eyes fell on a verse underlined with red ink. Jeremiah 33:3. "Call upon me and I will answer thee and shew thee great and mighty things, which thou knowest not."

Eliza's pulse raced, as the words seemed to jump off the page into her heart. Was it possible God meant these words for her? Surely, it was her imagination. Why would Almighty God want to show her anything? She left Him behind the day she drove away from Goat Hill. She read the scripture again. "Call upon me and I will answer." Bitter tears rushed forth like an uncapped well. She wanted to believe . . . oh how she wanted to believe.

She slid off the bed and fell on her knees, feeling an urgent need to pray—but it had been so long. Would she know how to begin? Cleo's words, uttered years ago, came back to her. "Honey," Cleo had said, "you're more of a slave than I've ever been. Turn it loose, give it to God. Pray the Lord's prayer every night, until you mean it."

Eliza had ignored Cleo's pleadings. But now, with her eyes closed and her hands tightly folded, she began, "Our Father, who art in Heaven, hallowed be thou name. Thou kingdom come, thou will be done on earth as it is in Heaven. Forgive us our trespasses as we forgive—" She stopped and stiffened. *Mama had no right . . . no right at all.* Her heart felt as if someone had reached in and slashed it with a knife. The verse in Jeremiah 33:3 pricked her conscience. *"Call upon me, and I will answer."*

Eliza threw her head back and wailed, "Lord, you say you'll answer me when I call? Well, I'm calling. Where, Lord . . . where are the answers? Show me. Show me those great and mighty things." Her chest heaved as she sobbed. "Oh, God, what's wrong with me?"

She dropped her head and finished the prayer ". . . as we forgive those who trespass against us."

Eliza sobbed, "Oh, God, I've been so wrong. Mama and I both made mistakes, and said cruel, hurtful things to one another, but I've missed her. You know I have. I wanted to come home, but I was too stubborn. I've grown hard and become obsessed with bitterness. I wish I could beg Mama's forgiveness, but it's too late. Why did I wait? Forgive me, Father."

The prayer of David, which she learned many years ago, came back to her remembrance. She uttered the words, "Create in me a clean heart, oh God, and renew a right spirit within me."

She rose from her knees, and felt the heaviness lifted. She

heard no voice from heaven, saw no angels appearing, or lightening flash from the sky. She still had questions, but in God's timing the answers would come. He promised. Faith had made a home in her heart.

Eliza stood. Clutching the red shirt, she walked back to the window and once again ran her fingers over the initials. A sense of peace washed over her. "Thank you, Lord for showing me the etchings on the glass. Kiah did love me. He really did."

Nothing else seemed important anymore. Why should she bother to dig up secrets and open old wounds? No reason at all. Did it really matter why he left? He was gone.

She rose and took one last look around the room, before picking up her shoes and walking out the door. Her eyes moistened as she imagined her mother's voice saying, "Eliza Lancaster, put on your shoes, you look like a Loudermilk." How she longed to hear those words just once more. If only she could let Mama know how much she really loved her. It felt good to love again.

The clouds had disappeared. She didn't remember ever noticing before how much brighter and more beautiful things appeared after a summer rain.

As she approached the manor, she stopped to speak to the last guests who were preparing to leave. Uncle Henry sat in the car, waiting for Aunt Merle, who was still talking to the departing guests. Eliza smiled when she discovered that Aunt Merle didn't seem to realize she'd been gone.

Eliza walked into the kitchen, surprised to see Cleo sitting at the servant's table, eating supper. Her heart sank. *Why isn't she with Daddy? Unless . . . unless he's gone?*

Cleoda stood and wiped her hands on her apron. "Oh my soul, Miz Lizzie, where've you been, child? Hobart's done searched high and low for you."

Eliza's pulse race. "No, no, Cleo," she screamed. "Did you tell him? Did you tell him I came back, Cleo?"

Cleoda smiled. "Well, you go tell him yourself, sugar. Your Daddy's awake, and he's been asking for you. It's a miracle, that's what it is. Ain't nothin' short of a miracle."

Eliza's eyes widened. She grabbed Cleo in a tight hug and kissed her on the cheek. "Guess what, Cleo. God answered your prayer."

"He sure did, honey. Mr. Will woke up in time to see his baby."

"No, not that prayer. The one you prayed for seven years. Thank you for praying. My heart isn't heavy anymore. I feel so light, I don't know if I can keep my feet planted on the ground. I love you, Cleo. I love everybody."

"Oh, glory be. I love you, too, sugar, but is you all right?"

"I'm better than all right, Cleo. We'll talk later. I need to see Daddy." She ran through the house, and leaped up the stairs. Her heart pounded fiercely against her chest as she ran to her daddy's bedside, gazed down at his pale, gaunt face and kissed him on the cheek. From the corner of her eye, she glimpsed a figure standing at the foot of her father's bed. She looked up and felt the blood drain from her face.

Chapter Thirty-Three

"Kiah?" Eliza's knees wobbled. So she was right. Her mother had been responsible for his leaving and now that Alamanda was gone, he'd come back for her.

As much as she wanted to throw herself into Kiah's arms, and to hear him say he'd never for a moment stopped loving her, she knew there'd be time for that later. A whole lifetime. At the moment, her dying father deserved her undivided attention.

Kiah acknowledged her presence with a simple head nod; no doubt, his way of showing respect for her dying father. His gaze remained fixed on the figure in the bed. When his eyes glazed over with moisture, Eliza thought it touching that a former employee would think so highly of the man he worked for, so long ago. Yet, it wasn't surprising, since everyone loved Will Lancaster.

"Daddy," Eliza hunched over her father's bed.

Will slowly lifted his hand and stroked her face. "Lizzie, my little Lizzie. I knew you'd come back," his raspy voice barely above a whisper. "I asked the Lord to let me live long enough to see it happen. How are you, baby?"

Her lip quivered. "I'm fine, daddy."

Will turned his head toward Kiah. "She looks good, doesn't she, Kiah?"

Kiah slowly shifted his gaze toward Eliza. "Yes. Yes, she does look good."

She swallowed hard. "It's good to see you, Kiah." The words from Jeremiah played in her head. *Great and mighty things? For sure, Lord. This is definitely great and mighty.* She felt eighteen again. It amused her that Kiah seemed to have difficulty finding words, but words weren't necessary. His very presence spoke volumes.

When her daddy closed his eyes, she assumed he'd fallen asleep. She looked at Kiah and mouthed the words, "But why . . . why did you come back?" She wanted to hear him say he loved her—had loved her for seven years. Without waiting for his answer, she eased up beside him, laid her hand on his and whispered, "I'm glad you're back. I never stopped loving you, Kiah."

He jerked away and glared as if she'd slapped him. He turned and stormed out the door.

Eliza's heart sank. *What was that all about? Why is he doing this to me?* Unable to control her emotions, she laid her head across her father's chest and wept.

Will slowly opened his eyes and gently stroked his daughter's hair.

"I'm sorry, Daddy. I'm okay. Really. I suppose I'm just tired.

It's been a long day." At the sound of someone approaching, Eliza raised up and wiped her eyes. She sucked in a breath when Kiah walked in the door. He appeared much more composed than when he flew out of the room like a chicken with its tail feathers on fire.

As calmly as if nothing had happened, he said, "Is he awake?"

Biting her lip, she simply nodded.

He eased up to the bed and gently caressed Will's shoulder. "Liz, you asked what I was doing here. I think you have a right to know." He looked down at Will and raised a brow, as if seeking permission to speak. Will nodded.

Eliza formed a thin smile. "I know why you came back, Kiah. Why is it so hard for you to admit you love me?"

"Liz—" He cleared his throat. "Mr. Louie sent me a telegram saying my father is dying and he requested that I come. So I came."

She grinned. "You mean *my* father."

He turned and walked over to the window. "No, you heard right. I said my father."

"Oh." The skin around her eyes tightened. "Then your father lives nearby? You never told me." Questions flooded her mind, so fast she didn't know which ones to ask first. "But how did Louie know your father was sick . . . and how . . . how did he know where to find you?"

Kiah's eyes glazed over. He spoke slowly, "Liz, Mr. Louie and I have kept in touch through the years." He walked back over to the bed and gazed into Will's moistened eyes. "You see, Liz, Mr. Louie works for my father."

"But you aren't making sense, Kiah. Mr. Louie works for—" Eliza glared at Kiah and froze. Her tongue stuck to the roof of her dry mouth. Why would he say such a thing? She refused to believe it. His father? *His*? She shook her head furiously. She wanted to scream, "No, no, it can't be so." But she knew it was so. The pieces fit. Eliza blinked rapidly. "I . . . I need to sit down and—"

When she came to—lying on the floor—she looked up into Kiah's face. He held her head in his lap. His blue eyes watered. "I'm so sorry, Liz. I wanted to tell you before I left, but I couldn't for obvious reasons. You okay?"

She nodded, but she knew she was *not* okay. She'd never be okay. How could this be? Life had played a cruel joke. "Please help me up." Eliza stood and stared into her father's weary eyes. The muscles in her face twitched. "Is it true, Daddy?" She wanted him to deny it. *Kiah is my*—the horrifying thought was too painful. She clasped her hand over her mouth, hoping not to throw up.

Will nodded. "It's true, angel. Alamanda insisted I keep the truth from you, but the time has come to dispense with all secrets. Please, come closer and hold my hand. Both of you."

Eliza walked up to the bed and clasped her father's hand.

Will slowly turned his head and motioned for his son.

Kiah reached out for Will's gnarled, arthritic fingers, tenderly massaging them.

Will's face paled. "Water." He whispered. "I need water." Kiah quickly turned loose of the hand and reached for a glass. With his father's head cradled in the palm of his left hand, he placed a straw to his dry lips. Will choked as he drew the water through the straw. With his head back on the pillow, he made a gurgling sound and closed his eyes.

Eliza stepped back. She gasped and mouthed the words. "Is he—?"

Shaking his head, Kiah pulled out his watch to check the time.

Will opened his eyes. His face lit up. "Kiah, where . . . where did you get the fob watch?"

He held it out for Will to see. "Mr. Henry gave it to me, years ago." Kiah's face suddenly distorted. "He insisted I take it. I know it sounds crazy, but it's the truth."

Will's voice trembled. "I believe you, son. He gave it to you, because it's yours."

Kiah's brow creased. "I don't understand. Mr. Henry seemed to think so, though I told him repeatedly that it wasn't mine."

"Yes, it is. The watch was my grandfather's, who willed it to be passed down to the eldest son. It was my father's, then Henry's, and now—as the oldest son in the family—it belongs to you."

Kiah bit his lip. "I shall treasure it always—or at least until I have a son of my own." He rubbed Will's cheek with the back of his hand. "Dad, you need to rest. I'll come back later."

Will reached for Kiah's hand. "No, please. Don't go."

Eliza swallowed hard, hearing the only man she'd ever loved, claiming her father as his own. The knot in her throat tightened.

Will said, "There's something you both should know."

Eliza cried, "Don't, Daddy. You don't have to explain." She turned her back to her father, in an attempt to hide the agony, which rose from her heart to her face.

"My precious, Lizzie. Come hold Daddy's hand. I can't rest until you know the truth." Will's chest rose as he struggled for each breath. "Lizzie, I've loved you since the day you were born. You must know that."

Her gaze locked with her father's. "I know, Daddy."

"Please believe me when I tell you that I couldn't have loved you more if you'd been my own flesh and blood."

"But Daddy . . . I am your flesh and blood." She looked at Kiah and whispered, "He's confused. It must be the medication."

Will slowly shook his head. "No, my little Swamp Angel . . . not confused." His words were slow and deliberate, stopping occasionally to draw a short breath. "Hear me out, darling."

She swallowed hard.

"Angel, your mother eloped and married Leonard Loudermilk before you were born. When your grandfather found out, he had the marriage annulled, but shortly afterward, he learned she was pregnant. So Mr. Gid quickly came up with a solution to the problem. I was the solution."

Eliza gasped.

"Ali and I were not in love, but we both had our reasons for agreeing to Papa Gid's proposal. Then you came along. You were the sweetest, most beautiful little creature I'd ever seen. From the first moment I held you in my arms, you were mine. Oh, how I've loved you, my darling."

She could hardly breathe, but she bent down and held her face flush against her daddy's. The room closed in on her. *Did he say Loudermilk?* She raised up and looked into his eyes. Her voice quivered as she fought back the tears burning her eyes. "So Mama had a little Loudermilk? That's funny, Daddy. Isn't that *funny?"* *No, it's not funny. It's not funny at all.* Yet, in spite of the tears, she snickered. "No wonder I couldn't seem to keep my shoes on."

Will made a weak smile. "Honey, Leonard was a good man—he loved your mother—and I always knew that she loved him. But I suppose she loved the Gladstone money even more. Papa made it plain he'd disown her if she stayed with Leonard."

"But I don't understand. Mama always acted as if she hated the Loudermilks."

"Not all of them. Only Mrs. Loudermilk and the children she bore him."

The bitter truth began to sink in. *I'm a Loudermilk? No. This can't be. Will Lancaster is my father.*

Will said, "Alamanda acted as if she hated Leonard, too, but I wasn't fooled."

Eliza needed time to absorb the shock. She'd received too

much information. "Don't talk, Daddy. I can see it's difficult."

"No, Lizzie, I can't rest until you know. I've prayed to live long enough to tell you the truth. I should have told you sooner. Please hear me out."

She swallowed the pain. "I'm listening."

"Honey, regardless of what your mother said about the Loudermilks, Leonard was as fine a man as ever walked the earth." Will coughed until his pale face turned blue.

Kiah poured cough syrup into a spoon. "Open wide, Dad." He slipped the spoonful of medicine into Will's mouth. "Doc Griffin said this will help clear the congestion."

"Thanks." Will swallowed the syrup and smacked his lips together. "Where are you, my little Swamp Angel?"

She stepped closer. "I'm here, Daddy, but don't try to talk."

Will shook his head. "I must, angel. I owe it to Leonard. Fennie told my son about me, and I'm grateful. For Leonard's sake, I must tell you about him. After all, he gave me the most wonderful gift in all the world."

Eliza rubbed her hand across his forehead. *Alice is my half-sister. Jeepers! This means I have a whole slew of siblings.*

Perhaps it was being able to unload such a heavy burden that caused Will's voice to grow stronger. "Leonard worked on the Morris farm, and when you were a baby, I'd slip you up there sometimes, so he could see you. I didn't feel it right not to let him see his own child. You belonged to both of us. I won't ever forget the way he cried the first time he laid eyes on you."

Lizzie cringed. "Don't try to talk, Daddy." *Daddy*? Never had the word stuck in her throat before.

Will reached over and patted her hand. "As you grew older, I was afraid if Ali found out I was taking you to see Leonard, she'd snatch you away from me. Of course, he saw you around town in the coming years, and I know he must have been as proud of you as I've always been. He never had much of anything in the way of material possessions, but Leonard Loudermilk sure loved his family, and that included you. In my way of thinking, a child can never get too much loving."

She hoped she could speak without crying. "But Mama said the Loudermilk children were orphans. So when did he die?"

"I think Ali pretended he was dead, long before the fact. I suppose it hurt less that way. Leonard died from lock jaw the year before you left home." Will heaved and gasped for breath. He clutched his throat. "I . . . I . . . thought . . . you . . . should know."

Eliza's heart hammered.

"Give him another swallow of water, Kiah."

Kiah reached for the water. Holding the glass in one hand, he reached down to lift his father's head. He slowly sat the glass back on the table, and gently laid Will's head on the pillow, before turning away and walking toward the window. Eliza followed him with her eyes. His shoulders began to shake.

She walked over and stood beside him. He turned and with

tears streaming down his face, whispered, "He's gone, Liz."

"I know."

He wrapped his arms around her and together they wept. Kiah pulled the sheet over his father's face and he and Eliza walked downstairs to break the news to Cleoda and Hobart. Cleo broke down and sobbed.

Hobart said, "I'll go bathe him and lay him out for the viewing. Mr. Will done told me which suit he wanted me to dress him in. I'm real sorry, Miz Lizzie. I know how much you loved your daddy, and he sure loved you."

Kiah whispered. "Want to take a walk, Liz?"

She nodded. With her hand in his, they strolled down the path, leading to the old Shanty. Both were quiet, as they entered the deserted log cabin. Kiah spotted Miz Mattie's Bible, laying open on the bed.

"I need to give this back to the owner," he said, picking it up.

Again, she simply nodded. For years Eliza had longed to be with him, to talk with him—and now words somehow seemed inappropriate. They walked out of the shanty in silence. The bitter-sweet moment seemed too reverent, too sacred to mar with mere words. The love of her life had returned—yet, she had lost the most wonderful father any girl could ever hope to have. How could one moment in time be filled with such overwhelming joy and unbearable sorrow all at once?

Liz reflected on the words in the book of Jeremiah. Faithful to

His word, God had shown her great and mighty things.

Kiah put his arm around her waist and together they followed the path leading to the creek. They sat down on the big rock, where they'd sat many times in the past. Kiah picked up a stone and skipped it across the water.

Eliza could see the pain on his face. She felt it, too. *We've lost our daddy.* The thought caused her to shiver. She had an uncanny need to console him, though her own heart was splitting in two. "Kiah, I'm sorry you didn't have longer to come to know him. He was a wonderful man . . . a great father."

His eyes stayed focused on the water. "I know." His voice cracked. "Mama told me all about him." He sighed. "I'm glad I found out for myself he was everything she claimed and more." He slung another pebble across the waters. "Liz?"

"Yeah?"

You know what I'd like to do?"

"What?"

His eyes twinkled with a look of mischief. "I'd like to go swimming and race you around the bend."

"Are you kidding??"

The water splashed, no doubt from a small fish catching a bug, and it reminded her of the first day they swam together and Bonnie mistook Kiah for an alligator. She laughed. It felt good. It wasn't forced, but came from a heart weighted down for seven years with unforgiveness, but had now been set free.

She jumped up, kicked off her shoes and slipped out of the bolero she wore over the halter-neck red dress. "I'm game, but you'll have to promise to keep your eyes closed. Remember, Kiah?"

He cackled. "Remember? I remember everything about you. You tried to shock me, you little tease. Just like you're trying to shock me now." He skipped another pebble across the water. "Liz, you know what all this means, don't you?"

She made a thin smile. "Tell me."

"It means we shared the same father, but you aren't my sister."

"I know." Her eyes glistened.

"Liz?" He skipped another pebble across the water.

"Yes, Kiah."

"I love you."

"I know."

"Eliza Virginia Lancaster, will you marry me?"

She threw her arms around him. "I thought you'd never ask."

This time, he didn't pull back.

Epilogue

Eliza Lancaster wrote the following announcement and had it printed in the morning paper, August 15, 1939. The townspeople were greatly amused—once the shock wore off.

Mr. William Hezekiah Lancaster IV departed this life on Tuesday evening at dusk. He leaves to mourn his darling daughter, Eliza Virginia, and his beloved son, William Hezekiah Grave. The interment will be held in the Gladstone Cemetery, at four o'clock on Thursday, the sixteenth day of August in the year of our Lord, nineteen hundred and thirty-eight.

Had Mr. Will lived, he would have had the privilege of seeing his two children, whom he adored, come together to be united in holy matrimony. The wedding will take place on Monday August 20, on the banks of Sandy Creek at sunrise.

Robert Loch, the new owner of The Tribune, raised his brow when Eliza presented him with the announcement. But she said not to worry, because before Hobart could pull out his harmonica to play "*Here Comes the Bride,*" she guaranteed that no one in the county would find reason to object to the marriage. News travels fast in little towns.

THE TRIBUNE

Society Page

Grave-Lancaster Vows Exchanged

Miss Eliza Virginia Lancaster became the bride of William Hezekiah Grave, on the morning of August 20, at a sunrise service on the banks of Sandy Creek in Goat Hill, Alabama.

The ceremony was performed by the Rev. Rufus McDougald, Pastor of Glory Road Church on Hog and Hominy Road.

The bride is the daughter of the late Mr. William Hezekiah Lancaster IV and the late Mrs. Lancaster. The groom is the son of the late Mr. William Hezekiah Lancaster IV and the late Miss Fendora Grave from Pascagoula, Mississippi.

Nuptial music was provided by Mr. Hobart Jones, who played *Here Comes the Bride*, on his harmonica. Mrs. Mattie Williams sang a beautiful rendition of *Whither Thou Goest*.

The stunning bride wore a flaming red Chanel. The lovely halter-back, tea-length dress had a fitted bodice and flowing skirt. Floral anklets fashioned from tiny red rosebuds adorned the barefoot bride's ankles.

A reception was held on the grounds of the Gladstone Manor,

where Mrs. Cleoda McRawlins prepared breakfast for the huge crowd. The menu consisted of scrambled eggs, grits, cat-head biscuits, fig preserves, fried ham and red-eyed gravy.

The happy couple are spending their honeymoon in a little getaway, which they simply referred to as "The Shanty."

ABOUT THE AUTHOR

Kay Chandler is a multi-award-winning author of Southern Fiction with a speaking ministry called LIFE ROCKS. An enthusiastic motivator, she shares personal experiences seasoned with humor, to illustrate that life rocks when God's in the center. If you'd like to have Kay visit your church, civic group or book club, she can be reached by email at kay@liferocksministry.com. Her Facebook account is Kay McCall Chandler. Kay and her husband, Bill, have retired and moved back to their hometown in lower Alabama.

If you've enjoyed this little romp with Lizzie and Kiah, a favorable review is always appreciated.